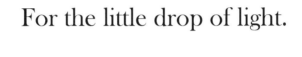

For the little drop of light.

The Hundred

Be where you are.

You are not in the future. You are not in the past. You are right here, right now. You can't be anywhere else. You've never been here before and you will never be here again. It is the only place where anything can ever exist. It is the only place where you will find lasting happiness and your elusive, not illusive self.

Chapter One

The burning ball of light began to melt. Drops gathered and formed at its base awaiting their turn to descend into the darkness. One by one they fell. Down and down I fell, splitting the dark below. Excitement shimmered through me as anticipation engulfed my entire being. Burning at my brightest, I noticed a light appear from below. It was growing, racing faster towards me.

The drop of light shimmered before it fell into the dark pool of liquid mirror. It did not feel afraid as it descended into it, though it should have been. For what that black mirror liquid represented was far worse than any imagined imagining. It represented a loss of light, a place devoid of luminosity. It represented a strangling density of limitations built by words like time, space, gravity, subjectivity and impossibility.

As the drop of light sank into the dark shiny liquid its displacement bore a corresponding drop of its own. As the little drop's dark opposite fell back into itself the energy created a single vibration which caused the thick black pool to pulsate and form a small circular ring framing the spot where both drops had fallen in. This motion sent out a wave carrying the expelled energy outwards to create a larger, lighter ring enclosing the first. Then another and another, again and again until finally the ring became too faint to see.

Deep down under the surface as the energy finalised the distribution of itself in the liquid mass it returned to its originator, and as it did the little drop of light shimmered. This was to be the last time it would shimmer for quite a while. As the drop of light sank like a stone further into the depths of darkness the viscous liquid began coating every beam of light emanating from it. And when it was done, the drop was a decidedly different being. It no longer shone as a small burning ball of light. Now instead, it hid, peeking from behind a cloak of reality called Life.

At first the new ball adapted to its new self and surroundings. It thrived through love and affection and saw its new world as a magical place weaved from the fabric of its home. However, when caring and kindness were held back, replaced with isolation and indifference, when understanding and compassion were forgone for punishment and correction, a new evolutionary development of our ball was needed to maintain its survival. So a point of reference was created to give weight and balance, a heavy anchor for the storm. Thus the first building block went up, the first of many, many more, eventually culminating in the creation of a new kind of fortress. Unfortunately it was this very act of protection which led us to forget ourselves and the truth of our reality.

After a time our little shiny ball had built up quite an array of protective shields surrounding and covering its outer shell, each one representing a lesson learned, a piece of knowledge gained, all combining to form a viewpoint, a unique window to the world. But when something happens during development causing a crack to appear a very peculiar thing occurs. Layers are dispatched and dispersed to cover said crack, and more and more, until a very recognisable mound exists, one that cannot be ignored.

And it is this mound, this reinforced protective layer, which ironically was to become the shield's one chink, its one flaw, ultimately leading to its downfall. Because as long as it lay in relative disguise, seamlessly parallel to its host, it stayed hidden under the radar. But in its arrogance of dominion it naïvely forgot itself, forgot its place as a part, and not a whole, and that was to be its undoing.

The thread's end popped out inviting a tug that could unravel it all, beginning an unstoppable chain reaction that nothing could halt. And not just stopping at one fortress, but like a beacon warning tower igniting along the dark landscape, a domino effect would ensue, one that would continue until the last one fell, until the night was set alight, ablaze with the burning flames of enlightenment.

But for now all that has not yet occurred and our falling drop of light is still falling.

I felt a shiver as I met with the other ball of light. When I sank into it I realised it was not another ball of light, but the exact opposite. It was everything except a ball of light. Though as I fell further into it I felt a strange completion. A faint vibrating pulse of energy then surrounded me and we became one. Before I could understand what was happening my reality changed into the simplest form it could.

I enjoyed the peace simplicity brought and my gentle introduction to the senses. I grew and expanded as my reality did and soon forgot my original self, feeling a truth of belonging and belief in my new existence. I lived and breathed its ways without question until that truth I had built my life upon blew away. It was then that I closed myself and hid the key. It was then that I learned how to cope in my new reality called world. And it was then that my real story began.

My life meandered along following tracks previously formed before me. Nothing was special, nothing was terrible, most was manageable. But then a blinding light decided that that was not all that was meant for me. It shone so bright it nearly erased all the life I had begun to call my own.

∞

When the lights intensity began to fade a lattice matrix emerged from the white. Long bars of light created shadows that framed and defined squares forming a uniformed and somewhat familiar pattern. I tried to remember from where, but the deeper I sought, the more familiarity kept its distance. My concentration moved to the edge of the matrix where the squares ran out. Reality bent as a third dimension jutted out towards me. I followed it and was greeted by a far more unsettling one. Faces.

Faces were everywhere. I was lying down. Lying on the floor of a room. A room scattered with unknown faces belonging to unknown bodies. Then the bodies began to stir. I'll never forget that first hand fear laid upon me as its icy fingers coiled around my neck. My eyes darted above the faces. I was trapped, trapped in what seemed like some long abandoned, long forgotten office space. It wasn't big, only ten by twenty, twenty five metres long, and there were no windows, just doors, three of them. A pair on the shorter wall to my left and a larger one on the right of the wall opposite me. More were waking now. The silent few had become the vocal many.

Where was I? How did I get here? What was the last thing I could remember? Nothing came, nothing at all. My memories, where had they gone? Fear's grip tightened. What had happened to me? To us? Us... My blood froze solid as I remembered him. My throat constricted. Every breath became harder to release. I scrambled to my feet, frantically scanning the shapes on the floor, my head aching from a heavy haze.

Thoughts battled violently competing for dominance. I hoped he was and wasn't here. My eyes searched and searched in desperate desperation. It was as my belief began its downward slide that I heard him call for me. In that moment I couldn't have conceived any other. I caught him in my arms as we embraced each other in the centre of the nightmare. I squeezed his little body as tight as I could and told him not to worry, that Mamma wasn't going anywhere.

The whole room was now awake, and beginning to comprehend what they had awoken into. I knew people and I knew panic, and the two did not mix well. We needed to find shelter from the unavoidable storm that was brewing. But there was nowhere to go. We had nowhere to run, nowhere to hide. We were caught with the beast in its snare and all we could do was wait for it to stir, wait for the inevitable, wait for the communal nightmare to commence, for the self-fulfilling prophecy of panic to fulfil itself.

I didn't know what to do so, like a frightened animal, I ran for the best cover I could. Stumbling across the room with him tight in my arms I pushed through all the sitting and standing bodies and headed towards the bottom corner near the twin doors. A corner, was this the best refuge there was? It wasn't good enough. I didn't know how to keep him safe. I could feel panic's paralysing poison oozing. But I couldn't allow it, I couldn't indulge, I was not alone. I shook away the venomous predator and sat with my back against the corner wall, eyes on the room, my baby's face shielded over my shoulder, knees bent tight in against his little back.

I just sat there watching as every bloated fantasy of who we were, how much we mattered, the impact of our lives, the clout we carried, what we amounted to, what we knew of truth, our power and our strength, watched it all wither under the unremorseful glare of this new reality. Everything we had strived for, everything we had accumulated over the course of our lives had not saved us from this fate. In every moment that passed we seemed to outgrow all we had grown to know, like some path was disintegrating behind us, never to be used again. Every skill and every piece of knowledge we had acquired seemed so empty, so useless, so utterly worthless.

What were we doing here? What had happened? How had we just been sucked up and spat out onto this dirty canvas? Was it our fault? What had we done? What choices had led us here? What choices had been made and not made? What no, what yes, what maybe, what hesitation had brought us to this moment? If we could be so effortlessly swept from our lives and blown here, to this place, then what control did we have over our existence at all? What real control did we have over anything? Was this all just to remind us that our perceived power was just that, perceived? All just to show us that we were not the gods we thought we were? How were we going to react? Just how many degrees of thought separated us from our savage self? How many links of intolerance would we have to pass before we descended to the buried barbarian beneath? And what did it lay beneath? A veneer? A veneer of what? What part of us needed to be threatened in order to crack it? What needed to happen to stir the beast? And where lay that divide? Would we now fall into a new set of parameters of reasonable behaviour? Would we now rationalise a new yard stick, a new moral compass to adhere to? And how far could our rationalisation stretch? At what point would we decide it was at its limits? Would we even know when we reached them? Or would we simply recalibrate and begin the new range of measurement under the guise of desperate measures? Would we just sit back and allow our thoughts to prescribe unimaginable terrors, leaving ourselves powerless to stop them? Would we just continue to permit the horror show of the mind to screen the fevered, fear driven orgy with our conscience bound and gagged, deemed too soft for the fight? But what fight? Against whom and to what end? There was no battle. Yet, I could see in their eyes, they were ready for war.

There was no time to question thoughts once insanity took the wheel. Like any herd, it only took one. A man yelled, a woman screamed and then terror sank its teeth in and locked its jaw. All around me the room crawled with panic and retched with fear. One after another, they choked on the endless unknowns now redefining their existence. Madness force fed madness. Blind panic led blind panic. And then they all just ran. Ran from the lunacy, ran from the moment, not even realising that they were just running further into it.

Now we were at the mercy of fear's full fury. Almost obscured by all the rushing were two thick columns in the centre of the room. Every few seconds I could hear the nauseating sound of bodies smacking off of them. But still the frenzy continued. Thud after thud, people collided with walls and each other. Yet the mass mayhem marched on. They all looked so alien, so unhuman. But they were just people, normal people. Normal people who now resembled a swarm of bees stuck in a cookie jar. I held his head tighter on my shoulder and sang into his little ear, sang anything I could that would take us away from here. I had to shield him from the darkest shade of humanity. People are not beastly rabble, they are quite the opposite. But here, in this box, that's all they seemed to be.

All around us was a rotting of reality, a decomposing of ideals, decorum in decay. What was happening? Is this what happens when you trap a group of human beings in a confined space? They immediately resort to fight or flight? They just devolve? It all just dissolves? Everything we've become, everything we've grown to be just disappears? Leaving what? Do we then descend into what we pretend we are not? A savage? Would this room fill up with feral fury? And here I was, alone, in this brutal unstitching of society. No, worse, I wasn't alone. Maybe I too would have no choice but to devolve and become what I pretended I was not. I didn't know, I didn't know anything.

In our highly orchestrated lives we rarely find ourselves in a situation where we don't know what to do, where our mind does not offer up one option, one idea, one iota of anything. My mind had abandoned me and left me to fend for myself. So I had no choice but to simplify my solution and become as hard and impenetrable as I could. I imagined a cage of solid steel bars surrounding him, shielding him. No matter what I saw, what I heard, I just visualised my strong, impenetrable self. At least I had that, at least I had him as my purpose, as my direction but those poor people, they had nothing. They just had their panic and their fear, their freshly shattered conceptions and perceptions, alone, loose without instruction.

The swarm moved and swayed around the room desperately looking for an escape where there was none. I don't know which was worse - the room or the room's reaction to the room. It was unbearable to watch but I had no choice. I had to keep watch, track the storm. Though not all were feeding it. There were a few who had not been swept up in the madness who were clinging to the fringes of the tornado. There were even one or two who just watched where they woke, despondent, silently witnessing the horror unfold before them, perhaps stuck in complete belief that the only plausible explanation was that this scene was not real and they would soon awake. But I was not in anyone's dream or nightmare, as much as I wished I were.

The noise reverberating down the wall from the large metal door was excruciating. A hill of hands clambering, scrambling over each other, each one trying their best to open a locked door, each having distrust in the person previous, distrust of their skill and adeptness, while holding complete and unwavering faith in their own. Some struck and kicked at it, cursing its indifference. But all they received was more pain.

Another mound was building around the doors to our right. I'm sure I saw the same people go back and forth between all the doors. Perhaps they were hoping that they hadn't quite pushed or pulled the handle enough, that they and everyone else hadn't managed to jiggle it hard enough. But of course they had. And rather than admit it to themselves, they persisted with their lunacy and the stampede continued.

People had degenerated into a mindless mob, performing the same ritual over and over again, not even stopping or pausing their madness when one fell, just moving around them, over them, through them, blindly continuing, stubbornly stuck on repeat. The injured dragged themselves to the walls, clinging onto them like vertical life rafts. The edges of the room began to fill as more and more were kicked to the side. The weak whimpered as they huddled along the perimeter, trying to burrow themselves into the wall.

An overwhelming swell of nausea swallowed me as dizziness circled like a vulture, waiting for my surrender. I felt unbalanced, not just mentally but physically as if gravity had somehow liquefied and was swishing and swirling around me. It felt as if the room was falling, tumbling through space, twisting and turning through time. Reality seemed to be distorting on every axis.

11

Everywhere was chaos, pure and utter chaos. Humanity and everything that word meant had been forgone. Forgone for what? Continued existence? But as what? And at what cost? I tried my best to shield my son. I did not want his vision of the world to be tainted. He still believed it to be a place full of wonder and magic, where evil existed solely in the pages of comic books. I wanted to keep that precious view protected for as long as I could. I wanted to protect it forever. I wish that were possible. I wish it were possible for every child. Then what world would we find ourselves belonging to? Certainly not this one. There was no way I was going to allow his delicate bubble of belief to burst, not here of all places. The pieces would be far too small to have any chance of ever being put back together. Besides, it would be such a false estimation of our species. We are not what we do, what we say, what we experience. We are not our actions or reactions or even our decisions. We are more than that, far more, and we cannot be judged, condemned, just written off in a moment of madness, or even several.

And just when it seemed these moments were beginning to pass, a new ingredient was added to the cauldron, despair. As options were finally believed to be exhausted people's mindless racing and chasing slowed, adrenaline drained, and they began for the first time to look around at one another. Until then it had all been a very personal battle against the moment, a very self-centred cyclone of hell with strangers merely scattered around like objects, no more relevant than furniture.

But now they were finally realising that others too were chained to the same experience. Nothing was said. Looks of fear were exchanged, noticed and noted. This small shift in perception had a big effect on the room. All the mirrors reflected their anguish back at them confirming a truth they did not want to recognise. The reality they had been refusing, fighting, hiding from, was here.

Now it was real. All of it. The room existed and we had to accept it. There was no other choice. But words do not quite do justice to the horrendously difficult task that is. To accept a nightmare is far harder than to not accept it. So now, pressurised into accepting something they could not, would not, people fought to reject it all the more. And so, inevitably, the room finally caved in on itself.

People turned on people. They had gotten the war they had wanted. But it was clumsy and awkward, brutally and uncomfortably real. It was indiscriminate and aimless, and it was everywhere. I had never in my life seen true terror before. It was not the same strain you find in a horror movie. Maybe that's because it can't be acted, because when you're truly terrified there's no room left to act. Terror isn't found in a scream or in an overly dramatic gesture, terror is found in the eyes. Terror is found in a face that contorts to such a degree that it becomes entirely unrecognisable. Like werewolves they morphed into their other side, their underside, the side they never knew existed. They became their worst nightmare.

Pupils dilated, eyes protruded, people shed the social graces we vigilantly contain ourselves within. Mouths hung open, tongues became visible, saliva escaped without acknowledgment or care. People look very different when they no longer care who's looking. They take on a very different demeanour when they no longer care about keeping themselves together, keeping themselves in check. I had never been exposed to such an abandonment of grace, such an exodus of civility, except, that is, when my grandparents died. They both suffered greatly towards the end and did not have a care in the world for their behaviour, physical or otherwise. But at least they had the feeling that peace was looming, waiting for them. These people did not.

As I stared at the unravelling of humanity's evolution before me, I had a ridiculously superfluous thought. But even though I acknowledged its redundancy I still sheltered in its escapism. I realised that I was being allowed to witness a world before our own, that I was being given a chance to catch a glimpse at pre-civilised man, to view a jagged, ragged world where impulse and desire ruled, where only instinctual emotions dictated, a turbulent tempest of a time before rationale and reason had yet to even appear on the horizon.

All around me were Neanderthals in jeans and loafers, shirts and ties, skirts and stilettos. It felt like two worlds were colliding and combining, like the threads of string theory's string were fraying and unwinding. I just wanted to close my eyes, block it all out, the room, the people in it, everything, just to escape for one moment, to be somewhere else, anywhere else, but I couldn't. If I was alone maybe I could have curled up into a ball and blocked it all out, but I wasn't. I had to be on my guard, keep my eyes open. Though everywhere I looked, the sensory bombardment of human horror blinded me like popping flash bulbs. And even if I closed my eyes the images burned inside them like dark room negatives. I couldn't escape them. There was no escape. No escape from this room or this reality, not even for a second. It was all around me. It was everywhere. We were drowning in it. I was drowning in it. It was too much. It was all too much. I needed it all to stop. It had to stop. I was going to make it stop.

My scream was so full and unrestrained it set my whole throat alight. My cry hit every wall and every corner, every ear and every eye. It hit the moment hard and killed it dead. A strange silence fell. Perhaps my madness was simply madder than theirs. I don't know. But they all just stopped. Every single one of them stopped. Stopped screaming, stopped shouting, stopped running, stopped pulling and pushing and shoving and stomping. They all just stopped. Just stopped and stared. Stared as if I had just screamed in the middle of a theatre.

I held my boy closer as I caught my breath and stared back at each and every staring face. How dare they? How dare they look at me that way? They had been the ones to lose themselves, not me. They had been the ones to choose the easy option and allow themselves to spin so terribly out of control. Still they stared. Let them stare. I had nothing to hide, no veil to protect. I felt raw and I didn't care. I stared right back at them all. They were the ones who needed to feel the shame and the embarrassment of their actions, not me.

And then they did. Slowly they began to look at themselves, to take a long hard look at themselves, at what they had done, what they had become. It was as if I had smashed a curse and they were now beginning to regain themselves. However after they had all looked at themselves and each other, they again looked to me.

I didn't care if I had made a scene, the scene had already been made. I wasn't embarrassed or apologetic. I had always been a calm person, pragmatic and conformist, but this, this was where I got off. Chaos on top of chaos? What was next? This was all crazy enough already without everyone adding in their own. I had had enough. I stood up with my boy in front of me. I don't know what it was that compelled me to do so, I didn't have anything to say. Maybe I just felt I had to make a stand and my brain took it literally. So with no direction whatsoever I found myself standing with every eye in mine.

I stepped back a little and squeezed my son's shoulders. What did they want from me? Just because I had managed to control the room for a whole second, now I was expected to grab the reins and somehow ride us all to safety? Well that wasn't going to happen. I was no one. I couldn't even protect my own child. As my heart began to turn itself away my eyes caught others brimming with despair. In that flash I was one of them. I felt their fear, their loneliness. They were all going through the same trauma I had been so desperately trying to shield my son from. But they had no one to shield them, no one to protect them. I saw the frightened child hiding behind each pair of eyes. Everywhere all I saw were orphaned, forgotten and abandoned children begging to be embraced, to be kept safe, to be rescued. My turning heart stopped as I reluctantly took a step forward. Faces that had been painted with dark disparagement now began to reveal flecks of hope, hues of possibility.

My voice, still raw from my burning scream, broke as I tried to speak. I cleared my throat. My mind was trying to unbalance me, to pierce my confidence, make me doubt myself. I closed all the interrupting thoughts away, they were of no use here, and focused on all those cowering children lost behind adult eyes.

"Can anyone remember how they got here?"

A wave of worry flowed across a sea of struggling faces. They were all, just like me, swimming against the current, hoping to catch a glimpse of a shore they couldn't see.

"No, I can't either. But maybe we will, soon. I found my son. Maybe there's some of you who, in all the confusion, haven't yet found each other. Why doesn't everyone line up along the walls so we can all see one another?"

People began lining up. No one said a word. It all felt very strange. Like we were standing in line, waiting for some impending something. Stranger still, much stranger, was the fact that every single one of us standing up against those four walls fitted exactly, perfectly. As if the room, the space, the walls had been tailor-made for us, for this moment.

Reunions tumbled into the middle of the room. They cascaded over each other like emotional stage performances, all the while watched by an audience of despairing eyes frantically searching for their own. Which, for nearly all, never came. The joyous faces seemed so out of place against the sorrow filled ones lined up behind them. That contrast created such a chasm between us, making the odd feeling surrounding us even odder. Some of the spectators chose to vicariously live through the joy on stage, allowing their hearts to drown in the overflowing emotions, possibly sensing that this may be their last opportunity to ever feel that flood of feeling again. Yet others, too broken and torn to partake, instead chose to look away, to extinguish their hope and protect their hearts.

The players on the stage, although aware of the spotlight soaked around them, didn't care who was watching. They didn't care how exposed they seemed, they were. They didn't dare stifle their powerful emotions, instead they swam in them. A mother reunited with her daughters, brothers finding each other, husbands and wives huddled in sobbing embraces. Many, many people were missing, but the ones that weren't, the ones that were found, did not let go. They did not return to the line. They just held each other, fixed to the spot of their reunion, clinging onto that reality, holding it tight and not letting go. And we all just watched, a crowd of peeping Tom's, unashamedly spying on the naked emotions screening before us. There we all stood, an arena of dashed hopes surrounding the victors. We stayed like that for quite a while, longer than we should have I suppose.

The people lined up against the wall were all silent in their sadness, well, most of them anyway. The few that weren't, the few that did not adequately restrain themselves, that did not contain their woe, inconsiderately allowing it to spill out into the room, those were the ones everyone wished were not there. They were the ones piercing our barely inflated dingy. Their recklessness was threatening to sink the room. We wouldn't last much longer with these weights dragging us down. I didn't know who it was going to be, but I knew someone's patience would soon fall. It was only a question of when, when their rage would escape its restraints.

It ended up being a man, about my age, on the wall opposite me just a few people down from the worst offender. He calmly stepped forward from the wall and turned towards her in an attempt to stare her into submission. His stare spoke with words that could not be heard, only seen deep in his eyes. But when she did not heed them, he spoke them through screams.

I suppose it was an attempt, although probably in vain, to release some of the pent up anger and frustration that had accumulated to such an unbearable degree. He was, of course, far too loud and went on for far too long, but no one stopped him. No one knew how, or maybe no one wished to. Maybe they all supported him in their silence. The unfortunate recipient just stared at her aggressor with tears rolling down into her open mouth. Nothing he said was personal, he did not know her, he did not wish to cause her pain, but her irresponsible outpouring of grief was threatening to remove the precarious plug from the room.

Unsurprisingly, he could not control the force of the flow of his trapped emotions which, once released, soon became passengers aboard that very same runaway train that hers had. After a while when that realisation hit, he stopped. And then he did not make another sound, and neither did she. Though she could not stop her tears from streaming silently down her face as she breathed as quietly as she could curled in against the wall. Everyone stayed quiet. We all stayed quiet together. Even the reunited stayed quiet as they sat on the floor. Nobody knew what to do. Nobody knew what was next. I looked down to my boy. He was pointing at each person in turn while quietly muttering under his breath. Before I could even think, I spoke.

"How about we do a head count?"

"What for?" a voice shouted.

"For something to do, unless you have any other ideas?"

So people began counting people. And then recounting. I was nearly finished my second count when my boy excitedly exclaimed the result many of us had dismissed.

"It's one hundred, Mummy!"

The people who had refused to take part in the head count now took notice. My son's figure was checked and double checked until people stopped counting and became very still.

One hundred. Exactly one hundred. One hundred of us trapped together in that small space. Just hearing that number did something to the room. It changed things. It allowed more doors of probability to open up, and other more palatable ones to close. What did this now mean? The wall provided assistance as people fell back against it. Eyes fell and rested on the floor. It was a place where thoughts could be thought without intrusion. Grave and heavy thoughts, thoughts without end, conclusion or reason, just weighty and overpowering. This was the only piece of information we had and it didn't add anything at all, it only seemed to take away.

What was this? What in the hell was this all about? What was happening? And why was it happening? Why us? Why were we all here? Soon the unbearably heavy loads needed to be unloaded.

"One hundred..."

"But what does it mean?"

"I don't know."

"What are we doing here?"

"Where is here?"

"Well this must be some sort of exercise, or routine... something."

"I don't know what it is, but we've got to find a way out."

"Yeah, something just ain't right."

"Something?!"

"We definitely need to get out of here."

"No, we need to wait to see what all this is, to find out why we're here."

"What?"

"Well, we haven't been told we can leave yet."

"Are you serious?"

"We haven't been told anything!"

"Exactly!"

"Are you all just waiting around for directions? What, you think a guide book is just going to drop into your laps?! You *can* function without instruction!"

"We don't know what to think, okay?"

"Well, maybe that's why you're here."

"What?"

"To learn to think for yourselves."

"Well then why the hell are you here?"

"Calm down, guys."

"So you really think we've been brought here to do something?"

"What on earth could we possibly have to do in this place?"

"Well, why else would we be here?"

I could hear the same rhetorical questions, the same unanswerable questions, the same desperate questions all drifting aimlessly around the room. They floated about like an oversized beach ball. The same thoughts, the same conversations bounced around to everyone, everyone except us. We just sat cross-legged in our adopted corner space and I did all I could to keep his bubble of reality intact. Everyone else's was lost, destroyed, lying in tatters on the floor. If I could just keep his safe space guarded, keep his innocence vibrating at the same frequency, then maybe I would have a chance of keeping his childhood from ending. I could not let that happen, not here, not now. And that is all that concerned me. That, and getting out before my odds of success became too small for any amount of positivity to resuscitate.

When you become a parent you lose so much. Children really do take your life away, but they return it back to you with added meaning. Though, through protecting your new heart, you lose the ability to protect the very thing you have been diligently guarding all your life, your own. You enter a terrifying new terrain, where for the first time you are forced to immediately surrender your defences without question. You become what you have always tried not to be, vulnerable and exposed. Your bundle of joy has given you the first gift of many, an Achilles heel.

But the gifts do get better. Not only do you acquire never-ending patience and the ability to multimillion task, but you receive the privilege to witness a Polaroid develop into a picture. That is an incomparable magic trick that lasts a literal lifetime. But there's something else that a child can gift you which nothing in the world can. New eyes. A chance to restore a sight long lost. A chance to press the reset button on your view of the world. Because as you help guide the blank canvas to find its way, to find itself, it can simultaneously help you to. And this opportunity, if taken, can change your life and help you to regain, to retain the magic, the innocence, the wonder for the very world that took it from you.

For that is what we all aspire, whether we know it or not, to be relit, to have that awe and sparkle sprinkled back into our lives. So if we join them in their world, allow it to encompass us in our own, we can relight our dwindling spirit, and shine as we once did. For that is all they wish, to see our light ablaze with theirs, dancing together, playing for as long as the day will allow.

So our conversation topics varied quite a bit from everyone else's. We spoke about dinosaurs, astronomy, and, of course, Sherlock Holmes. I was forced to escape with him into his reality and the pressing issues within it. What exactly was inside a black hole? How did Moriarty survive the fall? And if dinosaurs were feathered, would a T-Rex still look as scary? It was, in fact, the greatest gift he could have given me. Even if only for a moment, I had escaped the room.

But soon the volume of the hundred increased, booming into our hideaway retreat, storming across the drawbridge, flooding our castle of conversation. The quiet questioning had turned into unignorable interrogation and now I had no choice but to listen. Groups formed along the walls and around the corners and the reunited merged with others to form a large centre group. Thrust back into this reality and its accompanying anxiety my idle mind was relishing the exploration of beastly possibilities lurking in the future's moment. As I looked around the room trying to distract my attention, something caught it, something we had all somehow managed to miss. Pinned high on one of the columns were a few sheets of paper. So I walked over and pulled them off. Though as I did a large man, who was leaning against the column, turned around looking at me as if I had just pickpocketed him.

"Hey! What have you got there?! Give it to me!"

His stare contained such hostility as if all items within his proximity were, by default, his property. I was going to say something to that extent but decided against it. I recalled him and his manner during the chaos.

"Hey! I'm talking to you!"

He grabbed my arm and pulled me back. It was obvious he was used to getting his way, used to pushing people around like dolls. But we were not in his world anymore, we were in the room's. And although he may well have been one of its most physically dominating citizens, minus his scenery and life story, he was just another jerk. It did not matter who he was, what he'd done, who he knew. Here, no one knew him, or any of his backstory, however colourful it may have been. His face held a look of confusion when several men intervened in his manhandling of me. His reaction to them, however, was not one of anger, but of mild amusement.

"Easy, fellas, easy. I ain't got no beef with you."

"I think you need to take a step back."

"You do, huh?"

"Afraid so."

"And who's doing the asking here, exactly?"

A young, but burly boy, a little taken aback by the lack of command his presence seemed to conjure, answered, albeit somewhat apprehensively. The middle aged man just looked at him and smiled a cold smile, revealing a few of the nefarious hues his life had held. Instinctively the young stag, feeling his footing to be less secure than he had presumed, softened his stance and took a step back, though all the while keeping his eyes locked upon the predator in front of him.

And although some members of the audience were hungry for the next scene to unfold, ultimately, sense had to intervene. Which it did, in the form of a short, stout, bald man. The peace keeper smiled at both men as he, quite amusingly, stretched up and placed his hands onto their towering shoulders.

"Guys, guys. There's no problem here, is there? We don't want to set off a bomb in a sub, do we? It ain't gonna end well for anyone. No one here wants any more trouble thrown onto our plates. They're all full enough already, right?"

The men edged away but their stare stayed stuck and the room stuck with it. Was the atmosphere that tenuous? Would we have to navigate people's drama as well as this room's? Was every step going to be upon eggshells? And I thought I had it hard with the wind changing whims of a child. As if he felt his ears burning he ran to me. I took him in my arms and he took the sheets of paper. He flicked through them but as there were no pictures he soon gave them back. I scanned as he did and then turned to my attentions to the second sheet, running my finger down it, stopping halfway when I saw something I hoped I would not.

"What have you found? What is it?"

"Lists. A supply list... and a people list."

"As in, an 'us' people list?"

"I guess. Both our names are here."

"Please, read it."

I read out all the names on the list. It was the weirdest name call I had ever been a part of. I don't know if people were happy to hear theirs called out, no one confirmed their name when they heard it. Now it didn't feel like a mistake. We were meant to be here. We were on the list. The harried hundred now became the hushed hundred. Everyone stayed quiet for a while contemplating the many why's on offer. It is a strange thing to ask questions with no answer. But yet we still did it, repeatedly, as if after the hundredth time of asking that somehow the answer would just materialise. Then someone broke the sombre silence.

"So what's on the supplies list?"

"Just looks like bomb shelter rations. There's some dried food and water, blankets, a medical kit and a radio."

"So where are they?"

"God knows."

"But why would we need them?"

"Because we're obviously going to be here for a while."

"I hope not."

"Maybe they're going to arrive?"

"Unlikely."

"Maybe they forgot."

"What if they're already here?"

"Yeah, where?"

"I don't know. But if they're on the list same as us and we're here, then they've gotta be."

"Genius."

"Well at least I'm doing something!"

"Not that much."

"Could we all please return to the current conversation?"

"Okay, well they're obviously not in this room and we've tried all of the doors, so..?"

"So how about we try them again?"

"Why?"

"Yeah, there's no point."

People closest to each of the doors pulled and pushed and one of the three opened. It was the one nearest us.

"That's impossible."

"It was locked, I checked it myself."

"We all checked it."

"Maybe it was just stiff?"

"Maybe this whole thing is stiff."

The man who had opened the door coughed as he entered the space beyond it. A fluorescent light flickered. Others led by bravery or curiosity followed and out they came with boxes and large water dispenser bottles. The supplies.

The room rushed to the open door to be presented with a small space with two cubicles at the end of it. To the right there were a pair of sinks filled with dirty water. It was not the nicest bathroom I had seen, but it was certainly not the worst. After disappointment had subsided that the door had not led to a way out, we soon realised how vital a find it really was. The ramifications of one hundred people and no bathroom would not have been pretty.

So we had found the supplies. I don't think people knew how to react to that. I'm sure that our future selves would see this find as lifesaving but now, in this moment, it all just felt very unwelcome. I felt like a spoilt child on Christmas Day complaining over the wrong coloured bike. But I wasn't happy, I wasn't happy about any of it. And I couldn't shake this eerie feeling that had been following me around. It sat in my gut like some bad clams, plotting its next move. I watched as people began ripping and tearing at the boxes. Hands grasped and grabbed, items were cast aside in favour of other more appealing possibilities, which were then always discarded with the rest. I turned away. I didn't want to join the frenzy.

"Mamma, I'm hungry."

A small tug from behind forced me to reconsider. I bent down near a pile of crackers and scooped up a couple of packs. Suddenly the lady who had been creating the discarded pile looked at me. I looked back and she spoke.

"We can't have a free for all, we've got to have some order."

A full figured woman, with a voice pouring with warmth, spoke before I could.

"Two little packs won't make such a difference. It's for your boy, ain't it?"

I nodded. And the lady begrudgingly allowed my crackers.

"Now she's got a point though. We do gotta get organised. If you let me see that list, I can maybe try to get things a bit more in order."

I was fine with relinquishing all control. Whoever wanted it could take it. I gave her the sheets and I gave the crackers to my hungry chick. Before I could sit down with him, a tall man with slightly greying hair approached us. He was carrying an old white case with a big red cross on the front. I remember thinking how archetypal it looked, so iconic in its shabby state.

"You found the med kit. That's great. There's probably a few people who could use a bit of attention."

"Can I speak to you for a moment?"

"Me? Yeah, sure. I was just about to sit down anyway."

"In the bathroom, if you wouldn't mind."

I did mind, but before I could formulate a response, the warm voice spoke again.

"It's alright, honey, you go ahead. I'll keep your boy here with me. He can help me with the counting, he looks to be pretty good at that."

I reluctantly left him eating and counting and followed the man with the case into the bathroom. As soon as he closed the door his demeanour changed. Fear flickered its flame of fantasy forcing me to scan for a weapon. However, when he began to talk I knew my suspicion was stemming from the wrong branch.

"It's all just very strange, very unorthodox. To begin with, it is a *very* old model. I remember it from my college days. It's a medical field kit, certainly not designed for places of work. But that is beside the point. The point is what I found inside it."

He pulled back his hair as he searched in vain for a place to sit.

"I was expecting the standard contents, which I found, but I also discovered a few additions. Prescription medicine, very specific, no patient's names but the two bottles are pretty important to the people who need them. Heart and post-transplant medication. These are not here by accident. Christ, these weren't even in existence when this kit was packed. And then there's the base."

He pushed his thin silver glasses to the top of his nose. I took a breath to say something but nothing came.

"The bottom of the case looked odd, a little shallow, when I pushed down on it, it popped up."

He softly shook his head as he looked up at the ceiling.

"Well, of course I immediately came in here to explore it further, which I was glad I did because-"

"Sorry, but why are you telling me all this?"

"Why?"

He took a deep breath and released it as he looked directly into my eyes.

"Because you have a young child. You are the only one here who has much more than your own self to protect. You cannot lose yourself or indulge in melodramatics. You have no choice but to remain as calm as you can and keep yourself together. You have the most to lose in here, and so that is why I can trust you."

I breathed out a stubborn sigh. His rationale was sound but I still didn't want to play leader.

"So, what did you find?"

"I found anti-venom."

"Anti-venom? Okay, that is a bit strange, but not as crazy as I was expecting."

"Well this type is very rare and I find it quite alarming that it's been provided."

"You really think there's a snake crawling around here?"

"I don't know what to think, do you?"

I took it as rhetorical.

"That's not all."

He pulled back his hair again and looked to the door.

"There was also a gun."

"A gun?"

"A tranquilliser gun. But with a very powerful sedative. Two doses."

"What? Why?"

"I don't know. But it's beginning to paint a very grave picture."

"Maybe there's been a mistake. I mean you said yourself it's an old kit, maybe it was just left here."

"In a place of work, with such specific medication, anti-venom and a tranquiliser gun?"

"Well, when you say it like that, I don't know. We better get back. So you're a doctor then?"

"Of sorts, yes."

"Okay, well, you keep the case on you and... and we'll just have to see how all this plays out."

I walked back into the room. With this new layer of truth overlaid things looked different, felt different. Yet to the room, nothing had changed. Some people were sitting, some were standing, some were talking, some were not.

"Well, they can't keep us in here forever. That would be insane."

"It seems quite evident that our definitions differ."

"But there's no reason for it."

"Obviously we're proof that there is."

"Sometimes, there just ain't a reason."

"I think, in this case, there clearly is. It's not simply picking a burger off a menu. They didn't do this on a whim. This must have taken a great deal of planning, an incalculable amount."

"But still, for what? Why?"

"Jesus! Stop asking that!"

"I'm just saying out loud what everyone's thinking."

"Not everyone."

"Yeah, rather than asking the unanswerable maybe we should go straight to what we should do about it."

"He's right. The reason doesn't really matter that much. It's just a useless detail."

"Exactly."

"Useless detail?! Have you all gone mad?! How on earth can you make a decision on anything before first knowing what it is?!"

"Hey, easy, man. Listen, it don't make a difference why we're here. We're still here and we still gotta find a way out."

A young girl cleared her throat as she tried to speak over the clutter of chatter. Her first few attempts failed, but once a few of the louder men had noticed her pretty presence they soon quietened.

"Well... well, maybe all this is a good thing?"

"Jesus, a nut job! A pretty nut, I'll give her that, but a nut still the same."

"I'm serious, maybe we've been chosen for a reason."

"What? Are you high?"

"Hey, whatever you're on share it around!"

"Yeah, I'll take two!"

"Well, I don't want what she's on. I'm happy with my untainted reality, thank you very much."

"I'm not on anything. I'm just saying that all this could be a real opportunity for us to come together, to... you know, bond."

"Is she for real? You really expect us to huddle round and sing kumbaya?"

Sniggers sang their own collective song as the girl, who had suggested loosening Pandora's lid, turned a rosier shade of pink.

"I just meant that maybe we should treat this experience as a chance for connection. You know, a coming together to generate some sort of a unity, like maybe begin to initiate and instigate a bit of what's been missing from the world?"

"Yeah, you're right. Hold on I'll just get my bongos."

"Joke all you like but it's your fear and resistance to the unknown that keeps you separated, and alone."

"Will someone please change the channel?"

"Maybe we're being punished."

"What?"

"Maybe we've all done something really bad and this is our sentence."

"Speak for yourself!"

"Just think about it for a second, it explains a lot."

"Ridiculous."

"There's no way any governing body would permit this form of cruelty as penance."

"No? They just stick with the 'Gu-Gu, Gua-Gua'."

"The what?"

"Political penitentiary workhouses, aka capitalist or communist concentration camps."

"Alright, parking that particular train of thought for a while. So do you guys really believe all this is a sentence?"

"Well, I can tell you there isn't even the remote possibility that I would have performed any kind of unscrupulous act which would have warranted this manner of chastisement."

"Well, I can tell you that if you did, you wouldn't remember."

"My God, maybe that's why our memories were wiped."

"Makes sense."

"Nothing crueller than pressing the erase button on your life."

"Shit."

"What? You guys, that doesn't make any sense. Why would they erase the memory of what we did? Surely the punishment is living with it."

"Not for some people."

"Well, okay, but tell me what sense does it make to delete the memory of a person you want to send to some freaky form of solitary confinement? How is that punishment if they can't remember the life they lost?"

"You don't think this hell is punishment enough?"

"Are you insane?"

"You know what I mean. It doesn't make complete sense. It's not airtight."

"What is?"

"Well, I think I could still be right."

"Alright. Well then, what did the child do to deserve this form of punishment?"

"Oh, yeah. I forgot about him."

As much as everyone tried to untangle the thread, they were always left defeated. But that didn't stop them from trying, not for now anyway. In the centre of the room a small crowd was doing their best to keep themselves busy by over-organising our find with my son enjoying his new job as head cracker counter.

"Mummy! I've counted all the crackers, twice! There's 598!"

"Wow, that's a big number!"

"He's been a mighty fine help. You got yourself a good boy there. Me and my girls were thinking, why don't we get some refreshments out there? Might help folks a little. I'm Missy by the way, just in case you ever wanna holler out for me!"

"Thanks, Missy, that's a great idea. I'm-"

"Sorry to interrupt, but could I trouble you for some water?"

The doctor gave me a strange look that I didn't understand. Missy helped me pour a cup of water and I brought it over to him and the older man he was kneeling beside.

"Thank you. Here you go. I'll leave them with you. Just take them as you normally would."

The doctor stood up and I took it as a cue to go to the bathroom.

"No, we have to be more casual. There are a lot of tilled minds in here fertile for conflict."

I hushed my voice, "I can't believe he... that's... I don't know."

"Now I just need to find someone with a bad heart. I'm going to do some rounds, check on people's bodies and minds."

My head was haemorrhaging questions. I turned to return to Missy when two brawny young guys dressed in grubby blue overalls blocked my path.

"Can we talk to you for a minute? We were thinking-"

"We had a great idea!"

"It may not work-"

"It's definitely going to work!"

"All we can do is try-"

"We have to get behind-"

"That door and see-"

"So we're going to break it down!"

"Well not the big one, that's a reinforced steel security door, which seems a little out of place in an office but the small one's-"

"Just an internal door!"

"The hinge pins aren't accessible from this side but-"

"So we're going to smash the hinges off!"

"Without tools, it's gonna be a bit-"

"But there's an old bracket hanging off that wall, so all we gotta do is-"

"Obviously it's going to take some time just to remove it and we have the problem of-"

"We had the problem of the hammer sub, but the old fire extinguisher in the bathroom should-"

"It could work, but it could also be a bit dangerous-"

"But we're willing to give it a go-"

"If you give the go ahead."

"Me?"

"Yeah, it's cool, right?"

"Sure, do whatever you can."

"Great! Let's do this!"

As the two brothers catapulted themselves and their high-octane energy over to the locked door, I saw disposable white cups being dispersed behind them with water and nuts and those dry crackers. It looked like the world's worst picnic. I turned to go find the picnics little chieftain when I walked into a broad chest.

"Hey," he spoke so casually as though we were just meeting at some party.

"Hi."

My politeness kicked in before my brain could catch up.

"So, what you make of all this?" he smiled, again my brain seemed too slow.

"Just as much as you I suppose."

I tried to side step him but he read my mind and met me there.

"Yeah, it's all pretty crazy isn't it?"

I couldn't believe he was still talking to me.

"That would be one word for it."

I stepped the other way.

"Hey, hold on, wait. Listen, I've been racking my brain, and I can't put together from where, but you feel really familiar. Have we met before?"

Have we met before? He wasn't, he couldn't be? Here? Now? I took a step back to get the full picture of this guy standing well over the boundary line in every sense of the word. He looked like he had just come from the wild. He wasn't dirty, just completely unkempt. Though as I looked further at his untamed curly sun-bleached hair which had that annoying unstyled style about it, I suspected it and his short scruffy beard were all part of a carefully orchestrated look. And with his tanned skin radiating like that, it couldn't have been real. And his eyes, the blue of his eyes looked so unreal, so liquid, like it was about to pour out. I stared for a second, half expecting it to.

"You do know me, don't you?" he said through his perfect white teeth.

Maybe I had stared too long. I did not know him. I certainly would have remembered if I had seen this before.

"No, sorry. You must have me confused with someone else."

"No, I don't think so. I really feel like we know each other."

His warm hand wrapped gently around my wrist as I turned away. I was so shocked that in this day and age someone could be so forth right and brazen. Maybe it was his age, youth usually does come with an excess of bravery. But as much as I knew I had to leave, as much as I wanted to leave, my body wouldn't listen. I couldn't move. It was like I was stuck in his moment.

"Why won't you tell me?"

He softly squeezed my hand before he slowly let it go. His hand was so hot. His stare was so penetrating. I couldn't release myself from his lagoon eyes. They had caught mine and taken them prisoner. I felt myself drift towards his blue waters, float towards a future I could not see. No, no. What was happening? What was wrong with me? I came to my senses and tore my eyes away. Then just as I was about to turn away he pleaded into my eyes.

"Please, it's me. It's Leo. I'm here too."

"I don't know what you're talking about. I don't understand, I, I..."

A big bang followed by a scream of celebration provided enough of a distraction for me to untangle myself from him. The brothers had knocked one set of the door's hinges off. I disappeared into the middle of the crescent crowd that had formed around them. I looked over my shoulder expecting to see the mass of golden curls close behind, but they weren't. My eyes subtly swept across the room. I couldn't see him. Where was he? Who was he? What was he doing? You can't just do that, you can't just come up to someone without warning. There were rules, even here. Especially here. He looked like someone to whom rules did not seem to apply, one of those free birds, flying and fluttering wherever the breeze took him. Well, not over here to me. There were boundaries, I had boundaries and he had to respect them. He could keep his intensity over there and I-

A heavy bang interrupted my stream. The door, the door was now unhinged. But while all eyes were fixed straight ahead to see what was behind it, mine were not. Where had he gone? I looked around again. The brothers shimmied and pulled the door free. The crescent crowded closer and I was pushed towards the entrance of the door. The light from the room raced impatiently ahead of us. It wasn't an escape, though I doubt many thought it was. It was just a storage cupboard. A small space crammed with rubbish, as many small spaces usually are. I could see all kinds of junk, from all kinds of eras. Yet men rushed forward, treating it as Aladdin's cave instead of what it really was, a decades old dumping ground. Everything came out. Old cleaning equipment, tools, broken things like clocks and shelving, some candles, a big roll of old printer paper, bulk packs of soap bars, toilet roll and then, the pièce de résistance of junk, an old television set. The commotion it created was a bit over the top, but I suppose it was more about what it represented, a symbol of home. They rushed to plug it in and turn it on, but slumped down when inevitably it did not. I turned to go and finally find my son, when the radio came into my mind. Where was that radio?

I saw the short bald peace keeper flicking through the mass of mess, swaying from side to side, picking and plucking at it. He looked like someone who knew what he was doing. And although I didn't have a clue what he was doing, I knew enough to know that he did. He knelt down at the television set beside the blue dungaree brothers. They spoke with such gentle bedside manner as though it were a patient of theirs. It was decided that they were going to attempt to revive it. Any guy who had ever hung a picture was now sifting through the clutter, squatting at different angles of the set, nodding and agreeing, humming and hawing. It was a good way for the testosterone to be channelled I suppose, a very good way. I decided not to ask about the radio yet, to leave them to their optimistic mass tinkering for now. I headed back to my worker bee who I was sure was eating more than his fair share of rations. He was chattering away to Missy's grown up girls. He seemed to be okay. I don't know how, but he really seemed to be okay. Children are so adaptable, so bendy. They're like Plasticine, fitting into whatever mould or shape they're placed into. I wish I still possessed that virtue. How did we lose it? How did we become so rigid and brittle? So immovable and unpliable? To cope in our lives? But how does inflexibility help us to manoeuvre the chaos of life? Maybe we should all take a little leaf out of our children's drawing pads and be more chameleon-esque, learning and growing in our ever changing environment, in our ever changing times.

Missy appeared and handed me the sheets of paper, bringing my attentions with them back to the room.

"It's okay, you can hold onto them."

She pointed to the back of one of the pages where there were scrawled calculations and a number circled at the end.

46

"Well that's good news I suppose. It looks like we won't have to be here for more than a few days."

But Missy's smile was feigned, her eyes told me that. They confided in me her real sentiment, her real aura.

"I just wanted you to know, that's all."

I hadn't recognised or understood that faint flicker of fear that danced behind the glaze of her russet eyes, until, that is, it leapt into mine. Fear is one thing, but fear mixed with famine is quite another. When those rations ran out, patience and politeness would soon follow. It would just be a matter of time until we would be left with only the primal versions of ourselves, versions that there was no rationalising with, no talking to, no protecting ourselves from, and more terrifyingly, no coming back from. A suffocating pressure descended. My old foe dizziness returned, like some agenda armed avenging angel circling, jesting, playing soothsayer to what lay ahead, wilfully whispering a path of the most extreme, the most obscene, the most frightful and cursed any human could fear to tread. No, no, we wouldn't, we couldn't. Well I couldn't. There was no way I was going to dehumanise myself to such an unfathomable degree, to fall to such a place of desperation, of complete destitution, to a place of such madness. I would rather die clean then live dirty. Some stains cannot be washed out.

What trade could be worth that? It would be a dirty deal with the devil, a poisoned pact. You would be left with a life littered with mutilated memories that would haunt your very being. What kind of an existence, framed by what you took to have it, could ever be called living? A sickness would infect it, one which not even time could cure. The images would not simply fade into the background, they would never go out. They would distort and fester, torturing you far worse, far deeper than the deed you did to make them. You would rot from the inside and live already dead, already damned.

You would then wish you had been one of the first to go. What fate could be worse than being the last? And for what? A few more days or weeks of what? An existence more tormented than this one? Maybe I was too weak to dive to the deepest depths of survival. Maybe I was a coward, but I had no problem admitting that. There were lines in some sand I would not cross, not even to continued existence. Because the thing with life, is that you come with it. You can never really ignore that fact. Every single shitty little thing you have done to keep it, mend it, elevate it, justify it, you take with you. It all sticks, all the dirt accumulates. That filth builds up, tarnishing your lenses, ruining the view. And when all is quite said and quite done we, every one of us, still need to clear our heads, clear our minds every night before we fall into the serene scene of slumber. The harder it is and the longer it takes, the less peace we're permitted. There's a high price to pay for some trades and sometimes both ends of the stick are pointy.

Though however hastily I could make the decision to walk down this road of emotional preservation to maintain my humanity, there was one curve along my path which I would have no choice but to yield to. My son. I had responsibility over another life, one that looked to me for protection. And that added a level of complexity I could barely comprehend, let alone contemplate. What choice does a parent have? Do you allow your child to die alone or together with you, or first? Which was the lesser evil? All options were sickening. I couldn't bear to take even one step toward contemplation of any of it. I would entrust that harrowing hell to my future self. That choice was left, and it would be the only one I would take.

I looked around at all the now slightly more known faces. Were we really about to enter the colosseum? Was this just the waiting room? Or were we already there, on the bloodied sand, oblivious to who we were, of our role, our part to play? Play. Could this be any further from it? Though my mind soon reminded me of the distinct possibility that perhaps, outside, where cold indifference ruled, there would be some who would see it as a game, and quite a sporting one at that.

I looked around again. There were a few standouts who, if I had been a betting lady, I would have favoured. But they were very much the exception, not the regular rule. I was certain that the room most probably housed many a skilled hunter from the boardrooms and the bars, but I imagined not many were prepared for the brutality that was brewing, not many equipped to enter the barbaric arena of survival of the fiercest. Perhaps it was because we were no longer living hand to fist, instead safely nestled in our soft uterine environment of plush pods of personal comfort, that our feral fierceness had, like our coccyx, slowly died out. We were no longer bred for battle. Our natural habitat of the savage savannah had been renovated, made over to become the slick suburbia that it is today. Our new plain of existence bore no resemblance to the one which bore us, it had been developed, as had our adaptations to it. Our survival instincts had evolved, become more civilised, more suited and booted to our time. Simplistic savagery had become defunct, just another splinter sanded down in Darwin's dream.

Now battles are won and lost remotely, without getting so much as a finger dirty. We destroy people with cleverly worded lines shot in safety from behind shields of LCD. We stalk and torment, hunt and catch our prey, all within the largest net there is. In this great century of ours we believe ourselves to be the ultimate warrior, the true predator, deserved of our place at the top of the food chain. Kings of our kind. But now, here, it was becoming clear how very premature our estimations may have been.

We, although still in costume, were off the stage, sans backdrops, and it was now plain to see what we were. We were all show. We were a show that we believed we needed to perform in order to exist. And that's all that we were. Every aspect of our being displayed our chosen character, our chosen self, confirming to all, but especially ourselves, who we were and our solidity in that. Our whole identity was constructed upon foundations of fear. Fear of rejection, of ostracism and thus instead of embracing and exuding our own original self, we procured copies of other copies, gathering as many parts to our personality as possible, piecing together our preferred Frankenstein of fortitude, the least susceptible to failure, the most resistant to ridicule. Yet we are all playing this masquerade together, all dancing a representation of replication, parading our choice of individuality as we continue to perpetuate the pageantry of personality, all just mimicking madness. We believed our identity to be solid and impermeable. But now, in here, we were being shown, that in truth, it was nothing except a highly elaborate illusion, a flyaway figment of our own creation.

All our notions were being challenged, all our opinions opposed, all our comprehension countered. The whole game had been reset - the rules, the players, the everything. We were no longer in Kansas, that was for sure. And there would be a fierce fight for those ruby slippers.

I looked around again. Youth, from a physical standpoint anyway, obviously had the upper hand. But I did wonder, if somehow the room had managed to level the playing age, would it have been my generation that would have held the advantage? Perhaps then the real contenders would have been the ones hailing from quiet nursing homes and quaint retirement villages, the products of a bygone era of true struggle for survival, and not their progeny's progeny who lived in a time where survival rested upon strong signals and smart software, hits and likes, tight tresses and tighter dresses, jumpstart juice and jock-in-the-box jesters.

What had we done with our chance, our ticket, our generation? Had we traded it all, our reality, our authenticity, our lives, for a fabricated fantasy? For a life filled with fleeting flickers of fancy that seem only to fan our fire of desire? All for an existence as satisfying and thirst quenching as a sea water spritzer? What have we become? Do we even know, or are we just whatever is in, so as not to be out? Are we simply whatever is trending, this season's cool, today's top tweet? Are we merely mindless minds, grown up children still following every Pied Piper peddling the promise of acceptance? Are we really that easily led, that obvious? Are sex and drugs and rock and roll just different types of bait? Just worshipped worms wriggling on a hook, writhing seductively to a hypnotic beat as we float comatosed towards it, anaesthetised in our dopamine induced stupor? Solely shoals of fish swimming to where the warm waters take us, waiting for our beloved bait to just drop into our mouths, all the while oblivious to the line attached? Is that all we are? All we think we can be? Just a craving to be satisfied? A world of walking, talking itches longing to be scratched? A land of lazy lap dogs yearning, praying, begging for our master's touch?

What were we? Did we even know? Did we ever? What was this place and what was it doing to us? What truth was it unearthing? What was its plan? What did it want?

This room, there was something about it, something very odd. Even the atmosphere felt different. *You* felt different. Some things seemed to clear while others just clouded up. Things felt messy, yet organised. It didn't make any sense. None of this made any sense. It all felt very abstract, very conceptual, very unfinished. Something just didn't sit right. There was so much that didn't make sense. Like those supplies, what were they for? Where did they come from and why were they hidden?

Why the hell were we here? And why hadn't we been questioning things more? I felt I had somehow drifted off at the wheel and now the noise of the hard shoulder was waking me. Were we really just mice in a maze blindly accepting what we had been given without even a second thought? Had we already become institutionalised? Were we already? Or were we just clinging for dear life onto a raft of civility, the only thing preventing us from being at the mercy of rough seas?

So many questions asked, so many still to ask. Why were we locked in this space with rations and supplies that looked so old they could have been here before this place was abandoned? And why were our names written with the list of supplies? It didn't fit. If we were meant to be here then why all the extra hassle to make things appear older than they were? And why not give any explanation or indication as to why we were brought here? Why keep us in the dark? And where was that radio? It just didn't sit right. It was like two scenarios were playing simultaneously, like two fabrications were being squashed together, intertwined, but they were not the same, like a projection overlaid on a projection. Either, I was seeing through some gap, seeing something missing, or I was the one that was missing something.

"Are you okay?"

Without seeing whose mouth the words were coming from, I lied.

"You look like you're connecting the dots to something."

I turned to face the questioner who was, again, well over the boundary line. I stepped back but the wall prevented my retreat as he moved closer. My body began to betray and disobey me. I was very disappointed that my female feathers were that easily ruffled. He wasn't even my type. I went for tall, dark, serious, professional men. Not blond beach bum boys. I tried to shake off this ridiculous feeling but with every millimetre he advanced my body fizzled, dissolving, disappearing into the moment. As my blood rushed faster it generated a heat I had never felt before. I bit my lip as so not to show its quiver.

"So," he said in the coolest way I had ever heard that word spoken.

"So, what?"

I attempted to imitate his calm demeanour as I felt my own slowly float away.

He stretched out his arm and pressed his palm on the wall behind me. My brain had now ceased all ability to correlate and compute. I felt stranded on a blank page of reality without any lines to guide me, just floating without direction. My skin crawled with a sense of irritation mixed with something else that I hadn't felt for a very long time. I was simultaneously more comfortable and uncomfortable than I had ever felt before. What was happening? I looked up at him, but had to shield my eyes. His glare was too much, like a burning solar flare. He was too much. This was too much. I felt trapped, even more trapped then being in the room. But I wasn't trapped. I could leave his personal space whenever I wanted but something in me, something deep inside, refused to allow it.

"So, do you remember me now?"

"No."

I had to speak as monosyllabically as I could, at least until I got a hold of myself.

"Why are you being so stubborn, so closed?"

My voice could only muster a whisper.

"This is hardly the time or the place."

"What about the place of time?"

"The what?"

I looked up into those light blue waters and felt the immense depth behind them.

"Well, we don't know the place, but what about the time?"

The practical side of my brain kicked in and saved me from drowning. Routine, safe, familiar tasks and possessions. Time, what was the time? Instinctively, I went to get my phone from my pocket but, of course, it wasn't there. I looked around. We had no belongings, no nothing at all. I felt naked, stripped of my identity, completely exposed and I happened to be with the one person who I knew wanted nothing else. Maybe that was his plan, to leave me completely disarmed.

"We're on our own now. No reminders of our past life or guiding hands of time to direct us."

"Past life? Don't say that, you talk as if we're never going back."

"Back to what?"

"To our lives."

"What life?"

"Our life, I mean my life. You may not have had one while drifting around the world, but some of us did, still do."

"Are you one of those people?"

"Yes! Yes I am and I think it's very inappropriate for you to be talking to me like this."

"You do whatever you feel is appropriate."

I didn't move. "What do you want from me?"

"I want you to find yourself and tell me who I am."

"What? What are talking about? I know who I am and I'm sorry that you don't, but I can't help you. Maybe we did meet once, a long time ago, when I was young and free but I'm not anymore and don't really care to remember that part of my life."

I ripped myself away from the wall and out of the cage he had me in. I walked away, in no particular direction, just away. This was all crazy enough already. As I stomped off, I ran out of road and hid behind a column. What was happening? I needed to get it together, to rein myself in. Yet for as much as I pushed my thoughts away, like a boomerang they kept returning. I didn't want to feel it, but I couldn't help it, there was a distant yet distinct familiarity about him. It wasn't from the line up, I never really noticed him there. It was from my past, but I couldn't place him, or us, or anything. It was so frustrating, like a broken splinter you can't find.

My legs got a small, short squeeze from behind. I turned to see my little man. I scooped him up into my arms and stayed squeezing him until my inner strength had returned and my arms had lost theirs. Holding hands, we made a beeline to our little corner. All I wanted to do was just curl up with him, shelter in his love, in his world. We snuggled up close but were soon interrupted by a cold shiver rising up through me.

"Mummy, I found a big box of blankets. We can go get one if you want."

"Good idea, baby, let's go have a look."

He took my hand and brought me to the box of blankets. There seemed to be far fewer there than we would need. We were going to have the fun task of organising the distribution of the too few to the too many. But I couldn't begin to try and work that out now, the circuits of my mind had already melted. But, of course, the irritation of curiosity soon got the better of me. I would just do a rough count. I walked my fingers along the side of the pile. As I got deeper into the box, it became harder to count so I lifted out the chunk I had counted and put it to one side. It was looking like we were going to be very short. As my heart sank I noticed a lump near the bottom. There was something hidden in one of blankets. I carefully unwrapped it inside the box. What could have been hidden in there, and for what reason? Then as it fell free, so did my first smile in the room. It was the radio.

I flicked and fiddled the dials. It was an old one but it still looked to be in pretty good shape. I needed it to work, I needed it to speak, to talk to me. And then it did. But it was not what I had wanted to hear.

".... is still instructing civilians to stay indoors as they prepare for the inevitable and imminent attack. Remain calm and in your designated housing. Do not attempt to leave your shelter without instruction or permission. Residents are advised to stay away from windows and

doors and seek underground shelter where possible. Do not leave your residential area to seek out family members, friends or supplies. Stay where you are until further advised. For more information call emergency line 918. Do not approach or apprehend anyone. Report all unusual activities to the authorities on the emergency line. Updated information will be added in due course. This is a repeat warning. All citizens able to receive this message are recommended to be on full alert. We are now in a state of emergency. Marshall Law will go into effect this evening at 2100 hours and remain until further notice, with no exceptions. The government is still instructing civilians to stay indoors as they prepare for the inevitable and imminent attack. Remain calm and in your designated housing. Do not attempt to leave your shelter without instruction or permission. Residents are advised to stay away from windows and doors and seek underground shelter where possible. Do not leave your residential area to seek..."

The strength in my hands drained away as I felt the weight of the words emanating from the small black box fall with it through my fingers. I watched its fall, watched it tumble through its new awakened reality as it took with it our own.

As the radio made its descent, time seemed to warp and slow down, for a moment I heard faint music in the distance, and then the loudest bang returned time to its correct speed. The radio bounced back up, gracefully pirouetting in the air before completing its final landing.

Everything had changed. In an instant we had shifted an era. The air, the moment, it was all different. Everything now had a loud silence to it, like I imagine it must feel after experiencing a close quarter explosion. Except for my breathing, my breathing was loud, too loud. I held my breath, and then I heard it again, the music. It was so quiet and seemed to be coming from such a distance away. But where was it coming from? What was it? What was happening? What had just happened?

The weight of realisation sank in me like a steamroller over a meadow, pressing each delicate petal to the ground. I felt reality stiffen and cement all around me, as if even the world appeared to halt its spin. Time and movement seemed alien now, like we were caught here, in this moment, forever; that this had become existence.

I felt so helpless, so paralysed. All I could do was look and watch. Watch the room, the pain, the shock, the sorrow filled faces attempting to express and squeeze out their grief. We didn't know how to process it, we didn't even know what 'it' was. I felt lobotomised, like a piece of me had been removed, stolen, declared ineffective and now I had to cope without it and somehow make it back to shore.

This new reality felt far colder and harsher than the ambiguous unknown we had before. This felt solid, concrete, absolute and far beyond us. And worse, it left us powerless to do a damn thing. Because here we all were, safely tucked away in our 'room'. Feelings of shame and embarrassment were born from our complete selfishness. Guilt over our former self-centredness was now haunting us, reminding us of our lack of humanity. This was a real disaster and it went far beyond our own little lives. It was everything and everyone we had on the outside. And here we were complaining about our dire situation when beyond our four small walls the real hell was about to be unleashed.

The reunited clung tightly to one another but the others, the others had no one. They only had the few scattered memories of all the people they may never see again, not just because they were trapped in the room, but because their loved ones were not. They leaned in against the walls and the floor, some curled up to both. Whatever solace and comfort they could take from the room, they took.

Imagination, as always, lent its helping hand in giving us complete freedom to visit any reality of horror we wished. And that was where we went, torturing ourselves over and over again, trapped in a world of worst case scenarios, snowballing into a crescendo of complete loss. We were lost, in every meaning that word summoned. The little we thought we knew, the basics of what we thought the room was and what we had to do, had now been taken away.

With this new truth superimposed onto everything it had all changed. Our direction, our perception, our instincts all now had to be rearranged, rebalanced, repolarised, recalibrated. The game had transformed and now we had to get to grips with the new rules.

We had to understand that, no matter what, we were not returning to our old lives, they were now gone. We had to accept that everything we held dear outside this room would never belong to us again. We had been cut adrift, marooned in a life raft floating out on the open sea, watching our ship sink into the horizon.

We were not the captives we thought we were. We were the survivors. We were going to have to pull together and realise that now we were all orphans of the room. We had to allow the room to adopt us, to embrace us, to protect us. We had to realise the true nature of the beast. That it was not the enemy, the cruel captor we had assumed it to be. That it was, in fact, our saviour, our only hope. And now we, the fortunate few, had to be grateful, indebted to it for saving us from the storm beyond. We had to accept that no matter how long we were going to survive in here, it was to be far longer than we would have survived out there.

Now that our prison had become our haven, and our damnation our salvation, the axis of our world had again been reversed. Our precarious plain of perception had inverted. And as we sat on the ceiling looking up at the floor we realised that now we had a new set of parameters to adhere to, a new identity to accept, a new reality to call our own. But how do you welcome captivity? How do you embrace imprisonment? How do you adopt a freedom once believed to be a limitation? What were we now? Who were we? And most importantly, why were we here?

Chapter Two

Disillusionment is a funny word. What does it mean? That the illusion has disappeared? That the version of what you thought was reality has now become the illusion? The etymological analysis of the word is to be free or freed from illusion. Therefore does it mean that what you believed has been discovered to be an illusion or is it simply the way you now view it, that it's reality in yours has disappeared? Either way its existence becomes extinct. But a new illusion is born from this quandary. A gaping gap is created between the betrayal of the old and the mistrust of the new. And because neither ground feels solid you are stuck in a form of limbo where your reality is on hold. But you must jump to the new and let go of the old. Though irrespective of which ground holds more stability, more truth, it is never easy to jump over that chasm. But jump you must. You cannot live your life paralysed between two worlds. Though only you can make that bounding leap. You cannot be pushed, even if it is in the right direction, otherwise not only will it serve to exacerbate the feeling of displacement, but it will also invite a powerful and destructive force to come to your defence, vengeance.

When a human being feels forced, their instinctual response is to produce an opposing force against it, to create a balance, an equilibrium, so that all will be well with the world again. But it won't. Because all we are trying to do is mask our helplessness by creating a phantom feeling of empowerment. Nothing changes, because when all the huffing and puffing is done, deep down we still feel like we're losing. But what is it we feel we are losing? The race? The game of life? The struggle for power? Exactly what is it that we want to win?

Winning and losing. Is that all life seems to amount to? With every single moment of time now being categorised, judged, decided upon, declared as to whether it is a pass or a fail, how can any true or pure perspective not be lost in the never ending search for the ultimate perspective?

The ideal of 'if you're not winning then you must be losing' is not only tragic but dangerous. It stifles life by imposing a ranking system of things, moments and people. It declares an impossibility of there only being more than a handful of great things, great times, great anythings. It pushes the belief that amazement and wonder is rare, and that normality equals banality. But surely no one would consciously choose to live in a world with those set parameters? And really, isn't it all completely relative anyway? Seeing as we are not clones, that we have all been bestowed individuality, our own path, complete with our own bespoke set of experiences, we must then see that it is here only to give context to our story. And it is this context that creates the judgement of the moment and the verdict within it. An opinion is solely a single pin pushed into the map, a view from just one point, not the whole. The only reason for our obsession with gaining collective agreement is ultimately to reaffirm our perception of ourselves and of the world we have created around us. Through gaining approval, support with what we have done, what we have said or thought or chosen, we are given kudos that we have decided correctly, that we are what we think we are, what we hope to be. The more people we have in our corner and the more people who concur with our beliefs, the more confident we are in those beliefs and, more importantly, ourselves. Though unfortunately because taste and opinion are such fly-away, disposable creatures born in one moment and destined to die in the next, so do our pinned hopes, our confidence and our security. And instead of learning from our pain we immediately seek solace from it by chasing the very thing that brought us to it. Once again we ignorantly venture forth in a desperate search for a way to replenish our precious elixir of security. Out we go into the fields to till once more, renewing the cycle of cultivating compliments, confidence and completeness.

In the room we had no followers or supporters, virtual or physical. Here we were alone. We had to make our own decisions without assistance or support. Here we had to function cut off from society's cord, from society's numerous cords, and somehow find our way, our own way. We now had to exist and manage and live without an instruction manual, without any rule book, without a search engine. Marooned between these four walls we were doomed to think for ourselves, and for those not accustomed to it, it was a very unnerving state in which to reside.

Nevertheless, here we all were, the fortunate shipwreck survivors adrift at sea. Were we glad? Were we sad? I don't think any of us knew what we were. It was all new. But that's the problem, isn't it? We don't like unknowns sneaking into our world uninvited. We don't trust 'em and we don't like their kind skulking around. In our lives we make damn sure to keep them to an absolute minimum by bundling ourselves up tight in our beloved blanket of routine. But here the room had left us completely uncovered, unclothed and unprepared. No safety nets, no ropes, no paddle.

Because we had spent our lives living in a grid of compartmentalisation and categorisation, we were finding it very taxing relating to the whole situation. How could we possibly compartmentalise the room without incurring great difficulty? Our introduction to this place had been so horrendous and yet now we were supposed to welcome it with open arms? We were caged, yet saved. Loser winners. That's what we felt like and that's what we were. Stuck between two polar opposites, yet not in the middle. So we fell between the paradox. Too scared to settle on one thing for too long, too scared to stay, too scared to jump, like some fearful frog procrastinating its next leap as it slowly sinks the lily pad. We leaped between what we knew and what we thought we knew and got tangled up in both. This contradiction of identity was quite literally tearing our selves apart.

This inner conflict was bound to over flow into the room and because we weren't sure how to act, where to pin our point of perception, we leaned on others. Though not in a supportive 'lean on me' way, more in an 'attacking and ripping apart' way, whereby in dissecting and destroying another's stand point we would then somehow be more convinced of our own.

So not surprisingly the room fell into division. Both of the opposing groups stood defiant in their dividedness, as so many often do. Divided over a difference of opinion on something that men have fought and died for since the second pin was pushed in, belief. The two parties were separated by their belief into the believers and the non-believers. One group trusted the radio's words implicitly. They were to be depended upon, relied upon and thus acted upon, to be used as our North Star to help guide and show us the way. Whilst the opposing group vehemently believed the radio announcement to be completely untrustworthy. Though when it came to the exact details and reasoning behind their non-belief, there seemed again to be more division. Some questioned the timescale of the message, the dangers of following information that may no longer even be valid, while others questioned the very nature and reliability of the message itself. Suffice to say, every faction and faction of faction were united in one belief -

that they were undoubtedly the righteous party and therefore by default all others were not. Immaterial of who held the true reality, saw the true truth, the room was very much divided and therefore acting upon the radio information proved quite difficult. I found it hard to completely ignore the radio announcement. I felt I had to take some regard in it. After all we had no additional pieces of information and even if it were old or fabricated, it was still a clue. So I sat on the believer's side, though on the fringes, with both ears open to every soap box speech.

It's interesting to watch people with opinions. How ferocious they protect them as if it were their own kin. How painstakingly they strive to convince others of the truth absolute in their words. My mind drifted on a gust of thought as I wondered if every act of violence was simply protecting an opinion. How terribly tragic if that were true. No one should have the right to inflict pain upon another just because their pin is in a different position. What need is there to defend words? If a creed speaks to you surely nothing and no one can undo the connection you have experienced. You cannot change thoughts with violence; thoughts can only be changed with thought. Surely each and every person should be allowed to hold any view they wish. Should that not be a fundamental basic right? We may seem to have freedom of speech but is it really permitted and supported within all moments of life? Freedom of speech is merely expressing a personal opinion, not ruling it truth or law. How can it be that this medium of expression can lead to injury or even death? Opinions are the same as perspective and every pin is subjective. And that is a great part of the beauty of our big wide world - its sacred subjectivity, its complete individuality. Otherwise then we would just be one entity wandering the earth alone doomed to never see, speak or experience anyone or anything different from ourselves.

"We need to keep it all in perspective."

"Perspective? I don't even understand what that word means anymore."

"How can you have perspective in a vacuum? That's what all this is, isn't it?"

"I mean we need to keep our eyes on the prize. Nothing has changed. We're still trapped. We still need to find a way out of here."

"We need to listen to the authorities."

"What authorities?"

"Yeah and what authority do they have in here?"

"Every authority! They're the authorities!"

"Authorities of what?"

"How do you even know that it was them anyway? It could have been anyone broadcasting that message."

"What?"

"Like who?"

"What, like the attackers?"

"No, maybe, I don't know."

"Or more likely it could have been made by whoever set this whole thing up."

"Maybe they're the attackers."

"What? Why would the attackers capture us and then broadcast a fake radio message and... It's just too loony."

"Well welcome to the loony-bin man, 'cause it don't get much loonier than this."

"Oh my God. What if he's actually right and we really are stuck in a loony-bin? Maybe that's it? Maybe that's what all this is, that we're all psych patients and this is our new ward."

"Or maybe this is where they do their experiments on us, hidden away so no one can find us."

"You guys are crazy! Your imaginations are letting you create ridiculous conspiracy theories! How could the message not be official? You're forgetting that they gave an emergency number."

"Yeah and how are we supposed to check that?"

"Well they didn't just make the message for people without phones!"

"Unless they did, 'cause they knew we ain't got shit in here."

"None of that matters, it's a digit wrong."

"Didn't you listen? They said it's a new one."

"Why would they bring out a new emergency number in the middle of an emergency?"

"Well maybe because they're getting too many calls."

"Then why not mention that on the radio bulletin?"

"Because they can't mention every little thing! Explaining themselves is not on their priority list! We're in a state of emergency people!"

"I think the attacks have already happened and this is the fallout from them. We're in the fallout."

"So you think we're POWs instead of evacuees?"

"Depends on who won."

"Us or them."

"But who is the them?"

"Does it matter?"

"Of course it matters! We need to know who we're up against."

"They're all the same anyway, it doesn't matter who it is. And how can that piece of information change anything about what we're going through here?"

"Any information is good information."

"What, like the radio message? I wish I had never heard it."

71

"That radio might be the only thing that keeps us alive. God, you people need to wake up and realise that we're in a situation that we can't get out of. Do you understand what that means? We all need to keep our eyes and ears open to anything we can. We're on our own now, maybe even more so than we think."

"So what are we supposed to do? Just sit and wait?"

"For the moment anyway."

"What choice do we have?"

"Yes, it's best to stay put and just wait."

"Wait? Wait for what? To be rescued or captured? I can't do that, I won't do that."

"Yeah I ain't gonna be no one's sitting duck."

"Well in case you haven't noticed, we haven't got many exits to choose from."

"We got the way we came in."

"That door's reinforced steel. Without the key no one's going anywhere."

"God."

"So how long you think that transmission's been broadcasting?"

"Could be hours or even days."

"Days? It can't be, we would have heard something before we got here."

"When did we get here?"

"What do you mean?"

"Well when did we arrive?"

"Today, just earlier, earlier today."

"Yeah, we just arrived."

"Have we?"

"What?"

"Well can you remember exactly when we arrived?"

"Well we weren't exactly conscious at the time."

"Okay, well then from when we woke up."

"When did we wake up?"

"Before we got organised, a while before. I don't remember exactly. But definitely not days."

"So what day is it?"

"Today?"

"Yeah, if yesterday we were just going about our lives, completely oblivious to what a shit heap tomorrow was gonna bring, then what day was yesterday's tomorrow?"

"It's, it's..."

"Yeah?"

"I, I..."

"Tell me!"

"Leave him alone!"

"Hey! Don't touch me! I'm not touching anyone so don't touch me! I'm just trying to get you all to see that this is a little more fucked than we realised. It goes beyond that fucking radio. Something's messed with my mind and I want to know if its messed with yours too. I can't remember a God damn thing!"

"Hey man calm down, we're all in memory limbo. We're all stuck in the same crappy boat."

"Listen, everyone's nerves are understandably frayed. I think we're all well aware of the grim reality of the situation. We're trapped in a place where we can't tell when one day ends and another begins. We have no clocks, no daylight, no nothing. To make matters worse, alarmingly, we all seem to have mislaid our memories and to cap it all off we have been given no indication, clear or otherwise, of why we are here at all. But it could be worse still. At least we're not alone. At least we are all in this, whatever it is, together."

"Look, all I was trying to say was that we're just taking everything as fact, as certain, as real."

"What else are we supposed to do?"

"Question it, question things, question everything! If we can't trust our memories, if we can't trust what's going on inside our heads then how the hell can we trust what's going on outside them?"

A communal silence fell. He had a point. And he had another.

"We need to open our minds and look beyond what we've been given. We're keeping ourselves preoccupied with bullshit! We're concentrating on the wrong things! We think we know a little but we don't know a damn thing! It doesn't matter when we got here! The point is we don't know, we don't know anything and we can't keep pretending that we do. It's just fantasy! We need to keep the canvas clean, be open to any answer, to any truth!"

"Any answer? We need to knuckle down and get some answers instead of waiting for them to drop out of the sky."

"You're not listening to me! This could all be anything! We're minimising our sphere of perception to what we deem plausible under the circumstances. Well there are no circumstances! We're not in Kansas anymore! We don't know where we are, we might not even be on our planet!"

Muffled laughter was stifled as fast as it erupted.

"Philistines! You're all so bound by your expectations, you're blinded to anything else!"

"Hey, hey, relax, relax."

"Relax? How can I relax? I'm trying to expand and stretch my mind as much as possible to try and catch something, anything, and you think I'm going too far?!

We could be trapped in some sort of infinite flux! This could all be a simulation! Who's to say that it's not all been happening over and over again?!"

"What?"

"What did he say?"

"It doesn't matter, he's crazy."

"What's he saying?"

"I don't know. I mean I heard it, but I still don't know."

"He's really lost it now."

"I liked the alien scenario better, more blockbuster."

Laughter was not stifled this time, no one cared about disrespecting a mad man.

"He is right, in part. We have got to look at every plausible possibility. We can't base our entire reality on just one unconfirmed transmission."

"Can we afford not to?"

"Y'all can stay arguing all day. I don't care what's real. I just gotta get outta here."

"I think we've got to keep listening for updates."

"Well we can't keep it on, it'll drive us all mad."

"We should leave it in the bathroom and anyone who wants to check can go check."

"I really think we should take heed of what they're saying and just stay put. There's a war happening out there, the least we can do is listen to them. They're risking their lives for us."

"I doubt very much the voice you heard is doing any life risking."

"Well what trouble does it take for us to just do our part and leave it at that?"

"Do our part and leave it at that? Just our freedom, our lives, which I remind you is the very reason brave people give theirs."

"Well there don't seem to be any point in arguing, we got no place to go."

"We don't even know where we are."

"We're probably in some government owned building used as an emergency safe house or something."

"Or we could be underground."

"We're in a high rise office block. That's hardly going to be underground."

"Then where are the windows?"

"Covered over and sealed for protection."

"In this state of emergency they had time to plaster the windows and then carefully and seamlessly make it look like part of the old wall?"

"No! Yes! I don't know!"

"That's the point, we're making hypotheses upon hypotheses! It's all just unfounded speculation!"

"Well isn't that all science is? And we've used that as the foundation for our whole world."

"That's different."

"Is it?"

"We should do a vote. Make it democratic, like all successful societies."

"Successful societies? Are you for real? There's no such thing as true democracy, or a successful society for that matter."

"Are you serious?"

"He's right. A perfect democracy cannot exist, but neither can a communist one."

"Alright, listen, we're not trying to create a perfect society, democratic or not, we're just trying to decide what to do. And we should probably leave politics out of it."

"First rule of a successful dinner party, no politics."

"Lady, this ain't no dinner party, in case you hadn't noticed."

"Yes, I am well aware of that fact, but my point is only strengthened by the environment in which we find ourselves. This may not bear any resemblance to any dinner party I have ever hosted, but being ten times the size and without entrées or Bellini's, the atmosphere is going to be far harder to control and guests are going to get far feistier far faster. We certainly do not need an argument to start with political pedanticalness."

"What are we voting for again?"

"Democracy."

"But what can we do? I mean, after we vote? What is it for?"

"Yeah, won't we just be in the same situation we're in now?"

"Well, except we would have killed some time."

"We're stuck here regardless of anything, voted or not voted."

"I can't just sit here and do nothing, I've got a family out there."

"We've all got families out there."

"So what are we going to do?"

Their conversations ran in circles like the ever-avenging ouroboros, infinitely at war with itself, infinitely consumed with a quest for righteousness, destined to be forever caught within its own reins of retaliation, unable to escape, unable to forgive.

I stayed quiet on the periphery watching the speeches spiral. Missy joined us as I think she too felt the futility in their words. She decided to distract herself and my son by teaching him pat-a-cake. I watched the strange scene before me of oil and water; separate yet together. A light-hearted world of innocence encased within a heavy-hearted world of experience. And now the experienced were becoming irritated. Their anxiety was chipping away at their foundations, destabilising the shaky scaffolding surrounding them. There was pacing and tapping, fiddling and scratching with nervous nail biting, restless hand shaking, sporadic head twitching and repetitive blinking, all the many quelled ticks were now emerging as the effects of withdrawal were hitting. You could see craving choreographing the same dance moves around the room. But which beat of the dangerous drum of addiction forced their dance, conducted their trance? Which rhythm of withdrawal was now animating them, puppeting them now that their mainline maestro of melody was gone? Maybe it wasn't anything as dramatic as the obvious heavyweights. Perhaps it was the smaller, more habitual routines that were proving the most difficult to cope without. A morning cuddle, a favourite mug, a drive to work, a familiar tune, a friendly smile, a trip to the store, a family dinner, a goodnight kiss. Perhaps we didn't even know how dependant we were on the content our lives. Every day we strived to change them, improve them, polish them, perfect them, but maybe they already were perfectly the perfection they were supposed to be.

I think until now we had been quite oblivious to the multitude of coping mechanisms we had all been administering, not even the slightest bit aware of the numerous walking aids we were availing of at every step, not realising how dependant, how hooked we really were on our various seemingly harmless vices that we were now slowly becoming conscious of. If our addiction is never tested then how can we see its full power? If we feed it we never get to see it starve. We never get to see its hunger, its real strength. If the beast is kept fed and locked away does it cease to be a beast, does it exist at all? Is a functioning addict still an addict? If the locks were removed the released beast would probably take great exception to the disregard of its existence. And it would in no uncertain terms make quite sure its presence was felt. Maybe he is the one that flicks the switch. And maybe he is not the best choice of guardian for it. To avoid at being at the mercy of this creature of chaos we must remove all our bannisters to see how we really cope in this reality called life, how we really feel about it, instead of just postponing the reveal, prolonging the poisonous zeal and continuing to exist in our haze of desire.

Now clouds of craving were descending and a mist of madness was rising we would have the greatest challenge yet to overcome, ourselves. I saw a man feverishly scratching at the wall as if it were an itch. His eyes were red, his obsessive stare intense. He seemed to bear a closer resemblance to some character from a dark underworld than one from our own. Maybe he was a smoker or an alcoholic or worse, he could have been detoxing from anything. There were a hundred of us after all, a perfect census of society. A thin speckled slice of our civilised world. Just like one of those ice samples collected in one long tube, bands and waves of dirt and bubbles, mud and stone. We were those contrasting bands, all so different, all meshed together, all coping in the best way we could, in the best way we knew.

The bathroom was finally empty so I decided to take the opportunity, but at the exact moment I went to stand I felt something. I wasn't sure what I felt, or if it was even real. But when I looked around the room and saw the same doubting eyes looking for confirmation, I knew we all couldn't have been imagining it. Then it happened again and more heads perked up. I looked down to Missy and my boy, their frozen faces echoed my own. But what could we do? Where could we go? What possible cover could we take? We were stuck in a storm in a bottled ship. There was no escape. Then the big one came. People who hadn't noticed the other two warning shots were thrown right off their feet. I grabbed my boy and pressed us tight against the wall. I could see the room out of the corner of my eye. Everyone was fixed in their positions, as if concreting themselves to the floor was somehow going to make them immune to the shake. The rumble was accompanied by such a growl it felt as if the room was going to collapse in on itself. The ferocity of the noise was terrifying and it had us surrounded. It sounded like the room was being twisted apart, like a baby with a Rubik's Cube. The walls moved and swayed buckling under the pressure. Cracks ran across the ceiling raining down thick showers of dust. No one moved or spoke a word. After it seemed to have stopped our own personal aftershocks hit. We had believed ourselves to be relatively safe and secure in our stronghold. But now, now all bets were off. There really was no safe place. But we had to hold our panic at bay a little longer. We couldn't allow ourselves to surrender just yet, we had to be poised for action and reaction. Breaking down is not a good survival mechanism. When was the next one coming? We all braced ourselves, wincing for the next wave. The threat, the anticipation was worse than the happening, like the almighty pre-plaster removal angst. We stayed frozen in our gargoyle positions, poised, waiting, waiting for something we didn't want to happen, to happen. The alertness you feel in a crisis is unparalleled. It is of course terror tinged but contains such a presence of being that it nearly hypnotises you with its lure. I felt myself surrendering to its power, flowing into a feeling of such an almighty strength of self, such an unshakeable force of being. The irony was not lost on me as a secret smile seeped out. I tried to shield it, to hide it, but of course on my cover up my eyes landed upon the very blue waters I did not want them to. He mirrored my smirk, which I then instantly snuffed out turning back towards the wall.

Just as the tension and our grips were losing strength, the large fluorescent tube lights flickered and flashed, sputtering as they fought to stay alive, until one by one they accepted defeat. The darkness poured into the room like thick paint, covering us all. I could feel it envelop my skin, fill my pores, steal my reality. The air felt viscous, like it was coagulating. I didn't have any fear of the dark, I didn't have any irrational phobias at all. But now I felt like a claustrophobic agoraphobe. There was just too much and not enough. I had never been exposed to such a darkness. I imagine not many of us had. In the city the lights always found a way. Even in the countryside it never reached this level. It was as if here, wherever we were, light had now ceased to exist, as if it had been made extinct. Now we were submerged in the lonely strain of isolation that only complete obscurity can bring. It was an uncanny experience. I held my son close, though he wasn't scared. Strangely many children aren't, it's normally the adults who are but who hide it well. Perhaps it is due to our excess of experience over innocence which warrants us, demands us to consider all risks as possible.

My ears zinged as they seemed to unfold, allowing all the sounds to enter. That was what surprised me the most. When you're down a sense, especially the primary one, the others really do seem to answer the call. Maybe I just noticed them more without the limelight hogger, sight. Now I could hear breathing, so much breathing. All types, fast and shallow, deep and slow, all kinds of wheezes and whistles. I could hear people rubbing their face, stubble being scratched, the bathroom tap dripping, and faint music... that music again, where was it coming from? Was I the only one hearing it?

Another sense stormed the stage shoving my thoughts aside, smell. The room smelled. No, it stank. I couldn't believe I hadn't noticed it until now. It was a stench. A stench with multiple sources battling for superiority. Stale, dusty, damp, mouldy, the smell of the old, of the forgotten. The dank smell wafting in from the bathroom was blending with the room's multiple offerings to create a cocktail so rancid, so repulsive that it made my stomach heave. There was no safe place to find clean air. Even the walls had a smell of their own. Their smell felt hazardous, like we should have been wearing masks. But that wasn't all. There was more and it was airborne. The air was full of it. All I could smell, all I could taste in every breath was the hundred. I could smell their panic. I could smell their fear. I could smell their rotting of reality. It was an unimaginably oppressive cloud to be immersed within, such an unyielding mist of putrescence which clung to me like a film of filth. The air felt warm and humid. I felt I was breathing the discarded breath of the hundred. I tried to breathe less. I felt ill. I closed my eyes, trying to block it out. I had still had my eyes open. I don't know why but it felt strange to close them, like I was conceding. But when I did, my final sense really kicked in. Touch. My fingertips became so sensitive. I could feel every stitch on my son's shirt. I could feel the tiny hairs on his arms, his calm pulse, his soft breath. My aural sense demanded my attention again as a wind of whispers blew around the room.

"Is it over?"

"Where's the aftershock?"

"It's wasn't an earthquake."

"Well what was it?"

"It had to be an earthquake."

"It's not like any I've ever experienced."

"Then what was it?"

"It was the attacks!"

"You think that's what happened?"

"Makes sense."

"I hope not."

"You mean you'd prefer them to happen to us as well as an earthquake?"

"Maybe they won't affect us?"

"You heard the radio message. Anyone who can hear it is going to be affected."

"Yeah but we're in a safe house, right?"

"Why did the lights go out like that?"

"Yeah, why not all at once?"

"Maybe they're on a circuit or something?"

"A circuit? Are you an electrician?"

"No, but I've seen these types of lights before."

"We've all seen tube lighting before."

"It doesn't matter. How do we get them back on?"

"Did anyone see a switch?"

"You can't just switch them back on if there's been a power cut."

"Is that what we're going with, a power cut?"

"Maybe the grid's down?"

"Maybe the whole city's down."

"If we're even in the city."

"They'll come back soon."

"What if they don't?"

"Then, well then it's all just got a whole lot worse."

"I didn't think that was possible."

"Oh God."

"What are we going to do?"

People seemed more forthright with their opinions under the invisibility cloak of darkness. We had to do something, though I had no idea what. I could hear another conversation, a planning and plotting one. It was the brothers. I told my son and Missy that I was going to see what I could do. I stood up with determination trusting my heightened senses to guide me. But they did not, and after a few steps I tripped. As I was falling a warm hand grabbed mine and a familiar tingling fizz consumed my body.

"Don't worry, it's me."

I knew who it was, I knew that feeling.

"I was okay." I detached his hand from mine.

"I can help you find your way."

"You can see in the dark?"

"I saw you fall."

"I wasn't exactly soft-footed."

"Are you okay?"

"It was just a small trip."

"I mean, are you alright?"

"Yeah, sure. Why wouldn't I be?"

"Don't worry, the lights will come back."

"How do you know?"

"They just will. I don't know when, but they will."

"You don't know that."

"They always do."

"But you don't know for sure, you can't. You've never been here before."

"Light always returns."

The warm hand found mine again, preventing me from processing what he had said. Was I hearing something he wasn't saying? The intensity of the fizzling increased as my thoughts decreased. I could feel myself drift into autopilot mode. It felt so easy, so natural. No. I couldn't lose focus. I couldn't fall. I shook my hand away from his and stepped forward into the unknown. I felt for the wall to my right and soon my fingertips found it and followed it to the door frame of the bathroom. I felt past it towards the planning voices.

"We can't do that."

"Will it work?"

"We can't."

"Will it work?"

"Probably but-"

"But nothing. It's our only hope."

"No, the radio is our only hope. We can't sacrifice it."

"It might not damage it."

"You don't know that. We could lose it."

"Look, we have candles, we have darkness, it's the only way."

"We can't, we can't risk it."

"We'll just need it to burn long enough for the paper to light."

"Well we can't make that decision. It's up to everyone."

"Alright, let's ask the room."

A piercing whistle split sensitive ears and the darkness surrounding them. Now people had their radio referendum. Everyone had to choose between light or darkness, information or radio silence. We didn't just have to arbitrarily pick sides or pick a theoretical truth; we had to set fire to a bridge. Now that the choice was directly in front of us with a substantial risk on the table, people weren't so quick to make their allegiance known. It was no longer hypothetical. A decision with an immediate and irretrievable consequence had to be made. The present for the future. The reality we had or the one we would have.

It is not often in a life crammed with choices that a decision is made which really impacts our lives. This wasn't just one lump or two. It was quite possibly life or death. We also had to decide how we were going to cast our vote. Democracy in the dark is a very tricky thing to achieve. We were nearly pushed to a vote on how to cast our vote. We were going around in circles. Then a voice ended the motion sickness.

"Hey, has anyone checked the radio since the shake?"

Silence answered.

"Okay, so how about we listen to see if the message has changed? If it hasn't, we go through with it. If it has, we wait another hour and check again."

No one agreed. But no one disagreed. So as silence again answered, the radio was turned on.

"...has been destroyed. All lives within the red danger zone have been presumed lost. If you are receiving this message you are outside the red zone. Do not make any attempt to enter the red zone. Preliminary reports show an unknown bio hazard has been deployed. Those

believed to be exposed are strongly advised to isolate themselves as a precaution until a field medical facility has been established. The amber zone is now under quarantine. All inhabitants in the surrounding outer zones of yellow and green are advised to evacuate as soon as possible. Those in the yellow zone must do so within six hours and those in the green zone must do so within twelve before the quarantine area is expanded. Head away from the city and bring identification, limited supplies and belongings. Checkpoints are being set up where you will be further notified. This will be the last broadcast. Breaking news. The city has been destroyed. All lives within the red danger zone have been presumed lost..."

The broadcast was so much louder in the dark. The words seemed to ripple upon the darkness and ricochet around the room, doubling the resonance, doubling the impact. And though there were a hundred of us sharing in the fall out, this time we were each forced to experience it alone. Without the lights, without our sight, we couldn't mirror our grief, we couldn't share the weight. The darkness had separated us from each other, split our dysfunctional family apart.

"What zone are we in?"

"We have to leave."

"What zone are we in?"

"How the hell are we supposed to know?!"

"We need light."

"We need to get out of here."

"We could get the light back at any moment. The back-up generator is bound to kick in soon."

"How the hell do you even know there's a back-up anything?!"

"We need to get out of here."

"We can't leave. We have to stay put."

"We were told to stay where we are, it's contaminated out there."

"But maybe we're in the yellow or green zone?"

"Then we really gotta get out of here!"

"Why would they put us here with no means of escape and then expect us to somehow evacuate ourselves?"

"Why would they put us here in the first place?"

"It doesn't make sense."

"What does?"

"Maybe everyone's been evacuated already and they're all in rooms like us, probably in this very building."

"Then why would the radio message tell people to evacuate?"

"Maybe they didn't get everyone, how could they?"

"Why the need for all the secrecy, all this cloak and dagger stuff? What is being protected? What are they hiding? What aren't they telling us?"

"What do they ever?"

"Those poor people."

Sniffs and sobs were quietly trickling around the room.

"Doesn't anyone think that it is a little strange how quick the new message came after the attacks?"

"Maybe they were anticipating it."

"Perhaps, but how could they already have the preliminary reports? How could they know it is an unknown pathogen? And why dramatically declare it the 'last broadcast'? What a strange decision, don't you think?"

"Yeah, why would there even be a need to announce it? And hold on, how can it be the last? There never is a last."

"Because maybe the enemy is listening."

"The enemy is hardly going to stop listening in just because the announcement promised to be the last."

"Maybe there's nothing left to say."

"Of course there is. It's not like they're all abandoning ship!"

"Unless they actually are and that's the thing they're holding back on announcing."

"What do you mean?"

"That we've lost, and they're not coming back."

"Then we're all refugees?"

"That's completely ridiculous, you can't displace an entire population."

"Well, we don't know the extent to which this pathogen has spread, how dangerous it is, how many places were hit."

"Oh my God, this could be nationwide."

"We don't know anything yet so let's not speculate on the worst."

"Well at least now we know the message is up to date."

"And what the shake was."

"No! No we don't! We still don't know anything for sure! The shake could have been our response to the attacks! The credibility of the message has not risen due to an updated version!"

"Yes, he's right. If we look at it clinically, this doesn't actually prove anything."

"What? You guys are thinking yourselves away from the reality of the situation! Look, they said there were gonna be attacks, then we got a hell of a shake, then they tell us there's been an attack, that's pretty water tight to me!"

"We're going around in circles again! We're not voting on whether the radio is reliable or not. We're deciding whether or not we want to risk the radio to get some light on in here."

"I would say that the integrity of the radio message is integral to our decision!"

"I thought the decision was already made. We heard a different message, so we don't touch it for an hour, right?"

"So we're all going to wait for an hour to hear a new message that the old message said is not going to come? Either way you cut this shit cake, we're gonna need light more than we're gonna to need that radio. Anyone who doesn't agree, just say."

Silence again met darkness. So the team quietly took it as their cue. I could hear the short bald man working on dismantling the radio, most probably with the tools he had singled out earlier. How strange, I thought, that he had somehow foreseen their use. As he did, he explained to the brothers how he came to know transistor radios so well. Their team searched in the darkness for the printer paper and the candles and suddenly a plan was in motion. It took him a while to get the show ready but he had been entertaining the crowd with stories of his father's old tranny and the wrath they had often incurred forsaking boring family occasions to listen to the big game.

"Here goes something," he said as he did something no one could see.

Then the dimmest of deep scarlet glows appeared. It cast such a warm, almost ethereal light in the dark. I suddenly got a strange flash that maybe the creation of our universe had not been too dissimilar. Why did it have to be such a boomingly brash beginning? Why not calm and gentle, small and soft? So as I watched, mesmerised by its delicate beauty, I pretended I was witnessing the birth of our reality. It felt so comforting, so familiar. As the glow focused its force, gathering its power, a short thin line of bright red shone like a strand of Venus' hair. Its soft light soothed the obscurity and made us remember ourselves, the parts we could remember. As it glowed brighter with the red turning into an amber and then a gold, the darkness, like a ghoul, was banished into the corners of the room. It seemed that even the smallest light had the power to defeat the darkest dark. Finally we had perspective again, visually at least. The boys softly teased the paper over the hot wire. It burned but it did not light. A strand of smoke coiled around the room. Every eye stared at the stubborn old paper refusing to light with every mind realising that this may be the last sight we would ever see. I looked down at my sons beautiful face. I wanted it to be the last image burned into my memory. Just as hope was exiting and disparagement arriving, a gust of flame flashed the room. It looked like the air had caught fire. It was beautiful, and it blew me and my deprived senses away. It was shocking to see so much light interrupt the darkness, to see so much vivid colour erupt in bland beige. It was quite something to see a living breathing entity being born in such a place.

We all rushed over to see the show, to see the beast sway. From a distance we must have resembled a clan of cavemen crowded around the springboard to their next evolutionary step, completely hypnotised by their new discovery, their new source of power, their new weapon against the brutality of the world they found themselves in. Shining, smiling eyes glazed over providing a hundred pairs of mirrors for the flame to admire its reflection in, to marvel at its boundless beauty of form, to worship its wild wonder of awakening.

The capricious flame danced before us, reaching out and expanding its new self so gracefully, so vibrantly, so uninhibitedly. Its merry shadow skipped and twirled around the walls of the room to a song all of its own, its own ode to life, its celebration of birth. I felt such honour to be present for its beginning, to witness the dawning of this impish sprite of light who had spontaneously and unwittingly broken into our fortress. Though it all seemed very peculiar, like it wasn't supposed to happen, like it was a little off script. Which, of course, made it all the more exciting. I felt like a naughty child in church as a stifled giggle burst out of me. This moment was one of the rare few where you realised, whilst in it, how rare and extraordinary it really was. I yearned for its frolicking freedom. It held such unparalleled passion as its spontaneous creativity expressed itself with every stretch. It was more than inspiring. Its truth and fluidity filled me, I felt it complete me. I felt I was a great light, a part of the greatest light there was and I had found my brethren.

A new conformist flame was born from its wild parent. It was a small single flame which stood still and regular, securely fixed upon its wick. It had no dance or song. It had been tamed, its spirit broken, its freedom sold for the price of existence. When they were confident their new recruit had been adequately lit, they wafted and waved its predecessor in the air like a flag until it defiantly claimed the paper for itself forcing them to drop it to the floor. Feet appeared and began stomping and stamping. I wanted to stop them but I couldn't move. I just watched as they attacked and extinguished the very life they had created. As I saw the brave embers on the floor burning their brightest, gasping for breath, grasping for life, my sadness bore a child of its own which fell slowly down my cheek before dropping to the floor. I felt such a great ache for the courageous flame and its brief but invaluable existence. It had gifted the room light and returned our sight. It too had gifted them to me, but internally, in a way I had never known. And our gratitude to our saviour, our servant of vision, was to dismiss it, to snuff it out, just discard it once we had gotten what we wanted. I felt that I had been part of a crime, that my inaction was just as bad as their action. I felt myself begin to fall. Strong arms interrupted my descent and held me close. I had no strength to push him away. I needed a moment to steady myself. Once I had, I turned to walk away. His warm hand caught mine and turned me back to him. I shook the sadness from my eyes before I looked into his.

"It's okay, you don't need to hide your grief from me. I too drifted into its spirit, danced with it, became it."

All I wanted to do was fall into his broad chest, collapse into his strength, become weightless, but I stayed strong.

"I... It's just fire."

"Was it? Was that all it was to you?"

"Yes! Yes that's all it was!"

"Did that flame not gift you more? Did it not give you great joy and a complete lightness of being? Did it not elevate your spirit with the infinite aliveness of its essence? Did you not lose yourself within it, live a life, even for just that moment more free, more joyful, more your own than your own?"

"No! I don't know! I don't understand what you're saying!"

"I think you do but you're too scared to admit it. Let me just ask you this. Did you feel a piece of yourself perish along with it?"

"Why are you doing this to me? What do you want me to say?"

"I don't want you to say anything. I just want you to say what you feel."

"I just want to be alone!"

I regretted the words as soon as I heard them. My stupid reflex action. But I couldn't take his intensity, his insistence, not now, not after what had just happened. I pushed past him to the bathroom. As I closed the door all I could hear was cheering. I felt sick. My stomach turned as I gagged. I twisted the dirty taps, trying to drown them all out. I twisted and twisted those stubborn old taps until my hands hurt. But I could still hear them, hear their celebrations. Celebrations over a death, the death of the only thing in the world that I had completely understood and that had completely understood me. I knelt on the hard, cold, tiled floor and wept, wept for my friend, and the piece of myself that died along with it.

Chapter Three

As a new generation of controlled offspring were born the room began to take on a different mood. I don't know if it was just the ambiance that the candlelight had conjured but it did not feel like the same space we had been trapped in. An hour ago, we had the lights and only the first radio message and the mood was low but now, even after all that had happened, the density in the room seemed to dilute. Was it just because we had won that battle over darkness? Was it just because of that one little victory that the air now held such buoyancy? Even the smell seemed to have dissipated. Things felt lighter, yet they certainly were not. I didn't understand. I didn't understand anything anymore. My head felt scrambled, like it couldn't correlate, like it couldn't create order. Were we really destined to be trapped in solitary confinement with a bowl full of people? Was this really happening? I tried to wrap my brain around it all but it was too much. I started to feel unbalanced. I tried to repeat my silly calming mantra, *it's not real, it's all in your head, it's no deal, it's all in your head.* Obviously it didn't work. I don't think it ever had. As ridiculous as it sounds, there is some truth in it. It is after all in our heads where we process and generate, where we create and formulate, where we piece together our reality. Everything, all of it, has to pass through there.

But what if our processing machine became faulty and we weren't even aware of it? What if we were looking at everything the wrong way? What if we were lost when we felt found and found when we felt lost? What if we weren't ourselves? What if we weren't here at all but somewhere else entirely? What if we were in a dream? And perhaps, not even our own. How would we know? How could we find out? Would we even want to? How different would it be to real existence if we had never experienced it? Would we even mind? Surely imagined existence is better than no existence at all, even if you are just the creation of someone else's dream.

I looked over to my son making hand shadows on the wall with Missy and her girls. Always making lemonade. I watched the wall and the strange shade they were casting upon it. In their reality of play at this very moment how real were those shadows? How did they feel as the deities of a new world? I watched the various, sometimes dubious looking, animals rejoice at their vicarious host creators. They were animated, but were they alive? They so seemed to be. In the world of the wall, which I may add had more eyes than just mine rested upon it, they were quite certainly alive. Two dimensional creatures born from spirits too complicated for their comprehension, yet how different was their situation to our own? Were they real? Were they really alive? What does alive even mean? We immediately submit the standard answer of living is breathing yet, not all life takes breath. Is there not more to it than that clinical response? Does awareness classify existence, life? While locked within our own cage of consciousness how can we possibly comment on who or what has it? How can we know for sure whether anything has an awareness outside of our own? By simply coming into being, by simply just being a part of what is, is that the prerequisite for being alive? Where is the line drawn and who does the drawing? Did every single thing have a conscious nature about it and did we impart that conscious nature simply by perceiving it? In that way does everything contain an aliveness, some form of sentient existence? If anyone could have heard my thoughts my liberties may very well have been in jeopardy. Was I going mad? Had I already? I slumped down on the hidden side of the far column so that the only portal of awareness I cared about wouldn't have to watch his mother try to collect the pieces of her brittle self. Thankfully I was alone, except for a man sitting on the left side of the column and a husband and wife on the right. I felt so vacant, so lost, so completely disjointed from everything, from anything. I just didn't care anymore. I just didn't care. I felt more alone than I had ever felt in my life. In a room full of people, I was drowning in loneliness.

The strange thing was that all this didn't have a thing to do with the room. Obviously it had been a catalyst, yet I don't think it was the trauma of the whole ordeal that was causing me to feel this way. In actual fact I felt strangely distant from it, unattached. That was the bit I didn't like, the feeling of separation. Separate from myself, separate from reality, but how could that even be? How could I be apart from me and my life? Who was the me that was apart from it? Was that the real me? I felt adrift in an ocean of oceans with nothing to hold onto, nothing to help keep me afloat. Yet, that flame... that flame had reached something in me. It had touched and awoken something deep inside. It had uncovered a part of myself I never knew I had lost. I needed to think, but nothing was coming. I needed to explore and expand this new territory but my mind just kept drawing blank pages. Like chasing fireflies in sunlight, it was just too faint. It was all too distant, I couldn't grasp at any of it, and then I heard the music again. It was beautiful. An unknown composer with an unknown composition, yet more familiar than any piece I had ever heard. It carried that same breed of honest truth that the flame had possessed. I closed my eyes and instead of questioning its origin, I allowed it to enter. It was very hard to keep myself open, to lower my drawbridge. But once I persevered I felt a healing, like I was being mended from the inside. Relief flowed up through every part of my body and as it reached my eyes, it cascaded down in a waterfall of cleansing.

"Beautiful, isn't it?"

I looked around but no one was there.

"So quiet you doubt its existence."

The voice was coming from the man on the left side of the column. He peeked his head round but I knew that tone, those words and the weird way they made me feel. A learned response of recoil shot up but it felt feigned and programmed.

"What are you talking about?"

"The music, what else?"

He could hear it too, typical. However this time instead of running away, I decided to play.

"How do you know I was listening to it?"

"Because I could hear it too."

"Okay... so where is it coming from?"

"The same place as everything else."

"And where is that?"

"The place where the flame took you."

"How do you know about that?"

"I just do."

"Any other things you just know?"

"A few."

"Any you'd care to share?"

"Any you'd care to hear?"

"Why did you speak in spirals?"

"To catch you."

"To catch me?"

"To catch the girl inside the girl."

"What do mean the girl inside the girl?"

"The girl who has been imprisoned."

"What?"

"I want to help her free herself."

"From what?"

"From whatever has got her so stuck."

"And what do you think that is?"

"Only she can know."

"Well I hate to disappoint you but there is no damsel in distress for you to valiantly save. I am trauma free, no deep regrets or supressed guilt or anything."

"Really? Okay, well if you're sure. I'm very happy to hear that."

"Good."

"Good."

A silence seeped in, slipping sneakily without invitation, squatting down between us like some ugly troll just staring at me. I couldn't stand it any longer, so I didn't.

"So, what are you in for?"

"Life."

"Me too."

"But it's okay. Life's good, no matter where you're standing."

"Not really."

"No?"

"Definitely not."

"Why?"

"Because life can't always be good. It's like a barcode. When you're in the dark bits, it's never great. Actually, it's really mostly dark bits with slivers of light."

"Really?"

"Yes. Actually it's more like that near impossible task of capturing the perfect selfie. You're always trying to find that angle, your best side. There's only one and it's a bitch to find."

"Interesting. So you think there's just one angle of perfection, of happiness, just one way to see life at its best?"

"Yes, but you can't just choose that view, it's not something that you can consciously go and find. It just sometimes happens. Like super brief flashes if it."

"But wouldn't it be better if it were just one continuous flash?"

"Well obviously, but that's not really attainable."

"It isn't?"

"Not for us mortals anyway."

"But surely if that flash exists, it must exist in order for it to be found and felt all of the time?"

"I think you're being a little over optimistic, and perhaps a little naïve."

"You consider those words to be related?"

"How can you not?"

"Okay, well at the risk of sounding like a terribly naïve optimist, I think it's our supreme purpose to live within that flash every single day of our lives. I think it would be an absolute waste of life not to dedicate our life to it. Wouldn't you want to push your curtains aside if you awoke to a beautiful sunrise streaming through the gap in the middle? Just because the full view of the sunrise is obscured, it doesn't mean a sunrise can only be that sliver of a scene. We're just peeking through a slit of life and making judgment calls on it without getting to see the full picture."

"Right, but you can't just dedicate your life to chasing something that's impossible to find. It's not like people aren't looking, they are."

"Has it worked?"

"Well that's exactly my point. It's an impossible task."

"Not if you know what you're looking for."

"Which is?"

"Freedom from preconceptions."

"But we need presumptions to navigate the world we live in. To not cast blueprints onto things would be to fly blind, to journey without a safety belt."

"And what would be so terrible about that?"

"You wouldn't be protected, and that's dangerous."

"Isn't it more dangerous to be protected when you don't need to be?"

"What?"

"When you hug your child, do you do so with a bullet proof jacket, goggles and parachute? Well, why not? Because it is safe and those very safety providers would end up damaging your ability to connect with him, to increase your bond. Sometimes we need to go into life unarmed. Sometimes we've got to leave all our weapons at the door to truly feel what life really is, what life really feels like."

"Maybe emotionally you might be right but that's as hard as not protecting yourself physically. It's not easy to open up. It's far easier to stay protected, closed."

"In the short term maybe. But it's not something we can keep up forever. We've got to let go of the wall sometime. I think it's just easier when there's a choice, and quicker. Life is so special and it's just such a shame if we never get to see it."

"I don't know if it's all special all of the time."

"I think it is, every single second. I think it's just us who are the ones who can't see it all the time. Because we incessantly and obsessively evaluate and review it we are left with a paltry portion of perfection which always leaves us hungry. But life is special, all of it, because it exists. Because it is happening right now. At this very moment life is in existence, happening right in front of our eyes. And even more wondrous than that, you are here experiencing it. You exist as an awareness that is perceiving it at this very moment. You are aware. You exist. Now come on, it doesn't get more wondrous, more miraculous, more magical than that."

"Magical? That's just pretend."

"But magic is just perception."

"No, it's deception."

"Maybe, but it is still perception. To cavemen a simple lighter would certainly have held magical properties as would the person mastering it. Fifty years ago hand held computers existed solely in the realms of sci-fi shows, back then our ordinary phones would have seemed like magic."

"But we know they're not. It just depends on advancement, on time."

"You're right, magic is time dependant. Take an ordinary carrot growing in the ground. If time were sped up and we could see the seed manifesting itself into a

110

fully formed carrot, we would proclaim that this seed held magical powers. But because it happens so slowly, on a different time scale to us where we don't see each detailed step of its gradual appearance, we simply pass it off as ordinary, as normal."

"Come on, a growing carrot is hardly magical."

"Isn't it?"

"Really, Leo?"

"Well, the fact that contained within the seed is all of the intelligence needed to create and form a complete carrot makes it pretty magical to me, immaterial of how long it takes for the reveal."

"I have never met anyone who sees a carrot as intelligent or magical. Things grow everywhere every day and have done since before our time. It's nothing new, it's the most normal, ordinary thing there is."

"Things are only normal because it's what we're used to, because of the parameters we have come to accept."

"What?"

"We are accustomed to accepting what is within the parameters of existence. Which on its own is not so serious, but when we then brand and mark things based solely upon their frequency of occurrence, we do something very destructive. We devalue our world. We suck the colour from it, disregarding the magic. All these wonders, without even having the opportunity to defend themselves, are suddenly stripped from their wonder and baptised as ordinary, as nothing special, just written off because they are the norm. How can we dismiss magic just because of the high frequency at which it occurs?"

"Well, rare does equal special."

"So a hundred flying pink elephants is less magical than one?"

"I'm not even going to answer that one. Regular things are regular because that's what they are."

"But can't you see that in thinking that way not only are we shading our lives, changing them into monochrome, but we are closing a door of perception, just taping it over with words like 'understood', 'standard', 'common'."

"Well, that's because they are. A carrot is a carrot. Things are what they are."

"Are they? To past civilisations the stars were not the balls of burning gases we now know them to be. They were celestial. The sun was deemed a God. The elements were entities that wielded power and energy. Lightning was believed to be a product of the gods. Things we regard now as trivial were once worshipped."

"That's because they didn't know the truth."

"Truth. Possibly the most subjective word in existence."

"I think you've got that backwards. How can truth be anything else but completely objective?"

"Because everyone has their own version of it."

"No, truth is still truth is still truth, immaterial of what anyone believes to be true."

"But in the world of the believer, it is their truth. How can you say that does not exist?"

"Because it isn't real, it's just their opinion, it's not fact."

"So when people were persecuted for considering the world to be round, what truth did they suffer at the hands of?"

"Well, obviously not the real truth."

"So how does truth matter if you are contained within a world of untruth? Surely then its authenticity becomes immaterial? Take Galileo with his outlandish ideas and perceived untruths. In the world in which he lived, not his subjective world but the law of the land world, he was sentenced to house arrest for his heresy of belief that the sun was fixed and we were not, with his innovative findings banned from publication. No matter what the truth was, he was still stuck within the confines of a reality where it was not. So therefore, what is truth? And how does its objectivity matter in a world of subjectivity?"

"Okay, I know what you're trying to say but that's a very isolated incident."

"Is it? History is streaked and splattered with examples of people who have killed and died in the name of their truth. Some have even been executed because of their knowledge of a truth that has not yet been revealed, burnt at the stake because their intelligence, their insight made them untrustworthy otherworldly beings. And perhaps more commonly people have lost their lives fighting for or against a truth they believed was worth dying for. Objective truth inevitably becomes subjective."

"Perhaps you're right. But you've verged off the magic path."

"Okay. How about electricity? We all use it on a daily basis without a thought to how magical a thing it is."

"It's just moving electrons, Leo."

"Just because we have named them electrons it doesn't mean they're not magic. We don't know where they come from, why they were born. We have not created or invented them but just found them already in existence. Just because we have learned to harness the beast, it doesn't mean we fully understand it. Knowledge of how it behaves doesn't take away from the mystery of what it is."

"True. But it doesn't make it magic either."

"But what is magic? For a child learning about the world, magic is in all things. It is only with an increase in experience we declare things not to be. Knowledge may make us aware of things, may help us to understand their behaviour, but it still does not explain them, their origins, their essence, their reason. We don't know the reason for any of the things in our world, not really. And the more we try to explain them in greater detail, the more we are eluded by their why. The very reason for our own existence is still the source of such divided speculation. Even after centuries of thought, of ideas, of disagreement, of wars, we still just don't know. We still don't know the truth of our existence. We're all just going about our lives not even the least bit bothered that we have no idea of the truth of our selves, our reason, our why."

"Well, I think we have a pretty good idea."

"We do?"

"Well, I suppose it's not concrete. It's still a bit wet."

"Until it dries then it's just subjective truth isn't it?"

"Okay, you've got me there I suppose. The ultimate objective truth of our existence is still subjective."

"And yet we still sacrifice ourselves for the sake of subjectivity."

"What?"

"We still kill and die over perception. Don't you think it's just insane that people have died over a dispute of ideas?"

"Yeah, you're right there. It's complete madness."

"It's because belief and truth are both caged in the mind of the perceiver that they are both subjective."

"Alright, that does seem to be true, I mean a truth."

"Cute. So the question is how can we, captives of subjectivity, claim to know whether magic does or does not exist? We can't see all, know all, be all, so we can't really have a forever view on anything."

"Okay fine, but I thought we were talking more about fairies type magic."

"Well to a child fairy magic is quite real. In their reality it definitely exists."

"Yes, but we all know it's not true."

"If you saw a fairy would that change your opinion?"

"Come on that's ridiculous. It's never going to happen. You don't really believe in fairies do you, Leo?"

"I try not not believing in anything."

"So you believe in everything then?"

"In a way, yes, until it's disproven of course."

"That's crazy. How can something that doesn't exist ever be disproven?"

"How can something that does exist but has never been seen, be proven?"

"Leo, no more spiral staircases. What you see is what exists. Simple."

"The layer that you see covering everything is just a fine mist. What you see is not all that exists. How can it be? Even purely at a scientific level we can only see a fraction of what's there, and not solely on the micro or telescopic scale. The electromagnetic spectrum has shown us just how little our primary sense can actually sense. If you stretched this spectrum to circumnavigate the globe our naked eye wouldn't be capable of seeing any further than our own arm's length. Things exist far beyond our comprehension of them. They don't need us to see them in order for them to exist. The question is not whether fairies exist but more if you came across one, would you even be able to see it?"

"What? Of course I would."

"The indigenous people of America could not conceive of such an unknown as a naval fleet arriving on the horizon and so did not see them. It was only when they were alerted by their Shaman that they then saw."

"But I know what a fairy looks like."

"You know how?"

"Leo, everyone knows what a fairy looks like."

"But how if you've never seen them before?"

"From fairytales of course. Make-believe things are just fantasies from someone's imagination that caught others. Fairies, witches, sprites and elves will never exist outside them."

"Not necessarily. For example, sprites and elves don't just exist in storybooks."

"Come on, Leo."

"No really, they exist in the skies, tens of kilometres above us, above storms, bursting their plasma all over the stratosphere in displays bigger than any fireworks we could ever create, illuminating the darkness above the grey clouds. Of course they are not the creatures you are thinking of, but what I'm trying to explain is that we can't know the all, the everything, there's just too much. But in order to know the most, we have to accept that we can't and will never know the all, well not yet anyway. It's beautiful. The way and wonder of the world is just magic, pure magic and we are so blessed to be a part of the great chorus of the cosmos."

"Maybe you're a little bit right that the world is more magical then we allow ourselves to see, but that make-believe stuff is just that, make-believe."

"I'm not saying that it isn't. I'm just curious to see what your mind allows you to believe, if you would believe the most unbelievable thing even if it crash landed into your reality."

"Okay, well if a fairy crashed into me then I suppose I would have no choice but to believe in them, well that one anyway."

"So your staunch view can be changed by a single experience?"

"Well yes, I mean I don't know. I suppose, if I had proof. What are you getting at?"

"What I'm saying is that we cement all our beliefs into fixed categories, of real or unreal, yet from one moment to the next they could switch sides. So therefore how can we know anything for sure, take anything as certainty? We can't. Because we can't possibly see everything all at once. If a belief can be so easily changed then why are we so adamant in fortifying them?"

"Because we need to build a structure of reality to our world."

"But why?"

"Because otherwise we would just fall through it."

"So you're saying we need to create a platform of reality to walk upon?"

"Yes."

"So then that platform is created only by thoughts and ideas?"

"Well, yes."

"But if beliefs can change, how can they ever really be real?"

"I don't know, because it just is. And at the end of the day, aren't we just an accumulation of all our thoughts and ideas? I think, therefore I am."

"I think we are a little more than that. And I think it's more correct to state I feel, therefore I am. Thought can be borrowed, stolen, copied, feelings cannot. They are the only things that are completely unique, the only things that are really real. You feel an embrace, a smile, sadness, joy. You don't think them. We are not just these thinking processors, we are entities of experience feeling our way through life. You can't think a feeling, you can only feel a feeling."

"You can. I think about my feelings all the time."

"Yes, but that's not the same as feeling the feeling. Thought cannot capture its entirety because, like a nose that cannot hear, thought cannot do a job it is not created to do. All it can do is to think an opinion on the feeling. Thought cannot feel. Thought cannot be who you really are because you are quintessentially moved and guided, not by your mind, but by your reactions to a thought. These reactions take the form of feelings. Our behaviour is then guided by avoiding bad feelings and following the good ones."

"I suppose you may be a little right but I feel I've been led into a bit of a trap."

"I'm not the one trying to trap you."

"No? Who is?"

"You are."

"Me?"

"Yes."

"Well that's crazy, why would I want to trap myself?"

"To keep yourself."

"To keep myself from what?"

"To keep yourself from escaping."

"Escaping from what?"

"Yourself."

"God. Leo, you're sounding like you've just come from an unbirthday party."

"Maybe I have."

"Well then in that case, please give the Mad Hatter my regards next time you see him."

"I knew the two of you were acquainted. The March Hare also speaks very highly of you."

"Well I don't usually speak very highly of him. He's a little unstable you know."

"Yes, I did have a feeling something wasn't quite wrong."

"Don't you mean right?"

"Do you?"

"Do I? Could we please maybe tear ourselves away from the tea party and have a proper conversation?"

"Okay. I'm a bit rusty, how does this go again? Oh yeah, so how's the weather?"

"You know you're blowing your human cover by discussing the most discussed topic in the only place you can't."

"Don't you think that's interesting?"

"What, the depths to which your lunacy can plunge?"

"I was thinking more about the fact that the cliché topic of conversation of mankind is something that we have no control over?"

"I suppose it's more interesting that way."

"Isn't it funny that surprise can only be felt over things that we have no control over? We have to be out of the control loop in order to really enjoy the ride."

"Yes, I guess that is a bit strange, especially because as a rule most of us quite like to be in control and usually don't have such a great affinity to change or the unknown. But yet we wouldn't go and watch only one movie over and over again, eat the same meal forever, have the same day repeat for eternity. That sounds more like a nightmare than a dream."

"So which do you have?"

"Sorry?"

"The nightmare or the dream?"

"Of what?"

"Your life. Are you happy?"

"How is someone supposed to answer such a loaded question?"

"Loaded? With what?"

"I have a feeling that maybe you've been missing from the world for a little too long. Like you've literally been living in a cave or lost in some jungle somewhere."

"You could say that. But you still haven't answered my unloaded question."

"Fine. You want honesty? I'll be honest. I'm not unhappy."

"But isn't that the same?"

"The same as what?"

"Not being happy."

"What? No! I said I wasn't, never mind. I mean I'm content, it's all quite satisfactory, nothing really to complain about."

"I think you have confused the meaning of content a little."

"No I haven't. Content means, you know, that you're alright with things the way they are."

"I think you're closer there but I don't think it's the same as satisfactory, I think it's the opposite."

"But that's unsatisfactory, which is bad."

"Is it? Only if you deem satisfactory as good."

"Oh God, spirals spirals! Okay, go on, I'm sure you're just dying to give me your revised definition. What is it?"

"I believe true contentment is a feeling that has no opposite, no rival. It is a state of being where you feel an acceptance of anything that the moment brings. Where you possess a sense of such peace and happiness that nothing more can be added to elevate it. A place where everything is equal and nothing is separate. Though I think that finding and feeling true contentment is very rare in our world, though it shouldn't be."

"And you know this because you've had first or second hand experience?"

"A bit of both. So why aren't you completely happy with your life? Why don't you feel my meaning of content?"

"Oh. Well nothing major really. Just the general woe we all carry, the usual amount of allocated sadness."

"The usual amount?"

"Yes, but a very manageable grey cloud, no thunderbolts or anything."

"So you think that's acceptable?"

"Well everyone has a cloud."

"Does that make it any more palatable?"

"It makes it easier to know we're all in the same boat."

"Are we?"

"Of course we are! We're all glued by gravity to this watery ball of rock, aren't we?"

"Yes, it is gravity that keeps us glued to this reality."

"This reality? Seriously? Newsflash, there is only this reality."

"So which reality was it where you wept for the flame?"

"I don't know what that was."

"Have you ever felt it before?"

"No, yes, I don't know. It was familiar but I can't remember from where."

"Like me?"

"Yes. No. I don't know! You're a very pushy person, did anyone ever tell you that?"

"No."

"Well, they should have. I have, there, now you know."

"Okay."

"Good."

We stayed trapped in that awkward moment of silence everyone dreads, everyone except him, I suppose. Fine, I decided to play again.

"So, where is this music coming from?"

He smiled and then spun out from his wall in one effortless fluid movement, ending up directly opposite me. I wasn't expecting his close quarter arrival to happen so quickly. I wasn't properly prepared. I had been careful not to look directly at him very much, to avert my eyes from getting caught in his gaze, but now I had no choice. His unavoidable beauty was even more apparent cast in such soft lighting, as I suspected it to be. His tanned skin seemed to exude a glow of sensual well-being and in the candlelight his blue eyes seemed to actually contain a sparkling essence moving within them. As his mouth moved around the words he was creating, every so often his lips would part displaying his perfect teeth. This had an extremely unnerving effect upon my blood stream. It seemed to create a surge. What was I on? I felt drugged. Was I drugged? He was now staring at me awaiting a response. My mind's replay function was defective. Shit, caught.

"Did you?"

"Yes, did I..."

"Did you think on it?"

"Yes, yes, I did, quite deeply."

"And, what happened?"

"Oh hard to explain, you know, to put into words."

"Did you just space out on me and try to cover it up?"

"Yes. But I'm listening now."

"You know, you miss the movie when you've got the commentary on."

"Yeah, yeah, I know, stuck in my head. Sorry, please go on."

"That's okay. I was just saying you should give it a go, revisit those feelings that the music and the flame gave you, try to remember where you have felt them before."

I closed my eyes and tried, but zilch.

"Nada I'm afraid. There's nothing."

"Try again."

"But there's nothing there."

"If there's nothing there, then nothing will happen."

He needed to see proof. So I closed my eyes and really tried. I summoned the feeling and drifted into it. Flashes of different pages from my past flickered by me. I couldn't believe it.

"The music... I have heard that music before, many times before. I remember it quietly playing as a soundtrack to my earliest memories. Crawling on my grandmother's carpet, sinking into the strange psychedelic swirls, and then in my pram mesmerised at being able to see the shape of the wind as it trickled through the trees tickling the leaves, laying on the cool grass drifting away with the ever changing, ever morphing cloud beings. It all feels like a dream I once had long, long ago. And just before I woke up here, I think I felt it too, and then I felt it when I..." I paused as I realised my words were being heard.

"When you what?"

"Nothing."

"It's okay, you don't have to say it, there's no need to admit it."

"I'm not not admitting anything. There's nothing to admit. Nothing is going on, nothing is happening here. I don't feel anything. I'm not doing anything. You're always pressuring me, why are you always pushing me?"

I had to exit, my head was deep fried. I needed to go back to my boy, my little man, my island of remembering. But when I looked to our corner wall I saw he had fallen asleep beside Missy.

"He's fine."

"You don't know him, you don't know anything about him, about being a parent."

Leo stayed silent.

"I have to go, I need to talk to people, decide what we're going to do."

"If that's what you want."

"What I want? When does that ever come into anything? When do I ever have a choice? Honestly, I can't even remember what that feels like."

"You have every choice all of the time."

"No, no I don't. I never have a choice. That's what happens when you take responsibility, when you grow up. I'd love to bum around the world, free to come and go as I please but I can't."

"Why not?"

"Are you listening to me?"

"Every syllable."

"Then you don't understand a thing! Wait until life throws you in a blender. Then we'll see how put together you come out."

"How do you know it hasn't?"

The cheek of him. Comparing his miniscule challenges to being a single parent. I had several knockout responses lined up but I decided not to use any of them. My desire to expel myself from the situation overrode my desire to be right. I turned away from him and walked towards the brothers and the short bald man gang. They were still trying to fix the TV. As they worked they talked, using the tinkering as some sort of stress relief exercise.

"But we don't even know what zone we're in."

"Does it matter?"

"Of course it matters, we could die out there."

"We could die in here too."

"We're safe here, we know where we are. Out there we'll be lost, completely exposed."

"But we don't know where we are and won't know until we get out there."

"There's no talking to you. You're too young to understand."

"Too young? You're only five years older than me!"

"Guys, guys. Listen, you're fighting over something you can't see. There's no obvious way out, so for now we're stuck. But it won't hurt to see if we can't find one."

My presence hadn't halted the brotherly bickering so I used the short bald man's referee skills as an opportunity to wedge myself into the conversation. I did what any polite person would do to announce my presence, and cleared my throat. How silly we all still use these commonly declared false gestures as accepted customs of civility. I knelt down by the set and the short bald man.

"How's the patient?"

"This one's got a bit of work to be done on her. But I'm afraid the little guy's a goner. We might get more light out of him, but no more words."

"Well we know everything we're supposed to, don't we? So you really think there's a way out of here?"

"Well we can see the way in, maybe there's another way out."

I looked around the ugly room. If there was another way out, it was being very coy. The doctor caught my exit searching eye and nodded at me. I hadn't checked in with him for quite a while. He walked over and I stood up.

"Hey, so how's everything going? How is everyone holding up?"

"Frazzled, shell-shocked, some restlessness and nausea, all to be expected under the circumstances. Physically, nothing too serious, nothing life threatening. Aside from cuts and bruises, it's mainly headaches and abdominal pain, the physical manifestations of the expected mental symptoms of anxiety and stress. We've also got a few mild forms of dissociation. We'll have to keep monitoring over the next twenty-four hours and then we'll start to see how they're really coping. At the moment most people are still in civility mode, reacting to everything within the parameters social etiquette requires. But with time that will drop. In severe cases we might have to prepare for the worst as some may exhibit a complete inability to regulate primitive drives. But hopefully it won't get to that stage."

"Oh."

"But..."

"But?"

"But I'm just speculating. Studies have only been done on situations involving prisoner of war camps, hostages, concentration camps, and of course penitentiaries. But not here in a situation such as this."

"Oh good. Well we can't really compare our situation to those."

"No we can't. However, we are in an unknown location with a large group of people selected by an unknown captor, for an unknown period of time, for reasons unknown. Off the top of my head, I cannot think of a single study involving a situation with so many people and so many unknown variables. Therefore, any guesses as to how we will cope are just empty stabs in the dark I'm afraid."

"So what can we do?"

"Provide something more powerful than any doctor can prescribe, hope. Even just a glimmer should help. Just some form of direction would even be enough to carry people through. But we can't stay like this for long."

I said nothing. I didn't want to continue this conversation anymore. I felt all the symptoms he had mentioned begin their assault. My skull suddenly felt smaller than my brain, stomach acid spilled up my throat as my mouth filled with saliva. Did the doctor just play soothsayer? Was that really waiting for us, a dystopian nightmare, an adult Lord of the Flies?

"And how are you feeling? I haven't really had a chance to check on you yet."

I felt like my organs were failing. But somehow I managed to rustle up enough energy for one passable line.

"I'm fine. You go see the rest first. I'll catch up with you later."

"How's your boy?"

"He actually seems okay."

"Looks like he's waking up."

I looked over to my unfurling little ball and my anxiety dissipated. My brave little soldier. I sat down close to him as Missy took a leave of absence. I lifted my angel's head up onto my lap and listened as he voiced his opinions of the day. He had been such a trooper, and it was late, or maybe it just felt that way. Either way he had had enough and wanted to go home. He wasn't alone. It had come to that time where I was going to have to fill him in on what was going on. He had a right to answers, we all did. So I told him about the game. I told him that, even though I wasn't supposed to say anything because it was against the rules, it would be okay because he was so good at keeping secrets. I told him that we were lucky enough to have been chosen for a great competition. I explained that it was all televised as I pointed to the super small secret cameras in the ceiling lights and that many of the people in the room were just actors. But there were some, like us, who were really playing in the game. But we didn't know who was who. The point of the game was to enjoy the experience as much as possible. We were marked down when we got cross or upset or made other people cross or upset. And we got marked up when we were happy and made someone else happy. I told him to remember how lucky he was that we were given this opportunity to get the prize. That out of thousands of entries, only one mother and child were picked. After I had explained it all to a very pensive nodding head, he had only one question. What exactly was said prize? Under pressure, and off the top of my head, I said tree house fort. I didn't even know what a tree house fort was, but he certainly did. And so ended the press conference. After we had gone to the bathroom, washed faces and brushed teeth as best we could, he snuggled in for his usual bedtime story.

"Once there was a little boy called Fionn who dreamed of visiting the sun. No one else had this dream, they all dreamed of visiting the moon or the stars or Venus or Mars. But Fionn didn't care for those places, the only place he wanted to be was the very brightest place he could see. And even when people told him what a silly idea it was, he still held that longing, he still felt that belonging.

One night as he was just about to fall asleep he heard a noise in his room. He opened his eyes and looked around and saw a little drop of light. It seemed afraid. But Fionn, used to making friends with small scared animals, softly asked him why he was in his room.

"I have gotten lost and can't find my way home." said the sad little drop of light.

"Where do you live?" Fionn asked.

"I live in the great ball of light."

Hardly being able to contain his excitement Fionn whispered, "The sun?"

"I don't know it by any other name than home, but it is lost and so am I."

Fionn thought for a minute. "Well, it sounds like the sun. That's the brightest thing in the sky."

"You mean it was." the little drop of light sniffed. "Now it's been replaced by dark and that strange white crescent."

Fionn slowly got down from his bed and sat cross legged across from the sad little droplet.

"We call this crescent the moon. And the moon does replace the sun, every night, it looks after all the small stars."

The droplet edged closer to the cross legged boy. "Are the stars the moon's children?"

Fionn stopped himself from correcting the droplets idea. After all, he couldn't be one hundred percent sure that they weren't. "Maybe they are."

"Will they ever find their way home?"

"I don't think they are lost. I think they are in their home, the night's sky."

"But I must find my way home. That is where I belong." The droplet edged back a little as a new question arose which he had to ask the little boy. "You don't think the stars are... are maybe lost little drops of light like me?"

Fionn being old enough to know the importance of his answer, but not being old enough to know what it should be, decided it was best to be as honest as he could.

"I don't know. But I don't think that they are sad or lonely, lost or forgotten. I think they have a very important job. They help people find their way. They guide them and make the darkness less, well, dark."

The drop thought for a minute. He was a little scared and a little excited. "So how do the drops of light become stars?"

Fionn smiled as he leaned back on the side of his bed. "Well I suppose they have to leave the sun like you in the day and then fly up to the sky at night."

"The day?"

"Yes the day. The day is the opposite of the night. Just like the moon and the sun are opposites."

"So the sun is not gone?"

"Not forever no, just for the night. And then in the morning it comes back up from behind those hills and guards the day."

The little drop of light shimmered with happiness. "So in the morning I can go home?"

"If you want to, of course."

The drop thought for a moment. "Do I have to choose now?"

"No, and I don't think you ever have to choose."

"Really I can have both?"

"Yes, I think so, but not at the same time. You can't have everything at the same time, then you wouldn't really ever have anything at all."

The drop of light was quiet for a moment. "So how can I have both?"

"Well I think that you can be with the sun in the day and then at night you can join the stars."

The drop shimmered again. "So what do I do now?"

"I suppose you have to wait for the sun to come up."

"Will you wait with me?"

"Of course."

"Thank you so much. Not just for waiting with me but for helping me find my home and giving me a dream to dream. How can I repay you?"

"You don't have to. It makes me feel happy to help you to find your home and your dream. And waiting up with you 'til sunrise, that's a little bit like my dream."

"What is your dream?"

"My dream? My dream is actually to visit your home, the sun. But I don't think that it will ever happen. Sometimes the magic is in the dreaming."

The little drop shimmered. "But we can go to my home together."

Fionn smiled at his new friend's kindness, but he secretly knew that all the people had been right and it was an impossible dream. "I don't think I can. I'm afraid it's not possible."

The droplet moved closer and hovered in front of him. "Well we can't fail in trying? So why don't we try?"

The two new friends spent the night talking and laughing about each other's worlds. As different as they seemed, they were inside both very similar, both a little afraid, both a little brave, but both quite happy.

When the night began to disappear and the stars with it, they knew it was time. They didn't know how they were going to make it to the sun, but what they did know was they were going to try their very best. The little drop of light moved towards Fionn's chest and paused for a moment. Fionn closed his eyes and smiled as the small drop of light shone into him. The light spread quickly through Fionn's small body and then as his frame turned into light the little drop moved back from his new friend and watched as Fionn's whole body shone brighter and brighter and then grew smaller and smaller until he too was a little drop of light.

The two flew and spun around each other laughing and playing, continuing their spiralling dance all the way to the sun. When they got there they paused.

"Here is my home. Shall we go in?"

The new drop of light shimmered as they fell into the great ball of light. Fionn's dream had come true and he danced and swam in the warmth of the bright light. It was even more wonderful then he had imagined it would be. He sang with joy and soared with happiness. And after a time when he had soared and sang and danced and swam more than he ever dreamed possible, he stopped. And his little friend asked him why.

"I have stopped because I have lived the life of a drop of light within the great ball of light. I now know what it feels like. But I don't yet completely know what it feels like to live as Fionn the boy, and then as Fionn the man."

"But I thought this was your dream and I thought dreams were meant to last forever."

"Dreams are dreams because they have no rules. They can change and grow and become what we want them to be. Just like you don't wish to always be a star, I don't wish to always be a drop of light."

"I understand." But the drop of light was still a little sad that he was going to lose his friend.

"Don't be sad. We won't really be that far apart. We will still see each other. You can always visit me anytime. And whenever I look up at the stars I will know you are up there living your dream. And whenever I look up to the sun I will know you are home and I will remember the wonderful time we had there together. So you don't need to be sad because we will always be together, day and night."

The two drops of light swirled together and just before they parted the little drop of light repaid Fionn for his kindness.

"Keep your drop of light. Keep it inside you, keep it bright and never forget that it is there. Then you will always have a little bit of your dream with you."

Fionn shimmered as he left his dear friend and the great ball of light.

As the months passed he would often look up at the sun and the stars and see his friend shimmer and the little drop of light inside him would shimmer back.

As the years passed and he grew into Fionn the man, he realised that everyone had a little drop of light deep inside them, but they just didn't know it yet. He felt very fortunate to have met the little drop that night who showed him who he was and gave him the chance to find his own light. And so he made it his new dream to help everyone he could to find their own little drop of light, no matter how deep it was hiding within them."

I continued the story long after he had fallen asleep, I think I needed it as much as he did. The reminder of our routine gave me a feeling of familiarity and security. I also had a bigger audience than I expected and it wouldn't have been fair not to finish it. I tried to join him in his soft slumber but I just couldn't let the room go. So I just stayed sitting next to him watching the scene change before me.

People were now starting to lay down and the room was quickly shrinking. Vertical people take up so much less space than horizontal. It really was going to be very tight. As there were only half the amount of blankets that we needed people decided to take sleeping shifts, if they wanted a blanket that is. The blankets were thin but they were bigger than I expected and you could fit two underneath them, comfortably even, if you snuggled a bit. It was an interesting fact that everyone could have slept at the same time, if we had all just gotten close to a stranger.

As the first shift went down the room got cooler. At first I thought it was just me as I was wearing quite light clothing. But then I noticed other people rubbing their arms as they walked around. Maybe it was just the fact that we had lost so many of our upright radiators. I checked my little one who was wrapped up in his blanket like a cocoon. He was very warm, he always was. I stood up and as I was rubbing my shoulders a blanket fell on them.

"You look like you need more than just a blanket, sugar, but I'm afraid that's all I got for now."

"Thank you, Missy. Thank you so much for everything. How are you doing?"

"I'm doin' fine. Don't you be worrying yourself about me. I'm a survivor. I'll make the best outta anything I'm given. In fact, I got a treat for breakfast tomorrow. We're fixin' to have oatmeal with raisins and everyone's gonna get half a sweet slice of canned peach. It's gonna set us up real good for the day."

I just hugged her. I don't think she was expecting it but I didn't care. Here embarrassment felt so out of place.

"It's okay darlin'. I'm just here doin' what I can. It's not much, but keepin' peoples' bellies happy is as good a start as we're gonna get. Gives us all a fightin' chance against whatever it is we got ourselves into. Now, now,

141

you'll be alright, honey. You got that survivor gene inside you too."

"I'm not so sure."

"Angel, you gotta learn that you can't carry the whole room on your shoulders, it'll break 'em. Take it off for a while, it ain't going nowhere."

"How can you be so calm and cool with everything that's going on?"

"Oh, honey, I ain't gotta choice."

"What do you mean? How can you not?"

"Well, I got no choice but to look on the bright side, 'cause that's the only side that there is. It's the only side that's lit, the only side that's real."

"I don't understand."

"It's simple, sugar, real simple. If you're in a dark room with only a candle burning what d'you see? Of course it's that swinging flame. You can't see the dark because it's too dark, it's not possible. The dark ain't meant to be seen, that's why it ain't lit. You get it, sugar? It took me a while to really understand, but when I did it changed everything. I got my granddaddy to thank for that. I remember him always saying to me. 'Missy, you gotta see the big picture and take those hosses blinders way away. You gotta step back and see the whole world, see that sheen shining across it, see the glint in its big blue eye. It don't care what you think about it, it's too big and it's too beautiful. You can make it as scary and ugly as you like, see it any which way you want, but you ain't changin' a thing, you just makin' yourself, makin' your world that way. Honey, life is left and life is right, always has been always will be. You just gotta stay in the middle, keep walking your own line, no matter what other folks be saying to you, you just keep on walking. And then no matter what shade you find yourself in, you'll always see the sun that made it.'"

The golden brown in Missy's eyes seemed to melt. They looked like bowls of dark honey about to be poured. Though when they did, the honey ran clear.

"Poor granddaddy lived a heavy life for his size but always managed to have enough room to carry a smile with him. It was 'cause he saw the light that he never felt the dark. And you gotta do that too, sugar. No matter where that road of yours takes you, you gotta keep walking it and feel that hidden sunshine even when no one else can, especially when no one else can. That's a gift we gotta cultivate, not eradicate. You'll be alright, you just gotta believe you will first."

"Sounds familiar."

"That's only 'cause it is."

"Maybe."

"Now you do me a favour and go find that doctor, make sure he's okay. He's so busy lookin' after everyone else he's forgettin' himself. We need him, and he needs to be lookin' after his own self before he can be lookin' after anyone else's."

The doctor appeared just as I turned to look for him. He too had noticed the drop in temperature.

"I am a little concerned about the suddenness of the drop. We lost the lights a few hours ago. If the heating had also gone we would have noticed it sooner. The sleeping shift going down is not enough to explain it."

"Well it can't go down too low. We're not in winter!"

"Aren't we?"

"What? What do you mean?"

"Well, can you tell me what month we're in?"

"Of course, it's, it's... this is ridiculous. How strange, it's on the tip of my tongue, I just can't, uh, it's... Okay, that's really weird."

"I have been trying to remember the season since I got here, just the season. I have been attempting to piece back my memories to the most recent event or moment I can remember and, well, I'm having great difficulty."

"Well it must be spring or summer because look at how I'm dressed."

"I don't know why we're dressed the way we are. I'm not certain these are even our clothes. There's much more happening here than we think. I can't put my finger on it, but something is very wrong."

"I'm trying my best not to ask too many questions that can't possibly be answered right now. I'm just trying to deal with what's going on at the moment. There's more than enough happening right now to deal with."

"I understand that, but we still have no idea why we are here. We cannot stop thinking about that and just concern ourselves with keeping busy."

"We're not just passing time. There's things that need to be done, need to be organised. We've only just arrived. Plus you know it helps people to keep themselves and their minds busy. I don't need to tell you this."

"And what will happen if they don't?"

"What? What will happen? Well, the room will fall."

"And then what would happen?"

"What? I think you need to go take a rest. You've been going constantly. Here take this and go lie down. You'll feel better after a break from the room."

The doctor didn't reply. I think he had clicked onto autopilot, but he took my advice and my blanket. And now exhaustion and cold were to be my loyal companions until the shift change. I sat next to my sleeping angel, closed my eyes and tried my best to turn off from the room. But I couldn't. I just couldn't switch off. Even in normal life it was never that easy. It was never easy to halt the incessant stream of nothing and everything. So how on earth was I going to do it here? And not so much as a cup of chamomile. My head felt full, jammed, as if it were the grand central station of thought. Yet I couldn't board any train. They were just going round and round. What did my head want me to do? Just wait on the platform and exist in this limbo of conflicting worries? I felt a rising weight come over me, an immense pressure constricting me. For a second I thought I was becoming paralysed but it wasn't a physical paralysis. I tried my mantra and any and every calming technique I had left in my memory banks. Nothing worked. It was coming again, like birthing contractions, waves of anxiety, of disempowerment. I tried to occupy my thoughts with light things, happy moments of the past, future's dreams, but they all just blew away in the gale force winds of woe surrounding me. Thoughts of the faint music flittered away from me like downy feathers on the breeze. They just seemed so childish and silly, so escapist and ridiculous. What was happening? I felt my self spilling over the lines. Nothing was happening, nothing had happened. It wasn't real. Just as I managed to hold anxiety at bay a new wave hit. Sadness. Immense sorrow was building up for no discernible reason. Leo was right. There was a sadness inside me, inside us all. A secret sadness that we tried our best to hide from the world, hide from ourselves. What was this mass melancholy we all shared? What had caused it? Where had it come from? I didn't know, but I knew that being here in this room was not helping matters. This room was melting the mask we had so skilfully created. It was causing it to droop down and reveal our truest, most tortured states of being. What a hell of a place for that to happen. Just as I felt my hands begin their shake and the lump in my throat become too big to swallow, I felt a wave of warmth cascade over me.

"That was a beautiful story. I haven't heard it for a long time. Do you mind?"

He sat down before he had even finished asking. But I didn't protest. My cold body welcomed the usual rush his presence produced. His body was generating such a heat that I could feel it radiating out, surging towards me. We weren't even sitting that close. We were on separate walls of my corner. I felt there was some kind of symbolism there but I was too tired to find it.

"It was really nice to hear it again. It's been a while. My mother used to read it to me. It was one of my favourites, still is. Obviously I didn't understand the full meaning of it back then but it still captured me and my untamed imagination. It really is a beautiful tale."

"My boy loves it too, even if it is a little too optimistic."

"Interesting that you would see it that way. I don't think there is such a thing as too optimistic."

"Really? You don't think optimism lifts you up for a greater fall?"

"You really believe that?"

"Of course you don't. Difference of opinion comes from different paths trodden. My boots are just muddier than yours. Trust me, I know a lot about being thrown high and not being caught."

"I'm sorry that you have come to know so much about it. But I really believe no matter what happens, the worst thing you can do to yourself is become pessimistic. Things only get worse when we lose hope. How can anything get better if we give up?"

"You don't give up, you get real and see the world for what it really is. Things definitely improve when you become more realistic. You don't get hurt as much. You take your blindfold off."

"You think being realistic is a cure for blindness?"

"Of course. Otherwise you would still believe in your ridiculous childhood fantasies. You have to let them go."

"Why?"

"Seriously? Okay, because every single one of them only serves to bring you pain in the end, to remind you that life is no longer a big fun game, that dreams don't come true, and that you're not special."

"Wow. You really believe that?"

"Wake up, Leo. That's what the whole world believes because it's the truth. Happy endings are fairy-tale. Dreams are for kids. And actually, now thinking clearly about it, I think it's unforgivably cruel to make our children believe in happily-ever-afters if we ourselves don't even believe in them. How unkind a thing it is to fill a child's head full of fantasies and fairy dust, only to have it all taken away."

"I think all people are doing is trying to keep children's dreams alive."

"Why, so they can believe lies and then have to accept the world as a crappy let down? Would you tell a child he can fly just to keep him optimistic? Why cultivate something of no use, of no value? Optimists are just children who never learned to grow up, who decided that instead of joining the real world that it would be easier to run away into a fantasy. Well it doesn't exist. Optimism causes nothing but pain and disappointment."

"I'm glad you're being so candid, but I can't agree with you. I believe that humanity has benefited immeasurably from optimistic people. Dreamers, thinkers, creators, they all had to be optimistic that their ideas would succeed. Any advancements and inventions had to come about from a positive outlook on a new idea. We're existing in a world where we're surrounded by examples of wondrous human feats, all because they dared to dream and then dared even further to act upon that dream. And more than likely against all odds and with very few, if any, sharing their vision. Alone, swimming against the tide, facing obstacles, ridicule, hardship like no other, all in aid of a belief, a belief yet to be founded, a belief in the impossible, a belief whose only proof of existence lay in their imagination. Carving something new is never easy. There's no manual, no trail to follow, you have to go by feel and hope for the absolute best, and that's the only way you'll succeed. Anything less and you'll most likely fail."

"Maybe you're right, and maybe for those kind of people it worked. But that's not really a practical way to live day to day for a normal person."

"It isn't?"

"Come on, Leo. You've got to wake up a little to the real world. You're living in a fantasy."

"I don't think I am the one living in an imagined existence."

"What? You think I'm the one that's living in an illusion? Please. I live in the real reality, in a world of brick and stone, cause and effect, nothing fictional about it."

"Okay, if you're certain."

"Of course I am. And so is any sane and rational person."

"Okay."

"What do you mean okay? Aren't you going to fight your corner, tell me how I'm the delusional one?"

"No, I don't think so."

"Why not?"

"Because truth never needs defending. The blue sky may obscure the stars in space but it does not erase them."

He was trying to trick me into agreeing with him. Well I wasn't going to. Anyway anything else I said would only be just repeating myself. He was stuck in his optimistic twenties bubble and maybe it wasn't my place to pop it. So I just let him continue.

"Okay, let's take your story. The child's impossible dream came true."

"But that's just a children's story."

"But most children stories are just metaphors, allegories for life and our struggles within it. We all do have a drop of light inside of us."

He put his hand on my bent knee and squeezed it. The tingling of energy scattered through my leg prompting a literal knee jerk reaction.

"What do you want me to say? That you're right and I too believe in fairies? Well I can't, because I don't."

"I don't want you to say anything. I just want to show you your light, that little drop hidden inside you."

I shuffled to the side. Why was he so stuck on that?

"What's wrong?"

"Why do you keep mentioning that drop of light?"

"I don't, but it is true."

"What is? That there's light in all of us? That we're all made of stars? You sound like a fridge magnet. Your unwavering belief in all that mumbo-jumbo is a little full-on."

"Why are you being so hostile?"

"Well if I'm so hostile then why are you still talking to me?"

"Because I see your light, even if you don't."

"I think maybe you're seeing things, a lot of things that aren't there."

Leo took a breath to say something but chose not to. I wish he had. At that moment I could have taken anything he said. I was in full deflector mode. Seconds passed as he seemed to cautiously select words. He could select the smartest troupe he had, he was still going down. But as more seconds passed, so did my zealous need to engage in battle. He still hadn't looked at me and I still hadn't broken my stare. Then finally he broke his and met mine.

"You know the author that wrote that story-"

"I don't want to speak about her."

Leo paused before he spoke. Maybe something inside of him knew.

"You know, you never told me your name."

"Well you're the one with all the answers. I'm pretty sure you can connect the dots."

"No, but that's... you can't be. Oh my God. I'm so sorry."

He had such pity in his eyes, too much.

"God, I'm so sorry."

He rubbed my shoulder and looked into my eyes. I didn't know what he was looking for with such sorrow in his eyes.

"I can't believe you're L.C May's daughter. I didn't even-"

"Not quite what you expected?"

"No, no it's just that-"

"What?"

"Nothing, it's just very strange. You don't realise how much The Manual changed my life."

"What? The Manual for Joy? I can't believe you even know about it. I can't believe anyone does. With a name like that it's hardly surprising it didn't sell. Well you're probably the only one who read it."

"No. No I'm not, not at all. It changed the life of the person who gave it to me and the person I gave it to. Your mother's book was like a skeleton key unlocking all kinds of doors in all kinds of people."

"I'm surprised you even found a copy. As far as I know it only went to print once."

"Yes, yes I know it did. The copies that are left are like gold dust. Lighthouses of literature scattered across the world. The ones left in circulation get shared and passed around, never kept. As much as I would have given my right arm for a copy of my own, I couldn't. To keep it just seemed like the exact opposite thing to do once you've read it. You just have to trust that it'll return to you if and when you need it. You know, it's actually found its way back to me six times in completely different ways, from completely different people. Those words..."

His voice quivered. The unshakable shook. I don't know why it made me happy. Maybe because it showed he wasn't perfect, that there was hope for us all. He cleared his throat and continued.

"Those words were like the soundtrack to my whole journey of self-discovery, of life, of reality. She was the greatest teacher I have ever known. It was her honesty, her sincerity and her complete and utter authenticity that helped me to understand so much about myself. She didn't claim to know a thing, she just wanted to explore and took you with her. She served as a guide through the hedge maze of the mind, showing its fallacies, its traps and tricks but all the time in her own genuine, unpretentious way. I just can't believe you're her daughter."

"At least now you know where you know me from. I'm the shadow of your idol."

"I wouldn't say that at all."

He stared into some moment passed and smiled.

"God, I imagine you grew up with copies just strewn around the house. So when did you first read it? What did you think? How amazing it must have been to be able to peek inside your mother's hungry young mind."

"I've never really read it."

"What? Never?"

"Well, I mean, I flicked through it years ago but it was all just gibberish."

"Gibberish?"

"Isn't that what you call words without meaning?"

"It was in those meaningless words my life found its meaning."

"Well, perhaps you saw what you wanted to see, read words you wanted to hear."

"Maybe. But even if I did, those words still had to be there for me to read into them. Lines still have to exist for you to read between them. I found so many answers to questions I never knew I had."

"But isn't it just a load of questions? How can you find answers in a book of questions?"

"Because in asking those questions I answered my own. Your mother's book has switched on so many light bulbs in so many people. Literally everywhere I have travelled I've met people whose paths have been crossed by it and I've travelled to some pretty 'out there' and remote places."

My mind suggested a comical quip about my confidence in how 'out there' these places of his were. But it seemed a little tainted with bad taste and my conscience wanted to keep a clean slate.

"Weren't you at all curious about her? About the book? I can't believe you never read it."

"I didn't realise there was such an underground following, or any following. I suppose to be brutally honest, it felt a bit strange to read it, like I was snooping in her diary. I didn't really want to know the uncensored version of my mother."

"But you have the rare opportunity to basically visit a parent when they were young, get a real idea about what they went through, all their thought processes, their hopes and fears, soak in their point of view. I would have thought after everything that happened that you would have been dying to read it."

"What? What do you mean?"

"Nothing, I suppose it just feels very weird that I know things about your mother that you don't."

"She wasn't my mother when she wrote it."

"No, but she would have been around our age, just a girl going through everything everyone does but having the bravery to honestly admit and express it to herself. Reading her book is like having a conversation with yourself. She asks all the questions that you're too scared to, points out all the preposterousness of the world, and yet does it all with her flag of transparency flying high. And her dreams, so much symbolism. I don't think she was even aware herself how much. Especially since she didn't even realise what she was creating, what it would become."

"Maybe I'll take another look at it again one day."

"And what about The Next Natural Step? Did you ever see it?"

"No. I've never heard of it."

"Really? God, it was probably just lying around, the only known copy, unbelievable."

"It was a book?"

"Not just a book. It was the book that inspired her, the guide for her journey. It was her Manual. She found it in some book fair. No one knows where it came from and, adding to the mystery, it was uncredited. The author just wanted it to have... what was it again? Oh yeah, 'an aura of magic and mystery surround it, like a message in a bottle washing up on the shore'. All we know from it is what May, sorry, your mother, quoted or paraphrased. I still can't believe I'm sitting with her daughter."

"Well, it's true. Now can you stop? I feel like some carnival freak show act."

"Sorry, it's just a very strange coincidence."

"I really don't think it is. But, just in case I'm in a room full of L.C May fanatics, I'd rather you kept it to yourself."

"Lips, sealed."

"So..."

"So?"

"So, can we change the subject?"

"Okay, how about your father? I don't know anything about him."

"Nor do I. Well not after he left. My father, my father was another temperamental artist. He was a painter, unknown of course, who sailed away to pursue his dreams without anchors of responsibility. Enough?"

"Sorry."

"Why do people always say that? It infuriates me. Sorry, sorry for what? How am I supposed to respond to that? Am I expected to comfort your sadness with 'it's okay, it wasn't your fault'?"

"I think I was aiming for honest empathy rather than sympathy."

"Well I don't need empathy or sympathy. I've had to get on with it on my own. It's too late now to ask for help."

Leo stayed quiet.

"Anyway, I never speak about him."

"Is now also never?"

Who was this guy? I didn't even speak to my therapist about my father. Why did he think he was so special? Just because he had a pretty face? Just because his eyes could pierce armour? Well it wasn't going to be that easy to crack me. I was a little tougher than that.

"So you must have creativity sparkling in your DNA coming from parents like that. I would love to see you express yourself in an art form. I bet you'd be mind-blowing."

I was fully loaded, ready to shoot down his line of questioning, so this kind of compliment of belief in me left me a little disarmed.

"Oh, I'm a terrible artist really. Nothing I have ever drawn has resembled its inspiration. Actually I just remembered something, an old something. Funny how it decided to surface here and now. I remember one afternoon my father was rushing out the back door to catch the perfect light and my mother, who was busy writing, asked him to take me with him. Excitedly I grabbed my paints set and pad. He had already left so I rushed out the door running as fast as I could to catch up to him. I remember the noise his tubes of oils and brushes made clanging in that rusty blue tool box he used to keep them in. We walked for what seemed like a forever. Well he walked, and I just tried to keep up. Finally we got to an enormous cornflower field. But he didn't stop until we got to the very centre of it and were engulfed in an ocean of blue. The amber sun draped the moment in such a warm glow. It soaked the scene with a honey haze transforming the world into a painting. I remember imagining, and secretly hoping, that the hundred insects flying through the golden spotlight were all subjects from a far off magical kingdom making their way to grand gathering. How silly young thoughts can be. Once he had set his easel and canvas up, he began trying to 'steal the beauty' as he used to say. I tried my best to mimic him but of course failed miserably. Seeing my disappointment at how different our representations were, he tried to ignite in me some of his passion by explaining about the magnificent sphere of colour that encases us everywhere we go. But that just made me giggle as I imagined a giant hamster ball rolling through the field. I was too young, and he was too serious, but I'm glad we had that moment in amongst the cornflowers. You know, my interesting interpretation of that sphere of blue was stuck up on our fridge for years. I wonder where that ended up."

"I can just imagine the scene of the two of you immersed in a field of warm blue creating art together. It would have been wonderful to have seen both of your interpretations. I really would have loved to have seen some of his work, experienced his style."

"Well, you know the pictures in The Little Drop?"

"Of course, they're iconic."

"Well, they were his."

"Wow, of course. That makes sense. They were really inspired. Why wasn't his work credited?"

"He said it wasn't real art, that they were just illustrations."

"Really? But illustrators help sculpt the platform for our imaginations. They paint the scene for our dreams to play out. If that's not art then I don't know what is."

"He said that he couldn't fully express himself within any kind of parameters."

"But that's what art is, expression within our subjective view with the tools and the talents we have at our disposal. There is no such thing as limitless art. I think if an artist wasn't limited by something he would have nothing to say, no voice, nothing to comment on. You have to feel confined to need to break free. You have to feel repressed in order to express. I think artists are just people who have decided to express their emotions through creation rather than destruction."

"I wish you could have given him that speech."

"Maybe he would only have heard what he wanted."

"You know he never even saw any of the success. He left before it was even published. Maybe in some way he felt she was selling out, and that by staying he would be too. But they had no money. We were in my grandparent's old house in the country, living off the vegetable garden. We had nothing. They couldn't live on air, not with a child. You know I always thought that when it became successful he'd come back. I really believed that if it got big enough it would somehow reach him, even if he was in the farthest corner of the world. I used to imagine him walking past some small bookshop and stopping as he saw the cover, his designs proudly displayed centre stage in the window. In my daydream he would stop in his tracks and he'd remember us and come home, but he never did. I suppose maybe it was its success that pushed him further away. The only thing I ever heard of him was that he died in Paris, penniless and alone, just like a real artist supposes he should. Maybe that was the closest he got to his dream. But it was his choice to leave. He chose his path. If he had stayed he certainly wouldn't have died poor or alone. We would have all been together. We would have made a life together, we would have been okay. We would have made it. If he had only just stopped identifying with being this tortured artist he would have had the chance, the platform to showcase his work. He could have had it all. If he had just had a little more patience, if he had just been a little stronger for just a little longer, if he had just waited and instead of running away..." I stopped because I knew if I continued tears would soon replace my words.

"He obviously felt he had no choice."

"You're the one who said we always have a choice. He made his and we were obviously not important enough to be picked. Protecting his pride and his principles meant more to him than protecting us, protecting me. That was the biggest life lesson he could have imparted to his dear daughter. That love does not keep people together, that there are no happy-ever-afters and that life is not your friend. You've got to be tough, look out for yourself and not let anyone in."

"Is that what you're teaching your boy?"

"Don't be ridiculous. He's far too young for that."

"So as a parent when do you decide to break it to him, break his reality?"

"I don't know. I suppose I'll know when I get there."

"I really am sorry that you had to go through all that."

"It doesn't matter. It's all in the past now. It wasn't my life he ruined, it was my mother's. They really were two pieces of the same puzzle. When he went she shut down, closed off a piece of herself. Her wonder, her belief, her lust for life left with him."

Leo stayed silent, maybe sensing that there was a little more venom left to squeeze out.

"He was what he was. Like everything you take the good with the bad I suppose. Though it was the good bits that made the tough bits so tough. If he had been all bad then maybe I wouldn't have cared so much. Maybe it all would have been easier. My father was a very complicated man. He was a strange person to live with. It was like he was two people, like there were two characters fighting within himself. It was very confusing as a child to grow in an environment of such extremes, to be exposed to such varying degrees of reality. He would chop and change from one second to the next, blowing whichever way the tempest would carry him. And because you would never know what side you were going to get, you were never fully relaxed, always a little on your guard, which muddles you up a bit I suppose. It's a pity because I adored him, like any daughter would but you see, after a while you'll stop eating even the most delicious cherries if every other one you bite into is filled with maggots."

Leo's hand stretched out to my knee. Then it all just came out. Funny how just a little understanding and compassion draped in tenderness at just the right moment can open even the most stubborn of strongholds.

"I remember the night he left. I pretended I was asleep but I wasn't, I was wide awake. My father was more of a temperamental artist than my mother. Well, he showed it more anyway. When he was up we were blasted through the stratosphere, sailing the stars together. But when he was down, it was like a solar eclipse, just cold and dark. The mass of his bad moods was enormous. The whole house sunk under the weight. You see he blamed everything and everyone else for all his problems, his unfulfilled dreams, his artistic blocks, his bad luck, his unresolved issues, his anger, everything was everyone else's fault, never his own. He never took the blame for anything, never owned up to his mistakes. He was perfect and therefore by default, everybody else was not. If he was always right how could anyone else be? I think perhaps he had accumulated so much blame, so much weight that he had been dodging all his life, that maybe he thought if he were to admit even an ounce of it, it would all just come tumbling down and crush him. That night, that last night was after a particularly heavy day of his immense gravity. I suppose my mother had finally had enough of his indulgence. She had never stood up to him like that before. He had always been the shouter, the aggressor, but that night it was her turn. I think that it was because he had never seen it before that it came as such a shock. But it had been such an accumulation of years of tongue biting, of being the calm one, of walking on egg shells, that really it was a long time coming. To be honest, even though I had never seen her lose her temper, it still wasn't as scary as when he did. But some people can only give it. Nothing she said was over the top or exaggerated. She actually kept her cool while she lost it. She never called him names, or swore or smashed plates or anything as dramatic as that. It was just out of such desperation, such exhaustion, that she finally engaged in it. She just wanted him to get himself back together, to stop all the up and downs, to just stop the rocky rollercoaster of emotion he had been taking us on. She just wanted to pull him out from his mist of me, find the real him, the soft side. But sadly it was his soft side that took all her words, his soft side they hit, his soft side that bled. Maybe it was that feeling of abandonment and disrespect that allowed him to convince himself to go. You have to understand, my father was a dictionary example of someone who relishes in cutting his nose off to spite his face. I think because it's a form of self-flagellation that perhaps he felt in some fucked up way that by punishing himself he was rebalancing the equation, clearing his conscience. Like some sort of messed up attempt at redemption.

Abandoning your family, yeah that'll balance the books. He was just too self-centred to ever think outside of himself, outside of his pain. He just couldn't, and that's why he didn't even acknowledge the innocent by standers that he turned into victims along the way."

"It's very hard for most people to think beyond themselves, to have thoughts outside their head. It's like a prison, they just don't realise it. I don't think he was consciously trying to hurt you. He was just acting from what his instincts showed him, like a wounded animal."

"But he was a parent, and when you become a parent you cannot continue to be the sun in your solar system."

"I think it's naturally more prevalent in women to be apathetic, to be the understanding ones, to express difficult emotions, to open up. For men, especially those for whom their lives outside their family takes up a greater part of their time, it's far harder to let that self go."

"He was too immature, too selfish to be a parent."

"You have to remember people are just coping the best way they can. They are carrying so much weight that any extra that gets thrown on can cause them to act completely irrationally and out of character. It's like we're all camels, one straw away from a broken back. Life is very hard when we carry the weight of it. How can you possibly expect people to be free to be themselves when they're continually living at their breaking point?"

"Well, he still shouldn't have acted the way he did."

"As strange as it seems you can't really judge people on how they act. They are only a product of actions themselves. Even if they make mistakes or start wars, big or small, you cannot reasonably find blame in them alone. They are only carriers of a disease that they didn't create. You must look at your parents' parents to see why they acted the way they did. Maybe your father's father was cold and unsupportive and did not see merit in the arts. But that was not his fault either. Maybe his father as a child had had his head in the clouds and his father worried about him drowning in the cruel world when he was gone and so cut his wings. But it wasn't his fault he crushed his child's dreams. He did it because he believed it was the right thing to do, because maybe his father, struggling to feed too many with too little, learned that life can only be fought with grit and imparted that knowledge with vigour upon the children who survived. This pattern of protection was passed down from our earliest ancestors, a baton of belief in what would increase our chance of survival. It has all been done with love at the core but the message has been out of date for some time and has now become a threat to our survival. We have come to the point where our initial response is a red flag, threat. And when we live that way, day after day, we can't help but end up engaging in altercation after altercation. But I'm swaying from the point. I just think that to place blame on someone and say how could you have done that to me, how could you have made such a bad decision, doesn't alleviate your pain like you think it will, it just serves to make the other person feel more of their own. We must stop the cycle by no longer making people feel bad. We must forgive and forget. Nothing ever goes seamlessly. If it did, then nothing would really happen and tales would not be so tall. So next time you feel anger or hate towards someone, for just one moment imagine how much pain they must have had inflicted upon them in order for them to make such a hurtful and senseless decision. Pause and give thought to the perceived monster in front of you. Consider what amount of horror made that person become the way they are and how inflicting more pain upon them will only serve to push them further towards the dark, and you with them, adding more darkness to the world, to your world. To truly get over something, we must rise above it and gain an understanding of the whole picture from all sides, not just our own. True compassion is rare because you must leave yourself to achieve it and we all, especially the ones who are carrying great pain, find that a near impossible task to do. Why? Because in order to slip into someone else's shoes we must first leave our own and the heavy weight pinned upon them. This then makes us question the reason we were carrying around so much weight in the first place if in one second we could have lifted it all away. Understandably people don't like to feel tricked or stupid, and so avoid it at all costs. Though what they need to realise is that by bullishly continuing down the wrong path, in an attempt to prove that it was the right one, all they are proving is that they would rather burn a bridge than walk across it. Time and time again our pride prevents our retreat. We display our folly when, with knowledge of the true nature of that road, we still make the willing choice to continue down it instead of cutting our losses and changing paths. It is only when we see our folly that we lose it. When you admit your mistake you are no longer the person who made it. All we need to remember is that every moment is new and within it you are given all the tools you need to change. So if you are finding the weight you are carrying restrictive then you must at least admit that it makes sense to maybe start removing it."

"But by just letting it go you're admitting that it wasn't important, that your pain wasn't real."

"By letting it go you are saying that your life, this moment, and all your future moments are worth more than proving the depths of your pain."

"But that still doesn't make it fair."

"No, no it doesn't. It wasn't fair. You didn't deserve it. But life has a track record of testing us to our limits to help us find where they are, to find how strong we are, to help us become the untouchable. You know it wasn't your fault."

"No, not directly, but I know I was the catalyst for their implosion. They imploded into one another because of the pressure I put them under, the pressure of responsibility, financially, emotionally, physically, everything. I took away their freedom, their chance to evolve and grow into the people they should have been.

They could have done remarkable things with their lives. They were so creative, so talented, but I came along and stopped their ride dead."

"Their ride didn't stop. It just changed."

"No, it stopped. I was never made feel that I ruined their lives but I know I did. They could have been anything, done anything."

"They did, they were your parents."

"Yeah, fulfilling job that turned out to be. Full of pressure and thanklessness."

"Maybe they were supposed to prep you to be the one to do the remarkable things."

"Well then they failed, didn't they?"

"I wouldn't think so."

"You don't know me. You don't know what I've become, what my life has amounted to. I am nothing special and I have done nothing special."

"I think you're very special and I think you're the only one that doesn't know it. I think that's the biggest mistake we all make, not seeing all of ourselves. We only see a portion, the pieces that need to be fixed. It's a real shame. That's really the biggest loss to humanity, not only the non-realisation of our full potential, but the non-realisation of how much of it we have."

"I don't know. I don't know anything anymore. This place... This place jumbles everything up. I can't think the way I used to. I just feel so out of sync, so out of place. Where the hell is this place? And God, why are we here?"

"The same reason we're anywhere else."

"Leo, I'm too tired for riddles."

"It's not a riddle, it's fact. We are where we're supposed to be because we're where we are."

"I meant more literally."

"Well literally, I don't know where we are. I do know we're not supposed to know yet, but we will. Soon enough most probably. After we've done what we're supposed to."

"Which is?"

"We'll know when we're supposed-"

"Yeah, yeah, when we're supposed to know, I get it."

In a way, he was right but also annoying. Acceptance is more comfortable than resistance I suppose.

"Well you know what they say, whatever you resist, persists."

"Well then I suppose I'll have to accept that we're trapped, and then we won't be."

"Well you never know. After all it's all just a state of being. If you feel it's your choice to be in here then suddenly you're not trapped."

"I think that'll be a little harder to sell to myself. Hey, you know the doctor's pretty freaked out. He can't remember the month or even the season, and neither can I for that matter, can you?"

"Nope."

"And you're okay with that?"

"I'd prefer to be okay with that than not, wouldn't you?"

"I really don't know how to answer that. Leo, you can't just be an ostrich and hide away from reality. It doesn't disappear when you're not acknowledging it."

"It doesn't?"

I had never met anyone who could go from sage to toddler from one moment to the next. He was so infuriatingly annoying, like sand in sun cream, or sandwiches, or eyes, or anywhere. That was it, he was sand. Maddening, irritating, incensing sand.

He also tended to do the whole staring into the eyes thing, relentlessly. I mean really, who does that? Well except children and weirdos. For the rest of us sane adults there were these unwritten eye contact rules which everyone seems to abide by, and it all works pretty well. Didn't he know that? Obviously not. Though I suspect there were many unspoken laws of civilised society that he did not adhere to, or probably hadn't even heard of. Thankfully though I didn't find his stare as uncomfortable as most people's, well, okay all people. But why is that? Why is it so hard to maintain complete unyielding eye contact? Why do I squirm? Why do I feel hot and pressured and constricted? What part of it makes me feel so uncomfortable? What am I so afraid of? What am I avoiding? Connection? Maybe that was it. To connect you must be exposed, lower your shield, surrender, all things that terrify me, and most people I would imagine. I wonder did our ancestors always address people directly eye to eye, self to self? Or did they too cower away and allow their insecurities of inadequacy to take over preventing true unity? I doubt it. Maybe it wasn't so much the complete surrender that terrified me, but what would happen next. I didn't know, and that was the scary bit. I would not be in control. The controls would be frozen as I drifted into the black hole. Double the unknown, double the fear. As he spoke I tried my best to keep his stare within my own, to not be the first to break it. Every time I got a little better, but it was still a challenge. Yet with my boy it never was. Perhaps because I was always defenceless with him and I suppose, quite possibly, because when he was a baby I spent hours losing myself in the electrical storms brewing in his eyes. I looked into the somewhat similar storm before me. Who was he? What was he doing to me? Why was he exposing me? I wasn't ready.

"So what are you, like, Toto, biting at the curtain, pulling the veil of reality away? Well maybe I like my veil, maybe I don't want it ripped away, maybe it keeps everything protected."

"You mean keeps you protected."

"Well... Yes. And what's so wrong about that?"

"It's the wrong you that's being protected."

"Stop talking like that. I can't understand a thing you say! Just speak normally, just say what you mean instead of this infuriating quickstep of words, no one's listening, no one cares."

Leo stayed silent.

I wasn't about to fall into that pit of silence again. So, I decided to continue with my attempt at a civilised conversation, maybe he might even learn a thing or two.

"So, anyway, the doctor's also pretty worried about our clothes, that they might not be ours. What do you think of that?"

"I don't."

"Oh for God's sake, can we not have a real conversation?"

"I thought that's what we were having."

"I can't talk to you. You're impossible. You're really going to have to open your eyes a little about what's going on here."

"I'm being as aware as I'm supposed to be. If you can't do anything about it then why bother worrying?"

"That's completely nonsensical."

"What is nonsensical is to keep flicking the switch of a broken light."

"What? Well then tell me what you think is going on here."

"I think we're here to learn something. Life always brings us to places we don't want to be to teach us what we don't want to be taught."

"Sometimes I wish I could peek into your particular vista. It must be some view."

"You can."

"Right."

"Nothing's stopping you. It's not just mine, it's open to everyone."

"Alright, fine. But I don't have the energy to do any travelling tonight."

"Hey why don't you just turn in?"

"No, I'm fine, I'm fine. I'm just a bit frazzled."

"You're exhausted. You really should get some sleep and just let go of the room, for a few hours anyway. You know you're going to need to be corpus mentis for tomorrow's big bag of tricks."

"I can't. What if something happens?"

"What, like getting drugged, kidnapped and taken prisoner?"

"Yeah, something like that."

"Go on, it's okay, close those heavy weight lids. I'm on a different time zone anyway. My body clock thinks it's afternoon tea. Don't worry, I'll keep an eye on you guys. Anyway, I haven't got anything else planned for tonight. I'm cool with just chilling here. You know, it's actually a pretty hip haunt, very exclusive. No one, absolutely no one can get in, or out for that matter."

I mustered as big a smile as my depleted energy would allow. For the first time in a long time I felt the possibility of trusting someone. I just hoped life wasn't tricking me, trying to catch me out. Either way, I couldn't fight anything anymore. I had nothing left so I allowed my lids to drop for a second. I couldn't hold everything up and drift away. So away I drifted.

I awoke from a lovely dream to find myself still in the room. The lights had come back on, so that was good. The room was silent and I was curled in towards the wall, but not in our spot, and my son was not next to me. I turned around and my heart stopped. The room, it was empty. No one was there. They had gone. They had all gone. I somehow managed to get to my feet but then fell towards the column in front of me as a new breed of panic hit. What had happened? What was happening? It was becoming harder and harder to breathe. I pushed myself off the column, stumbling towards the other near the bathroom. And that's when I saw it. The television. It was sitting on a small wooden table, like the one my grandparents used to have, just broadcasting static. They must have fixed it. I fell to my knees in front of it, fiddling and flicking all the buttons and dials, begging it to show me something, anything. But it did not. I banged on it, harder and harder, but still nothing. Defeated I fell back against the pillar, a little too hard. I rubbed the back of my head, it felt wet. The sticky crimson stuck to my fingertips. I tried to rub it off but it wouldn't go. I screamed and shouted. I don't know at what or who but I didn't know what else to do. Then the static disappeared and was replaced by something else, something I did not expect to see. I stared at the screen and saw a girl staring back at me.

I moved my head left and hers moved right. As my hand cupped my mouth in disbelief, so did hers. I searched the television set trying to work out where the camera was hidden, but the source of the feed seemed to be coming from the centre of the screen behind the thick glass. But how?! I scrambled to my feet and as the girl stood up faces began to appear behind her. Leo was there. He smiled as the rest came into view. I saw my son with Missy, the Doctor and the brothers. Every face of the room was there. I looked behind me but was met with nothingness. I grabbed the set and shook it. "Where are they?! Where are they?!" The girls face was nearly taking up the whole screen but I could still see them. They were looking at her on her knees with such pity in their eyes. Their eyes were over flowing with sympathy, why? Why?! Where were they?! I screamed again. "Please! Please let me go to them, I'll do anything!"

As the words left my lips I felt a need to take them back, but I could not. My feet felt cold. I looked down and saw the water rising. I don't know where it was coming from but it was coming fast. Before I could even register what was going on, it had reached my knees. The television was still on even though the water had now reached it. I looked into the screen but there was no water there. It was now getting higher. I pushed the TV off the table and stood on it. But the old television set didn't sink, it just floated up to the surface of the water, still broadcasting its feed. The water just kept on rising. Now standing on the table was useless. There was nowhere to go. I just watched as the old television set floated past me, its power cord tugging at it like a dog on a leash, pulling it down as the water rose above it. It looked so surreal, like the rules of physics had forgotten themselves. But there was a strange familiarity about it, as though I knew that like this curious floating balloon, I too had gone as far as I could. Just before I closed my eyes and surrendered I caught a glimpse of the television screen through the water. The last thing I saw was myself standing together with everyone else, shaking my head with those same pity eyes.

Chapter Four

I awoke from a terrifying dream to find myself still in the room. The lights had come back on, so that was good. The room was silent and I was curled in towards the wall with my boy who was still asleep. I turned around and my heart stopped. The room, it had changed. The shocking red flicked my survival switch. I gently got up, carefully treading through the bodies to get closer a look.

I stared and stared. I just didn't get it. What was it? It was so strange. I had never seen anything like it before. It was impossible to see where it stopped and where it began. It didn't matter where I started, I just couldn't get a hold on anything, it just kept slipping through my fingers. What was it? What did it mean? Round and round I read, emphasising different words, trying to squeeze out as much sense from them as I could. Every time I felt I nearly had it, that the meaning was only a few words away, it hovered just out of reach. I felt like the poor greyhound chasing the stuffed rabbit. It was so irritating and yet, so addictive. I must have read it a hundred times but I still never got anywhere. The flower design in the centre of the large circular ring of words only added to my confusion. I tried to use the letters in the petals as a code or some kind of tool to help me see what I wasn't seeing. But any and all ideas I tried just left me more frustrated. Each of the eight petals contained a letter, with both sides mirroring each other.

Live? Live? It didn't make sense. But it wasn't just the words that didn't make sense, it was the meaning of the whole charade. What was it for? To show us we were not the forgotten evacuees we thought we were? But why the dramatics? Why such a grand gesture? To remind us who is the cat and who is the mouse? But who *is* the cat? My mind began to buckle. I couldn't stop the surging so I just let it pour.

My flurry of questions fell so furiously it seemed to avalanche over my mind and into the room. I could hear my thoughts being spoken outside my head. Was I imagining things? What was real? I then found myself in a place, in a space I had never been. I, or more my mind, was transfixed upon the wall. It wouldn't release me. I found myself floating in the place where one moment ends and another begins, where things are simultaneously moving in slow motion yet at great speed. And it was in this bizarre space where I had my first sense that something was wrong, very wrong with the room. Something beyond the obvious, something else, something far bigger, but as soon as I tried to unwrap it, it was gone and so was my moment between moments.

.....the wall of reality will fall into freedom for all in one key is the serpent is your death of skin of the looking glass of the door of illusion of time tock ticking over tomorrow is today is yesterday is away to be born in a storm of light of day of night of stars that twinkle colours of view only red writings on the wall of reality will fall into freedom for all in one key is the serpent is your death of skin of the looking glass of the door of illusion of time tock ticking over...

The wall released me and I fell back. I felt outside it, outside it all. I felt displaced, a refugee of the moment. Voices vortexed expanding to a swirling whirlpool of reaction, of dissatisfaction, confusion and fear.

"Oh my God."

"What is it?"

"What does it mean?"

"It means someone was in here."

"What have they done?"

"Why would they?"

"What do they want?"

"I don't get it."

"What is it?"

"I don't understand."

"What does it mean?"

"It means we haven't been locked away and forgotten about. Someone definitely knows we're here."

"Oh God."

"But why?"

"What is it?"

"Is it a message?"

"For who, us?"

"Who else!"

"But why leave a message that we can't read?"

"To make a sport out of it."

"To keep us busy."

"We will have to try and decipher it."

"Decipher what? It doesn't mean anything!"

"There must be some code or algorithm, some way to solve it."

"But what does it mean?"

"What it means is that we're a whole lot more fucked than we thought we were."

"Jesus, what is this?"

"What do they want?"

"Why won't they just tell us?"

"Because they want us to work it out."

"It's all just a game, isn't it?"

"A game?"

"Does this look like a game?"

"What else could it be?"

"What is it even written with?"

"It's not..."

"No, it looks like paint."

"Who cares?!"

"No, it's not paint, or pen, it's like-"

"It looks like it's been stamped on."

"But it's handwritten."

"I've never seen anything like it."

"But this must mean that there's definitely a way out."

"Well of course. How else did we get here?"

"No, I mean that maybe this is our way out. That all we need to do is solve this riddle and then we get to go home."

"All we need to do?! It's impossible!"

"This changes everything."

"I knew there was something fishy about the whole thing. It was all too staged, too-"

"Listen, we don't know anything yet."

"We know that someone planned this all along."

"We don't know that for sure."

"So it's just a bit of honest graffiti, someone got a bit bored last night?"

"What about the attacks? How does this fit in, is there still a state of emergency?"

"Of course there isn't."

"Why wouldn't there be?"

"Are you serious?"

"Well I don't see what one has to do with the other."

"I hope that everything has been part of a game or whatever it is. I don't care what happens in here, as long as out there it's safe-"

"Speak for yourself."

"Isn't anyone a little concerned how someone came in and out without being seen?"

"Maybe they gassed us? It happened to my mother once. They sprayed this stuff on her while she was sleeping so they could rob the place."

"Maybe no one came in. Maybe they just went out."

"Oh my God."

"Or neither."

"What?"

"You mean they could still be in here, hidden as one of us?"

"It would make sense. Have an eye and ear on the inside."

"Hold on, let's just relax a bit. The last thing we want is a witch hunt."

"But we can't just allow a witch to-"

"We can't start suspecting and turning on each other either."

"We all woke up together."

"Some could have just pretended."

"Some?"

"Yeah, there could be a few of them in here."

"Oh God."

"Where are they?"

"Who is it?"

"Maybe you're the plant? Or you? Or you?"

"We could all be plants and you could be the only one who's real. Listen, we can't get distracted. We have to keep calm and try to deal with one thing at a time."

"Exactly what a plant would say."

"Oh for Pete's sake."

"We don't know a thing about each other. It could be anyone."

"We could do interrogations."

"Yeah, we could hold suspects in the storage cupboard?"

"That could work."

"Listen to yourselves! We'll be driven mad with suspicion! It'll never end! It will be impossible to determine anything as fact. We'll just keep dividing ourselves until there's nothing left."

"He's right. We should just take it that someone else came in and left. It's the safest, most responsible thing to do."

"But how did they come in? We were all sleeping in front of the doors!"

"That proves it."

"Yeah, it's gotta be an inside job."

"We can't possibly know anything for sure."

"There are ways."

"Listen, if we go down this path of doubting each other, we won't come back."

"With enough persuasion, anyone will give us whatever truth we need."

"This is crazy. Are we seriously considering this?"

"We need to know."

"Yeah, I don't think we have a choice."

"You're right. If we want to survive, we don't have a choice. Therefore it is imperative we honour and respect people's privacy and freedom as much as possible, and crucially, people's honesty and integrity. If we wave the value carried upon people's word then we will have no currency of truth at all. It all becomes meaningless, we'll be left with nothing. We cannot split ourselves and turn against each other. We must not lose the trust between us, immaterial of the grey non-truths that go by unnoticed. Trust is the only thing protecting us from dissolving into the abyss."

The room was silent. I think even the people that didn't agree saw that it was a better bet to shelve this fear for now.

"But why? What's it all for?"

"Has anyone ever seen Battle Royale?"

"What a completely irresponsible thing to even mention in here!"

"What is it?"

"It's nothing that should be spoken about ever again or even allowed to enter our subconscious."

"Why don't we try being a little more pragmatic and a little less dramatic?"

"Well at least now one thing's for sure, we know we gotta get outta here. And now we know there's an in and an out, all we gotta do is find it."

Some people started frantically looking around, searching for something, anything.

"Let's all just relax for a minute and not do anything crazy."

"That's probably what they want, to divide and conquer."

"Listen, if this whole thing has been set up then obviously they have complete control. There are no mistakes, no variables except for us of course, you can't plan what a human being will do. All I'm trying to say is that I don't know what choice we have left except to just to ride it out."

"Just ride it out? Isn't that the same as doing nothing?"

"Ain't no way I'm gonna just sit here and do nothin'."

"Maybe that's why they're doing all this, just to see what their only variable will do."

"I swear to God, when I find out who's behind this..."

"Calm down! You'll only antagonise them!"

"Yes, they could be listening or watching."

"Most likely both."

"I just can't believe it, I can't. It just doesn't seem right. No one could do this."

"Well they've done it sweetheart, 'cause we're in it. The world ain't full of rainbows and unicorns."

"But they could have hurt us and they didn't. At least that's something."

"Yeah, they don't want their fun to be over."

"So you really think this is all some sort of game?"

"I've heard of crazier things."

"It would be impossible for that to be true. It couldn't stay a secret. Someone would tell."

"Maybe we're the first."

"Or maybe no one's ever been left to tell."

"Oh come on now. This is getting ridiculous."

"How about instead of burning our energy up on extreme theories, we use it to solve this bloody thing?"

Most people agreed, then disagreed, then agreed again. Hypothesising was a waste of energy and we all had to conserve as much of it as we could. Missy and the girls took this as their cue to make the special breakfast they had planned. Of course we went over to help, or in my son's case sneak an early portion or two.

The room was now alive with ideas and meanings and answers. People do love to untangle the knot of a good riddle, to get to the root of an enigmatic enigma. Especially when it's one they can't solve. Why is that? Is it just the challenge? The egoic buzz we get from solving

189

it? Or is it instead akin to our preference for wrapped gifts over unwrapped ones? Is it all about the anticipation, all about the moment before something becomes a certainty? Are we possibility addicts, addicted to the paradox reality created just before the unveiling when it is all things at once? Why is that conundrum of quantum field theory something that we feel an affinity towards? Is it somehow a fundamental part of who we are, what makes us tick? What makes us tock? The unknown of infinite possibilities, all existing within a world of pure imagination.

Imagination. A word that is all and nothing. A word that cannot be anything else other than itself, yet it holds all things. How do you possibly quantify the unquantifiable? It is a mystery, an unknown dressed as a known, deemed understood by labelling it as just another part of who we are. But what part? Where does it start and where does it end? If a part of us is so unbridled and free then surely how can other parts not be? How can rigidity exist as malleability or vice versa? Every single one of us uses it on a daily basis to help us through the day, some more constructively than others. Some use it to make themselves happy, some use it to make themselves sad. Some use it to create, some to destroy. Some use it to speculate on the future, some use it to try to comprehend the past. But not enough of us use it in its truest form and implement its real power, its greatest magic. Though we all used to once, every single one of us. It's just that that time was fairly long ago and since we hit double figures it became a less important pastime, a less valuable way to spend our lives. Daydreaming was condemned as idle folly and we were told to get our heads out of the cumulus. But where else should they be? In the undergrowth? Six feet under? In the past, in the future, in facts and figures, information and details, dots and dashes? Surely unlimited fantasy of thought is a welcome and deserved break from all the busyness? We are, after all, creators when we conjure our daydreams. So to prevent and restrict the wielding of our own true power and identity is inhumane, an utter abomination. It's amusing that in our current society some of the most revered people are the ones who can make-believe the best. We celebrate their ability to create an illusion, to trick us into believing a false reality is real. So then, what does that show us about our true nature? That we revel in the unreal. That we take great pleasure in immersing ourselves in fantasy and delight in experiencing worlds that are not our own. If we are innately drawn to that which we are akin to then we must admit that there is a distinct possibility that the very essence of our essence is composed of pure imagination.

We are obsessed with adding gravity to our lives, obsessed with never allowing ourselves to get too carried away, too weightless, too free. Perhaps we do it for fear gravity will be administered sneakily without our knowledge and catch us by surprise. It is possibly that fear of falling, of being pushed that keeps us and our poor feet firmly on the ground. The weight of gravity effects us in many ways. Not just physically and emotionally, but spirituality. Though it is quite possibly the internal weight that we carry that impedes us the most. How can we feel uplifted or elevated if we don't allow ourselves to soar, to fly and live without gravity internally, in the only place where we hold any true power over our environment. Interesting that the word gravity has also grown to adopt the meaning of severity and seriousness, instead of more positive ones like energy and force. Maybe meanings just evolve and adapt to suit the needs of our time. After all, words exist as our servants. Their sole purpose is to serve us, to help us portray and provide meaning. They help us describe things that are not tangible, not visible. Words are like little containers that help us bottle images so they can be understood in order to connect with one another. Communication is the invisible string that keeps us connected, bound to each other through understanding. Words contain so much, they are the most powerful tools we own, they transcend barriers and create worlds. Their importance is unrivalled, unparalleled. Without them we would be lost. But obviously words are of no use when they do not make sense. And unfortunately, in the room, there were quite a few that did not.

"My brain hurts."

"I just can't read it anymore."

"All the words make sense by themselves but together, it's just such a jumble."

"Maybe it's a creole language of some sort?"

"It's not the words that are foreign. It's the meaning of them when they're all put together like that."

"Maybe it doesn't even mean anything."

"Yeah, what if it's there just to see how long we'll waste our time on it?"

"I can't look at it anymore."

"I think we should leave the ring of words and look closer at that flower in the middle."

"There's not really much to go on though."

"Yeah, it's just four letters."

"Maybe it's a key to unlock the ring?"

"That would be clever."

"I hate these things."

"I actually really love a clever conundrum, stretches the brain muscles."

"I prefer to stretch real muscles."

"L, I, V, E. What do you think it means? Do you think it's a word or is it an acronym?"

"How the hell are we supposed to work out what the letters stand for? They could be anything! It's impossible!"

"Maybe it just means what it means, live?"

"And what does that mean?"

"I don't know, but instead of seeing what the letters could stand for shouldn't we just look at the word they make?"

"Live doesn't get us anywhere."

"Oh my God."

"What is it?"

"Read it again, but backwards."

"Shit."

"Why would they write that?"

"Because they are evil."

"Oh God."

"Hold on, why would it be written backwards? Why would they bother?"

"Maybe it means that the opposite of live is evil?"

"And again, how does that help us in any way?"

"Yes, that's not really anything new. Live has always been evil backwards as the word devil has always been lived. It doesn't mean anything."

"Yes, we're looking at it too simply. It must be some sort of code to unlock the riddle."

"Well, if we're trying to find an algorithm then obviously we need to look at the letters separately, not as part of a word."

"Maybe its roman numerals?"

"Roman what?"

"The number system used in Europe before our own Arabic one."

"Arabic?"

"So, L would mean fifty, I one, and V five."

"Separately yes, but together it denotes the number fifty-four."

"Like Studio 54?"

"Yeah, we're in one of the torture rooms of Studio 54, 'depraved urban decay'. Very sexy."

"Well what could 54 mean?"

"God knows."

"The number of hours we have to be here, or days or weeks or years..."

"Maybe it's to do with us, like, 54 of us signify something."

"What? That literally makes no sense whatsoever."

"Well at least I'm trying!"

"Well try harder!"

"Enough bloody bickering! Let's just solve this thing!"

"Alright. Well I don't think it means 54, because there is no value for E in roman numerals."

"Maybe the E signifies something else?"

"Musical note?"

"No, that wouldn't fit in with the numbers."

"Well, it could be that it's the fifth musical note, fifth letter in the alphabet? If the V does stand for a five then that's a bit of a coincidence."

"Perhaps. It is the most used letter in our language, and it also appears in many others, old and new."

"What has that got to do with anything?"

"If they wanted to give us a number five then why the hell didn't they just write a number five?"

"Because then it wouldn't be a puzzle, it would just be instructions."

"Well, I like instructions! They're simple and solid and you can follow them. This whole thing is just... unnatural!"

"Isn't E derived from the Greek letter epsilon?"

"Isn't that some letter in German?"

"No, it's Italian for the letter Y."

"Y, like why?"

"Fifty, one, five, why?"

"Five hundred and fifteen, why."

"For crying out loud, if they had wanted us to see a Y then why would they put an E?!"

"He has point, unfortunately."

"How many times are we gonna try and guess what it is?"

"Well, in mathematics epsilon means a small undefined quantity."

"But how does that fit in?"

"Also, the sign of e signifies exponential."

"There's also the e mathematical constant."

"The what?"

"What if it meant all of them? Small exponential constant?"

"I think we're getting a little too focused on the possible meaning of one letter."

"Maybe it's E for eggheads."

"Who said that?"

"Does it matter?"

"Does any of it?"

"I don't think the petals mean anything."

"Unless they're the code to steer us through the words?"

"Listen, let's just forget the bloody flower!"

"If it even is a flower."

"Oh for God's sake."

"All I'm saying is that maybe it's something else."

"Yeah, looking at it now it actually looks more like infinity symbols."

"Yes, four of them. Infinity, infinite, four... four dimensions of reality?"

"Have you all gone mad? You're drowning in detail! You've lost all perspective by looking at it through a microscope. We need to stand back and look at the big picture here."

"Which is?"

"We're in a game. We're the mice in the maze. But the maze is not this room, they've made our minds into the maze. And the cheese is not just freedom from these four walls, its freedom from ourselves, from our man-made selves."

"What? What's he saying?"

"I don't know, something like we're robots or machines or something."

"Cool."

"So what, you're saying that this is some kind of social experiment?"

"It seems pretty obvious to me."

"All this just to see how we tick?"

"That seems a little far-fetched."

"Does it? I think it makes perfect sense. If you really think about it, what better way to cleanly analyse human behaviour than to trap a group in a room, dissolve the path they were on, basically delete their identity, throw stress into the mix and see what comes out? It's the clearest way to examine how human beings work together, if they'll collaborate or just end up antagonising each other."

"Antago-what?"

"What you're doing."

"Okay, let's not be taken down a road we'll regret."

"That's probably what they want."

"That's probably the whole reason for it."

"Shit."

"Is that really the only option, the only plausible explanation here? That we've been put in some nightmare just as an experiment, material for someone's thesis?"

"Maybe there is another explanation. And maybe it's the simplest one. That we're the ones behind it. That we chose this."

"What the..?"

"Are you crazy?"

"Perhaps, but that's beside the point. You have to admit what I am saying isn't outside the realm of possibility. It could be that we all signed up for this."

"Absurd."

"Is it? Maybe it's been our decision all along. It would make sense, explain how we could suddenly all go missing, lose our short term memories."

"And why on earth would we do that?"

"Yeah, what possible motivation is there?"

"You think we did it for the money?"

"What? No, no, this whole thing is probably costing an obscene amount of money as it is."

"So you're saying, that what, we all must be crazy rich?"

"No! I don't know, possibly, but that's not the point."

"So what is the point?"

"Yes, why would anyone in their right mind choose to subject themselves to all this?"

"Yeah, especially if they're filthy rich."

"Well maybe, maybe we wanted to feel again."

"Feel?"

"Yes. Feel our lives, appreciate them and the things within them. Maybe we all, all one hundred of us, had grown complacent in our existence and lost the joy of life. So perhaps we decided to do this to get some of it back."

"So you're saying we did all this just to gain perspective?"

"Pretty elaborate lesson."

"So, by your rights, this is all a fantasy of our own creation and therefore we shouldn't be scared or worried at all, shouldn't take any of it seriously?"

"Exactly."

"Well, you know that's impossible to do."

"Never mind impossible, it's insane."

"You might see it as risky but-"

"What you're asking is beyond risky. It's like walking along the edge of a skyscraper with your eyes closed."

"It's completely reckless behaviour."

"You're saying bring a water pistol to a gun fight. Do you think we're fools?"

"No, no I don't. But why does there have to be a fight? Maybe there isn't a fight at all, we have no proof. We're just making assumptions based on fear and believing them to be fact."

"I tell you what I know is fact-"

"You can't expect people to look on the bright side of the beast."

"Is there any other side to look? It's especially when things seem at their darkest that we can't afford to dive into the dark."

"What we can't afford to do is continue to listen to people like you."

"So you'd rather choose to act as if we're living in a nightmare?"

"There's no choice involved. We're captives. We've got to be on guard, ready for whatever's coming next."

"By imagining the worst outcome?"

"It's called being prepared."

"No it's not. Being prepared is not living in an illusion you're piecing together in your head. Being prepared starts with actually being aware of what is happening, being here, not lost in your thoughts of what could happen."

"Well maybe, but that still doesn't mean we have to believe that this is our game and it's all going to turn out rosy."

"But it hasn't turned out anything yet! And until it does, I'm going to conserve my energy rather than allowing worry to sap it away."

"You're asking us to put our guard down."

"Why is it up at all?"

"This guy's not listening. Why are we all still entertaining this crap?"

"You can't ask people to walk through hell pretending it's heaven."

"No, but given the chance to guess where I am, I will always believe the moment innocent until proven guilty.

I would rather make the mistake of thinking hell is heaven than thinking heaven is hell."

For a moment the room held a strange silence to it. His words made everyone imagine the utter atrociousness of the reality of being in heaven believing it to be hell. But if you had been somehow convinced that heaven really was hell, what on earth could convince you otherwise? Even more heaven couldn't do it. What could possibly change your mind? You would be destined for all eternity to experience your own private hell within paradise. Could there be a more tragic and hopeless existence? And for just a second it forced everyone in the room to become a little more mindful of the colossal power their mind could wield.

"Man, you're one crazy son of a bitch but you got a point."

"But we're not in heaven or hell, we're in a room. Your analogy doesn't apply."

"It applies all the more because of the uncertainty of where we are. I'm tired of being scared, aren't you? It doesn't help a thing, you don't get anywhere. So I'm going to try not being at the mercy of fear and I'll let you know how it goes."

Even though his words had reverberated deeply within some people they still entered the next moment and, consciously or unconsciously, dismissed this guy and his ideas as quickly as he left to go to the bathroom, returning back to where they were and their fret-filled-questioning of everything. But he had a point. He had several. They could talk until the end of time about all the possible possibilities and credible connotations, build assumptions upon assumptions and then consequences of said assumptions but it wouldn't change what the truth was, a truth that we still had no idea of. He was right; screening simulated scenarios in our minds wasn't going to help. It was all just a waste of time, such a waste of energy. We're so cleverly tricked by our calculating mind into never switching it off, always double checking and double, double checking. Our mind makes each problem into a sphere, insisting to us that there is always another angle to look at, always another side to check behind. But you never run out of sides with a sphere, you'll never run out of corners to check, you'll just keep going round in circles forever, chasing a tail that you don't even have.

I felt a little disheartened. No one had properly listened to what he had said. They just rejected him and therefore everything he had to say. But maybe it was exactly what we were supposed to hear right now. Maybe we needed to loosen our tight grip, lower our shields a bit to see a view that had been blocked. He wasn't wrong; we didn't know anything for sure. We had to keep an open mind to everything. That would give us our best chance. But for some mind opening meant mind altering, which was not to be permitted under any circumstances. Convincing the room to change their perceptions did not seem to be a viable option right now. It's hard to change a view you have held for a long time, to tilt your head to a different angle, to a new direction, to a new vista. Then a thought occurred to me. Had I just been the kettle, calling out the pot? A voice spoke over my shoulder forcing my blood to pump faster.

"So what did you think about what he said?"

"He reminds me of someone" I said not turning around.

"And do you shun him like you do that someone?"

He whispered so close to my ear I felt the warm breeze of his breath tickle me sending those same fizzy tingles through my body. I was happy he couldn't see my face, it was too much to hide.

"Or do you agree with him?"

I dragged myself back down to the room and turned to face my close quarter companion. I found my personal space in his, but I didn't move.

"Well, I don't think we're all unhappy billionaires. But I commend his bravery in choosing to no longer be directed by fear. He's right though, it is tiring being shepherded about. It's so much less draining not being on your guard all the time but it's not for everyone."

"Why not?"

"Because some people can't just drop everything, just let it all go. They have too much at stake, too much to protect."

"But don't the most important responsibilities deserve the most clear-sightedness? Don't they deserve the ultimate protection?"

"Yes, of course, but it's not as easy as you make it out to be."

"It's not? But you just do it. You just let go of everything you're dragging around. You just realise that every bit of baggage being lugged from moment to moment is useless."

"Then tell me, why do we do it?"

"Because we feel that we have been hard done by, let down, and it serves to remind us of our perceived flightlessness. It reaffirms our decision to not ever try again and it serves to keep our feet firmly glued to the ground. But a plane can't stay grounded forever. It can't just keep driving back and forth on the runway. It can't go on pretending it's something it's not. Consequences will occur from it misuse, malfunctions and error messages will appear."

"Thanks for the interesting analogy. But I am not a machine."

"No, you're not. Yet don't you think we all seem to act a little more machine then man sometimes, all just responding with programmed reactions, just repeating the same tasks over and over again? You can't keep a bird in a cage, it's not natural. That bird, it just won't be right. It will eventually become lethargic and depressed or it will turn vicious and angry. It might survive, but it won't live. Every trapped being inevitably becomes numb or highly strung."

"Okay, but we are not birds and we cannot fly. Life is full of hardship. Every day we slog through the molasses trying not to fall down. We should be applauded for not falling, for not going under. We should be praised for carrying this heavy cross."

"The cross that we decide to bear is the very thing preventing us from being free. It is not just worn as a badge of honour to commend our bravery of surviving through it, but it has also become our shield, protecting us, sheltering us from venturing forth and far, preventing us from experiencing new experiences. It has become our excuse to stay caged, to stay trapped, to stay unhappy."

"That doesn't make any sense."

"You're right, it doesn't."

"I meant what you said, not what people do, doesn't matter."

He had a real way of picketing your position, of shaking it, seeing how rooted it was. It was best, maybe, to treat him like my son and sometimes allow him his little victories, his small fry, to save the big fish for me.

"Perhaps you're right. Even a broken clock has its moment, twice each day if I'm not mistaken. But, come on, you don't honestly think that we're all just acting, just pretending to be happy?"

"I think everyone is portraying the part they think they need to be, fulfilling a role they feel has been given to them, which, sadly, they have confused with their real identity. They're all acting because they've forgotten how to be real. This world and its monochrome filter has blotted out all our colour and reduced it all to grey."

"Well it's impossible that everybody is feeling the same thing."

"Do you really think people are so different? Everyone's still picking up the same frequency, it's just that some have the volume turned up and some have it turned down. Everybody still bears the ache of separation."

"Separation? Separation from what?"

"Separation from ourselves."

"How can you be separate from yourself?"

"When you have decided upon another."

"Another what?"

"Self."

I felt a small squeeze at back of my legs. I turned to see my little boy with Missy behind him.

"Oh, hello, my little love! How have you been?"

"Super!"

"Your boy's been a mighty help. I don't know how we could've managed it all without his counting skills. Here's yours, sugar, help keep your strength up."

"Thanks but I'm not really hungry. Did you have fun, baby?"

I bent down to his level.

"I had two peaches and extra raisins!"

He lowered his voice and bent in a little closer to me.

"I saved some in my pocket, Mummy. We can have them later."

"Oh my little sweetheart."

I scooped him up in my arms and gobbled at his neck and chest.

"Maybe I'll just eat you!"

His loud liberated laughter bolted through the room. I was proud of his ability to be so free in this place. Mid-snuggle, he put in a request I could not refuse.

"Please eat your breakfast, Mummy. I put the raisins in myself. Look! I made a heart!"

I looked down at the cold plastic cup filled with grey gruel. There was a bright neon orange crescent that seemed to be drowning in it with randomly scattered raisins floating on top. They resembled more an anatomical heart than a classically shaped one. I looked into his approval seeking eyes, his sweetness that always pulled me through the sour.

"Alright my darling, how about we share it?"

"Okay but I have to be quick because I'm helping with the clean-up."

He lowered his voice again and leaned in closer to my ear.

"I think I'm winning, Mummy! I haven't been cross at all and I'm making everyone happy by helping them. And I'm telling my best knock-knock jokes. I think you must get extra points if you make people laugh."

"Oh, I think you're definitely right there."

We gobbled down the tepid mush and the super sweet tinned peach that we would never have had at home. Before he left, he leaned in one last time and gave me his particular insight into the red writings.

"I love the new puzzle, Mummy! They did it really well. It looks like a really hard one. Everyone really believes it! But they're being silly losing so many points. But don't worry, Mummy, I haven't told anybody anything yet and I haven't been scared at all. I'm having a great time!"

"Well done, sweetie! We're gonna win for sure!"

"Shush, Mummy! See you later!"

"See you later, sweetheart!"

"Innocence brings such magic with it. As small children we really do see the world as a place of wonder, where magic is real because evidence of it is all around us. When you've never seen colours every single one is astonishing, there are no favourites. When we're that young we're still so soft, we haven't as yet hardened into realists. Experience has not yet triumphed over innocence. We're born without fear and though some may think that a hazardous trait evolution should have corrected, I think maybe we're looking at it the wrong way. I think there's a reason we come into the world the way we do."

"Do you ever wonder what a human would be like if they stayed that way, I mean if innocence was left intact?"

"I do. And so did your mother. She believed that we were all meant to stay that way. She believed there was this feedback of a cloud that we create within our bubble of reality that prevents us from seeing things how they really are."

"Like muddying the waters to try to get a better look?"

"Yeah, that's a very good analogy. And it's true, it's really true. Your mother read about this concept in that book, The Next Natural Step. It was called the mirror of reality. Basically we each have this mirror and we cover it, or patch it up, make it better, improve it with things we have learned or found out about the world. We paste on these improvements in the hopes that it will make our lives easier but it does the exact opposite. All you end up with is a distorted patchwork quilt reflection of yourself and the world around you. Your mother then decided to make the concept her own and added another dimension to it. She made the mirror spherical, a little like a disco ball, with each mini mirror or mirrored bead, as she liked to imagine them, representing one of those patches. And when you start to remove the programming in your head and the corresponding beads, the clearer your sight becomes."

"It's not really that simple though, is it?"

"The concept or the deprogramming?"

"Both. I actually remember her trying to explain it to me once. Do you know the story of how she came up with her mirrored beads?"

"No, I didn't even know there was a story."

"Do you want to hear it?"

"Do I want to hear a story about how my favourite author formed her core concept? And do I want to hear it told by her daughter? I don't know, do vegetarians wish that bacon grew on trees?"

"Okay, I'll take that as a yes. It was summer, a hot summer. My mother had moved from her writing desk to the kitchen table to catch the breeze from the back door but the screen for the door was broken so we went to get a new one. But they were too expensive so instead we got one of those pretty beaded curtains. I remember hearing the noise of my grandfather's old typewriter as I lay on the cool kitchen tiles playing with the new toy. I was mesmerized watching the sunlight dance upon the facets of the shiny beads, reflecting the light around me in a shower of rainbows and shooting stars. I remember the feeling of kneeling in front of it being surrounded by a hundred small smiling faces, each imprisoned in a world of their own. All these distorted faces were so funny. They were all me but I was not them. I called out for my mother to show her my great discovery but as usual, she was deeply engrossed in her words.

"Look, Mummy! It's lots of mini me's!"

"Yes, dear."

"No really, look!"

"Mummy's busy, sweetie. Hold on just a minute."

"But all the beads have my face in them, but it's not mine, it's a funny face!"

"Hold on just one more minute, baby."

"Please, Mummy. I want to see our faces together."

"Okay, darling. Let me see."

I remember how happy I was to see her smiling face embedded within the bead's reality. I was not alone, we were in this alternate universe together. I remember thinking that even if we had really been trapped within one of those beaded prisons it would have been okay. We would have been trapped together. I hugged and kissed her as I watched our many mini clones do the same. I found is so funny. It was so otherworldly. Then her smile changed into a small open mouth which of course made me laugh all the more. She stared and stared and I just giggled. Then she leapt to her chair and began to type. I was a little sad she had cut our playtime so short. But then after only a minute or two she came up behind me and scooped me into her arms, squeezing me tight as she kissed and thanked me. At the time of course I had no idea why. I presumed she was thanking me for having fun because she didn't really have very much of that anymore. She then did something that I will never ever forget. She went over to our small freezer shelf at the top of our old fridge and took out the whole tub of our precious ice cream. She placed it on the kitchen table and gave me a spoon and a smile. I could hardly believe my eyes. I sat down opposite her and ate until I was ice cream. I'll never forget that feeling of such freedom, no bowl. It's funny the things you remember, the moments that become memories."

"Thank you for letting me share that no bowl moment."

"Yeah, well there's not too many flashbacks left, I'm afraid."

"Even if I squeeze the tube? No family holidays?"

"We didn't really go on holiday, except once when we went to see the sea. I had never seen it before and was always curious about what water touching the horizon would look like. Maybe because I secretly believed that that was where the mermaids met. Anyway, I didn't like it and we never went again."

"Hold on, hold on, you can't just stop there. Why didn't you like it?"

"Well, it was September and the sea was just too rough. I swam out too far and lost my mother. I didn't think I'd ever see her again. I thought I was lost forever. It was too wild, too strong, too uncontrollable. It was the first time I can remember feeling real fear."

"I'm sorry that awful moment stuck. I hope it hasn't tainted the ocean for you. It really is such a magical space. So open, so untamed, such a place of healing. Its peace has helped guide me to find my own. I spent a great deal of my evolution wrapped up in the sanctuary of the sea. I find it to be such an inspiring place. Don't you think it's just amazing how such a powerless thing like water once unified can become so powerful?"

"I wasn't really thinking along those lines when I was cold, lost and alone. Plus I hate the wind and it's always so windy by the sea."

"You hate the wind? How can you hate the movement of air?"

"Air should be still and stable."

"But it's one of the most glorious feelings in the world to have the wind blow over you, for it to fill your lungs."

"No, it's horrible. It's like a force pushing and pulling you from where you want to be."

"But gravity lessens in the wind. If it's strong enough you can fall into it. It's the closest thing to flying."

"No, I hate it. And it whips your face."

I felt like a stubborn child. But I couldn't unstick myself from this feeling, this feeling of rage without reason.

"What's wrong?"

"What's right?"

"What's right?!"

"Yeah, what is right? Really, what is? I mean, the world is such a mess, everywhere you look it's just a mess. It's like it's just teetering on the edge of the drop off, just waiting for one more atrocity to pull it down. There are just too many problems, there's just too much to come back from. I really fear for the future my baby is going to have babies in. If there is one. I actually think it's a miracle that the world hasn't imploded yet, a miracle that somehow it's still going."

"I think it's a testament to how much strength we all have that, amidst all the shit everyone's wading through, we haven't completely lost it."

"Not long to go I'd say, if everything stays on course."

"You really think it will?"

"It's inevitable. We can't change. The whole world can't change. It's too late, we've gone too far."

"So you believe we're all doomed?"

"Well, it sounds a bit dramatic when you say it like that. But yes, I don't think it's going to improve."

"So you believe the destiny of the human race is to descend into a chasm of chaos of its own making?"

"Yes I do. Then we will finally face the consequences of our countless irresponsible acts of selfishness and greed. You reap what you sow."

"You reap what you sow, I've never warmed to the way in which that expression is utilised. Why does it always have to be implemented in such a negative manner? Why can't someone say it after somebody passes their driving test or as encouragement for someone actively trying to better themselves in some way. I always felt its use to chastise people is a little unfair. I think we all love to hand out blame, to ourselves and to each other. But blame doesn't change a thing. It doesn't change the past, what has happened. In fact it just makes things worse. Not only does it spread negativity, but it also serves to isolate and condemn the blamed. And because there's always a reason for blame, always somewhere else for the blame to fall, the blame game stays alive with everyone just passing it around whilst pretending to be perfect. But we're not. Not in that way anyway. And that's okay, it really is. We're all just feeling our way without a guide and I think it's a bit unfair to expect perfection all of the time. As a parent I'm sure you don't expect flawlessness. Children make mistakes. And all we are is grown up children. We're living live, there's been no rehearsals. We're all learning every day and so should be helping and forgiving each other instead of persecuting and penalising. I mean, we're all just trying our best, aren't we?"

"Maybe you are, Leo, but I think most people have been taking shitty short cuts. There's been more than just a few honest mistakes. We have all played our part in the ruin of this world. It's the trillion crappy things we've done to this planet and each other that has caused the mess we're in now, our tolerance of the status quo and the continual turning of blind eyes that's allowed all the evils to accumulate, to breed and fester, to have free reign over our only home turning it into the cessbowl we're wading in today. And it's been a long time coming. You can't just keep throwing garbage behind the hedge and not expect it to turn into a dump site. We've fucked up, we've fucked up good. The ones who I really feel sorry for are our future's generations. They're the ones who are the real losers in all this. They'll never get a chance to sow anything, never get a chance to reap a thing. They just get the crappy harvest we set, born into minus carrying the debts of our time. Now, how's that fair? You know, sometimes I really admire the people who have chosen not to bring children into this madness."

"You admire them?"

"Yes, I admire their bravery and selflessness."

"I may not be a parent, but I think to bring a child into this world requires an enormous amount of bravery and selflessness. I think it is quite probably the hardest job imaginable to teach a child about the current way of life and yet simultaneously inspire them to believe in a better way. I think it is the most courageous and altruistic of acts to create a human being and arm them with belief in themselves and the world, especially when it is at its darkest. For a person to tear off a piece of their heart, ignite it and strive to keep it lit to help banish the darkness of our world, well, I can't possibly imagine a more honourable and noble act for any member of any species."

I had nothing. How do you answer that? There is no answer, so I stayed quiet. Though the thought passed me that the world might well be a brighter place, dare I say it, if there were a few more Leo's in it, maybe even a litter.

"I think you should be immensely proud of yourself, all mothers should be. Contrary to popular belief it's your sex that holds the real power. You're the ones that can perform magic. You're the architects of the future. You have the potential to create life inside of you which, if I'm not mistaken, literally makes you goddesses."

"Now that would be a great Mother's Day card. I'm a little shocked at how astute you are. Have you recently transitioned? Seriously though, I never realised how difficult it was going to be. You only realise when you become a mother how hard it is, how much of yourself gets sucked in and not returned. You realise words like strength and patience are limitless and jugglers don't just exist in the circus. And I only have one. I literally cannot imagine how women cope with it all, how they don't just crack. And they do it all with no thanks or appreciation.

Maybe there should be two days a year instead of just one."

"Maybe we could petition that."

"Yeah, when we get out, if we get out."

"We will."

"How can you be so certain?"

"Because it's the only way to be."

"How did you get to be such an ambassador of positivity?"

"Well I decided a long time ago to be the opposite of my parents. Instead of grinning and bearing life, struggling to get through each day, I decided I was going to live my life for my life."

"Meaning?"

"Well, when I was younger this crazy idea came to me which made me look at my life and how I was living it in a completely new way. It's not a belief or creed, but it made me enjoy my life so much more. I suppose it was my first insight into realising that I had the ability to make my life sparkle, that that power was in me, not outside me. This crazy thought was, what if we had to relive it all? What if we had to do it all again and again but always bound by the same decisions and choices and feelings we had? What if the life we're making now was all that there was? What if all this was just us creating our heaven, our eternity. And everything, all of it, is all we have, all we get to experience for the rest of existence. Like we're building a holodeck, creating memories that will be the only moments we'll ever have. Kind of like you get to paint whatever you want but then that's all you get to look at. So I have to be happy with my day. No matter what's happening, I have to be cool with it. Otherwise my anxiety, my pain will reverberate through my forever. And so, when I get to the end of each day, I always ask myself would I mind living it again and again. And well the answer, so far, has always been the same."

"That's pretty out there even for you, Leo."

"Well I'd prefer to be out there than in here, wouldn't you?"

"Maybe I would if I actually understood what you meant."

"Out there is freedom, in here is confinement."

"Obviously yes, in a very literal sense but I don't think you mean geographically."

"I just mean that I prefer to be outside my head than in it."

"But how can you actually do that? All this being open, thinking positive stuff seems to be just another weight to carry around, just another project to add to the already over-crowded list. You try and you try and yet I can't help feeling I'm just stuck, like a hamster, on his never ending wheel of nowhere. I don't know, sometimes I just feel like what's the point in always doing the right thing, always being good. Where has that got me? What has life gifted me, what has been my reward for all that effort?"

"Your life's not quite over yet. You can't complain about the ending halfway through."

"So it's all for the ending? I have to trudge through all the crap just to get to an ending that I'll be too senile to even register?"

"I think you've taken it too literally. I mean, come on, your story isn't anywhere near over. You don't know what's around the next corner, behind the next door."

I looked at the only locked door. "No, I definitely don't. But I still don't think life is fair. Why do bad things happen to good people? Isn't it supposed to be the other way around?"

"You think bad things should happen to bad people?"

"Yes. No. I don't know, maybe. At least that would be fairer."

"So you believe bad people exist?"

"Of course. But I can only imagine how you're going to twist this to make me agree with you. Well, I'm not going to because you can't convince me that Mother Theresa and a serial killer are the same."

"I never said they were the same, obviously they're not. I just wondered if you believe bad people exist."

"Well I do."

Leo nodded a small nod as he looked into some distant distance.

"Fine, go on, tell me why I'm wrong. Everyone is inherently good and it's society and the toxic environment they evolve and grown up in which poisons them, not their true selves, right?"

"Yeah, something like that."

"Well even if you're right, how does that change a thing? Nice guys always finish last."

"Plato argued in quite articulated detail the pros and cons of being the just man. He even went so far as to create a fictional dream city in which to judge his hypothesis correctly."

"Did he succeed?"

"I don't know. I never got to the end of it. I actually got a little disillusioned. I thought he was setting his pupils up for a fall, allowing them to build up a completely erroneous castle, only to point out the decayed foundations. But the further I read the more I doubted my belief and his, so I stopped. I don't usually leave books unfinished but in this instance I felt I had no other choice. I felt sad because I didn't want it to be true, I didn't want such a great mind to fall so easily. So, instead of confirming it either way, I decided to leave it in the air. Maybe one day I'll go back to it again, and maybe I'll be surprised."

"So he believed that to be unjust was better?"

"Well, at the beginning they were in complete opposition with another who believed their views to be rooted in naivety. And maybe he was partly right. But I think it goes further than all that. I think ultimately it all comes down to whether we feel we're being watched, whether anything we do matters and whether or not we end up paying for our mistakes. Some people think that you get further ahead in life by cutting corners, that assuming the role of the unjust will guarantee you a richer life. However, some people who hold this belief are too fearful to uphold it. They believe that the comeuppance received in the afterlife will be one of such colossal damnation that the punishment for their crimes and ill will to man greatly outweighs any upper hand that they would have had on earth. So men will not become beasts for fear of the biggest beast. It seems our sense of conscience is cultivated externally, not internally. Which, I suppose, leads onto the only question that matters on this subject. If there were no consequences in this life or the next, would people become the beasts they're running from?"

"So you think everyone's just holding themselves back, simply damming the river?"

"I really hope not. I have faith in every human being, it's never too late to change. But I think the problem lies in the fact that we do not intrinsically trust one another. I would like to think that if everyone was given complete freedom to do whatever they wished that they wouldn't just take and keep but give and share."

"The funny thing is that that's the world we all wish we lived in, so why do we continue to believe the opposite? Are we the ones creating our worst nightmare?"

"Maybe it does have a little of the self-fulfilling prophecy about it. Or maybe it's just part of the great arc of earth and we're just living in one section of it. I hope for all of us that we're at the summit, or near it, we've all been through quite enough."

"But, Leo, how do you even know that there is an arc? It could all be a never ending up hill slog. Maybe we're nowhere near the worst the world can get. Maybe, for any kind of real chance, it really has to be brought to its knees and all its inhabitants with it. The world is spoilt, because we are. I don't know if there will ever be a comeback. If there's going to be a climax leading to change, a downhill to your arc, I fear it wouldn't resemble anything we've ever experienced, which I don't know is a good or a bad thing."

"How can it be a bad thing?"

"Because a complete shift of infrastructure, a complete transference of ideals and ethos could all just be too much for some."

"Even if the alternative is walking further into hell?"

"Better the devil you know."

"What a strange phrase. What does it even mean? Stay swimming in polluted waters because the alternative may be worse? That saying serves only to keep us all down by perpetuating a belief in darkness. There is no devil. He is literally and figuratively a figment of our imagination and that is the only place in which he has any power. There is no good or bad, it's all just happening and we're the ones that judge everything, label it, decide it to be so and so. We just need to stop, stop for a whole second and look at ourselves and our lives, the world, what it has become, what it all means, to just have the next thought. People are in a coma daze because they're too tired to think just one thought outside their cell. They are living in cages of their own construction and have managed to convince themselves of their fortune for even having one. But they need to at least acknowledge that there is an outside to their inside. And until that begins to happen, until they begin to see that they are not only what they think they are, we won't get to slide down the other side."

"So what is the punishment for being unjust?"

"The punishment is living with yourself."

"But they don't see that as a punishment."

"They don't?"

"How can they? They are themselves and they have made all those decisions."

"You don't know how a person feels when they are alone with their thoughts, what it feels to live with the selves they have chosen to be."

"No, but I don't think it's a good enough punishment."

"You have to remember that people do what they feel is best for their survival, for the survival of their kin. They don't believe what they do is wrong, otherwise they wouldn't do it. We all have our own parameters of conscience."

"But that's hardly fair."

"Well would you say it would be fair if the reality existed that when you die, your next life is living with yourself?"

"I don't understand, isn't that just what you were saying?"

"No I mean quite literally living with another you. But one that didn't know you were the same. How would your self treat you, how would they be and act towards you? Would it be a punishment or a gift?"

"That would depend on what kind of person you were."

"Exactly. So do you think that would be fair?"

"Well, I suppose a little fairer."

"So you think it's fair for them to be punished for being what they are? But how could they have been anything else?"

"But you said yourself we can always change."

"Yes, and I believe that. But I do think that there's not much intelligence in the potter blaming the pot for being cracked."

"Then why did the potter create a cracked pot?"

"The cracks create a door to suffering and suffering creates a door to peace. They are two ends of the same corridor, the corridor of transformation that separates us from ourselves."

"Not quite with you but I'll let you know when I am."

"It is only through the need to change that we change."

"Right, okay. But don't you think some pots are too cracked to mend?"

"It is never too late to nourish the sick withering plant, no matter how deprived. Its deprivation of sunlight and water can always be rewound, that is, until its death. But before that point is reached hope is more than a real possibility. It is a truth, a path toward the wholesome whole. We have all been malnourished in some shape or form. It may be more obvious in some than in others, but we are all suffering the same strain of pain. Yet all is most certainly not lost, it never was and never shall be. We can all be brought back to life, back to our life. With care and love and the cleansing and healing properties of the light of truth, we can all thrive. We just need to accept our divinity, accept our deity as not simply a being but more a state of being, a state from which we were never lost at all, a state simply forgotten about, that just slipped on our mind."

"Don't you mean slipped our mind?"

"No."

"Slipped on our mind? What does that mean?"

"It means the slippery banana skin of thought has prevented us from finding ourselves, from seeing ourselves, from being ourselves. It has hindered our trek and forced us to live on our bellies on a cold hard ground of reality."

"Jesus, Leo, it's all getting a bit heavy. I think I'm short circuiting a little. I need to take a walk."

But there was nowhere to walk to. The room seemed to reflect more anguish than I knew I had. It exposed an anxiety that I thought I had been able to subdue, to control, to submerge. Now that I had been forced to stay put, sit still for the first time in my life, just the thought of it secretly terrified me more than anything, in or out of the room. To be forced to be alone with my bleeding, gushing thoughts, to have them pouring out unchecked, unimpeded, was more than a maddening prospect. It was an invitation to hell. I had coped so well damming that strong stream of thought that now it was threatening to break free I didn't know what I was going to do.

As I paced my skin was itching with irritation and unrest, like it couldn't be still and just be. I was shivering with a feverish wave, not hot, not cold, but certainly not just right. I felt awkward, like every step was wrong, both over and under thought. It seemed as though I had fallen out of sync with myself. Like I had lost my step, my rhythm. I felt like I was out of tune with the soundtrack of the moment. Yet there was something pinning me down. I felt bound, chained to some force that was halting me, preventing me from detaching, keeping me pressed hard against it.

I needed to get out of the room, or maybe just out of my head. That was the real room. Distraction, distraction never fails. Where was he, the troublemaker of the room? He had found a pen and with the enormous roll of printer paper was entertaining a crowd with his hangman skills. He always won, it was uncanny. Though there was a very simple reason for it. He never let his spelling inability get in the way of showing off a big word he knew. His preference for using words he thought adults would prefer had left them all baffled. It was good to see bewildered faces coming from his charlatan con rather than from the red backdrop behind them. I smiled at him to which he returned a very confident grin, one that said 'tree house fort - in the bag'.

My feet led me back to where they had left. Though a little apprehensive as to what was going to come next, my curiosity for this oddity of a mind still forced me back towards it. He was full on in every way, except in the way that he was. Even impassioned he still held this aura of calm around him, like he was sitting in the back seat of life. Like he was outside it. He seemed to be the real puzzle in the room. I don't know what he did to me but he conjured something over me, as if he had spun a web that I did not trust myself to be caught in for too long. It wasn't him that I didn't trust; I did, implicitly. It was myself that I had concerns about. Every millimetre of him carried such unequivocal grace yet bore such a weight of masculinity my mind drowned in the overflow of correspondence from the senses. He moved in a way that was physical poetry, not just because of his blistering beauty but because of the perfection in the fluidity of his every move. He effortlessly and seamlessly projected one colour of a being, one kind of a species, one moment of time. But although he was beauty in motion I still felt an internal force persistently pushing him away. I felt he had revived an old battle inside me. Why was I so stubborn in my resignation? Why could I not completely concede? Was it because I felt I was being lured into a sting? Was it because it did not originate from me? Was it because I had felt my power being stolen? But what real power can be so easily disarmed? Is this power just a mental Zimmer frame to help us follow the bread crumbs our mind has laid? Are we that easily tricked and led? Are we so fragile and weak that we need to create a false idea, an image of power to hold onto when we feel powerless? But what use is a pretend life vest?

"Digging some deep thoughts there?"

"I don't know. Sometimes I feel my mind would continue to whirr even without me listening."

"Screw 'em, you don't need them."

"Ha, ha."

"Seriously, they're not essential to the program."

"Come on, thoughts are vital tools. They're our guide through this crazy chaos."

"Like a leash?"

"What? No! More like a helping hand guiding you through the dark."

"How is that any different? You're still being led."

"Maybe, but one feels much nicer."

"Thoughts serve to create blocks in your path. They're troublemakers. They've masterminded the madness of this world."

"That's ridiculous, people have done that, not this masked supervillain called Thought. Thoughts are an integral part of life, of the experience of living. Without them we'd be lost."

"Don't you think you'd have a better experience?"

"Absolutely not."

"Okay, imagine you are chilling out watching some film. Then halfway through someone turns the radio on. Can you still properly concentrate on it, give it your undivided attention? Your concentration, whether you like it or not, is compromised, it's split. It's impossible to follow the film, to be as immersed in it as you were before the radio was switched on. Well your thoughts are that radio. They steal your attention away from life, preventing you from actually living it."

"Right. Radio silence it is then."

Self-imposed silence is always more preferable to its opposite. It's like every second that passes you feel more and more vindicated, victorious. Sooner or later he would surrender. It was just a matter of time and, fortunately, it seemed that was the one thing we had in here. Though, unfortunately, I was not aware of who I was up against in the mute marathon. Minutes were gliding past. I would have given anything for a watch, just to see how much time had gone by. If I spoke first it wouldn't really count as a concession as I was the instigator. Well, that's what I convinced myself of anyway.

"So..."

"So...?"

"So...?"

"So... the embargo has been lifted?"

"Yes. Go on, I know you've got something defining to say."

"No, not really. I was just thinking how you'd really enjoy her book, both those books actually. Your reading list now has two."

"Yeah, I will, when we emerge from our burrow."

"Don't you mean rabbit hole?"

I laughed but he wasn't wrong. I did feel as if I had tumbled down after Alice. Something very strange was happening here. Something far bigger than just this room. There was a metamorphosis going on inside me, one that I was not engineering. It was like everything was all rehearsed, now just playing out in front of me and I was watching from the stands.

"Hey, Alice, you still there?"

"Where else?"

"You looked like you were lost in your own dream."

"I wish."

"So what's it like?"

"What?"

"Your dream world."

"Well, the opposite of here anyway."

"Go on."

"I don't know, Leo. I haven't given it much thought."

"Okay, let's rephrase the question. What would the world be like if dreams always came true?"

"You want me to take a trip to fantasyland?"

"You don't?"

"Alright, fine. So what would I think the world would be like if we could imagine anything we wanted?"

"Well technically I said dreams, not whims, but we can go with that if you want."

"Very gracious of you. Alright, why not? Let me see, dreams come true stuff. Well firstly, my hair would be curly. Too external?"

"It's your question to answer any which way you like."

"Okay, fine, I'll be serious. Well, there would be no more wars or battles or arguments of any kind because, well, we could just wish for what we wanted or even wish away the arguments. So that would mean world peace then, wouldn't it?"

"Would it?"

"No more fighting, I think, is the definition. Is it not?"

"On paper maybe, but I always thought of it as more of a feeling. A feeling of serenity, unity and harmony, of and for everyone."

"You would. Anyway, my answer remember?"

"Please, go on."

"Well, no one would have to get up for work at obscene hours ever again because we could just wish for money and it would appear. Actually we wouldn't even need money because if we wanted food or anything, we could just wish for it. Cool. So everyone's on holiday, no one's fighting and, of course, you could just go anywhere in the world on your holiday. There'd be no more airport security queues, in fact, there wouldn't be any security or police or army or anything because there would be no terrorists, no bad guys, no criminals, because they could just wish for the things that they wanted. Interesting."

"What is?"

"Well, that all the bad stuff that happens is just because people don't have what they want. And that it would all stop in the morning if they were given it. Well, in theory anyway."

"So you think no more bad things would happen?"

"Well I'd say so, unless I suppose, someone was really cross and wanted revenge and turned somebody into a chicken or something. There'd have to be rules."

"Rules?"

"Of course, otherwise God knows what would happen. I mean if everyone had the power to do and have anything then goodness knows what kind of mess we'd find ourselves in."

"Really?"

"Gosh yes, someone could even end the world if they wanted. Okay, I'm changing my initial answer. There wouldn't be world peace at all, it would all just get worse."

Leo just stayed quiet and shook his head.

"What, you don't think so?"

"I think that maybe you've just described what led us to the point where we're at right now."

"I don't understand."

"If suspicion and doubt forces you to make rules, they will inevitably constrict people who will then in turn attempt to compensate and so on and so forth. It all just becomes a self-fulfilling prophecy. Our fearful minds just won't allow things to just go how they'll go. It has to throw reins onto everything in order to prevent the runaway horse but, ironically, it is these very reins and their constriction that make the horse bolt."

"So even if we had paradise, we'd still mess it up. Great to know that there's definitely no hope then, even if dreams did come true."

"You're seeing it topsy-turvy. It's not what we've been given, what we have or don't have. The problem lies, lurks even, in our mind, our interface to it all. That's the part that's malfunctioning. So if that was fixed, no longer projecting a distorted image of everything, then it wouldn't matter if dreams came true or not, because we would already be living in one."

"You've lost me, but that's okay. I'm glad you've got it sussed, that's all that matters."

"Let me ask you a question. Do you exist when you're not thinking anything?"

"What? I suppose, I've never thought about it. Oh yeah, I'm not supposed to think about it. Well, of course you still exist."

"Which means you are more than your thoughts. That they are not you and you are not them and your life does not depend on them."

"Well, obviously."

"It may seem so but when clouded by our habitual reliance on thought it becomes less obvious. The problem, I think, is twofold. Firstly, we believe that we are the master and our mind is the slave, that is it a tool we use to help us in our lives. But it is not the tool, and we are not the master. We are manipulated and controlled by our thoughts in every aspect of our life. How? We give away our power by holding each and every thought in such high esteem, revering them, labelling them completely unignorable. By trusting all thoughts and regarding them to be of the upmost importance, we have decided to discard our filter and take it all in as truth. But it is as far from truth as it can be. And what truth is it even masquerading as? Truth of who we think we are, what we believe we are made up from, what we want and what we need? But how can thought add to who we are? It can't, it just takes away. We still exist without thought, without the voice in our head commanding us to where it thinks is the safe place. But thought does not lead us to the safe place because it doesn't know where it is. So it forces us to continue a search for a place it does not know, like a faulty satnav. The tragic irony is that we're running from the safe place in order to find it. And the saddest part is that we trust our thoughts, truly believe they are the only things that are really on our side. But they're not. They are selfish and dishonest and seek only their own preservation. They trick us into believing we are what we are, that we'll never change, that we have very little potential, very little strength and power, that we are small and nothing special. But we are more, far more than our thoughts allow us to believe. They don't want us to know the full picture of who we are because then the roles would reverse. But we can do it. It takes time but, little by little, we can reclaim our minds, recover control and regain consciousness. One way to begin to re-employ our filter is to think of your thoughts as trains and your mind as a station. With every thought that visits your station, you need to first decide whether or not it is contaminated. You must do an inspection to assess whether it is a constructive or a destructive thought. You need to ask yourself whether it will contaminate your station. The problem is that we have been led to believe that every thought is there to assist us. That every thought is us, is a part of us. Especially the negatively tinged ones concerning problems, worries, anxiety, stress... They are given preferential treatment over positive ones because of their seemingly urgent and important nature. Though what we fail to realise is that it is these very thoughts that are the source of the negativity. They cannot aid us in any constructive way in dealing with what will happen in the future. They simply serve to impede clarity. They are just trying to get our ear by terrorising us into listening to them, scaring us into remembering what went wrong before, intimidating us into agreeing with what they say will happen next. And the jewel in the crown of crazy lies in the minds ability to convince us that this pseudoscience has a solid foundation, that this forecast of fear is a fool proof defence mechanism to assist us in the war of worry. But the fact remains that no matter how much we look to the past to predict the future, we don't become any better at fortune telling. It's all just guess work. We have to remember that the past is not the only pool of possibility. It only serves to show us what was, not what will be. It's just there as a reference. You know, backstory stuff."

"Okay, I dare not ask what the second part of the two fold is."

"Passion does tend to carry you away with it."

"That's okay, I'll allow it. Passion's never a negative in my book."

"Now that would be one for the reading list."

"What?"

"Your book."

"My book? No, no I don't think so. I'll leave that to the experts."

"They weren't experts when they started. Plus, we all know everyone has a book buried inside them. It might take a lifetime to write and maybe only a few will read it, but the catharsis is supposed to be very healing."

"Then why don't you?"

"I might. I think I'm nearly ready. The sponge has almost reached its soakage capacity."

"You'll have to wear glasses. It's part of the dress code. You know, intellectual vibe."

"You've just reminded me of my two of two fold!"

"Go on, hit me."

"It's much shorter I promise. The other part of the difficulty in dropping your thoughts, and the identification and connection to them, is that thinking has become synonymous with intellect. Deep thought means you are an intellectual, and therefore someone to be respected and esteemed. But in my opinion, the further away you are from associating yourself with the thoughts in your head, the closer you are to true intelligence."

"Well that can't make sense. The greatest minds of our time have had to think for long periods to get anywhere."

"And where is that?"

"What? What do you mean?"

"Well where has thought brought us? Just to more thought about thought."

"That's just ridiculous. Everything has come from thought."

"Has it?"

"Yes! Otherwise we'd still be these animalistic buffoons who couldn't even start fire."

"I think you're confusing inspiration with thought. Thought can only be used to relate what unbridled inspiration, in the absence of thought, has gifted us."

"Right..."

"What I'm trying to say is that through thought and thought alone we only get deeper into the burrow. No thought allows room for intuition to surface. Just like you said, we're muddying the water instead of letting it settle. How can you see anything clearly in murky waters?"

"So then, we should just not think of anything?"

"Well, it's impossible to think about not thinking."

"What? Then how do you do it?"

"You can't. Well the thinker can't. The observer, on the other hand, is incapable of thought. It, much like looking out the window on a plane, can only be the witness to what is happening."

"So you're saying that in order to gain the ability to not think you have to become the thing that can't? Right, so you just sit back and observe. Well, that doesn't seem too hard."

"It isn't, as long as you're the passenger, and not the plane."

"Cool. I'll do it right now. It'll be nice to have a break."

"Great. I hope you do better than I did."

"How did you do?"

"Well most greenhorns don't get much past five to ten seconds."

"We'll see about that. Time me."

What is it they say? Pride comes before a fall? Well, I fell. Hard. Though really, deep down, I knew I was going to fail before I even started. I pretended to last over five, but in truth I don't think I even managed it at all. It was far harder than I imagined it would be, far harder. Zero thought is not quite as simple as it sounds. You can't think about not thinking, he was right, it was impossible. You can't think about anything. So what do you think about? What's on the stage? And when you do this observer thing where does your marker, your cursor rest? Where does your flood light of concentration fall? Nowhere? But how can it be nowhere? Or does that mean that it must be everywhere then? Secretly, I kept on trying. And secretly, I kept on failing.

"The trick is in realising that you can't think about the moment and be in it at the same time. You have to choose. You have to let go of the side of the pool and just swim. It takes practice. Just like any muscle, you have to build up strength by working on it. But it's worth it. Your mother had some really amusing observations about the whole thing, you should read them."

"I will, I will. If we ever get out of here, I think it'll be one of the first things I'll do. And if I come across an extra copy, it'll have your name on it. So, you don't think it's something you're born with? You know, writing."

"Actually, I believe we all have the same capacity to stream, to tap into the flow of imagination. It's there for everyone. Inspiration, innovation and vision are not selective. Obviously people have aptitudes in different areas, but I think, in most cases, the reason why someone excels is because they believe in themselves. Even training or honing of skills are things that serve to add to that belief. Maybe that's why sporting figures and performers are often quite superstitious. They follow the same patterns of routine before events to reconfirm their belief. Actually a lot of people avail of their daily routines to permit them a form of security, to give them faith, to help them trust that everything will be okay. So much work to convince yourself of a truth. Can you even imagine what the world would be like if we all held complete unfaltering belief in ourselves and life?"

"Wow, I wonder. Then would we have our peace on earth?"

"I think we'd be closer. The problem is we feel it's just too far a leap to reach that place of such belief. We just don't have faith that when we step off that ledge that a once invisible bridge will become visible. We believe we have been so let down by life in so many ways that we just can't bring ourselves to trust it anymore. That's why your 'better the devil you know' creed is now what we're all following. We think it's safe because we know where we are and we won't get any surprises. But life is always full of surprises. Its very nature is change. The tighter our grip, the more life will try to loosen it. All life wants us to do is to just turn around and see it, just see it for what it truly is."

"Which is?"

"Love."

"I'd really like to believe you. I mean, I was with you, I really was. But you're right, it's all just a step too far. I can understand, even agree with, a lot of what you're saying because it makes sense, but life is love? That's just too much. It's just airy fairy hippie hype. It's not real. It's just not true."

"I understand how, for now, that's your truth. But you asked and I told you what I believe to be true. I believe this world is not all there is and I believe it is not our true home. I believe we have taken this ride to give value to our true state of being and, of course, to have a hell of an experience. And if that makes me mad in the eyes of this world, then so be it. I am not from it and neither are you. But for now we are bound to it and to whatever experiences we are gifted. And so I will always dive into each and every experience and swim in its own unique colour, all the while trying my best not to think of consequences, connotations, causes and effects, instead just trying to keep my heart as open as I can and my centre core as relaxed and weightless as possible."

"Right, okay... well, I don't think you're mad mad, not like cuckoo mad, maybe more like... sparrow mad."

A small voice called out to me.

"Mummy! I've finished all my jobs and games and everything!"

"Well done, darling. What do you want to do now?"

"Missy said she'd tell me a story she used to tell her children when they were small. It's about a dinosaur picnic on the moon!"

"Oh wow, that sounds exciting. Can I come too?"

"No, it's alright, Mummy. I'll see you later."

"Oh okay, baby. Love you!"

"I know!"

"It's such a relief that he's seems to be doing so well, that he's so comfortable. It's incredible how far a child's belief can stretch, how they just accept any reality as truth, never questioning a thing."

"I think we also do that."

"Though not quite on the same scale, Leo."

"I don't know, I actually think our reality has been completely constructed from belief. I mean if you think about it, what is belief, what is faith? Isn't it just accepting something as fact without proof? We accept a multitude of things we've been told about our world, and all without any actual personal proof. We just take it all on faith. We accept the history and geography we have been given as well as all the science stuff, and all with very little first-hand experience. We take as fact what we have been told about the origins of the universe when, in truth, no one really knows for certain the reality of, well, reality. Just because we have taken these ideas and held them up as solid truths it does not make them any less of what they are, just a belief. And the length of time that these beliefs have been held doesn't make the belief any more solid. It doesn't make us any less gullible than a child who is told that he is living in a gameshow called The Room."

"But we're not children just believing everything we're told."

"No? Remember we are all grown up children and we have spent our lives being told to listen to the things we are being told. That's a pretty hard merry-go-round to leave. For the most part, we take everything we see, hear and read as fact. That's not our fault, it's just the way we've been trained to be."

"Well, I am not as naïve as you think I am, and neither is the world."

"Good."

"Yep."

"So what do you make of dreams?"

"What do you mean?"

"When we dream we experience the strangest of scenarios imaginable, most being completely implausible and unexplainable, right?"

"Right."

"So how come we buy it every time?"

"Because we're just dreaming."

"That's not an answer and you know it. When we're dreaming we don't know we are. If we buy the reality of flying pink elephants shooting rainbow stars across crystallised clouds of light, then it's not surprising that we don't question everything to do with this reality."

"Not quite the dreams I would have guessed you'd have. But there is a difference, Leo. When you're dreaming you're not in control."

"So you believe when you're awake you are?

"Of course."

"But how do you know?"

"What do you mean? I know because I can feel it, because I can create an effect from a cause. Perhaps a practical test is needed, one with a little punch."

"Oh, really?"

"There, your welcome."

"Thanks! A little more heavyweight than I would have imagined. But how do you know for sure that the will to punch me was your own?"

"Well who else's could it be?"

"The same else that makes the grass grow and the birds sing."

"What? Like instinct?"

"That's one way to look at it. Some may argue that we are all, as is everything in nature, predisposed to act in a certain manner, to become what we are meant to be."

"Something tells me that you have an upgrade on that."

"I think that it's quite a mathematical way to view reality, but there is an outline of truth to it. I believe that there is something else, a diviner and that we are the stick. A little like streaming, we're just watching the stream."

"But what does that even mean? That I'm just this lifeless sock puppet? I know I am alive, that I am real. I know this because I am the one who decides what I have for breakfast every morning, it's my choice. I wake up in a certain mood and my cupboard gives me certain options, and between the two, we find a way. So as much as I'm kind of understanding you, I can't agree. I am my own man, or I mean, woman. I am the controller."

"So if you're the controller, where does that control begin and end?"

"With me and my life, of course."

"So do you control the digestion of that breakfast?"

"Well, not personally per se, but unconsciously yes."

"Right, so you are not consciously in control of the internal workings of your body? Well, how about the cosmos?"

"Of course not."

"Okay, not the macro or the micro then. So where are the limits of your cage of control?"

"Somewhere in the middle, I suppose."

"So your control is very limited."

"Limited to me, but that's all that matters."

"So you control everything that happens to you?"

"Well, no, I can't control a car crashing into me or a bird pooping on my head, but I can control the inner workings of my life."

"So then it's impossible that your life would ever get out of control?"

"Well, not quite."

"So how, if you always have control, do you lose it?"

"Well, circumstances outside my control crash in."

"So what's in control then?"

"Everything else except me, I suppose."

"And when do you get it back?"

"When life decides I can!"

"Exactly."

"I don't mean life as in an entity, more just, you know, life."

"Sounds to me like you've just given life, life."

"Maybe."

"At the end of the day, if you really were in control of your life, how could you end up here, trapped in this room?"

"Touché."

"So therefore if you aren't even sure the control you have is real, how can you be certain of anything, especially life?"

"Well, then I suppose we can never be completely sure of the truth of reality at all."

"Perhaps. Though certain moments of clarity mingled with the surreal help tip the balance."

"What do you mean, tip the balance? Tip the balance of what, to what?"

"Of truth, towards the true fabric of reality."

"Come again?"

"I've experienced many moments which are not related to this reality, well, how we currently perceive it. They felt strange and foreign at first, but then contained such a deep familiarity, like a memory I had forgotten, that my mind failed to just brush them off. It's like they hit too deep to be dismissed. Sometimes life warps the moment for just long enough to allow you to peek around it, through it, over it. You get given a glimpse of the real picture and you gain a perspective you never knew existed. It's then when you really see just how big and small everything is. It's like you get thrown to a place where you've never been, yet somehow you feel that it's a place you've never really left. It's a very illogical and contradictory a thing to explain. God, it's so hard to define, to explain without context. Okay, it's like experiencing a moment where you feel like you're outside it, like you've just popped out and you're viewing it from some other place, some other angle. You feel locked out from the moment and how you would normally relate to it, and yet you feel more connected to what's happening than ever before. Like you're suddenly viewing it all while sitting rather than lying on the floor. Like you finally found your seat and it's the only place you were ever supposed to sit. You feel like time has paused and there literally is no past or future, that they are just illusions, impossible to conceptualise or reference to. The moment becomes so full that you don't need to look for anything anywhere else, like whatever is happening right now is all that there is and whatever you are in that moment, is all that you are. You feel like you have finally found yourself, finally met the real you and you haven't a care in the world because you know, you finally know who you really are and, more importantly, who you are not. Though it really is nearly impossible to explain it to someone who's never felt it. All I know is that your happiest, freest self inhabits the space between your thoughts. I'm trying my best not to sound abstract but I know I am. I suppose it's a little like slipping down a secret tunnel and finding yourself in a moment between moments. Does that make any sense?"

I nodded. I did know that feeling. It hadn't lasted long but I had felt it that morning with the writings. It was completely abstract but he had managed to describe it. Parts of his strange symphony were ringing true, for the simple reason that I had heard the tune before. Though I'm sure that if I hadn't, this mad melody of his would have cast doubt upon where its maker's sanity lay. Were we really that contrary? So bound by our experiences? Were we really moved and guided that much by what speed and direction the wind was blowing? Were we that flimsy? I don't know if that made me have more or less belief in freewill or destiny. But it did make me feel differently about them, that maybe they weren't quite the opposites I had thought them to be. So what moved and guided us then? In real life it always seemed to be those troublesome brothers the carrot and the stick. With the carrot of desire luring and the stick of fear scaring, it's no wonder we never stop, and it's no wonder we believe our lives to be full of purpose and direction. But how can they be if all they are filled with is chasing and running? We never get anywhere, we're just condemned to stay stuck in the maddening middle, living our lives in painful purgatory, caught forever in the space between two worlds. And no matter how luxurious we make this limbo of ours we will never shake its hollowness. We're still sentenced to the suffering of slavery. We may not have been kidnapped and chained to a ship to cross an ocean to shine shoes, but we have still had our freedom stolen, sold for a promise of protection. The oldest trick in the book.

I turned to see how the storytelling was going. Missy was talking and he was sitting and listening, and looked to be munching on something. He was such a clever charmer, making friends with those in power.

"What's so funny?"

"Oh nothing, politics pervades. Anyway, I think he's getting a little annoyed."

"Who is?"

"The bright red elephant we've been ignoring."

"Oh, of course. How very rude of us. An interesting development indeed. Not quite a Monet, but it has its charm."

"True. It is quite raw."

"Well obviously hanging in such a setting was deliberate in order to create that juxtaposition of bright and dull, life and sterility, passion and… what's the opposite of passion?"

"Unpassion? No that's definitely not a word… Hold on. No, I can't think of it. Well obviously it does exist. Maybe if we can describe passion then we'll be able to find its opposite there. What is passion? Maybe it's like desire?"

"I don't think they have anything to do with each other."

"How can you say that, Leo? Of course they do!"

"For one thing they never exist at the same time, they're in relay. Secondly, I think desire is a pre-booked ticket for a future show, leaving you ignoring the one playing."

"What would we do without desire? Desire is the get up and go, the thing that leads us through life. Desire is who we are, Leo."

"We aren't meant to be led around like beasts. Surely you can't think that's our correct state of being?"

"Well, we're not just being led about. The carrot is the good thing, remember?"

"You mean the unattainable is desirable?"

"But how can it be bad if it makes you feel good?"

"How can a craving be enjoyable?"

"Craving? I never put the two of them together before. It is a little like a craving I suppose, but much nicer."

"Is it? You are still creating an itch that needs to be scratched."

"But without desire we wouldn't want anything, we wouldn't do anything."

"You really believe we would just seize up? Desire is fundamentally an irritation masked as pleasure. It is frustration from not currently existing within the perceived superior scene. This, by default, then causes us to regard the current scene as inferior, a state in which none of us wish to reside. But if you remove desire, that need, that yearning for something other than what you have, then everything is on par with everything else. If you don't, your life will be predominantly a second rate existence of your own making. The addiction to desire is the same as the thrill of the chase. Because it has not yet formed into matter, become real, it still exists within our imaginations and therefore is perfect, the best. When the momentary fulfilment of desire does not live up to our extreme expectations we crash lower than we were before. And even if it does sometimes live up to it, the fleeting buzz of excitement soon dispels and we immediately look for another coat tail to chase. In order to achieve lasting happiness we must understand that it can never be preceded by desire, that it exists beyond it and to get there we must remove ourselves from our imprisonment within its vicious circle of promise. Stimulus response is not what's meant for us. We are more than just animals or machines. Would you rather experience fleeting sporadic geysers of joy or a continuous waterfall? The pursuit of happiness does not lead to it. It only highlights a lack of it in the current moment. Though there is one positive to desire. You gain the strength of the desire that you refuse. You just have to invert it to create a door to peace."

"What star system did you say you were from again?"

"I didn't, yet."

"Seriously, Leo, where the hell did you come from? You look, no offence, like some guy who used to be one of those angelic little cherubs, dangling from the sky but accidently fell to earth and then had to cope with living here, condemned to slumming it with the rest of us."

"I will take that as a compliment."

"That's it! That's who you remind me of! You're the Little Prince that grew up!"

"Now *that* can't be taken in any other way than well. Such a beautiful book. I'm a little surprised you've read it."

"Oh, only once when I was young. I don't remember it."

"Do you remember liking it?"

"Yes, yes I do. Okay, it's going on my reading list."

"Okay, well come on then, tell me what passion means to you."

"Alright, let's just see for a minute. Well I suppose it's energy, sensation, magnetism, a force that flows through you, a force that you do not consciously create. It's well, inspiration, you know, conducting a flow of energy. I don't know, I'm having trouble really pinpointing it."

Leo tried to hide his smile.

"You're doing okay."

A rush of electricity surged through my entire body defining the contours of my form. Waves of sensation flowed across my skin as my breath became too quick to keep. The blood in my veins ignited with a fevered fire of fantasy, of vibrancy, of ecstasy. The air around me, around us, illuminated as though each atom had been switched on. *This* was passion. And its power was immense. It had the ability to unplug the processing machine in your brain, press the mute button and shine a spotlight on only one space. Nothing else existed and nothing else mattered. For the first time in so long I felt it, I felt life. My eyes focused in on him as the edges softly blurred, like some old movie. Every time his gaze stroked mine the intensity of the moment increased, the air thickened as if the atmosphere was coagulating. Everything was heightened, sharp yet smooth. The sound of every word that danced upon his lips fell deep into my inner most being, rippling its warm waters.

"...perhaps passion is just one of those indescribable things, something with no discernible contrast, maybe because it's not tangible or temporal, but celestial. It's just love flowing through you, filling you, animating you. I suppose it's allowing that flow to pass through unhalted. It's getting out of the way, being able to remove yourself from it, just letting go of everything that prevents the circuit connecting. I think what it really is, is being a conduit for life's love and being able to leave it at that, with no questioning, no striving, no grasping..."

Grasping... grasping... a flash of immense beauty and light and home and everything and nothing stole my breath from me. I came back to the room trying to steal it back. I knew that place. I knew that light. I remembered it from a distant dream. But it felt so real, so right, everything aligned, it all made sense. In that flash I understood it all. Yet now, just a second later, all I was left with was the memory of remembering. But I knew that memory of a memory would never leave me, that it had now become a part of me, or more correctly, had revealed a part of me.

"Did you see it?"

"Yes."

"I knew that you would. Did it feel familiar?"

"Yes, very. But I don't know from where. Maybe from a dream I once had... or before..?"

"It's unexplainable, isn't it?"

"Yes, it's like I felt my whole self all at once, but how?"

"Yeah, that bit's always a bit confusing and can initially be a little hard to come back from. But you will, it will all settle. Don't worry you'll be there again. Just don't strive. That's the worst thing you can do."

"It all felt so real, more real than... than here. But how can that be? I've been here all my life and I was there, there for just a microsecond."

"Well, how long is all of your life compared to eternity?"

"A... microsecond."

"So can you see now how that makes all this even more special, makes this fraction of experience even more precious? Because it's only here when it's here and when it's gone, it's gone. And if we aren't even around to witness it, if we just stay caged in our thoughts, well then it's all a bit of a waste, isn't it?"

"I need to sit down and process this."

"No, no you don't. The only way you can process this is by using your mind; and we've already spoken about your mind never being satisfied, always wanting an answer, a problem to solve, it won't let you experience or enjoy anything, there's always a 'but', an 'if', a 'maybe', always something to keep you hooked, listening to its next line. It never wants anything to be solved or resolved because then it would cease to exist, and nothing ever wants that."

"But I need to-"

"You don't need to do anything except relax. Relax in this moment, not the previous or the next. You saw and felt what you were supposed to. But now you are not, because you're supposed to be here. Now is a new moment so enjoy the unique experience it has to offer. Bathe in the aftermath of clarity. This moment will soon be gone and replaced by the next. So drink its nectar while you can. And then, like all other moments that have passed, let it go. Look around you. New moments are everywhere, new scenes are being played out at every turn, all for you. A bright bard once wrote that all the world's a stage, and all the men and women merely players. So go watch, and go play."

"Hold on, I just want to go back there for second. Maybe if I just think on it for a while I can-"

"You'll never think yourself there. That's not what brought you there. You'll go back when you're supposed to. Be here, be now. There is a reality playing out right in front of you. Look, look around you at all the players caught up in this scene, so enthralled with the search for understanding, for meaning, for escape. So go join them. Live it. Live this now."

"I can't get involved in this stuff, not now."

"Listen to me. I understand what you're feeling and how important you think what you've felt is, and it is. It is the most important thing you will ever discover. But it cannot take you away from the here and now. That is defeating the point of it, of all this. After the first flash of awakening people erroneously dedicate their life to finding it for keeps. But that is not the reason for the insight. Its purpose is to let you know that this is not all there is, that there's more, much more. This new light does more than just illuminate. It banishes the darkness, allowing you to see the full picture. Everything loses its weight, its seriousness. You now realise that nothing holds any real gravity and that everything only matters because of its brief existence. We need to stop being the annoying back seat drivers and start enjoying the journey. We have to look at the scenes on each side and

261

actually live the ride, whilst remembering that that's all it is, just a ride. So with a light heart, go play! Play the game of the room, of this moment, and really live the experience because it won't last. It never does."

He softly pushed me towards the heated debate going on around the old television set and before I could catch them, unvetted words spilled out.

"I think the writings are a map out of here."

Eyes focused, increasing their intensity like burning spotlights. I took a deep breath without knowing what words would escape with it.

"I knew that there was something missing but I couldn't work out what it was. Then I realised that nothing was actually missing at all. The words were already there, they were just being shared."

The spotlights moved to the writings and rested there for a while. Then they returned, a little diffused, back to me.

"So maybe it's just exactly what it seems to be. Maybe we're not supposed to look too deeply into it at all. Maybe the door is actually our exit and the key is a key. So maybe we should be looking for this key, as well as the door."

"A key? Oh shit, yeah. There's been a whole load of them just lying around, but I never thought to use them."

"Oh-"

"Of course you didn't, 'cause you're a dip shit."

"Hey! Who you calling dip shit?"

"The dip shit."

"Guys, guys. Really, are we back in the school yard?"

"He started it with his shitchat."

"No, we're back in Kindergarten."

"Who the hell asked you?"

"Don't you tell me when and where I can speak!"

"I'll tell you whatever I friggin' want!"

"Oh my God, this is so frustrating! How has civilisation not crumbled yet?!"

"It's not far off."

"But *we* are, from the subject at hand, I mean."

"She hasn't told us anything that's gonna help get us outta here."

"I actually really think she's stumbled across something."

"I still don't understand it. But, in a way, it does make a little more sense now."

"It doesn't tell us a thing."

"Yeah, it's just gone from gibberish to jabberwocky."

"I don't know. Try reading it again. There's definitely something there, alright. I just don't know what it is yet."

"Come on, key is your serpent? There's no serpents in here and somehow I don't think they'd make a very good key."

I looked to my left. The doctor was looking at me. Some caught our exchanged glance.

"What?"

"What is it?"

"Do you guys know something?"

"Something about the serpent?"

The doctor stepped forward as he cleared his throat.

"Well, Ophidia Serpentes is arguably the oldest and most widespread symbolic creature in man's history. It has appeared in the mythology of countless cultures on nearly every continent. I cannot think of one successful civilisation who did not have it woven somewhere into its tapestry. Even in such a scientifically driven society as our own, we still have our chosen insignia for our physical preservation as the Rod of Asclepius. Although interestingly, and quite evidently a testament to our time's depth of attention, it is habitually confused with the caduceus. Which not only holds a very different meaning but also appearance. For one it is winged, with dual serpent entwinement and, and anyway, the serpent's symbolism may vary, yet the ideology of the circle of life remains. It is representative of death and-"

"Oh my God, it's an omen we're-"

"Death *and* rebirth. The notorious ouroboros? The balance and unity of dark and light, power, divinity, infinity, life force, birth, transformation, immortality, all the big stuff. Though I am not sure what relevance it has in connection with a key. Perhaps the security aspect? If you ever read adventure stories as a child you would probably be quite familiar with the practice of littering your treasure trove with a brood of snakes. They make excellent guards and will fight to the death if necessary, not to protect your treasure of course, but to defend their territory."

"Okay, thanks for the lecture, Grandad. But what has that got to do with anything?"

"If you know something that an encyclopedia wouldn't, then let's hear it."

Once again we locked eyes and once again the doctor spoke.

"Well, inside the medical kit provided, we were also gifted some anti-venom."

"Anti-venom?"

"What?"

"Like snake anti-venom?"

"Oh my God."

"What the hell?!"

"How much?"

"Twin vials, two doses."

"What?!"

"How long were you going to wait before telling us? Until someone got bit?"

"Jesus!"

"Who gives you the right?"

"Were you ever going to tell us?!"

"At the time it seemed like adding unnecessary fuel to an already wild fire."

"We just didn't want people to get even more panicked."

"Anything else you'd care to divulge doctor?"

"No, no that's all."

I looked at him but this time he did not look back. But others did. Paranoid others, fearful others, others who had had enough and wanted a release, an excuse, some way to express their amputated anger, their stifled frustrations. So they did. As soon as they lunged at the doctor, the brothers and the TV guys leaped to his defence and suddenly half the room was involved. It looked like some mythological beast fighting itself, arms and legs flailing, bashing and clashing into each other. It reminded me of a bar brawl, but stone cold sober punches were different, they were far more accurate and far more damaging. It had all come from nowhere. It was so shocking. From one minute to the next civility turned to brutality. I ran to my son who Missy had put in the box of blankets. I scooped him up into my arms and tried to navigate through the madness but I couldn't. It was everywhere.

What were we doing fighting each other? We were all in the same tragic boat, all equal, all equally screwed. I suppose after a day without any of our usual comforts and calming devices, even being trapped in a luxury hotel room would have taken its toll. The symptoms the doctor had predicted were coming on much earlier than expected. I thought we had more time. It felt like the wheels on our already decrepit cart were coming loose. The med kit, where was it? I saw a space and ran towards it but was blocked by a bloody face demanding answers. Where was Leo? I looked around but all I could see was the women lining the walls, edging away from the threatening tornado of testosterone. Missy and her girls were cowering in a corner. What were we to do? I turned my son's body away from the bloodied ghoul and braced for some kind of impact. But then I heard my boy giggle.

I turned around to see a man with a swashbuckling swagger wink at us as he came to our rescue. He was tanned with shaggy dark hair and a dark suede patch over his right eye. I remembered him from the name call. My heart had sank a little for him. How courageous he was to be so confident with such a loss, or maybe it was his courage that had led him to it. Either way, it was both a pity and a mystery. He skilfully fought the man and every other that came near us. But he did so in such an unusual fashion. His swings were hilariously exaggerated as he grinned with every pantomime punch. His act never dropped. Even when he was hurt he still winced in character. It was quite literally an unbelievable sight. Our brave eye patch saviour spun and spiralled around them all, effortlessly neutralising every threat, every danger. One by one or two by two, twisting and twirling them about, spinning them round and round in the most surreal dance ever danced. And he did it all with such ease, such fluidity and grace. Either he was a seasoned performer or he had been in far hairier situations with far hairier assailants or, quite likely, both.

It wasn't just his physical protection that I was thankful for but his wild eccentricity had also helped protect the tenuous illusion, helped mend the tear. It didn't just save my son's reality but I think it actually served to strengthen it. I'm quite sure that it was his theatrical performance that also helped to halt the rotation of a room spiralling out of control. All of his silly expressions and comedic swipes forced people to see the ridiculousness in their behaviour, like he was holding up a looking glass, forcing people to face their folly. Or maybe he just freaked them out. Either way, it seemed to work. As the wind blew out of angers sails all that was left of the fight were the original instigators and their verbal assaults. As the doctor stumbled away from them, one of the school yard bullies tripped him up. As he fell his thin round glasses slid across the floor. Another picked them up, walked over and knelt down by the doctor. As the doctors trembling hand caught air, his tormentor stood up laughing. He put the doctor's glasses on but then his laughter suddenly stopped. He moved them up and down, looking at the room through and over them.

"What is this? Some kind of prank?"

The younger brother helped the doctor to his feet.

"That's enough. Give them here."

"Sure. They're useless, to me, or anybody."

"Well not to me."

"Really?"

"Give them back to him. Now."

"Sure, I just don't think he needs them."

"What? Of course I do. I have worn glasses since I was a child."

"Yeah, yeah, drop the charade, pops. What, you thought they'd make you look smarter, more believable? I bet you ain't even a real doctor."

He threw the glasses at him.

"I-"

"Who are you really doc?"

His oppressor pinned him with his stare. Most people felt bad for the doctor who still hadn't put his glasses back on. They didn't understand the grudge this man seemed to have. But they were about to.

"You're not the plant, are ya, doc?"

Now the room stepped back from the view they previously held and began to see the doctor in quite a different light. Subconsciously sensing this shift in perception, he instinctively took a few of steps back from the auditorium now forming around him.

"Absolutely absurd... I..."

But then the doctor stopped as he saw the red writings behind them. He closed his eyes and opened them again, slowly blinking in disbelief.

"What's he doing?"

"What is it? Do you see something?"

"What's he seeing?"

"Nothing. He's just stalling."

"He sees something in the writings."

"Tell us what you see!"

"He could be dangerous. Stay away from him."

"Yeah, keep back."

"Do you see a pattern, doctor?"

"What is it? What do you see?"

But he did not reply. He just closed his eyes and began rubbing them. He then stretched one lid open as wide as possible and pinched his pupil. Then he tried the other eye, and back again. No one spoke, no one said a thing, everyone just watched. We didn't understand what was happening, what we were witnessing. The doctor started to become increasingly panicked as his rubbing became more and more furious. His eyes were red and tears were now falling from them.

"They must be there, they must be. It can't, it can't be, I... I..."

The short bald man was the one who broke the spectators' spell. I've often thought it strange how we become so inactive in a group. Yet alone, witnessing the same event, we spring into action without a moment's hesitation. Maybe when responsibility is shared by a group it dilutes. Perhaps that's why atrocities still take place.

"It's okay doc. It's alright."

He tried to calm him as best he could, but the doctor was becoming increasingly alarmed.

"No, no, no, no, no, no, it can't be! How?! How can this be?! I've been as blind as a bat my entire life!"

"Don't worry, there'll be some explanation."

"Explanation? Explanation?! What, that someone gave me laser eye surgery before I came here and then changed my lenses for glass? What the hell is going on here?!"

"Okay, okay, calm down. Just relax a minute and take a deep breath. Alright, can you remember your prescription?"

But the doctor didn't answer. His body just folded and fell to the floor.

The room held a new eerie feeling, like we were finally realising how twisted this thing really was. Everyone looked around at everyone else. Again we found ourselves encased within that certain strain of unnerving disturbance only the room could provide. Subtly those wearing glasses were secretly checking them. People were now beginning to look at themselves in a new way, with uncertainty. We all began questioning the things that we thought we would never have to, the things we thought we safe, solid, certain.

Who were we? What had happened? What was all this really about? Who would go to so much trouble? To such extremes? What kind of people? What could they possibly be getting out of it? The sheer organisation of it all, unimaginable amounts of time and energy pumped into, into what? What *was* this?

Any time we had any footing on the reality of the room it soon found a way to dislodge it. The only thing we knew for certain was that nothing in the room was ever certain. Nothing was what it seemed, or not seemed. The room wasn't just playing tricks on us, it *was* the trick, and it had not yet finished its show. But neither had the doctor. His muttering moans soon turned into screams. He directed his despair at the walls and the ceiling.

"Is this what you want? What you've come to see? A fucking show?! To watch a man turn mad?! Is this what you wanted?! Is this what it's all for?! To see the sane pushed to insanity? Are you happy now?! Have you made your big point? Well, congratulations! Yes, sanity is an illusion! But who cares?! Who cares if it's all just an illusion! How does it matter? How does it change a thing? How does it impact our lives? What you're doing, this, all this is what's impacting our lives! You can't play God! You can't play with people and their lives, their minds, their hearts, their souls! You don't know enough, no one does! You'll push too far, you'll create monsters! Or is that what you want? It's ignorance like yours that will kill this world! It's arrogance like yours that will burn it all down! You believe your work holds value, holds importance? You're so naïve! Your belief grows from the same sordid seed that spawned our history's villains! They hid within our cracks and turned them into chasms! As a member of mankind it's our responsibility to fill those cracks, to mend them, not to expand them, not to push back evolution and create more hate, more fires to put out, more chaos, more anger, more sadness, more pain! Why? Why?! WHY?!!"

The shuddering noise of his pounding on the large steel door demanded answers to questions his desperate howls knew were never going to be answered. I had never seen someone so saturated with desperation. I held my boy close and whispered to him that the doctor was one of the best actors in the whole show and here we had a big chance to win points. He nodded but still cuddled in close. The brothers and the bald man tried to subdue him, to somehow get through to him but he was no longer there. It was like he was stuck on repeat, caught in a loop of a moment, unable to exit from it. The med kit! Where was it? I ran with my boy still in my arms to Missy who was staring open mouthed at the deconstruction of our dear doctor. It took her a moment to understand what I wanted but then she produced it from the blankets box.

"You think he's been bit, don't ya? That venom, it's got to his brain, ain't it?"

"No, Missy. I don't think it's the snake venom that's got to his brain, but something far more poisonous."

Chapter Five

The doctor was sedated. I felt unimaginable guilt. It all seemed so wrong, like I had darted an escaped beast running free toward the wild. The room was happy that the unpleasant outburst had been stuffed out, relieved that the madness was over. But I knew better. All we did was postpone it, give it a rain check, but it was still coming. The doctor wasn't the only dark cloud in the sky, the only storm forming on the horizon, it was just that his broke first. Perhaps he really was suffering from the very symptoms he had described, or maybe, maybe he was seeing a truth that no one else saw. A truth we had all been shielding ourselves from; seeing the real room, the real reality. And it seemed to me that sedating the only person who did was the most foolish thing we could have done.

But fools do rush in, especially where angels fear to tread. And here, in this room, and out of it for that matter, hysteria always seemed to summon the fool in us, to shine the spotlight on the red suited brute perched upon our left shoulder, not the one clad in white on our right. Was I trapped in a room full of people being prodded by a red pitchfork instead of following the light?

I wanted to escape the room, now more than ever I wanted out of here. The thought that we were going to be in here for a forever, for our forever anyway, contaminated your consciousness like a virus. Forever never seemed so short, so finite, so final. Was this really the stage for my finale? Was this sad backdrop of grubby beige the last landscape I would ever see? Had we already reached the third act? Were these strangers the last characters I would meet? What faces would surround mine as I took my final breath? My son's beautiful face I hoped, or no, no I couldn't leave him alone. But the alternative? No, I would not be lured down that dark alley again. It led to nowhere good.

I stood in front of the red writings and stared at the circle, with desperate determination directing me. I searched for an in, some crack, some way to get inside it, something to help unravel it. I was certain there was an end thread. All I had to do was find it. I read until my eyes bubbled and my brain boiled. Was I really standing in front of Gordian's great knot of knots? Did this somehow mean I would I have to choose between the left and the right, the just and unjust, the Alexandrian way of the warrior or the philosopher's path of prophecy? Did impossibilities really exist? Was I the fool for even trying? Was the answer that there was no answer? I couldn't believe that to be true, not here in this maze so deftly designed, this labyrinth of lunacy.

I read it over again, *view only red writings, view only red writings.* Then I stopped reading and just looked, looked at the whole image as one being. After only a moment something began pulling my eyes towards it. I allowed my stare to sail through to the centre of the flower, beyond it, to sink as deep as it could. Then it seemed to drop anchor. I felt I had locked onto something, but I could also feel a tide turn, pulling and pushing me away. I wouldn't allow it. I knew I was getting somewhere, all I had to do was keep the moment alive. I dared not even blink. I needed to stay in it, to stretch the moment, keep it open for long enough for the words to make sense. I could feel my eyes burn as they wept but I would not, could not concede. Then, just as I thought I couldn't take it any longer, the red flower began to move. It slowly started to turn like a wheel. Then its turn accelerated. Faster and faster until my locked stare spun loose and suddenly the whole image came into view. The red circle of words framing the flower then too began to move, but in the opposite direction. The red ring twisted and inverted, with words doubling and disappearing into one another. The wall then seemed to fall away from the red, giving the image room for its next move. With the circle of letters still orbiting the flower it began to glow brighter and brighter before it then bloomed into a three dimensional being. Its bright scarlet petals, protruding on every axis, pointed at the orbiting words that now had formed into a sphere encasing it. I sank deeper into my trance as I allowed the floating sphere of red writings to encircle me. As the sphere spun around me the flower's ruby petals began to sway and stretch out, dancing on its own breeze. Then, as if playing an instrument, their tips, now sharpened, deftly stroked and plucked at words orbiting around them causing them to ignite and glow. It was magnificent. Its beauty consumed me. My eyes tuned into a type of trance as I became completely hypnotised by the burning words igniting all around me. For a second fear flashed before me, halting my surrender, but then I felt the presence of my playful friend reminding me of the light. I allowed myself to let go. I allowed it all to fall, everything. All the walls, all the fences, I allowed myself to let it all go, and me with it. As I dropped through myself I felt suspended by a buoyancy of spirit I had never felt. Then I realised I was wrong. I had felt this before, at the end of my nightmare dream. This was the light. I was in the light. Everything seemed to align. I understood it all. It all made sense. A beam of relief poured through me illuminating my darkened despair, exposing its shadows as just shades of light. I felt that I was connecting to a connection of connections. Suddenly I saw the whole, the absolute, the everything, the meaning, so many meanings. How ignorant I had been in my learned life, how selfish in my selflessness, how short-sighted in my open mindedness, how completely blinded and animated and ordered and ruled by my pain, by my suffering, by my martyrdom. How completely consumed by my... my self.

The unbearable pain in my eyes resurfaced. They were on fire, burning from within.

"Stay with it, you're nearly there."

His words echoed, ricocheting around the sphere, lifting me up, bringing me closer. I was so close. The depths of his voice swirled around me, peeling and revealing my layers, unravelling my bandage of bondage, discarding cover upon cover, showing me who I was not.

I felt my centre expand, blow up like a balloon, bigger and bigger until it grew beyond the barrier of my body until it had joined, superimposed itself onto the perimeter of the red sphere. In its core I saw my frame catch alight and my burning self reflect back towards me. The blinding truth of reality filled me. It was an all-encompassing light that shot out through every pore illuminating my new space, my new being. But it was too fast, it was too much, I couldn't take its intensity, I couldn't control it, I wasn't ready. I felt myself fall.

I awoke to find myself in the room. It was filled with silence except for a faint whistling of wind. It seemed to be coming from behind the security door. Without thinking I ran to it and pushed down on the handle of a locked door. It opened without resistance to reveal a long hallway of doors. Still without a second or even first thought, I opened one of them. Inside was a white circular room. It was polished to perfection but it too was empty. I hurriedly opened another, though all that was there was a black hospital bed in the centre of it. I closed it and then opened another door in the hallway. Behind this one was a large grey room. No one was there but it wasn't empty. It was full of an assortment of non-descript grey things, shadows of another life. I returned back to the corridor. The wind whistled louder now and seemed to be coming from the end, not that it was yet in sight. I ran towards it, past the door lined walls faster and faster, but the more I ran the more it stretched out in front of me. There was no end.

Tired and defeated I opened the door nearest to me. It opened onto another door filled hallway. The whistling wind was here too. I tried to open as many doors as I could but they were all locked. I needed to find the one I had entered from, but I couldn't. I ran back and forth in vain searching for a way out. Finally a door opened. Behind it a tight staircase spiralled downwards into darkness. As I stepped in the door closed behind me. Unbalanced, I slipped and tumbled down into the hard dark. When I got to the bottom I fell out through a door into a new hallway. But one with only two doors, one black, one white.

I opened the black one. It led into a black interrogation room. There was a black table in the middle of it with one black chair and a mirror on the wall to my right. I looked in the mirror. In it I saw only the reflection of the furniture, not myself. Then a black door seemed to appear on the opposite wall behind me. I walked to open it. As I stretched out my hand I felt its weight increase. I pushed through the heaviness and twisted the shiny black doorknob. I then found myself in a very different kind of hallway, one made of stone.

It seemed more like an old mining tunnel or some forgotten beast's lair. The roughly carved stone corridor curved around either side of me disappearing behind itself. Instead of doors, round jagged cave entrances lined the central crescent of rock in front of me. There was no light but it was not dark. It felt otherworldly and cold, void of warmth, as if they had never met.

I could hear a distant whistling coming towards me. Was this the wind I had been following? The gust forced itself through the narrow space completely overpowering me, disabling my strength, pushing me further and further down the curved corridor of caves. I ran to try and escape it but I couldn't, it never left me. It just continued to stalk me, blowing all warmth away.

I felt my presence was now stirring whatever lay behind those dark portals. I could feel a darkness being summoned, like the wind was waking it, inviting it to play. I ran as fast as I could around that cavernous cage but I didn't even know where I was going. I could sense something, something alive hidden behind those haunting holes. What was there? Was this its home or hell? Was it being held here, hidden away from the world? But why? Kept for what?

The wind swirled around me carrying sounds I did not recognise, obscure noises I had never heard. What was coming? What was on its way? Was it behind me? Was it getting closer? The wind grew stronger as I grew weaker. It was relentless, as if it were trying to blow out the light inside me. This was not where I was meant to be. This was not where I belonged. I had to find a way out. As if the gale heard my thoughts it increased its advance. Through the rushing air I thought I heard a snarl, then a deep growl. Off guard the wind threw my balance and pushed me hard onto the rocky wall. I winced as its sharp edges tore at my skin. Unable to fight the force of the gale, I pulled and dragged myself along the cold rough stone, whimpering every time its fury increased, desperately searching for the door that had brought me here, hysterically hoping that I hadn't ran too far round this wheel of wind. But when I finally found it, it was turning to stone.

The wall was slowly growing around it, claiming it as its own. I pushed and pulled at the handle with all the strength I had left. The sound of the cracking membrane of stone seemed to call on the gale to increase its ferocity. As the rock splintered and cracked around me the gust carried a hundred whispers of warning, threats of great ruin, disaster, destruction, and devastation. I tried to block them out as I pulled with all the power survival summoned. Finally the door broke open. I tumbled back into the silence of the small black room, struggling to close the door against the force of the wind. Once I had, I felt very weak, as though my elixir had been syphoned away. I struggled to stay on my feet, my life force still seeping, still leaking away. I grabbed for the back of the chair to prevent my fall, but it didn't. I hit the floor hard with my face slamming against the seat of the fallen chair. I tried to lift myself up onto the table but then stopped when I caught my reflection in the mirror. It was an old woman. She looked so strained, so tired. The lines in her face drew a picture of the sadness her life had held, with every crease etching the emotional journey her path had led her upon, each of her wrinkles telling their own tale of her personalised pain and her sacrificial suffering, all her anguish and misery wearing and tearing at her life, consuming it for itself, corroding her beauty, eroding her light. Her tragic torment gripped me, forcing me to face it, to somehow answer for it. I felt I was meeting death. But I was not ready to die.

I pushed off the table and stumbled toward the door pulling down on the handle as I fell. I collapsed on the floor of the hallway, instinctively kicking at the door with my feet as if it were the jaws of a great white. When it was closed I just lay there panting, contemplating what I had experienced with my mind questioning my memories, querying my belief. Had I dreamt the beast, the wind, the cave, the old woman? Had I imagined it all? I scrambled to my feet and stumbled towards the wall. The stinging pain in my arm and the blood marked wall answered my doubt ridden mind. I had had enough of the hallways and the corridors. It was time to leave. I turned to go back to the spiral staircase but it had disappeared. All that remained was the white door. I paused before my trembling hand reached the white handle. Where would this lead? What would happen? Would I make it back?

The white door opened up into an exact replica of the black room, dressed in white. It felt warm but fresh and light. I walked to the mirror and saw a reflection of a little girl. She had such a weight of melancholy hanging in her eyes that I wanted to comfort her. But I couldn't, she was only a reflection. When I looked behind her I noticed a white door. I knew this was where I needed to go, what I needed to do. Without hesitation I twisted the polished white knob and watched as the door opened. It was another hallway. But not one with walls or a ceiling or confines of any kind. It was just a long strip of floor hovering over an abyss. It seemed to be lit from within by a bright light which also illuminated its pair of handrails. It looked more like a bridge. A bridge of light. I was instinctively drawn towards it, to walk it, to connect to it, like it was created for me, for this very moment. As I stepped upon it my feet tingled as though the bridge were slightly charged. I felt a connection, a belonging as if I were completing the circuit. Finally I felt I was where I was meant to be.

It was only when I had taken a few steps across the white platform that I noticed the immensity of the dark surrounding it. The density of darkness was so great it felt like the air could barely contain it, as if it had become so dark, so heavy that it had nearly solidified. I walked forward trying to keep my eyes as rigid and fixed as possible but the further I got over the black ravine the more my eyes gravitated towards it. What was down there? What was lurking in the dark below? What was hiding, waiting to pounce? I had to check, I had to make sure. I stepped to the left and slowly leaned over the edge holding tight onto the railing. It was colossal, without limits or end, an eternity of darkness, nearly suffocating in its intensity. Every breath felt thick, viscous, alien. I felt compelled to reach into it to see if I could touch it. Then I saw something. Something moved, something split the dark. What was it? It was only a flash but I was certain it was some sort of creature, some sort of beast. Was it the same beast from the corridor of caves?

I stepped away from the edge. What if I had fallen? I had to be careful. Then I heard a displacement of space, a parting of air. It was close. I had to see what I was up against. I went back to the edge and leaned further this time. As I stared deeper my eyes widened and my pupils dilated adjusting my vision to the intensity of the void. I then began to see things, many things. Dark things, terrible things, frightful things. Things too dark for nightmares to even hold, things too dark for the mind to accept or comprehend. How could all this terror exist in one place? What could I do? How could I protect myself? I was completely exposed, completely vulnerable. What if I slipped and just slid off into the vast nothingness? I fell to my knees in fear of falling. I was alone.

There was nothing to hold onto except for the railing. I clung tightly to its post with my legs dangling slightly over the edge. I felt a soft breeze stroke them. I knew I had to move away from the edge, but I felt even more exposed there without anything to hold onto. So all I could do was look out into the sea of shadows scanning for a break in the pattern. But I couldn't see anything. I scanned and scanned the dark chasm checking every bit of it, but it wasn't enough, I couldn't see it all. I couldn't be completely prepared. Then I saw something fly underneath the bridge. I had to check the other side. I crawled over to it and stared deep into the all-consuming black matter. There was just as much to check on this side. How was I going to keep an eye on both sides? I crept back and forth, slowly sliding between the two. Then quicker, left and right, backwards and forwards. I was caught in such a constant cycle of catching the moment before and the one to come that there wasn't any time to protect the now. After a while I couldn't do it anymore, I couldn't keep it up so I stopped in the middle of the bridge and curled up into a ball, gently rocking myself between the two unknowns. I was stuck between two hells, but I was not in heaven. What was I going to do? But what could I do? The bridge was too wide to hold onto both railings. I had to decide. But which one?

Just as despair was drowning my depleted spirit, a light flickered, and I saw something I hadn't yet seen. At the end of the bridge was a rectangle of white. It looked like a door, a door of light. I had to reach it. Without breaking my stare I carefully got to my feet. I refused to allow my gaze to wander, to be distracted by anything. I locked it to the light ahead. Nothing was going to break it. As I began to walk forward I could feel something following me, stalking me, daring me to look behind, but I couldn't. I wouldn't take the bait. I had taken it so many times and it had not changed a thing. It had not served to save me, only to blind me. The longer I held out, the longer I didn't fall, the more I believed I wasn't going to. As much as my thoughts begged me to reconsider them, to turn around, to not give up protecting myself, I stayed strong ignoring their desperate pleas, choosing instead to concentrate on the only path out of here.

Then suddenly a thin thread of light appeared before me leading to the door ahead. It slid through my fingers like a fine thread of silk, glowing brighter as it passed through them. I felt a tingling energy exuding from it, welcoming me, guiding me towards its end. I was nearly there, just a little further, I was going to make it. Then the wind came. But it seemed to be coming from the door. Maybe it was already open. As I struggled to push through the racing, rushing air my eyes were momentarily diverted. I saw something in the darkness. Something worse than all the others things it had shown me. It was a vision of myself, falling. I didn't know what to think, what to believe. Had I already fallen? Was my mind tricking me or trying to help me cope with facing my demise by creating an alternative truth, an alternative reality? Had I already died? The immense force of the gale pushed me back down the bridge. It carried with it that whirling whistle of whispers. Those disturbing, sinister voices from the caves spoke with strength and power reminding me of my weakness, my fragility, my vulnerability. I could feel myself slowly submerging, submitting to the ghouls of the dark. Then my eyes caught a flash of the doorway of light. It had changed. A small figure stood in front of it, watching, waiting. It was a child. Without thought or hesitation and with only instinct guiding me, I pushed against the wind, through it, nothing would hold me back.

A thunderous sound broke the scene and my concentration. A loud cracking, a shattering, breaking and smashing sound was following close behind me. There was no turning back. I forced myself forward, supressing every will to look behind. I was almost there, just a little further. Then all of a sudden the wind seemed to abruptly switch direction and began pulling me in, pulling me towards the door of light. I looked up, the small silhouette had disappeared. Fear trickled into my thoughts, pouring its poison over them, tarnishing them, varnishing them, making them truth. Was this all a ploy, a ruse to get me to walk into my cage? Had I been tricked all along? Had I been fooled into running into the open arms of dark masquerading as light? Was *this* the nightmare? Had it only just begun?

I tried to fight the force but I felt numb to my commands as if my head and body were functioning separately. Which was me? I watched, powerless, as my body began to surrender to the force beckoning. My form seemed to almost float on the wind. It was beautiful. This wasn't wrong. This felt right. It was only the words in my mind that were repelling the light. My whole being felt a releasing, a belonging, a returning. I allowed my feet to rise up and closed my eyes as I finally fell through the door of light.

When I opened my eyes I was still falling but there was no wind. I knew I was falling and not floating because my body felt a weightlessness that can only be achieved from a great fall. All around me I was surrounded by the brightest light imaginable. But it wasn't blinding, it was soothing and comforting, familiar and calming. I felt free, yet contained, liberated, yet protected. A peace befell me, a peace I had never imagined existed, and yet, it felt like the most natural state of being I could possible inhabit. The serenity danced and spiralled in the air like ballerinas performing their piece just for me. Just as I imagined the notes they would be dancing upon I realised the volume of the silence around me. It was so full, like the air had cemented. A mischievous joy convinced me to be the one to break it. But as I spoke my breath, carrying the sound waves of my voice, seemed to shatter and collide with itself with all its echoes crashing into the light. Laughter spilled out splashing the scene reflecting around me like a kaleidoscope of diamonds. Every tone reverberated off each other to create another and another until, like a pebble bouncing on the surface of water, its force ran out. The stillness returned as I contemplated for the first time where I was and if I would ever leave, if I would ever want to. Though it somehow felt premature, like I was opening the present before time. The answers were not yet ripe to be picked, or maybe it was me who was not. Then the silence began to crackle. It crunched like virgin snow. The sound played on the air making it sparkle like falling diamond dust snow. It was dazzling, as though the radiance of the air was finally allowed to come out and play. It was so enchantingly beautiful, so majestically magical in its show of simplicity, a poetic prose of perfection. And here I was in the centre of it, orbited by this ignited energy, caught in this free flow of expression, happier than I could have ever imagined I could be, finally free.

To my delight the intensity of this place began to increase, magnifying my senses, magnifying the ecstasy. Then it began crescendoing, further and further, faster and faster, too fast. I feared it would reach a breaking point, that the scene would shatter. I held my breath, braced for its release. A loud bang sounded and my body met with a hard surface. All the light around me fractured, falling away like mirrored glass. All that was left was a warm darkness and that loud crunching again, though other noises were now joining it. Banging and knocking, hitting and hammering, and voices, lots of voices now too shared the aural stage. Then I felt a sprinkling on my face. I realised my open eyes were not open. Once they were, I saw my son's happy face munching crackers over my head. His eyes were transfixed and my mind, still misty from my nightmare dream and regulating realities, nearly managed to convince me of a sweet untruth. We were at home, sinking into the couch together, busy doing nothing. Becoming vegetables and eating everything else. Though as the memory of the bridge of light grew distant, so did my feigned belief in our lazy afternoon, and unfortunately reality finally took its seat.

The source of the clanging and hammering was coming from some kind of construction being built in the middle of the room. An ugly assortment of wooden shelves and slats created what could only pass as a contemporary abstract representation of suffering, or some kind of table. Either way it looked like it was in pain. When it finally couldn't take anymore its creators began their ascent and, once at the summit, began jumping upon it. After it had somehow not collapsed a tall man mounted it and our valiant swashbuckler climbed upon his shoulders, pushed on the ceiling displacing a large square tile, and then hoisted himself up past our perceived parameters of perception.

"Hey, Mummy! Do you want some of my cracker?"

"No, thank you, sweetheart."

"I still have those raisins in my pocket. Do you want them now?"

"How about we save them for later? Honey, what's going on?"

"The pirate's gone to get the snake."

"What?"

"The snake! They said it's in the ceiling so he's going to catch it. He really does looks like a pirate, doesn't he?"

"Honey, don't say that. He's got a hurt eye, that's all."

"I know, but his hair's all messy and he showed me his tattoos and I asked him if he was a pirate and he said that he was, but not to tell anyone. But it's okay that I told you, isn't it, Mummy?"

"Of course, darling. Don't worry, I won't say a thing."

"When you were sleeping he told me all about when he sailed around the world. Mummy, can we go sailing around the world? I want to see the seven seas."

"When you're older, honey, you can go anywhere you want."

"But why can't I go anywhere I want with you?"

"No, baby, we can't just go anywhere."

"But you said when I'm grown up I can. You're grown up, so why can't you?"

"Because I have you to look after."

"But can't you look after me anywhere?"

The lights flickered as they began their familiar descent.

"Mummy?"

"It's okay, sweetie, Mummy's here. Everything's going to be okay."

I did not feel okay about losing the light without knowing more about what had brought about this sudden expedition. But the room didn't panic in the darkness. No one uttered a word of worry. For a second I questioned my sight. Maybe because people's minds were already feeding on bigger prey that they simply saw the sudden loss of light as merely incidental. Men's voices then shouted up to the ceiling, but received no reply.

"Why isn't he answering?"

"What happened to him?"

"They took him."

"We've lost our only snake charmer."

"What are we going to do now?"

"Maybe he escaped?"

"Please."

"They took him to punish us."

"Or maybe by having the guts to go up there he was allowed to go free. Maybe this is our way out!"

Again deep voices shouted up at him, and again were left unanswered. No one spoke, not out loud anyway. But we all thought. Was he really gone? What were we going to do now? How stupid a decision it had been to break into the ceiling. If I had been there I would have told them as much. And plus, you never go alone, always in groups, that's pretty basic survival stuff. God, what kind of people was I stuck in here with? The only one that seemed to have any grit, albeit colourful grit, was gone. What was up there? And where were the candles?

We heard a scuffled shuffle coming from above the writings wall. The men shouted and finally got their, albeit muffled, reply.

"It's a maze up here. I've been following a... Hold on, this could be it."

"Be what?"

"What was he following?"

"Wait, how can he follow anything up there? It's pitch black, same as here."

"Maybe he's one of them?"

"Of who? What? No, no. He's probably found some kind of light up there. Maybe daylight?"

"I knew we were underground!"

"Hold on, we don't even know what floor of this building we're on."

"We don't even know if this building even has floors. We could be the only ones."

"Listen, this could all be in a lab, or even under water, there's no point just guessing for guessing's sake. We won't know until we get out."

"Do you really think that's what he's found, a way out?"

"Seems that way."

"Oh thank God."

"He hasn't found it yet."

A strange clanging noise limped above us, slowly making its way across the ceiling. What was it? No one said anything, but now we all wished the dark had waited a little longer to descend. My mind began preparing possible scenarios of what was making that unnerving sound. None were plausible, none were preferable, and all were worst case. I hugged my boy closer as some ridiculous futuristic mythological beast prowled in my imagination. Finally a dim warm light ushered the darkness away. At least now we could see what we were up against. Something long and thin caught the candlelight, shimmering as it fell down to the floor, closely followed by a pair of legs and then the body that belonged to them.

Everyone took a step back.

...the serpent is your death...

A glint glowed in his one eye as he smiled at the reaction his dramatic entrance had created. A tall man stepped forward, eyes fixed upon the new visitor to the room. To his surprise the eye patch guy picked it up and threw it at him.

"I don't know what it is, but it was impersonating our supposed slippery friend. It was the only thing up there. I've checked that whole space, as much as you can in that tunnel labyrinth. No green exit signs or serpents to be found."

"Let me see that. It looks heavy."

"Here, catch!"

"Wow! It is heavy."

"What is it made of?"

"Let me have a look. It's not iron, maybe brass?"

"Look, look at the handle. The design, it's the same as the flower on the wall."

"No, it can't be."

"Pass it over."

"It is."

"No way."

"It can't be the same, let me see."

"You're just reading into it. A flower's a flower, they're all the same."

"It's exactly the same! Look, eight petals."

"Coincidence."

"Somehow, I don't think we're gonna have a whole lot of them in here."

"So what do you think it is?"

"Is it the key?"

"Don't be absurd. It's just some sort of metal bar."

"It's gotta be the key."

"It's not a key."

"Come on, don't you think it's a bit strange that he found it when he was looking for the snake? He even thought it was the snake for God's sake! You can't get any more straightforward than that."

"I'm pretty sure you can."

"It does seem a bit of an eerie coincidence."

"Well that's all it is, and a loose one at that."

"Well I hope it is just a coincidence because the writings also say the serpent is your death."

"Actually, it says death of skin."

"Maybe that's like when a snake sheds it skin?"

"Well what does that mean? And how's that any better?"

"Shedding your skin is quite a positive thing, isn't it? You know, growth?"

"Can we use it to pry open the door?"

"No, it's no match for that beast."

"Well, what is it for then?"

"Something yet to come."

"A weapon?"

"Maybe for the snake or-"

"Am I the only one who still thinks it's a key?"

"It's not like any key I've ever seen."

"It looks more like a crowbar."

"Wait a minute. Hey, how did you see it in the dark? How did you mistake it for the snake?"

"I was wondering when you guys would get round to asking that. In my opinion, it's a far more interesting find than that metal bar. Because right now it could be anything, and that's always a good thing. You see, when the lights went, another appeared. A faint red one. I followed it around that warren of a place until it led me to this bar."

"What was it?"

"Where was it coming from?"

"I don't know what the light is. But it was coming from behind a wall in that corner."

I stood up and told my son to stay put and finish his crackers. I was already outside the store cupboard when everyone was making their way towards it. The eye patch guy was a little surprised to see me there but gave me an old fashioned kind of nod. I half expected him to tip a hat he wasn't wearing. We looked up, the ceiling wasn't as high in here, but was still too high. The makeshift table was called for. Once up on it he leaned forward as he pushed the central ceiling panel, but it wouldn't budge. He then leaned backwards against the end wall and pushed up hard on the back panel. It burst open. Nearly losing his balance he caught the edge of the opening. A strange red glow shone down from it as if it were a cursed treasure chest from some old low budget movie. He began to lift himself up into it and then stopped. His chest glowed red as he held himself there, motionless. He ignored all the questions, the cries, the pleas for answers. After less than a minute he let himself go and dropped down.

I asked him what he saw. But he did not answer. He just looked at me with a weight of woe that had seemed to flatten his light heart. I looked at him and his sore sadness trying to find the answer for it. He looked away and I moved out of his. He made his way out into the room pushing through the crowd. What had he seen? A fevered curiosity compelled me to find out. I lifted myself up just enough to perch inside. The red light zinged my eyes as they adjusted to what was in front of them. It was just four red numbers on a radio alarm clock. I sighed, quite relieved. Perhaps he was just in shock at seeing the time, or just maybe he was developing some of the doctor's symptoms. For me, it was actually quite comforting to see a familiar electronic device, even if it was a very primitive one. It reminded me of the old one my mother had on her bedside table. The time was obviously wrong; our body clocks couldn't possibly be that much out of sync. But why on earth was it hidden up here? Just as I was about to release my aching arms and drop down the last number changed. I blinked as my mind tried to understand what had just happened. Then I realised. What is the only clock you don't want to see? One that goes the wrong way. There were no more second guesses about why we were here. We were here in order to escape. We were planted in this puzzle for one reason and one reason only, to find the exit, before the timer ran out.

I fell back into the store cupboard toppling onto the short bald man.

"What's up there? What did you see?"

I just shook my head, I couldn't, I just couldn't speak. I saw him jump up and stretch to pull himself in. His face flashed red as he managed to hold himself up just long enough to see the changeover. A clear droplet fell from his brow down his shiny face of disbelief. The little bead glimmered as the red light shone through it, transforming it into a sparkling ruby as it slid off his face.

"But how? It can't be for us. It can't be."

I couldn't reply. As I left the storeroom, the crowd grabbed me for answers. They were scared. They wanted to know what could have made the brave snake hunter turn such a pale shade of grey. They bounced me around, faces in mine demanding answers. Just as panic began its icy trickle, a warm hand grabbed mine and pulled me free.

I let him hold me. I was barely able to hold myself. I felt sick. I had to tell him, but my tears were making it very hard.

"It's... a clock... but... it's counting down."

"How long do we have?"

"It's over. It's all over."

"Have we got enough time to get free?"

"Free? How? Where? We're done..."

"Come back to me! Bring yourself back to here, to now, where we still have a chance."

"A chance? We don't have any left. Not anymore."

"You can't give up. It's not over until the moment it is and we're not there yet."

Maybe, but we weren't far from it. I needed to be with him, I needed to spend my last day close to him, loving him. I ran to our corner and held his little body as close as possible. I needed his comfort, his love. My mind was constructing spiralling staircases of repercussions. It was all too much. Now it really was all too much. I squeezed him a little too tight as I tried with all my might to contain my desperation.

"Mummy! Stop it! You're losing points!"

"My sweet baby."

My tears began their flow. I wept for all the things that he would not. I mourned all the milestones his life would never reach, all the memories that would never be made. I wept for the purest love I had ever had the fortune to feel, knowing that he himself would never have that chance.

"Mummy! Please, you're losing too many points! Mummy listen, are our points shared?"

"My precious little baby."

"Mummy! You're not listening to me! Are our points shared? Because if they are then you're really pulling us behind. I mean I was quite far ahead, but now you're losing our lead. Mummy, are you forgetting? You can't forget! It's not real, Mummy! It's just a game!"

He held my face as he looked deep into my eyes, pleading with me to remember. But remember what? A fantasy? I closed my eyes to stop the stream but instead more tears poured out, rushing to be free. I felt I was suffocating, I couldn't breathe, I was drowning, drowning in my own sorrow, it was engulfing me and my whole world, like some great flood, covering, obscuring all remnants of what was, of what could be, obliterating any trace of reality, replacing it with another. Another, another what? Truth? Then something my baby said resurfaced and unstuck me from my mourning. What *was* real? What really was reality? Was it just our personal perception of the present moment? If all we have is a slice of a splice of time to call the now, then reality is only ever within the width of a needle point. Therefore what possible weight or mass can it really have? I had been wallowing in a fictitious reality, accepting a possible future that had not yet happened. And even if it did, why would I drag that reality into this one? Could it not stay in its own moment and we in ours, the one in which we were still living.

I wanted to spend what little we had left in his reality, in his world. And who's to say his one wasn't as real? Who's to say anyone's is any more real than anyone else's? No two people can share the exact same one. It is an impossibility. We each get our own and we each shape and form it by distilling the objective reality which surrounds us. We sieve every moment that we're given through a net we have spent our life weaving. This makes it very difficult for us to be comfortable with any experience that we have not already had. So, for the most part, these new possibilities fall through the cracks, without being examined, tasted or discovered. All that we are left with is what we've caught in our net of knowledge, and that is all that we keep. But we miss the opportunity to expand our parameters of perception every time we employ this filter, every time we continue with the same method of fishing in the same waters, catching the same fish in the same net. If we continue to be caught in this cycle our palate for life will never develop.

Understandably, we have all availed of this apparent aid to our survival, this bespoke interface which has been carefully crafted over the course of our lives. For it has been our only compass to navigate the stormy waters. It has guided us and our reactions and attitudes in every situation. It is what has caused us to feel pain and pleasure, what has prevented or compelled action. It has led us all our lives and it has shown us from what position we must view them, from where to watch the show. However, in truth, it has been our own insecurity which has forced us to pick a seat and stick with it. Our rigid interface is just doing exactly what is being asked of it, reconfirming our truth to make us feel more secure. It couldn't be more ironic that the end product of such a specific process could be believed to be the one and only, the whole, when it couldn't possibly be any more relative. How can a whole remain a whole when it has been rendered into a fraction of itself?

Perhaps instead of always feeling the loss of the half empty, it is wiser to feel the gain of the half full. For even if the looming calamity did strike, in the moment of its arrival we would, most probably, not even notice. So what exactly, then, did I have to gain by holding on to my old mechanism of reactionary behaviour? Besides suffering? So I decided against playing martyr. Instead I chose to play his game, to play by his rules, to make that reality my own, and to live it fully until its end. We were not going to be stalked by future ghosts, real or imagined. We were going to live. Live whatever time we had left and bloody well appreciate it. Live, for once, fully.

So we sat snuggled close together, witnessing the landslide of points, eating our smuggled raisins, watching the show. The game was an interesting one, that was for sure. We played a guessing game of who we thought were the best actors and what kind of commercials would be shown during the show's ad breaks. It was actually quite fun. We tuned in and out watching the players play. But although, for us, reality had a recreational quality to it for the others it certainly did not. People were, at first, quite pensive in their panic. Though I knew what was happening inside their minds. I had been there, many times before. And, in truth, mental torment is quite often far worse than physical.

I had a feeling that perhaps I wasn't the only one who knew that truth. Undoubtedly the room's cruellest and finest torture device was not the visible but the invisible. That relentless struggle against the sour-tongued demon who had taken seat in our minds, sapping our life force like some stubborn tick, impossible to evict. That tenacious tick spoke relentlessly of only one thing, like some distorted vintage vinyl, forever stuck in a loop. He never had anything new to say, he didn't need to. He just laughed at the fountain of fear he was creating by simply existing, by simply being the guest of honour at a party you did not want to host. He could not be ushered away or thrown out because, as he frequently reminded you, he had a right to be there, it was his party. This was his domain. He finally had a platform, a stage for his song, and he was not going to give it up for anyone. Silencing the chorus of continuous commentary was as gruelling and fruitless as climbing a mudslide. He knew he had a good chance of being right and he knew you knew it too. All he needed was for you to listen, to entertain his prophecies, to buy into the show. Then he would have you, have your ear and you would be deaf to anything else. The only way out was not to enter at all, to just swipe the screen when his popups of peril popped. No, it was too dangerous to ponder the fall while standing on its edge. Our fate would be our fate and delving into finding out how deep the ravine was would only serve to bring us to it. So, for now, somehow I had to ignore the avalanche of lava steaming towards us, pretend the gun pointed to my head wasn't loaded, ignore every instinct of protection and survival, disregard the approaching calamity and bury my head in the sanctuary of the sand. I knew that my best option was to resist defence. But how can you not flinch when an arrow is shooting towards you? I suppose the only way you can, by realising that it's just a phantom shadow shot from the bow of your mind.

"We've got to get out of here, we've got to get out now."

"That's what we've been trying to do this whole time."

"Well we obviously haven't been trying hard enough."

"We're going to die in here."

"Don't say that."

"We just need to find the door. That's all they want us to do."

"Maybe there is no door."

"Maybe they just want to watch us look for something that isn't there, just to see how long our hope will last."

"Why would they do this to us?"

"I knew this was all an experiment."

"One hundred people in a room, how do they get out? It's like some creepy show's catchphrase."

"What kind of mind could have possibly thought of all this?"

"There's thinking and there's doing. The question is more what kind of person would bring this to fruition, make this a reality?"

"But who could possibly even orchestrate such a thing?"

"The money that would have to be spent on this whole operation defies belief."

"Forget about the money. Think of the logistics, and I don't just mean the room. Just getting us all here. The organisation would've had to have been insane."

"I can't believe that someone would go to all this trouble."

"I can."

"It's all just too much, too much of a stretch."

"Hey there, dreamer? So do you still believe that we all booked up for this ride?"

"I don't know. It's feeling a bit too real now. If we are, we're stretching the shit out of it that's for sure."

"But why do all this? To what end?"

"To test us."

"To see how we all tick."

"That's not funny."

"It wasn't intended to be."

"Well, now I think it's quite obvious that we're part of a highly elaborate social experiment. But one far graver and far more ambitious than any before it."

"What if it's some kind of new underground gambling sport? Bet how many are left in the room! Who lives? Who dies? Who goes free? Place your bets now ladies and gentlemen!"

"That's some twisted shit."

"God."

"So we're just here to make people money?"

"You can guarantee that in some way or another we are."

"That's what makes the world go round."

"Isn't that supposed to be love?"

"Maybe back in the sixties, before we ate the heart out of it."

"Yeah, now it's all about the pulling and the tugging."

"The tug of war of capital."

"Well, money does equal freedom."

"No it doesn't."

"Of course it does! It makes everything easier."

"What? It just traps you, weighs you down."

"Typical answer from someone without money."

"Hey! You don't know me!"

"I know your type, you're part of the 'one love', money ruined this world, capitalist pigs blah blah crowd. Well, wake up, honey, those cute little boho shoes you're wearing were put into existence by the machine. Without it you wouldn't survive a day."

"That's enough, leave her alone."

"No, I'm sick and tired of these hippies spouting judgement on us hard workers who have grafted for everything we own. Not all of us were handed it on a plate, or handed anything for that matter. Most of these guys are just pretending to be the 'struggling artist' with daddy bankrolling their quest to 'find themselves'. I'm on my own. I haven't got anyone looking out for me. The buck stops at me. I'm that guy. I'm just trying to look after my family as best I can. I'm not some heartless sell out, I get up every morning because of my heart. Would I prefer to stay at home and play all day long with my kids and help my wife prepare lunch instead of eating with strangers who I spend more time with than my own family? Of course I would! I'd give it all up for that, but that isn't an option our society offers. You know the real reason these anti-establishmentists really piss me off? All they do is rip and tear apart at the only thing keeping us afloat without providing a viable alternative. What a cruel and cold-hearted thing to do. You can't tell a mother the water she gives her child is contaminated and not show her where the clean well is. You can't throw out the patched parachute without replacing it. And this is why there's such divides in the world, because everyone takes sides. No one admits that wherever you stand, you're still caught in the web. All we do is fight and pick each other apart. We should be connecting instead of disconnecting. All the shit of the world is because of us and our judgment, our inability to be honest with each other or even ourselves. People are angry, they're pissed off! Life is not going the way they expected it to and they're just looking for someone to blame, a scapegoat to unload all their crap onto. There are no enemies, no villains or baddies. We're all just people out there, every single one of us! We were all someone's child, we were all innocent once, until a product of life spewed its bile onto us. I'm just tired of it all, all the blame throwing, all the injustice, all the shallow hollowness of the world. When did we suck out all the cream, all the good stuff? When did it all get so empty? When did it all become so rotten?"

The woman who had inadvertently sparked his bonfire looked sheepishly up at him.

"It's not you, it's this room. You can't escape it. It gets in your head, under your skin, forces you to, to find exactly where your tether ends. Why? Why are they doing this?"

He knew no one had an answer but, still, he asked it all the same. Then a man did answer him, one who looked like he was missing a knife to sharpen.

"There are people in this world who view other people's lives as currency, an expendable resource that can be used when convenient."

A girl who looked like she had trodden the opposite path to the knife sharpener answered his answer.

"I just can't believe that such people exist."

"Well you better start believing it."

"Is there no side of this that ends well? Couldn't we be somehow mistaken?"

"Yeah, how?"

"I don't know, that it's all just one big misunderstanding?"

"Misunderstanding? We've literally got a ticking time bomb counting down above our heads. What's to misunderstand about that?"

"We don't know for sure that it's a bomb."

"Well do you wanna wait around and see?"

"Has anyone not thought that maybe it's a timer for how long we have to be in here?"

"In a sense it is."

"No, I mean maybe when it gets to zero the doors will open and we can all go."

Her optimism was met with cynicism, and then laughter.

"I just think we're all being very pessimistic."

"I think we're all being what we have to be."

"Yes, we have to be realistic, cautious. This isn't a game."

"But we don't know what it is. Why don't we just try, for once, to look at this glass half full and see what we come up with?"

"We're wasting time. You're more than welcome to wait around until the time runs out, but those of us who want to survive are going to try to find a realistic way out of here."

"So how are we supposed to use this key?"

"If it even is that."

"Well, it was provided so we've got to at least believe it's going to be useful."

"Provided? So all we gotta do is find the door that's also been provided, and just like in the pages of a fairy tale, the key will fit perfectly and we'll all be saved?"

"That attitude is hardly going to help matters."

"Well you tell me what is? Because I'm getting pretty tired of keeping my cool and pretending like we're not all gonna die in here!"

"We're not all going to die in here! We're going to get out!"

"How do you know that?"

"Because I have to. I have to believe it. Being human comes with a price, you never give up. Since the moment we first hobbled on two legs we have persevered through unimaginable difficulties, we have managed in the face of impossible chances, overcome inconceivable odds and all because we could not stomach the alternative. We are standing here right now because of never giving up, it's been woven into our DNA. We survive because it's the only thing we know how to do, the only thing we're certain of. So yes, I do believe that we're getting out of here, and I'll never lose that belief even if it means losing myself."

A strange stillness blew into the room. What did he mean? How could he choose belief over himself? My mind bubbled as I tried to expand a thought long enough for me to examine it. Was belief the same as hope? Was that just positive thinking? But hope seems more like insecure belief. Belief is belief. It is a certainty, a truth. I did believe in his choice but I don't think there were too many other subscribers. I looked around the room. Maybe I was wrong. Maybe there were more who believed in belief, who yearned for it, or hoped to anyway.

Just as I felt the mood begin to soften a faint buzzing hum intruded interrupting the peaceful contemplation. It was soon followed by the lights as they flashed their thought disrupting glare, disturbing the soothing moment of reflection entirely. Obviously we all preferred the candlelight. It did help to drape a warmer shade upon things, obscuring and smoothing the coarser aspects of our reality. But it was, of course, a relief to have the lights back. It felt like a glint of hope, even if it was a little too bright.

"And then there was light!"

"Maybe things are going to start going our way."

"Not while that clock's still ticking the wrong way."

Like the candles, people's precious ounce of faith was instantly snuffed out without a moment to breathe in the new scene.

"So what are we going to do?"

"How are we going to get out?"

The same old questions were being rehashed, reheated and served as fresh. We had been here before. We needed to accept that we didn't know, we just didn't, and re-emphasising that with inane questions wasn't going to give us any comfort, but quite the opposite. Finally someone with a sense of something else spoke.

"Listen everyone, let's calm down for a minute. We don't know what's happening or what's going to happen. We've all been chosen to be here for some reason. Maybe we've already guessed why, maybe we haven't even scratched the surface. And though some of us couldn't be more different, we're all in this together. At least now we're united in the belief that we do need to get out of this room, for the first time we have all one hundred minds pulling in the same direction. We're going do it, but I think we have to believe we are first."

"Belief? What an idolised version of ignorance."

"What?"

"Belief, hope, faith, it's all just rubbish, none of it's real. It's just there to keep us blindly plodding along without questioning a thing. It only keeps us from realising the truth, from owning up to the real reality, that we're all screwed. At least I'm brave enough to admit it."

"You really believe that?"

"No I don't believe it, I know it. I have a brain."

"So you don't believe in anything?"

"There's nothing that's worthy of such delusional thought."

"Not even yourself?"

"What?"

"I said do you believe in yourself?"

"How can you believe in yourself? It's just a self-created concept."

"The belief or the self?"

"Both. Illusion on top of illusion doesn't make it any more real."

The man left the conversation, storming out of the room to the bathroom. It was the only place of refuge we had. Though maybe bathroom escapism wasn't solely restricted to the room. Sometimes we all need a period of personal privacy. It really was a very strange experience not being able to leave the room or go anywhere. It sometimes felt insufferably suffocating. Though it wasn't necessarily a spatial claustrophobia we were experiencing because the room itself wasn't small. It was because of the people, they were everywhere. It felt like you were waiting in a large queue or stuck in rush hour, but one where nothing moved, and where the volume of people never receded. Maybe at a glance in very poor light it could all have been mistaken for a party, a never ending party for frightened amnesiacs. It sucked. There weren't many silver linings, no sugar left to coat. And although we had no real clue about the truth of our situation and whether or not we were being watched, being part of the herd of the hundred definitely made you feel observed. Eyes were always everywhere, watching, examining, inspecting. There was always an audience. Everything you did in here was exaggerated, every comment, every look, every thought. There was no space to let things dissipate. Living in our micro society was like being trapped in a snow globe, every bit of crap we created just polluted the room even more. Living and breathing in a vacuum wasn't easy. However, people expressing themselves seemed to help. Though now that the conflict had left the circle, and no one was pulling at the other end of the cerebral tug of war, the group's conversation split apart.

The room filled with voices, multiple clusters chirping and chattering over each other. I actually found it quite relaxing to tune in and out of. Maybe because it was the closest thing to channel flicking. I scanned the different scenes the room was screening. Conversation is great for procrastination and distraction. Talking the talk is always easier than walking any walk. Some talk was light, some talk was heavy, but all were preferred to silent contemplation. We all knew what we knew, but we didn't want to know it every second. So perhaps naïvely, and quite possibly stupidly, like an ostrich we buried our brains in the sand and watched it and time pass away, in a lucid haze of forgetting.

"I must be tripping or something."

"Hey, I ain't in your mind, man."

"Yes, I, albeit unexpectedly, concur."

"Well to me it's more likely than all this being real. Ever heard of Occam's razor?"

"Who's what?"

"Well, of course, but that still doesn't mean it applies here. You can't possibly, in all seriousness, believe that the simplest explanation for all this is your acid trip gone bad?"

"No way, no synthetics for me. You gotta go natural."

"Totally, dude."

"I can't believe what I'm hearing."

"I know, and that's exactly what I'm trying to tell you. It's too unbelievable to possibly be true."

"Oh God, please let me out."

The downside of our decided diversion, the flip of conversation becoming a form of entertainment, a selection of meandering matinées, was that they, unfortunately, could not be exited. We were stuck in a locked theatre. The channel button was glued. We were at the mercy of the whims of a hundred improv performers, and live jazz is not to everyone's taste. So at any given time there were half a dozen or so wanderers, just treading water, circling their cage like puppies at a pet store. Some people went to join the almost ever existing bathroom queue, though often to merely have a change, albeit small, in scenery. Everything we did was just for something to do.

Missy stood up to check on the doctor. He had been positioned near her column. The way she kept on checking and rearranging his swaddled blanket looked like she had been caring for him for years. It was like Mother Nature herself was moonlighting as Mother Nurture. She was the embodiment of nursing, epitomising the sweet nightingale of care. The gliding motion by which she checked his temperature belied the countless times she had done so before. I looked at her two beautiful daughters busy behind her smiling with their optimistic lightness of being that she had imparted upon them. They were the testament to her warm essence. I was relieved that she was looking after him so well. My guilt still infected me, contaminating my conscience. I wasn't yet ready to face him, even with his eyes closed. To the right of them outside the store cupboard, project 'Fix TV' was in full swing. I hadn't had high hopes for its success but I knew it was serving its purpose. The short bald man looked like a father with his boys. They could have been plucked out of any Saturday afternoon garage tinkering session. All that was missing were the beers. I looked around, what a little neighbourhood we had become.

The eye patch guy stood up to go towards the bathroom. But my son was not about to let him pass unquestioned.

"Can I see the key?"

"Honey, not now."

"Sure, I've got to first check the bathroom for alligators."

He returned with the ceiling's hidden treasure and sat down with us, entertaining my son with his flowered retelling of his epic quest into the atmosphere above. Though, unbeknownst to him, he was merely wetting my son's unquenchable appetite for adventure, and was shortly coerced into recanting some of his most exciting high seas voyages. I stood up to stretch my legs a little, as I wandered around the room I tuned into some of its more colourful conversations.

"You know I think I'd actually trade a tooth for a joint right about now."

"What the...?

"Yeah, I'd do it. I'd totally do it. Like, if there was some guy who could make that happen, who said I'll give you a joint for one of your teeth, I'd make that deal."

"What are you even..?"

"I'd say he's already on something."

"Who the hell would want your tooth, dude?"

"Gross."

"Or who the hell would trade their joint for one?"

"It would have to be my choice which, well I'd prefer it that way. Probably one closest to the molars, or one of those bottom small ones."

"Seriously, what are you?"

"I don't know which is more painful, the incarceration or the inmates."

"Hey, I'd totally do it for all of you, you know. Like if it was pure, we'd all just pass it around and totally, like, melt. This room would make the perfect hotbox."

"I really don't think this would make the top ten places to get stoned list."

"Come on, you know everything tastes better with a bag of weed."

"No, not necessarily."

"Depends how big the bag is."

"All I know is it would make this whole shit cake a whole lot sweeter."

"Make it a whole lot shittier is what it would do."

"Yeah I can't think of too many places that could induce a worse trip."

"No way, man. It would totally take the edge off."

"But you'll still be left with the same crap, just duller. Drugs don't solve shit, they just blind you to it."

"I don't know, man. They've solved a lot of problems on my road."

"Well obviously they didn't work too well if your road brought you here."

"Same as yours did, man, same as yours."

I hid my smile. Why do we secretly cheer the underdog, the little guy? Maybe subconsciously it inflates a belief that the odds of us being saved would somehow increase. So we continue the cycle, all in the hopes of our own salvation. But, in truth, our masked selfishness can't help but be a little altruistic, for every time we elevate another we elevate the world with them. From nowhere a fallen number eight tumbled into my head. Where did these unsolicited thoughts originate from? If you don't consciously think them, then where do they spring from? It's like some involuntary spasm, but in your brain. I couldn't subscribe to thoughts' existence being solely down to neurons and electrical pulses. It just seemed a little too simple and yet also a little over complicated. Anyway, back to my hijacker, did the number have anything to do with the symbol? What came first, eight or infinity? And who was the first to, well, use it? How did it become what it is today? Who decrees meaning? It seemed my involuntary feed did not yet include an answer, no complimentary counterpart followed, so I stopped thinking.

I looked back over to the man who had put his tooth on the theoretical table. As he began to laugh he pulled up his shirt sleeves. I don't know why my eye was drawn to the obscured inside of his left wrist, but it was. I could sense something hidden, my answer perhaps? Then I got it. He stretched his arms and exposed his inner wrist and the motif etched upon it. A strange chemical surged itself through me, it felt similar to adrenaline but less floundering, more poised and focused. That crude interpretation of a magic 8 ball seemed to change my physical awareness. I felt more awake, more alive, more myself. I also felt, as much as I tried to stifle it, a strong feeling that somehow I knew I was supposed to see it. That I was supposed to see my thoughts paralleled with reality, that I was supposed to notice that connectivity, and the great feeling of honesty surrounding it. And predictably life took me exactly where I guessed it would.

"Okay, Leo, so a really weird thing just happened. I was thinking about the connection between the infinity symbol and its numerical cousin and not really coming up with much and then, well, my eyes rested on this guy pulling his sleeve up to reveal, low and behold, a magic 8 ball tattoo. Weird, huh?"

"Interesting that it happened in connection with that symbol."

"That what happened?"

"An E.O.M."

"A what?"

"An eom. That's what your mother called them."

"Called what?"

"Extraordinary moments."

"Wouldn't it have just been easier to call them E.Ms? Seems a little grammatically incorrect."

"I'm not sure being grammatically correct was a deciding factor in her decision. It was probably more about trying to explain the bizarre feeling behind the bizarre moments that she found herself encased within."

"Fine. So why the need for a name?"

"It was because she had so many of these random moments that they no longer became random. They couldn't just be explained away anymore. They showed themselves to be something else, to be *a* something. And so, she had to label that something in order for it to be more than just a something."

"Okay. So what did she think they were?"

"She believed they were cursors, life's little lampposts."

"Strange."

"Cool."

"I mean, that she would believe that."

"Strange."

"What?"

"That you wouldn't."

"Why? Because I'm her daughter?"

"No, because you just experienced one."

"A coincidence is not proof that things are not what they seem. We're not in some late-night science fiction series."

Leo smiled. I didn't know if it was at my half joke half dig, or at some other Leo-esque thought he was having. But I wanted to know.

"What?"

"Well, it's funny because there are no absolutes, not really. We have no idea as to the real truth of existence. Just because we've done a lot of stabbing around in the dark doesn't mean we've lit it up any better. Things could be far more or far less complicated than we think."

"Like, what, we're all some otherworldly creature's science project?"

"Well, it's impossible to prove, or disprove. We just don't know. And it doesn't make things any more certain just because we think we do. We're like children in our treehouse creating the reality outside it, imagining it this way or that, all to feel a feeling of a truth. But there's actually more comfort in admitting that you don't know than you might think. It can be very liberating. When you don't close reality, tie it down, peg it to conform to what you believe it is, then there's room for it to show itself."

"Like a dog off its leash."

"Exactly. That's the only way you can really see the dog as it really is, by allowing it to be free to be what it is."

Around the room there seemed to be many canines sans collar. So I watched them, watched their unchained minds wander.

"Doesn't this all feel a little cult-esque?"

"Except for the being drugged and brought here against our will bit."

"So pretty much the same then."

"Can you imagine if we turned into some hippie commune?"

"The only hippie commune in a high rise block."

"Urban hippies. Very hipster, suits and beards, heels and daisy chains."

"Strange things communes. You don't hear about them anymore. When I was young they were springing up all over place."

"I suppose they're no longer society's idea of paradise."

"I don't know if they ever were."

"Did you ever visit one?"

"Once."

"What was it like?"

"Very different to what I expected. The evening I arrived was cosmic. It was like Dionysus himself had gifted the night to us, so much so that I remember swearing my allegiance as the sun was coming up, promising I'd never return to the metal kallipolis. I had experienced such a richness of being and a meeting of minds that I truly felt to leave would be abandoning my place in the world. But the next morning, or afternoon when I woke, things did not feel the same. I woke up to that certain agitated strain of hustle and bustle I thought I had escaped. People were rushing around, caught in a mirage of madness. Those same free beings were now scolding themselves for their debauchery, cursing themselves for the tardy start to their chore filled day. It was the last thing I expected to see, the last thing I ever expected to witness. Even here in this sanctuary of a place beyond the horizon of structured existence, we were still not far enough out of reach from society's sickness of stress and strain. I looked at the backdrop behind them, the beautiful mountains cutting up the blue cotton cloud sky, the deep emerald forests darkening in the folds of the mountain rock gleaming as the sunlight hit them. It did not match. Everyone was looking into the distance at a vista that was not the same as mine. They were all just muttering commands to themselves, racing to the next task, not even one taking in the wondrous splendour encompassing them. I just told my friend that for the first time in my life I felt the true meaning of disillusionment, and that if I stayed any longer it would eat up my natural hope and optimism for the world. It is a very strange thing to see a dream turn into a nightmare, makes you question the dream."

"Shit."

"Yeah. So here, with no blue skies or music or any of that good stuff, I think we've definitely been screwed over a bit."

It was an interesting topic of conversation. I day dreamed for a moment what that would feel like, running away from the world to create a new one. The sense of excitement and pride, before it inevitably waned, must have been pretty unbeatable. What righteous and utterly magical beliefs they must have held. We will make our own paradise and we will save the world! On cue, he heard my thoughts.

"So are you ready to run away and create your own Eden?"

"Is that a proposition?"

I turned to face my proposer, this time I did not hide my true reaction. He smiled as he squeezed my hand and for the first time I did not block his warmth. I felt a trail of energy flow through us, connecting us, like a complex infinity was being created. I stared deep into the black holes suspended in the centre of his pools of sapphire. The pupil of the eye is so perfectly black, it's the blackest black I have ever seen. It has such a bottomless pit quality, such a vast feeling of an infinite depth of forever, which just wouldn't work if it was any other colour.

"What are you thinking?"

"Of the perfection of the colour of the pupil."

"Well it is the apparent door to the soul, which is endless, so the according colour would have to match its endlessness. So you never answered my question."

"Create a commune? I think the idea of it is the most attractive and realistic part."

"You don't think it's possible?"

"I think it is very possible to start it, but I don't think it's very possible to really maintain it, to really live it."

"Why not?"

"Because people change. People's wants and needs and versions of peace and paradise evolve as they do. And if these type of communes preach higher thinking and evolution of the mind and spirit then surely it can't be a surprise to them that people change. It must be quite anti to their whole ethos to presume everyone will always stay the same, wanting the same, feeling the same. And even if you were aware of that inevitable change, how could you expect everyone to evolve in exactly the same way at the exact same speed? It's impossible. I also think it's a little arrogant to discard centuries of evolution of social structures with countless civilisations learning from previous generation's mistakes, literally societies standing on societies' shoulders. To refute all that, all those people, all that experience, immaterial of the creases, to ignore it all and start from scratch believing you alone hold the key to the truly civilised society, is well, a little messianic."

His laughter burst out of him like a jack-in-the-box.

"You don't agree?"

"No, I do, I really do. I think you're very right. Though, somehow, I don't think they would agree with you. The trouble is that they believe humanity can escape its problems by simply changing the backdrop. But you can't our run your problems. They, like your shadow, follow you everywhere you go. The solution is found internally, not externally. It's like forcing a herd of wild horses to run the Grand National. Even if they love to run and even if they are the fastest horses of all time, if they do not understand what a race is and what they have to do, they will never perform to their potential, they will never win the race."

"That's a strange analogy to use. I would have thought you would have used that imagery to describe how we, the wild horses, have been captured and thrust into a race which never ends."

"Yes, you're right, the thought did graze my mind that I might be taking an obvious allegory and distorting it, but I'm not a huge fan of obvious. And I think it fits. What I'm trying to say is that it doesn't matter how much optimism you have or how big you can dream. All parties involved need to be in a state of complete awareness, of the whole situation, of, as you said, inevitable change and most importantly of themselves. I think it all started to go wrong in these places when children began to pop up. In theory it sounds completely idyllic. No traffic or roads, just a nice community, freedom to grow and explore, learn and become. But in reality it is real hardship. It's not just running through wild flower meadows."

"I think at its shiniest it's basically the coolest, longest music festival imaginable. And one where you don't want responsibilities or stress, just fun and hanging out and being free. Which, as I know all too well, you cannot do with a child. Well, not for the first few years anyway."

"So how would you make the perfect commune?"

"I really don't know, Leo. Rules versus no rules, I suppose, is the big conundrum. If you're idyllically wanting to create a new way to live, a new type of freedom, then having rules just seems like it's defeating the whole purpose. But how could we survive without them? Even if you only adopt a few, you're still left with creating the fledgling of the very thing you were running away from. I don't think there is an answer, not yet anyway. Maybe the problem is that when people begin to know a little, they think they know a lot. And in a way they're right. It's true that in that moment, in every moment, you do know the most you have ever known in your entire life. But you also know the least you will ever know. The trick I'm slowly starting to realise is in admitting that you don't know it all. And the down fall of so many spiritual leaders is that they conceitedly believe they do. So they rule their kingdom under the guise of the all knower, imposing rules on freedom, creating a new treadmill of salvation where it is always kept just out of reach. How can they not see the irony in harnessing a free bird to help it fly? Strict rules and systems for inner peace with levels and hurdles can't be anything but stalling roadblocks created by those who don't know the way. Don't we have enough rules already? Shouldn't we be spending more time on wondering why that is? Perhaps all this optimism and good will should be spent on understanding why the ruled are so unruly so that eventually we can reach a point where we don't need the multitude of harnesses anymore, where we can eventually learn how to walk on our own two feet. Maybe instead of running away from the world to create a new one, we should start working on the one we already have."

"You're sounding like quite the philosopher!"

"I do listen, sometimes. Not much, but a little."

I tilted my head to the side and gave him a small smile. I felt so clichéd, like I was in some cheap romcom. Why had the moment just spoiled when it felt so right? Why do clichés have such a bad rep? They had to be born from somewhere and at that stage they were novel and fresh. How interesting that hyper success can lead to a downfall. Everything grows and everything decays. I suppose the cycle of life extends beyond the physical world. I turned to see how my little one was. He was in the centre of the room and seemed to be quite comfortable conducting proceedings. He looked like some mini ambassador at a function, introducing his guests to one another, keeping the atmosphere buoyant. His former nanny had now met his current one and they all seemed to be getting on very well. It looked like his hollow legs were coercing an early lunch. A crowd soon appeared around them reminding me of zoo animals conditioned to arrive at feeding time. I felt sad. I got a flash that we were, possibly even in our normal lives, more akin to the common hamster in the cage analogy then we dared realise, conditioned and trained by our habitual routines to expect our sustenance, our rewards, our lives delivered to us, never questioning the why or the how, taking it all on faith, taking it all for granted.

We have become a civilization of specialists. Like babies unable to fend for our complete selves, only experts in the niche we have burrowed into. All just cogs turning in a wheel of a world, never tasting colours outside our own, never experiencing new cycles, stuck in our own turning, our own rhythm, fixed to one spot, one view, never being afforded the chance to dislodge ourselves, to see ourselves separate from the whole. But what did all that matter now, here. We might as well have been transported back in time to the caves. At least then we would have been free in the wild, not trapped in this concrete cage. But we were. We were in the room and right now was the group highlight of the day, feeding time. I'm sure from the outside the food frenzy must have seemed very odd indeed, even from the inside it was pretty bizarre. But it was because we had been stripped of all pleasures, completely deprived of sensation, that a handful of nuts and crackers now held heavenly powers. Outside of here and this moment we would never have touched those dry old crackers. But in here, in this now, all I could see was people relishing and savouring their allocated portions, delicately nibbling away, carefully catching crumbs. Did we really need to have everything taken from us to appreciate anything at all? Were we really that spoiled? When did that happen? In only a generation or two we went from being grateful for what we had to expecting what we had not. The idea that this might be all the food left in the world, well, in our world anyway, placed such a great value upon it that it made us stop to take the time to actually enjoy it, experience the moment, milk it completely rather than just unconsciously spooning it in, like coal into a furnace.

Though the room had thrust us into obscurity of every kind, somehow in its darkness, it seemed to shine a light on our own. This place was an enigma of experience. I didn't know how I felt about it. I didn't know if the whole traumatic experience of it all had been a good or a bad thing. It had changed my life, there was no disputing that. But at what cost? I wondered, if it did end here would I die more awake, more aware then if I had lived a full life without it? Or was that just some crazy kind of cabin fever talking? I felt strangely distrustful of my thoughts, like they were being served to me and it was impossible to tell if some were poisoned. Maybe it was best not to consume them at all. As I switched my thoughts off, the lights followed suit. I called out for my son and as I felt my way towards his voice a strong arm aided our reunion and guided us back to our corner wall. My boy was quite impressed.

"Wow! You can see in the dark?"

"I haven't quite mastered that one yet, kid. But I'm working on it. You just gotta sense it out, trust your first impulse, your initial instinct. They're always your best bet, your most reliable source. You got to trust yourself kid. If you don't, who will?"

"Oh, I do, I do!"

"Good, good. You'll get there, you'll be alright. So do you know the real reason so many pirates wore eye patches?"

"No, no I don't."

"Well, it's pretty simple, for times like these actually. You see they always had to be ready for a below deck skirmish. Move your patch and hey presto, night vision."

"That's so cool!

"Yeah, pretty smart forward planning. A bit surprising when you think about the career choice."

"But isn't it silly to save one eye for worst?"

"Good point, though I suppose pessimism comes with the territory, especially when you raid for a living."

"But pirates stand for freedom, that's why they never stop sailing."

"You're right, kid, they are free. Though it depends upon what kind you are, if you have honour. Because if you don't, then the chances of someone coming for you are high."

"So all pirates with a patch have no honour?"

"Well, it's not that black and white."

I heard him scratch his emery board stubble as he searched for a way out of this. I felt bad for him, children can lure you into dead-ends of unanswerable avenues of thought before you even notice it. I knew he was debating the parent cop-out concession of complete agreement with whatever, leaving that little knot of knowledge waiting for your future self. Surprisingly, he didn't.

"Well, to tell you the truth, it's all about what choices you make. Your choices reverberate on life, they ripple it like when you throw a stone in a lake. So if you live without honour for the world, for yourself, it's going to come back to you. Those ripples will turn into waves and you'll live your life in stormy waters."

"Is that why you have one? Did you do something bad?"

"Sweetheart-"

"It's okay, though I might just bench that story for now, if that's alright, and ask you whether you've heard another. You do know the extremely curious tale of the mouse and the whale?"

"The mouse and the whale? No, no I don't."

"Really? Well it's pretty famous. In actual fact it was the mouse whose fame brought about this unlikely friendship. It all started on the docks late one night..."

As a small pair of ears tuned out every other voice, mine tuned in. No one was panicking. The guys still hadn't lit the candles but this time everyone waited patiently. I think that I had possibly underestimated the kind of people and the kind of minds that were trapped in the room. Maybe partially quenched hunger had played its part, as did the restored heating, though perhaps it was mainly because we now had the power to return our sight. Just having the ability to take even a margin of control was empowering. How much everything had been turned on its head. All our parameters of perception had been so inverted, so warped I hardly recognised their distortion.

The barest basics felt like luxuries. Luxuries. What a new meaning that word now held. Coffee and chocolate seemed like the most opulent elements in existence. I would never have thought to describe them in that way. In fact I struggled to avoid their temptation on a daily basis. But in that moment, in the dark, I would have strongly considered cutting a chunk of my precious hair for just one cup of bad coffee and a square of dark chocolate. Thankfully, the short bald man interrupted my insanity before it got out of hand.

"Sorry folks, we can't seem to locate the radio. I'm afraid we're going to have to wait in the dark for a bit longer."

Missy's comforting voice threw an invisible blanket of assurance over the room.

"That's okay, honey. We all know one another now, and we all know the room. We don't need any light to make us feel better. We got each other and we'll all be just fine."

Good old Missy. Her maternal warmth coated every syllable of every word like a honey glaze. She was the spoonful of sugar.

So there we all sat, together in the darkness. It was strange to be around so many people that you couldn't see. Did a hundred people exist if no one was there to see them? I smiled, though no one saw. In the dark your expressions were as private as your thoughts. It was so liberating to finally feel that no one was watching. I wished I could always feel this way. When I fully accepted the darkness an incredible feeling of comfort descended and with it an unparalleled sense of relaxation, like I was taking a hot bath. How strange that with your primary sense taken out you can feel more at ease. It didn't make sense that I felt so free, but I did. Obscurity is not usually synonymous with security but in that moment, I couldn't separate them.

A peace emerged in the dark as weighty shackles and masks were replaced by fresh candidacy and surprising serenity. I knew it wasn't just me, I could feel the change in the air. Perhaps this was because this time the darkness had almost been our decision. Maybe that's also why we felt that sense of liberty because, for a moment in the room, freewill seemed alive and well. And maybe it was also partly due to the fact that in the dark, the room really did cease to exist.

It's hard to imagine a conversation with nearly a hundred people, but it happened. And it was calm. We spoke of many things, not so much past but more future, namely what people would do if they got out. Except of course, for spending time with loved ones, it was the simple taken for granted stuff that everyone missed the most. Merely being able to go for a walk was a very popular suggestion. We were in a sense caged animals and as is often the case, when you can't have something, you want it all the more. Even if you were never one to just go for a walk, now you yearned for that stroll. Riding a bike, the subway or the waves, movement of any kind was craved. It meant freedom, as did just being alone. That was something we all needed. It was funny how frankly we all spoke in the dark, how it all just came easier. Forsaking sleep to watch the sun rise or simply being able to see the sun or a blue sky, or even a grey one. To feel the wind, any kind, warm or cold, it didn't matter. To just be able to feel the magic of energy moving the air around you. In a room so static and stale, wind seemed ethereal. Rain. That was quite a popular one. Just the thought of being caught in a spontaneous rain shower sent shivers through the room. To bear witness to the clouds unloading. To be part of nature, to feel life's ebbs and flows, to feel part of the world. Here we felt so very outside it, like had been cordoned off, exiled. Everyone wished to hear just one more song, or music of any kind, any piece, anything at all, to just drift and soar, to be carried away on a melody, all seemed to be the stuff of dreams. To hear strangers conversations and laughter, beautiful laughter, how foreign an expression that seemed here. To hear the outside world, to walk through a crowd, to walk through a field or forest, to dance, to sing, to just be a normal human being again. To have a shower, yes that received a lot of sighs. To brush your teeth, to brush your hair, to read a book, any book, to be transported away with it into a universe of its own so far away from this one, a safe fabricated illusory one which you could easily exit at any time by simply closing the book. To play an instrument, to play a game, to watch a game, to go for a swim to feel the buoyancy of water and to express yourself within it. To hear the traffic, the birds, the sounds of the day, the layers of noise that create the soundtrack of the city, of the countryside, of our world. The smell of a bakery, a cup of coffee, a flower, freshly cut grass, early morning air, late night bars, perfume, a loved one, the smell of home. Our senses had been so terribly deprived. How we longed to be able to use them to their full potential, to see colour and taste and smell the spectrum. To just get to live one day of our old lives, fully. To be given just one day back. To be able to really see, hear, smell, and taste it all, that seemed to be the dream, and that seemed more than enough. So why wasn't it ordinarily? Why was the mundane now so magical? How had mud been turned into gold? How had raindrops been changed into diamonds? Who had performed this alchemy? Was it us? Were we all alchemists and we didn't even realise our true powers, our true identity? Could we really just change our ordinary into extraordinary? Was it really possible? Was that what it was all about? Was that what all this was about? Finding our sight?

We all became quite pensively still in that darker than dark as we finally allowed a very grave realisation to settle, that we had all had a fog of unhappiness surrounding us, following us, haunting our lives. How was it that we could now see it so clearly? And why had it suddenly lifted? Was it just because in the darkness we could now see what we had, see how wonderful life was because it had all been taken away? How sad that we cannot muster appreciation naturally, that like a naughty child, to learn our lesson our toys must be confiscated. Would we ever get the chance to play again? Would we ever get the chance to not take it all for granted again? Would we ever get the chance to not run around like headless hydras? We are always in such a rush, all of the time, but to get where I wondered? Surely we can't be anywhere else except exactly where we are? Is it because we feel displaced? Or maybe just lost? Maybe we are all lost, all looking, searching desperately for a way out, a way home. But perhaps we're already there and we're just not seeing it. Maybe this secret escape that we dream of is an escape from our heads, not from our lives, from the camera and not the stage. Maybe there's nothing wrong with the scene, maybe it's just the observer, the critic that is finding grievance in greatness. Our life does not consist of just one plot line, it's not just one movie, it is made up by the million billion tiny things that happen. What we don't realise when we wake up every morning and go about our business throughout the day with all the errands and jobs we have to do, what we don't understand is that it is all the stuff that fills our day that makes our day. That is what life is made up from, that's the stuffing. It's all about the fluff and stuff. Life *is* the stuff of fluff. And our life is playing out live, every day, and whether or not we decide to realise it, it still continues to play on. It makes no difference to life if we watch or notice it, but it does seem a bit of a shame that we're sitting in the audience not watching the stage. By consuming ourselves with the thought that we need to first get somewhere, get to a certain place, a position, achieve a goal, before we can then finally relax and really live, is completely counterproductive. We are throwing our lives away in order to have better lives. This tail chasing paradox will never get us anywhere, let alone anywhere close to happiness. We must see that our only option is to move forward toward a current unknown. With knowledge of the despair the known has brought us, how can we not go? In our lives we get a handful of crossroads that really matter. We all knew this was one of them. We all knew what type of life we wanted. We wanted one that we were a part of.

As if on cue the bright lights returned, returning us back to ourselves and our position. The short bald man found the radio which was not lost at all, but was only hiding. Though I was glad that it had been. I needed that break of reality, we all did. They lit a candle and kept it burning just in case. It looked like a vigil in the corner, a vigil for what I thought, our lost loved ones, lost lives, or lost appreciation? I walked over to it. I don't know why, maybe because even though its instincts had been tamed it was still alive. I sat down near it just staring, fondly remembering my capricious friend. That all seemed like so long ago, was it really only yesterday? Was there a yesterday? Time seemed so simulated here, so counterfeit, like it was all just an act. It felt like something we had forced upon the moment in our attempt to categorise, contain and control it. Is time just a manmade rein we've thrown onto life? Just an illusion to make the illusion more real? Like that guy had said earlier, does illusion on top of illusion make it any more real? Again, my private thoughts were hijacked.

"So what do you think?"

"About what?"

"About what that guy said earlier, that illusion on top of illusion doesn't make it any more real?"

"Yeah, I don't know if it's as straight forward as it sounds. The illusion is definitely strengthened the more layers it has."

"But it is no more real is it?"

"No, I suppose it's not. But it can really seem to be. And if you perceive it to be more real, then maybe it is. Isn't truth all about perception, all about the perceiver?"

"Interesting. It's a truth. Is perspective only in the eye of the beholder? If you see something that is white yet in reality it is blue, as your reality is the only existence you have, how are you not correct?"

"Well, like truth, I suppose perspective is relative. You know, in this swirling storm of seven billion subjective realities moving and colliding with each other, it's a real wonder how we all manage to work together."

"The only way we can successfully share the world is if we all regard and respect each other's."

"Well, somehow I can't see the stars aligning and all our worlds joining the same orbit."

A little voice interrupted.

"Mummy, do you want your crackers now?"

"You can have mine, darling."

"No it's okay. I already had two packs, well actually, two and a half. I'll keep yours for later."

His voice lowered to a whisper as he leaned in.

"I've been helping with handing out crackers and lots of stuff. I think I've managed to get our lead back. I'm going to help tidy up a bit now and then can I go back to hearing about what happened to the Mary Celeste?"

"Of course, honey. And thank you for getting our lead back. I'll try my best to get a few points of my own."

"As long as you don't lose anymore, Mummy, I think we'll be okay."

"Alright, I promise I won't. Have fun!"

"You see how he is actually enjoying himself because he is living a lighter reality. The more you let the weights go, the more life tends to do the same."

"How am I supposed to keep him safe by just letting go? How can you be protected by letting yourself go? It doesn't make sense."

"When you let things go, you let go of the illusion of safety."

"I don't understand, then where's the safe place?"

"There is only one safe place, the place where truth reveals itself. Everywhere."

"Leo, you sound like a Zen desk calendar."

"Do you have a Zen desk calendar?"

"No."

"Maybe you should get one."

"Maybe I will."

"Good."

"Good."

I felt a little sheepish over my childishness, but I couldn't take it back and I couldn't back down now. I had chosen my road and I was stuck on it. I hated awkward silences, especially ones where I was the cause. There was literally no way out. We were just going to stay in this silent moment forever. I couldn't be the first to speak and I knew he wasn't going to. My stomach was in knots. He seemed serene. What would I even say? The longer the stalemate continued, the more painful it became. I couldn't take it anymore. It was only going to get worse. I had to jump, I had to kamikaze it.

"So go on, explain how protecting yourself is so irrational?"

"Okay, well imagine you're on a battlefield being showered with arrows, trying your best to protect yourself, trying to anticipate the next shot, which, unless you are a passenger on a certain Delorean or can slow time, is completely impossible. So you get hit, time and time again. But what if someone told you a way not to get hit, ever? That all you had to do was just stay behind your shield."

"Really? Just stay behind your shield? Where did you unearth that gem? The Art of War? Truly ground breaking, Leo."

"Wisdom only shows its true worth when it's put into practice. You know you can't knock something until you've properly tried it on for size, in spite of what its cover may show. The true wisdom here is expressed by daring to stay behind the shield and never looking round it, ever. But we always do. We're incapable of allowing only our current selves to be saved. We want our future self to be saved too. So we peek from behind the shield to see what's coming next, what's on its way. We justify it as thinking ahead, being prepared. We're just trying to prevent our worst fear, of being taken by surprise. But in fact it is this very act of protection that manifests the fear. By peering beyond the shield you leave yourself exposed, thereby, sealing the very fate you are trying to escape from. It is a self-fulfilling prophecy, and you are the prophet. Your fear becomes both the caution and the cause. But unfortunately we do not see it in this way. Instead we use the pain we have experienced to reaffirm our belief in the importance of checking for danger. We then decide to be extra vigilant, double checking this time, which inevitably leads to double pain, leading to triple checks and so on and so on."

"So you're saying believe that nothing will go wrong and never worry about the future and then all will be so, just like a fairy's wish?"

"No, I'm saying that you will always be given the solution to the problem in the moment you need it. One cannot exist without the other, they're inseparable. But we're always trying to get ahead of ourselves and life, racing to solve all our problems, juggling them all at once yet never solving enough to ever clear our minds. Thinking about what time your mail will arrive will not make it come any faster. We've fallen for the oldest trick in the book, we've bought the emperor's new hedge cutters. We're buying into an idea that we can get out of the garden maze by imagining that our imaginary hedge cutters are slowly snipping away at the bushy walls. Instead of solving the maze by understanding it and finding a way out, we are simply standing in a corner pretending to cut away at it, believing we are making headway and will soon be free. But it's all illusory. It is madness and we are paying for it dearly with the highest price in the land, the precious time of our irreplaceable lives. We cannot keep throwing away the present to work on the future. It's all in our heads. It does not yet exist. It's just an old hoax our mind manufactures to keep us busy. We cannot change the future in the present moment any more than we can change the past. It is out of our reach. The only place where you ever have any power is right now, which, coincidently, is the only place where anything ever happens, ever. When the future arrives in the form of the now, if you are present enough to witness it fully, you will always know what to do. What's there to lose?"

"Possibly your life."

"Really?"

"Well if you don't look when you cross the road or check your muesli for nuts if you're allergic or check your mirrors while driving, then what?"

"But all those things are happening in the present moment where you should have complete awareness. I'm not saying just walk around with your eyes closed. I'm talking about the incessant worry and anxiety that is produced by the same continued cycle of thoughts that are experienced before they are even proven to be needed. I didn't say you should become a potato and not engage with life. Then you'd already be gone because you wouldn't even be here. What I'm saying is very different from what you're hearing. The point is not to be a Vulcan and to live as passively as possible. It is to be aware and live as passionately as possible. You must become conscious that every one of your thoughts and feelings create a ripple effect on your whole life, including those surrounding you. Thoughts hold more power than people realise. They're not just these abstract, irrelevant things. They matter just as much as matter. They sculpt both you and your experience of everything. And their effects are cumulative. Like some snowball growing bigger with every tumble down the mountain, your thoughts grow in power the more you think them. They bully you into submission, obscuring your vision beyond them, leaving very little room for reason. If you spend your life expecting bad stuff, not only will you always find it, but you'll also find your life's never been lived, like a collector's toy on a shelf, never allowed to fulfil its purpose. We can't keep saving our lives, keeping them for best. It doesn't work that way. You can't save up time, it just keeps on ticking away. All you can do is choose how to spend it."

"Maybe so. But even if I could fully understand the talk I know it is nearly impossible to walk it. And I know that the world definitely won't, no matter how logical and wonderful the path may seem. People just won't make that leap."

"I don't believe that."

"How can you hold such belief in the opposite truth?"

"Because yours is only a current truth, not an eternal one."

"What does that even mean?"

"Just because it is night it doesn't mean the day has disappeared forever. You can't guess the ending of the story when you're only halfway through. We're not at the end, no voluptuous lady has yet sang her song."

"She may not have yet, but I can't see things drastically changing."

"Your mind tells you that you can't see what you've never seen, that things can never be what they've never been. But that's a lie. The exact opposite is true. Nothing you see is ever the same, nothing is ever repeated in the exact same way. A flower never blooms like any other. No two clouds are identical, even the same cloud never stays the same. Life is continual change."

"But how, Leo? How can it all change? It's just not what the world is looking for, what's in vogue right now. Popular culture couldn't be further removed from your 'truth'. People don't have the patience, the motivation, the time or the attention span. If you're lucky, people might glance at a flyer, but it's not like there's a pamphlet on peace."

"We all have our own personalised copy inside and outside us in every moment. We just need to open our eyes and see it."

"Well I don't see too many big flashing arrows or road signs pointing the way."

"You will."

"Yeah, when?"

"When you will."

"Oh God, I wish there was just a way I could cut out all the middle crap and jump to the end."

"And what kind of journey would that be? An explorer wouldn't feel the tremendous feeling of standing at the mountain summit if a helicopter just dropped him off there."

"No, but it would be easier."

"Maybe. But you know the best things are always those with the most backstory."

"Yeah, but a handrail would be nice."

"Did you ever try the blind test?"

"What, like brand versus supermarket's own cereal?"

"I mean a different type of blind test, one that your mother wrote about. I thought maybe she would have done it with you."

"No, what is it?"

"Well, it's where you evade your primary sense and therefore all programming connected with it."

"Right... meaning?"

"Meaning you close your eyes. By forfeiting your vision you are sometimes gifted another. You can obtain a certain presence because you have no choice but to. You're forced by your disadvantage to be as alert, as attentive, as sensitive as possible to everything that is happening in the moment. And that can throw you into awareness where an uplifting sense of well-being surrounds you because, well, you're just being, being yourself and nothing more."

"It's actually weird you said that because earlier when the lights went out I felt... doesn't matter."

"Go on, I'm listening with both ears."

"Okay, well the last time the lights went out and stayed out I thought I would feel this sinkhole of a feeling. But the more time that passed, the more relaxed I felt. This odd peaceful feeling kind of took me over. It was weird, but I felt free."

"Of course you did. You can't carry your past and future weight and be in the moment all at the same time. You only have one spotlight of concentration. And yours, in the dark, just moved from holding up your identity, your interface, your heavy shield of protection, to becoming aware of everything going on in the moment because that became the number one priority for survival, awareness of the now. Though unfortunately we don't normally have much awareness of what is happening. With our primary sense functioning we sweep scenes and then scuttle back to the burrows of our mind to analyse. But what we can't see is that this analytical part of ourselves is really just fear masquerading as foresight. Fear cannot exist in the moment, that is to say, you cannot have a fear of what is currently happening."

"That's ridiculous, of course you can. You see a snarling dog and you're scared."

"It is not the snarl that scares you but what that snarl could mean."

"Okay, but once you've been bitten, you don't just lose that fear."

"You do lose that particular fear. But because it gets so seamlessly replaced by the next one you don't feel the changeover. The face of the new fear has now become, what will happen to my bite? Will it get infected? Will I die? Fear is always future. It's the only place it has any power, and it is the only place where you don't, because it does not exist."

"So, what, I shouldn't be afraid of a snarling dog? How am I supposed to protect myself? Do I have to let him bite me?"

"You're misunderstanding me. I'm just trying to show you that fear is not the aid we all think it is. It can never assist you in the moment. The fear you feel does not decrease your chance of being attacked, in fact, it more likely increases it. Resistance to fear does not equate to resistance to action, to life. It just shows that you recognise that fear will never benefit you in the current moment."

"So you're saying that it's impossible to fear what is going on, because it's already happening?"

"Exactly. So what sense does it make to fear something before it happens? Because when it is actually happening, your fear about it always disappears, abandons you, to go in search for another. Fear is always psychological, it is never actual, because you are never in fear about what is going on, only what could happen. It has no power or dominion in the current moment. That's why it has to drag you to a fabricated future, where it can rule as emperor. The reason you felt a liberation in the dark was because you relinquished control. By just owning up to the fact that the reality which surrounds you is not under your control any more than your actions are as a part of it, your mind falls in line with your design. And with it persistent peace arises and is sustained, as long as the alignment continues. If your mind occupies the same time frame as your physical self you will be free and will remain so as long as it continues to be."

"So is that why you say the moment is the safe place?"

"Yes, because really it is the only one. But also even in the most practical sense. If you concentrate your spotlight only on the now, then you will always be the most ready, the most alert for anything that comes. And then, of course, you'll be protected from the crippling nature of fear and its ridiculous numbing and dumbing down of the senses. I mean, isn't that proof that we shouldn't be feeling fear? If something forces you to turn into a worse version of yourself then surely it is not for you. If it feels wrong then you must trust your instincts, your gut, and know it to be so."

"But how can I tell the difference between my instincts? The instinct to run or defend myself, and these quieter ones?"

"I think you just did there. They may seem quiet in the midst of all the feverish fear mongering but they too have a voice, the only clear voice there is. All we have to do is pause for a second to allow them some room to speak."

"But why the need to even have to do all this? I mean, why do we still spend our lives running around in a petrified panic when there is hardly anything that ever warrants such a response?"

"Because when we're just going about our non-life threatening day our workaholic mind lays predominantly idle, therefore in order to prove its existence it must seek work. It combines with our built-in primeval survival mechanisms to create grand fight or flight scenarios continually trying to save us from the fall."

"From what fall?"

"From falling into the perceived abyss, falling behind from everything and anything, falling down, tripping up, becoming vulnerable. Just preventing us, as much as possible, from finding ourselves in a threatening position where we are helpless, powerless to defend ourselves. But this heavy handed protection from predicted peril is, in actual fact, completely counter-productive to our survival in the long run. It is slowly killing us with its stress and anxiety. You see, we're no longer hunting and gathering on the savannah just living day to day, expecting probable danger around every turn. We have evolved beyond that but our instincts have not. And now living in the intensity of this twenty first century, full of its endless bombardment of attacks on the senses coupled with an impossible list of potholes to be memorised and avoided, it's a real wonder how we haven't completely lost the plot at all. The thing is, our physical body doesn't differentiate between the fear of being judged, worrying about bills or fighting for a promotion, and being stalked by a pack of hyenas. And it's all just gotten worse as now we're practically born into the race, nurtured in an arena of rivalry, competing with everyone and everything else, battling it out like an internalised version of the twisted gladiator games. And because our body has no conception of what reality is, except from the messages contained within the feelings we feel, when we face a challenge it reacts by dispersing the adrenaline and cortisol needed to give us the best chance to win the fight, even if it is only against a slow internet provider rather than, say, a sabre-toothed tiger. If caveman had been inundated with the same volume of challenges I don't think we'd be here having this conversation. Their nerves would have shattered and they would have starved to death. Yet here we are, submerged in a sea with never-ending waves of challenges, somehow still keeping it all together with only the glue of distraction. That can't be right, that can't be the furthest stage of mankind's evolution, and we can't all be okay with that. And the thing is, we're not, we just don't know it. We know something's off but because we don't know what, we desperately try to bury it. We're all just trying our best to hide that truth, all self-medicating to block out that feeling of wrongness, all carting out our different poisons, engulfed in our safety blanket of routine and identity, day after day after day, somehow just about managing to keep our head above the approaching wave, just about coping, somehow surviving with what little breath we have left. This can't be all there is, there must be more. We may very well occupy the throne as the most advanced being on the planet at the peak of its evolution but if we aren't even realising a tenth of the potential we possess, and not even questioning that, let alone putting the quest for the other ninety percent at top billing, it's hardly a wonder that we find ourselves, and the world in the position it's in. It's a real shame, but it's just the way the world is spinning at this moment."

"What? How can you say that? How can you just resign yourself to 'well, it is what it is' after everything you've just said?"

"Because it is what it is."

"I don't understand you, Leo. You're like a revolutionary without ambition. How can you stand by and let soiled food be served?"

"What do you think I should do?"

"I don't know, but you've got to do something."

"I am."

"What? What are you doing?"

"I am working on cleaning my lenses as much as possible so I can see the world, see life in the way you did in the dark."

"Well that might take a forever and how is that going to be of any practical help at all?"

"A solitary star in the night's sky can guide more ships than a coast full of lighthouses."

"I'm not really sure what you mean, but it doesn't really matter. I don't know, but what you've just been talking about it's true, it's all true. I do feel like I've been battling through life, and that can't be right. It's like you've just pointed out the shackles on my feet. I can't go on pretending they're not there and I can't keep it to myself. I feel like I just want to scream it from the rooftops, to just help everyone to see that they don't need to just survive, they need to live. It's all just such a waste. Such a waste of life, of living. It's all just so terribly sad."

"Yes, it is. But sadder still is not trying to unmask yourself, to deem the task too great and to choose retreat instead, to hide from your purpose, your path, your point for existence."

"So you think it's, what, to live without fear? By only being consciously aware and concerned with what is going on in the current moment?"

"For some yes, but it is not a theme in everyone's story. Maybe that will change. I don't know. I don't really know much about anything. I think that's what I have spent many years learning, slowly realising and accepting is that, to misquote that famous line, I now know enough to know I don't know."

"Well that's ridiculous, you quite obviously do know a whole lot more than most people."

"I know only what I know, what I have come to know. I can't know anything else and neither can anyone else. Ignorance is not something that people should mock. If the cloud has blocked the sun from the hillside, how can it be the hillside's fault?"

"But surely you have to suck up as much knowledge as possible to be the most informed version of yourself."

"I don't think that's necessarily true. I've realised on my journey that life is more about not knowing, than knowing. It's about moving forward and drinking the fresh flowing, not stagnant water. Those mountain dwelling monks really are right when they say you've got to empty your cup. You fill it, stuff it with so many things, some good, some bad, some even honest and wise and true. But truth is only there to help you realise that you have a cup, to help you recognise that you are a cup. Then when you do, you understand that you have to empty it. You have to throw it all away, dismiss any knowledge or teachers who have helped you along your way, understand that they can only help you on sections of your journey and must be forgotten once you have walked past their wisdom. Then one day I recognised that I wasn't the vessel I thought I was, but one without a bottom, without end, a continuous tube, a never-ending tunnel for experience to flow through. And basically, once you realise that, all you have to do is prevent yourself from blocking the flow, from stopping it. Maybe that's why you learn with the image of a cup, because you are closed, because you have clogged the pipe so much that it seems like a cup and it is not possible to conceptualise or relate to anything else. To see it you must learn to throw all the carefully accumulated treasure away. Then you will realise that your emptied cup is, in actual fact, bottomless. It is not for holding onto things, but for allowing them to pass through, a way for life to express itself, just a funnel for experience. Maybe the mental barrier to visualising a tunnel of being is as simple as not being able to allow ourselves to ever be empty, equating that with nonexistence. But if we were this solid block of a being then we would never change, never experience anything new. Our lives would be stale, uninspired. But by surrendering to being a portal for life to flow through we not only get to experience everything in its entirety but we also feel that phenomenal feeling of freedom and openness that comes with it, with that surrender of the concept of self. When we're a frame for the picture, we get to contain anything, we get to be anything. We do not lose our real selves, our awareness. In fact, we gain it. We gain the true awareness of what we really are, a being of experience, the being behind the experience. You won't disappear, you will only zoom out to become the entity watching the screen. It's like we're watching television but believing it to be our lives. But it's not, and although you may feel an affinity towards certain programmes, they do not, cannot possibly show you who you are. Your mother liked a similar analogy she found in that old book I told you about. Humanity is akin to a theatre of primates cowering at the screen, losing themselves in the picture."

"I suppose we are kind of doing that."

"God, what I'd give to read that book. I can't believe that you may have it just boxed up somewhere."

"I'll have a look for it and if I find it I'll let you know."

"You do that and you'll literally be my favourite person ever."

"That doesn't sound too bad, I suppose."

"It's a great position, good hours and benefits, you'll do well."

We reflected our smiles to one another. If we were anywhere else it would have been a lovely moment to allow to take root, to watch it grow, to see what flowers it would produce. We paused our interrupting thoughts and allowed the moment to breathe. Maybe we both imagined where the ship of now could have sailed to, what far off distant lands of exotic embrace and deep connection of being it may have arrive at. Maybe this way it kept its perfection, its purity. Daydreams are always perfect, never flawed. That's what real life is for. So for now we would rest in our cloud of imagination, creating magic together. He spoke about surrender, the beauty and truth within it, as well as the immense strength needed to achieve it. But right now, in this moment, it felt like the only option. Anything, everything else just seemed false. God, how I wished we could have mind melded. At least we would have been together there. The beauty of the blue of his eyes beckoned me to pour myself into them. I felt myself drift towards them being drawn in by their dominion of destiny. What was happening? I didn't care. I yielded to my instinctual emotions, they were too powerful to hold back, and they knew far more than I did. They knew the way forward, they would take control. I was too tired of playing leader. My brain seemed to seize and stall but no one was there to reboot. Did I even need it anymore? I was still conscious, still aware without my analytical calculator. It just felt like unnecessary weight, an anvil of anxiety that had been slowly crippling me my whole life. Now I felt as light as a feather floating on the summer breeze, happy wherever it took me. I never wanted that gentle gust to end. I wanted to be carried weightless on it forever, drifting around, flying free.

But, of course, it was never going to last, nothing free ever does. Cold reality sees to that. Eventually all its fugitives are rounded up, captured and imprisoned, sent back to the cell they broke out from. But this time with the pain of knowing the true measure of cold. Why must we fall from grace? Why can't we just feel good and stay there? Why must we be punished like moths to a flame, chastised for our affinity to joy? Why, like Icarus, when we touch our dream of joy must our belief melt away throwing us back down to earth? It wasn't fair. Every time you feel you make headway, you skid back down. Like a cruel game of emotional snakes and ladders. Why did it have to be so hard to climb the ladders but so easy to slide down the snakes? Maybe this was karma for the beast I had darted. Or maybe it was accumulated karma from every bad thing I had ever done. Well, I felt it, I felt that rough landing back to reality. Are you happy now, life? Have I been spanked enough? Can I go play now? Life answered me with its own breed of humour.

The shake didn't last long but, of course, we didn't realise that whilst in the middle of it. I was caught completely off guard, so was everyone I suppose. We had presumed since finding the writings and timer that there were not going to be any more attacks, or whatever they were, that we had passed that stage, but again we were wrong. And now we had to fully accept that nothing was certain, that anything could happen, and we were at the mercy of whatever it decided that would be. Thankfully, my son didn't receive the jolt of anti-freeze that I had. I rushed over to him but he and the eye patch guy were in the doorway of the bathroom pretending that they were aboard a ship in rough seas. It was so shocking to see them just playing in the middle of a crisis, that I didn't know what to say or do. I wanted to scream and shout and scold them for their recklessness. How dare they? Especially after what I had had to tear myself away from. They seemed so childish and immature. It wasn't fair. Why were they allowed to be so irresponsible, allowed to escape reality? But then I realised it was a spell that I was being put under. I was blindly following an order and one that was in direct opposition to my main objective. Above all else, I was to shield him from the serious, keep him irresponsible. That is what I swore to protect, his childish childhood. So scolding the only one who was unquestionably reaffirming that belief, plastering over any rips or tears so seamlessly, would have truly been the irresponsible thing to do. But I nearly did. Rage had given me a command and I very nearly followed it. It felt righteous and true. But now, after seeing through the smoke, I knew it was anything but. I had never realised the power anger could hold. It felt like a strength, a super human force rising up in you. I now understood the lure it had over people. You feel confident, secure, empowered and strong. You feel you are embodying the self you wish you could be all the time. You feel like your super hero self. But when the huff and puff deflates you are left only with your original self and the consequences of the actions of Mr Hyde. I thought I had gone beyond being at the mercy of wrath. I thought I was more evolved than that. But now as I felt the clouds covering the moon I was changing back, remembering what I had done. I felt horrible, disgusted with myself and the terrible thoughts I had had. Who was that? Whoever it was it was dark and desperate. Was it the devil on my shoulder summoning me to sacrifice myself so he could live out his lust for power? Was that the real battle warring inside my head? Was I just collateral damage? Was it that black and white? Was it that cliché? Was I the rope in this tug of war of reality? Or did I have a choice, complete control, and all I was doing with it was distracting myself, procrastinating? Was I really just stalling, taking the position of referee instead of picking a side? Was everything all my fault? Did I orchestrate and desire my own suffering?

Luckily, the sea dogs hadn't noticed the steam blowing out of my ears. Maybe because they weren't in the room. They were on their ship battening down the hatches, swinging from the rafters. I wish I had been in a better mood to appreciate how funny they must have looked laughing and shouting as the room was shaking and the people cowering. It would have been a magical memory to have been bestowed, not a catalyst for a meltdown. They rushed passed me, pretending to hoist up the sails, and then returned back to our corner spot, or maybe below deck, to continue the tales. A part of me wished to join them, to soak into their scene, to live it with them and sail away, far away from everything else. But something prevented me from abandoning this reality just yet.

I looked around, the room didn't know how to process the shake. It's a hard thing to have to decipher what is real after having questioned it so many times. Your brain is left a little sea sick after the wave after wave of opposing beliefs. So I think, in the end, most people just decided to allow all those waves to cancel each other out. It left a disturbing disturbance behind, but what else could we do? We just didn't know. We didn't know anything. And to find some sort of peace we really had to just leave it at that, recognise that truth. My mind kept trying to interrupt my verdict of acceptance, fielding questions I never asked, handing me reports of possibilities, reminding me of the stats of the rival teams, asking me who I thought was going to win, enquiring which I believed more plausible, advising me, counselling me, guiding me, directing me, and when I wouldn't engage, warning and threatening me. I didn't want to listen anymore. I didn't want to hear the swirling voices. I didn't want to play its game anymore. I couldn't, wouldn't win, I wasn't strong enough, there were too many variables, I would never know enough, I would never be able to know for sure, if I went in I would never get out, I would never escape, there would be too many voices to listen to, they would never end, it wouldn't end until I did, I couldn't, I just couldn't...

"So when's your birthday?"

"What?"

"What is the day that this world had the very great pleasure of welcoming you into it?"

"My... birthday? Oh, it's the twenty-ninth of February."

"Seriously?"

"Yeah."

"Oh my God, I can't believe that. You're a leapling?"

"Oh yeah, I forgot that's what we're called."

"My little leapling liebling."

A little laugh escaped me. I didn't wish it to, it just came out. He was so funny looking sometimes. He had such a silliness about him, such a contrast to the grey harshness I had just been swimming in. This colourful carefreeness felt so attractive, so bright in the bleak fog. Like his lone star in the dark sky, guiding me home. But what home was he guiding me towards? Was it just a dream, an optimist's opus? But what was the alternative? If reality was mine to create why wouldn't I rest, take refuge in warm, bright light? I didn't care if it wasn't real and I was, like my son, immersed in a make-believe fantasy. It was my life and I could paint whatever picture I wanted. And if I preferred bright and bold, loud and proud, if colour was more to my taste than monochrome, then let the walls of my reality pour down with rainbows and sunshine. The world, no matter how real, could keep its grey clouds and its grey skies, its grey days and its grey times, its grey suits and its grey ties, its grey areas and its grey minds, its grey faces and its grey eyes, its grey hearts and its grey souls, its grey ghosts and its grey hosts, its grey books and its grey looks, its grey thoughts and its grey matter. It didn't matter to me anymore. None of its busy busy-ness would ever be allowed to matter to me again. It had over-stayed its welcome. I was not going to play its game anymore. It was my turn to play mine. I finally realised that I had a choice, and that it was mine to make. I was not going to be bullied or terrorised into casting my vote. It was mine and I chose life.

"Leapling?"

"What? Yes... a leapling lady I be! So you'd better watch out! And quite appropriately I am wearing scarlet. Perhaps you are familiar with the tradition?"

"I am and I have received fair warning m'lady. But I'm afraid I have not a rose nor gloves nor even a spare pound to give. But, of course, the fourth I always have on me, a kiss."

"Well I believe that is the rightful assortment of compensation a lady should receive if her offer is declined, which it has of yet not been because no offer has of yet been offered."

"Indeed."

"So therefore I'm afraid we are caught in quite a quandary. You may not be able to pay that or any part of the compensation because such compensation is not yet required. As much as I would have appreciated such a gift, I cannot accept it unless I first ask you what I have not yet and you decline. Though I must also express the senseless nature of such a request, if prior knowledge of its refusal precedes it."

"Undeniable logic m'lady."

"Furthermore, adding to our quagmire, is that the law bound to such proposals is that they can only be offered during leap years themselves, not just by any leapling anytime she wishes, even if she wished so quite a lot."

"No exceptions?"

"Quite unfortunately, no."

"But hold on m'lady. If my memory serves me correctly, isn't this year a leap year?"

"Are you quite sure?"

"Quite."

"Hold on, I think you may be right. I remember, it is a leap year. Yes, we went to a fair for my birthday. It was cold but it was a great day. I can't believe I remember. It feels so recent. Maybe our memories are returning or maybe we haven't been remembering because all our days are so similar that they merge into one. But this day, this day was special. I remember we saw this huge tree on a hill behind the fair. We were trying to guess how big it was, how small we'd be standing next to it. On that hill it looked no bigger than his finger, he imagined being a giant and wanted to know if his calculations were right, if up close it would have been the size of a giant's finger. So up the hill we climbed. He's so spontaneous, and most importantly he follows through on his spontaneity. It really was a great day. He was so looking forward to it because then we'd officially be the same age. His birthday is the week before mine so it was a little like a twin's joint party. He's so sweet. He always wants to share his birthday with me. He's so kind and caring, sometimes I selfishly wish that he'd never grow up."

"Why?"

"Because then he'd always be my innocent little cherub."

"Maybe when he grows up he'll surprise you."

I looked over to his little face alight with glee at the story telling show screening just for him. It was his innocence that allowed him to experience a completely different reality to us all. It was immaterial if any of us had the right version, the right angle, his was far more pleasant, and truth be told, did it even matter? If I too decided to believe my explanation to him, would it really be such a foolish thing to do? Most especially if we weren't getting out of here alive. Wouldn't it then be madness to take a serious and grave approach and waste the last hours of life in a crippling fear, rather than optimistic excitement? When you're gone, you're gone and it won't make a scrap of difference then, but now, now it's all about the now. So maybe it was time to lighten up.

Perhaps Leo was right. Maybe then everything might begin to lighten up too. Feed the right beast.

"What are you thinking leapling?"

"Feed the right beast..."

"Ah, the parable from the mountain cave people."

"I don't know where it's from. But it does make sense. Though, like so many things, we just don't take them with us. Why is that?"

"Because the bud has not yet become too tight for the flower to want to open, the cocoon is still a sanctuary and not yet a prison. Sometimes we have to feel more pain until we take heed that we are going the wrong way."

"But it's the pain that we're following, like your checking behind the shield thing. We seek it out, we believe it to be here and then we find it. It's like we've confused the carrot with the stick. We're following the stick as it beats us, when just behind us hovers the carrot waiting to be noticed. How could we have got it so wrong? How could we have lost our way so much?"

"Because we were supposed to. Otherwise there would be no story, no tale to tell. Without the valleys there would be no mountains. Nothing would happen and it would all be a boring flat line."

"I meant it more in a rhetorical way, like I was having a deep opening my heart to the universe moment and you just kind of geese-pooped me."

"Makes sense that you'd be a leapling."

"Oh yeah?"

"Yeah, fills in a lot of gaps. So are there any special clubs where you can meet your brethren?"

"Of course. We all gather together in groups of 29, wear scarlet robes and at the stroke of midnight begin the serious traditional ceremony of eating birthday cake, like four years' worth. Then we collapse in a stupor, hallucinating on a sugar induced trip until we wake up and then just get drunk."

"So just your average birthday celebrations then."

"You know there is this town that welcomes all leaplings. I can't think of where it is, I've never been. But it does exist, I don't think I dreamt it."

"Maybe you should go, go and be with your people."

"Share our mutual pain of neglect and outcastedness!"

"Or your uniqueness. Oh leapling, if one could choose their own birthday, what better day? Leap years are always a cool year, 366 days, everything feels a little different, a bit off kilter."

"Not sure if I totally agree. So when's your birthday?"

"January first."

"Typical."

"Why?"

"Doesn't matter. So you're a curious Capricorn, now that makes sense."

"And you are a Pisces, which means you are naturally very creative and perceptive and I believe it is said that leaplings are supposed to be extremely sensitive to otherworldly things and hold a strong sixth sense."

"Really? Interesting. Not that I believe in any of that stuff."

"It's just as real as anything else."

"Now come on, Leo, I gave you more credit than that. Astrology is hardly astronomy."

"But the study of astrology is an intricate discipline that follows many rules and guidelines. It has be studied and learned like any profession. They're not just making it up as they go along. And I have actually met a lot of people who completely live up to their astrological stereotype."

"So you believe in psychics and mystics and palm and tarot readings?"

"I don't believe in anything per se, but I don't not believe either. It's all just different parts of the script. If it got in, then it's in, so I might as well listen. I'm not going to live my life based upon a path another has seen for me, but it can be amusing to see symmetry in certain things."

"Hmm, I still don't buy it."

"Sometimes you think too linearly. There is only hues of grey mein leapling, and I wouldn't have it any other way. Nothing has to be decided upon, labelled and categorised, deemed right or wrong. You don't have to have a view on everything or anything. Opinions only serve to separate us, they just create more distance between us."

"But you've got to have an opinion, some standing, at least on the big things."

"Do you?"

"Of course!"

"Why?"

"Why? If you have to ask that question, you wouldn't understand my answer. God, our opinions make us different, interesting."

"You really think an opinion on something makes you interesting?"

"If we all had the same opinion we wouldn't have anything to talk about."

"Maybe we would have new topics of conversation that didn't involve mental wrestling."

"A bit of a debate is healthy. That's how you learn new things."

"I don't think taking a stance is synonymous with learning. I think it cements you and your current ideology. How can you grow and change while holding onto a position?"

"That's ridiculous! Taking a stance on something doesn't stop you from growing and learning."

"The difficult thing with taking an opinion is that by making it your own you connect with it and then it becomes an adopted part of yourself, which then if threatened you fiercely protect. Thus making change, or diversion from said idea nearly impossible."

"So, what, we're all supposed to have no ideas of our own, just be vacant nothingness?"

"That's what you think the opposite of having an opinion is, to be a zombie? How many views does a small child have? When you are looking at a rainbow or anything holding great beauty, how many flooding thoughts and opinions come into that moment? None. Because if you're fully experiencing it, there's no room to think about it, because it would stop you from experiencing it fully. You can't experience the moment and think about it at the same time."

"Okay, fine. I shall be a blank canvas of opinion."

"And I shall marvel at your purity of expression. And people will come for miles to rest their eyes on such a masterpiece of possibility."

"Yeah, and it will be hanging in the emperor's dressing room, across from his new clothes."

"Poor guy. How ironic that it was his hunger to impress instead of express, his need to feel exalted, his lust for adoration and admiration that granted him the immortality he craved, as the butt of a parable, forever ridiculed as an example of false pride. What a legacy his vanity bestowed on him."

"I doubt he actually existed."

"Maybe not, but unfortunately countless people like him have, and do. Insecurity compels us to make the strangest of decisions. "

"I suppose that's the biggest chink in our armour that we spend the most energy trying to mend."

"But I think the way people are doing it isn't working. You can't sew chainmail with a needle and thread. Nothing that occurs externally will mend you internally."

"Well how then, do you darn chainmail?"

"You believe in your perfection."

"Yeah, like that's going to work."

"If you truly see yourself as perfectly what you are supposed to be then you won't care what anyone else sees."

"Still never going to happen."

"Okay. Can I ask you something?"

"Can I stop you?"

"How differently would you act towards life if you discovered you were the only one that actually existed?"

"Well, that's an impossibility, therefore impossible for me to answer."

"But how do you know for a fact that it isn't true?"

"Because there are seven billion people who would beg to differ."

"But what if their 'beg-to-differ'-ness was just part of the illusion?"

"Well, then it would be a very good illusion."

"Wouldn't it have to be to convince you?"

"Obviously, but it's not an illusion."

"It is impossible to know that it is an illusion as you, yourself, are in the centre of it. But it's also impossible to know for absolute sure that it is not."

"I suppose."

"So humour me. Crank up that great imagination of yours and tell me how you would act differently."

"Fine. Well, I suppose, it would be ridiculous to care about what anyone thinks or says about me. In fact it would be ridiculous to feel self-conscious about anything I say or do because no one is watching."

"And how liberating would that feel?"

"Very. But also, I imagine, quite lonely."

"Lonely?"

"Well, yes, if I was the only one that existed it would be pretty lonely."

"When a child plays with its toys, do they feel lonely?"

"I don't know, I'm not a child."

"When a child role plays with its teddies and dolls, giving them each a personality, a backstory, do you think they feel sorry for them not existing outside their mind? Or do you think they are happy to live through them, happy to have given them life by vicariously existing within them, being them?"

"So we're all puppets and there's only one puppeteer?"

"I don't know. But I know that I don't know which means I am open to whatever is the truth, even if I am the creation of someone else mind."

"That's sounds a bit defeatist, Leo."

"Does it? I'd say it's pretty idealistic."

"I don't really comprende."

"You can never lose if you don't mind what happens."

"But that's just abdicating your spirit."

"Actually I think it's accepting it."

"Fine, stalemate. We're allowed to disagree. We can't all be parroting the same lines. I believe that's what cults are for. Hey, that reminds me. You never really finished what you were saying earlier about the whole commune thing."

"Didn't I? You wouldn't, by any chance, be trying to change the subject, would you?"

"Well someone did once tell me of the futility of flicking a broken light switch. The bulb is missing so I concede."

"As you wish, liebling."

"I do and I wish to hear you speak of cults and communes and cabbages and kings."

"Cabbages and kings? Well, that is my mastermind specialist subject. Okay, well, I think fundamentally, and quite erroneously, these leaders tell people what to think and worse, how to do it, which can't possibly be right. Everyone has the ability to be what they can be, and surely that can't depend upon the approval or ideas of someone else. Plus it doesn't make sense that divinity could be more concentrated in one individual than another. Every glass is made of glass, there aren't some that have a higher percentage of glass. And why would there even be the necessity for a person to be seen as a deity? Think about it, even from a purely practical point of view, it can't be right for any one person to be worshipped or followed because it is a state that cannot be maintained. They, like everyone, will eventually die, therefore this template of a truth cannot be sustained, therefore it cannot be correct. I mean really, any organisation or person that requests you to pay for your freedom, be it physical, mental or spiritual cannot possibly have altruism in their hearts. And even if they supply their facts and figures, details and degrees to why they need your capital support, if it is more than the cost of a book or a movie theatre ticket then their only interest and passion in you is one of power, just a reflection of their own greed and insecurities. Not exactly traits that anyone would wish to exemplify. Besides, any belief that needs to be indoctrinated cannot possibly be in line with your design."

"Too true. But don't you think that, for some, it can help them?"

"Perhaps, in its purest state. But it's still all about the promise, the illusion of exalted freedom. That's the drug they're selling. And that drug is the very thing hindering liberation. It's the cork holding it all inside. Not just in communes, but the world. Everywhere we're offered a release, a step higher towards ultimate emancipation. But it is always fleeting freedom, never lasting. I think the people who pack up and leave society are doing so under the erroneous belief that by leaving the anxious world behind that their anxiety will be left there with it. But people looking for an escape from their dissatisfaction have no choice but to take it with them. A large gathering of dissatisfied people is only ever going to lead to one thing, mass dissatisfaction. You can't dispel dissatisfaction without first understanding the root of it. It doesn't matter if you change the backdrop. If the characters are still the same they'll still act the same. Like with so many things, it is an internal issue, not an external one. Each successive society's problems have always arisen due to the distraction posed by our combined internal struggles. If these are left unresolved each society inevitably breaks down to be replaced by the next. In a micro society, such as a commune, it takes far less time for the threads to unravel."

"So what is this internal issue we all continue to ignore?"

"That our dissatisfaction stems from our efforts to dispel it."

"But how can that make any sense? How do you get rid of something without getting rid of it?"

"By realising that no external event will ever deliver us from it. By realising that our greatest exploration lies within ourselves, the witness to everything. The anxiety we feel must be stemmed internally at its true source, not at an imagined external one. What happens is that we confuse our anxious reactions to things with the things we are reacting to. We load external things with a power they don't possess. Your thoughts about life, what is happening, what has happened, or what hasn't happened are the source of your self-punishment. How can we expect to relate to the world in any meaningful way if a cloud of anxiety restricts our view at every turn? How can we possibly hope to understand anything if we don't even understand the very being who searches for meaning?"

"But no one knows who we are, I mean, at the most fundamental level."

"No. But we can take the time to know what we are not. Our dissatisfaction derives from our insistence on confirming and reconfirming a lie we believe to be truth. The only reason why we keep trying to reconfirm who we are is because we are not certain, because we, at our core, know this vision of ourselves is not true. Why don't we just try pausing the panic for a whole second and pondering if this identity we are so fiercely upholding is in fact who we really are? We are protecting the very thing separating us from the freedom we crave."

"Which is?"

"Our opinion of ourselves."

"What do mean?"

"That we are slaves to the opinion we have of ourselves. And our lives are consumed by ensuring that everyone, including ourselves, agree with it."

"So why is it that we do that?"

"Because we don't know any other way. We truly believe the mask is the man. And we believe we will be destroyed if it is. People need to feel some solid ground before jumping into the unknown. It is completely understandable. That's why flashes of truth are such important lanterns along the path to help show us another way."

"Do you think we will ever find it?"

"I think it's an inevitable part of our story, but I don't know how or when."

"Well maybe this is the beginning?"

"Maybe. It will all flow in the only way it can. There have been beginnings before, many people through the ages who shared their energy in an effort to enlighten us, to save us from the fall. And, although most of their light fell on blind eyes, that too was part of life's course. Everything, all of it, is part of the same picture. There is nothing outside it and no pieces are missing. It's all just one mass of an idea, one animal, and it is beautiful and poetic, and romantic and tragic, and yet still holds within it a vein of humour. It's nothing short of a marvel."

"I wish I could see it, feel it that way."

"Remember we could never feel the complete comfort truth offers without first experiencing the discomfort of its opposite. It's there for everyone, but only if you want it more than anything else on offer."

"I do, but how can you, I mean how do you even start? Where do you begin?"

"By being as sensitive to the cues and road signs life gives you as you can. There is no absolute way to lasting peace and happiness. Just like life, it is an individual and completely subjective experience. You just have to be open to change. I suppose you first have to admit that it is change that you want and then be prepared that you might get what you wished for. But people are not inclined to do that, voluntarily anyway. If it does not seem vital then that's what it is, especially if there is any hardship involved. People are not only fearful of the change they crave but they also don't want to do anything too major to implement it. So they resign themselves to just complaining and condemning, it's easier. But it doesn't feel that great. Madness was once defined as continuing to repeat the same patterns while expecting a different result. Well, that's what we all do, daily. If you really don't feel 100% comfortable in life 100% of the time, admit it and then that's the beginning, you've just started your journey. Really and truly the first step on your path is admitting you want to go down it, admitting that you don't really know how to make yourself truly happy, because if you did you would always be happy. Then you have no choice but to admit that anxious thoughts have not helped you in their guidance, that their promise of protection and salvation has been an elaborate lie. You have to take heed of how much of your life you have burned thinking, living through a microscope, never seeing it as it truly is, never really being there to experience it. It's your thoughts about life that get in the way of living it. So if you can start to distance yourself from that fearful critic you can begin to slowly empty your life of all the things separating you from it. More intelligence exists outside of thought than within it and it's that intelligence we have to give our attention to. It's that intelligence that is in the know, in the now, not your analytical program that only knows what has been and that deals in forecasts and projections, calculations and estimates. Life wants nothing more than for us to see it, experience it, and see our arc complete."

"Okay, I'll take your word for it, Leo."

"Don't worry, I never took anyone else's word for it either. I had to find out for myself."

"No, I'm saying that I am taking your word for it. I'm really going to try. I do want it more than anything else."

"Do you?"

"Yes."

"More than your life?"

"What? Well, no, I mean, what do you mean?"

"Are you willing to sacrifice all that you know, all that you are?"

"I don't know... yes. Maybe?"

"You need to be certain, otherwise you'll slip."

"Well what exactly do you mean by 'more than your life'?"

"Would you be willing to sacrifice your identity, your reality, your life?"

"I don't know that's a bit extreme, isn't it?"

"The thing is, that if you want to feel different, then obviously you must expect to be different. If you want your life to change you must not be fearful when it does. You can't hold two perspectives simultaneously, you have to choose. And when you do, it's for keeps. The other disappears and with it all the other stuff that was attached. Your concept of self, your ideals, fears, persona, the whole way in which you relate to life will change. And so I meant what I said, it's an extremely important question. Would you sacrifice all that you knew, all that you were for the chance to be all that you are?"

"Who wouldn't when you put it like that? But your wrong about one thing, I feel as if I am holding two perspectives at the same time, and its hell. I feel so dizzy from jumping from one to the other. I'm just so tired of it. I've had enough of all the ups and downs. Why does everything always have to be so hard?"

"Because you're taking it all too seriously."

"What? But how can I take it any other way?"

"Life isn't serious, not really. Just remember all the tough bits are all just backstory stuff, context for your story, otherwise it would be a very short book."

"But it's all just such a trudge. There's just so much to overcome."

"You ask life for strength and then curse it when it gives you the opportunity to receive it. Every obstacle is there to help you realise that you can traverse it. Every trial you overcome strengthens you and your belief in what you can achieve. Each time the curtains close, it's only so you can learn how to open them again. You still know there's a world behind them, even if you can't see it right now. You did and you can't erase that memory."

"But there's just too much strain, too much weight, too much pressure."

"When the most pressure is applied the strongest material is created. A diamond starts its life as a dark, brittle object. But under great duress it transforms to become an impenetrable clear element worlds away from its former self and its humble beginnings. It is the hardship of its journey that brings about its new form. It is the extreme compression from its surroundings that forces it to change its makeup, to evolve, to become a new being that can now exist and cope within it, no longer yielding to its environment."

"Alright, but why does it have to be such a rollercoaster? It just gives you false hope and then you feel even worse."

"Why do people love rollercoasters? We're innately attracted to the thrill of the ups and the downs. There would be no mountains without valleys. Would you prefer it to be just from dark to light, with no gradual shading at all?"

"Well maybe it would be kinder."

"I think those flickers of light in the dark are the purest acts of kindness there is. They remind you of the day during the darkest nights."

"I don't know. I'm just tired, tired of the yo-yo."

"But without it, there would be no movement."

"No movement sounds good."

"You don't mean that. No movement is no life. It's like pressing the pause button."

"Well maybe I want to press it, take a timeout from it all. I just want to feel relaxed, to not feel any more stress. I don't want to feel uncomfortable in my own skin anymore. I just want to feel those flickers continuously. Why can't I feel like that all of the time?"

"Because you always do and so cannot do that now because then you wouldn't be doing this."

"What do you mean always do? I don't, that's the point."

"At this stage of your journey the sky may look grey but that doesn't take away the fact that the sky is always blue, and never can be anything else."

"But that's the point. I can't see the blue through the clouds. And if I perceive it to be grey, then it is."

"The clouds are there to enable you to see the blue sky."

"That doesn't make any sense."

"Without the clouds there would be no depth to the feeling of never-ending blue skies."

"Right, blue skies wouldn't exist without the grey ones. I get it. But what I don't get is the merry-go-round of reality. Why can't you just know and feel good the whole time? I'm just so tired of disappointment, I just can't anymore."

"Well you know the alternative and it isn't preferable."

"Giving up? Well staying in the dark sounds less painful."

"But it isn't. It's just that you have become used to that pain."

"Fine. So when do you jump?"

"You wait for life to show you."

"Life's taking its sweet time."

"When you're ready, you'll be ready."

"Are you ready?"

"Nearly."

"How can you be so patient?"

"How can I not?"

"It all just feels like we're life's lab rats."

"Maybe we are."

"Well, that's pretty harsh, don't you think?"

"Within the confines of this reality and our subjective perception maybe, but from the objective perspective, it's probably just as cruel as having a day dream, just thinking about an apple being eaten by a worm. You shouldn't feel so defeatist. You should feel fortunate that you've been honoured with seeing what's behind the curtain. Even if it was just a flash, you still saw, you still know."

"But maybe knowing is a curse. Maybe ignorance really is bliss."

"You wish you never saw?"

"I don't know. Maybe if it meant I wouldn't be aware of my suffering."

"But you would still be suffering consciously or unconsciously."

"Perhaps, I don't know. I don't really feel like I'm winning at anything at the moment."

"You will. It will all be worth it when you step out of the cave, and walk into that sunlight."

"So what is it that's holding me back?"

"Fear of more suffering, unvetted new suffering that you have not yet been acquainted with. I suppose the reason we don't allow ourselves to completely let go is because we don't completely believe, don't trust that we'll be caught. We still hold the belief that we are alone in this universe, and that very belief is what is stopping us from falling into truth. We've all, at some stage in our lives, felt exposed, abandoned, unprotected. And no one wants to feel that. So we orchestrate our lives as best we can to minimise them. But they are only there to be overcome, to be seen as false, and then replaced with the greatness of eternal protection."

"So basically it's the ultimate trust exercise, fall back knowing that you've never been caught before."

"Remember every time we felt like we hadn't been caught, it's still all been within the safety of the truth. Still above the safety net of true reality. It's incredibly hard to detach ourselves from our life and identity as its all we remember. But when you do, by realising that it's just a blink of an eye in a lifetime of blinks, that endangered species feeling dissipates and you feel your endlessness, your eternity. And that is when you become your natural eternal self."

"But if it's who I really am then why am I not feeling it when I want to? It doesn't make sense. It's not fair. It's just torture. I'm exhausted from it. Why can't I just let go? What is it that I'm even supposed to let go of?"

"Your driftwood self. You don't need to hold onto it anymore. You will not drown, you will know how to swim, you will be free. That piece of old driftwood is tattered and decrepit. It's breaking apart, falling to pieces as you desperately try to keep it together, keep it viable. This is what we are all wasting our lives doing, every single day, every single moment, keeping it all together, guarding our saviour from the sea. We drift along tortured by the fear that we may lose it, that the one thing protecting us will perish, and then by default so will we. But how could we? Your idea of self is only an idea that you have, it is not you. You don't need a conformation of you. You already are you. Yet still we continue the charade even to the detriment of our own lives. We disregard nearly everything else in our efforts to keep our floatation device intact. But it is already in ruins, it is already broken, because it was never solid, stable, real. It was found and borrowed, bought and stolen, constructed from bits and pieces we've collected along the way. How could our real self ever be manufactured? Your real self is just you. It cannot be forged and it cannot be broken. The tragedy of humanity is that we *can* swim. But due to our belief in the contrary we live our precious lives clinging onto our perceived only hope, floundering in a sea of delusion."

"You're right. But it's too hard to just let go of something you've been holding onto all your life."

"You're right, it is, and will be until it becomes impossible to hold onto and then we will finally find out that we always knew how to swim."

"Okay, fine. But I am trying to be as open as I can. Why is it so hard?"

"Because we feel exposed and we've spent our lives protecting our soft centre. But being open is the most natural thing in the world because it is our natural state of being. We all love love stories, why? Because it's an example of people opening up, surrendering to one another, proof of our capability to fall. That's why we call it falling in love. When you meet someone you have to put all your chips in, you have to bet on black or red and not hedge your bets. You can't bet on both. You've got to jump in with both feet. A very wise being once said 'do or do not, there is no try'."

"I think I need to watch those movies again, with new eyes."

"There's a vein of gold running through them, the force *is* strong. Funny how most people need wisdom to be packaged in a certain way, surrounded by the required frame in order for it to be seen, heard."

"'You must unlearn all that you have learned.' As a child that one was always my favourite, especially around exam time."

"It's just raw truth being thrown up like uncut diamonds onto a riverbank. It only becomes precious, acquires value, when it is seen by the one who recognises it."

"Yeah, like that Himalayan lily or some rare orchid. If you didn't know how rarely its bloom was witnessed you would maybe only give it just one second glance, but if you knew of the rarity of the moment you might spend the day losing yourself in its majesty."

"Exactly. It also works with the fear of something unknown. You fear what you do not yet know. You cannot defeat fear until you have named it. You must identify what it is you are most afraid of. Sometimes just the act of searching through all your petty fears will show you that they aren't as strong as you thought. If you no longer fear death because you see it as a transition, a returning home, then how can anything else hold any real power over you? When you finally turn around to face the ghouls that have been chasing you, you realise that that's all they are, ghosts. They have no real presence, no strength, no real foundation in reality. They are just phantoms of the mind. But because of our fear of the dark, of the unknown, we think that we're protecting ourselves by investigating bad thoughts when they cross our minds. But we will never get anywhere following them. There is no path through darkness to light, you just get deeper into it. Imagine you're in a field with an electric fence around it. You accidentally drift into the fence and the pain of hitting it shocks you so much that you begin to feel your way round and round, trying to find a way to stop the pain. But you never will by holding onto it. You need to step away from it. It's just there to show you not to touch it, to stay in the centre. You must make an oath to your true self that you will prioritise connecting with it over anything else, because, like fallen snow, it blankets every single thing."

"I am trying."

"Just don't give up. It will all be worth it, I promise you."

"I just wish I could shake this anxiety that just sticks to me like my shadow."

"That anxious feeling comes from being stuck between two worlds, the subjective and the objective. And because the concept of the objective is created while still stuck within the subjective, immense confusion cannot be avoided."

"That's what I feel alright, confused."

"We're living in the world from the inside out, when we should be experiencing it from the outside in."

"I don't understand. What do you mean, inside out?"

"I mean we're blocking our connection by hiding in our heads, instead of allowing the outside to enter us so we can feel. What is richer, the world that surrounds you or the one you choose to surround yourself?"

"But I don't know how to get out of my head. I can't very well decapitate myself."

"No, but you can start by admitting you are far more than what rattles around in there."

"I know I am. But it would be nice to find an off switch."

"It's there, finding it isn't that hard. It's the flicking of the switch that's the tough part. You first have to get to a place where you trust life enough to switch off."

"Okay, so if everyone in the world understood this whole thing, all got to that place and flipped that switch, what would happen then?"

"God, I can barely even imagine, it's just too much. It would be some world, one I'd be proud to belong to, that's for sure. A dreamer's dream."

"But what would it be like? I mean, how would we all coexist? What would the template for this new world be? How would it all work?"

"That's the same as asking me what a new fruit tastes like by just giving me its seed. We cannot possibly know until the seed has been sewn and the plant has grown."

"So you don't know?"

"No, I don't. I cannot even imagine what kind of a world would be grown from the seed of global realisation, though I suspect a far sweeter one."

"I don't know if it's actually possible to change the whole world."

"You're right. At the moment it isn't possible. A new world cannot grow within the same mental construct, from the mind-set that built the old. For a new plain to exist a new plain of thought must first be born to bear it. No true change can ever occur until those that can bring it about have themselves first been changed."

"Have you?"

"Been changed?"

"Yep."

"Since I began reading your mother's book I'd say I've been a different edition of myself every year."

"So where are you now, Leo?"

"I've managed to reach a place of no pain which, I think, is the rest spot between the two. I am as conscious as I can be at this point of my journey. I think our first challenge is to reach this zero, this nonplus place, where we are no longer subject to the whims of the wind cutting us off at our feet."

"Great. So we're all in the minus then?"

"Yes, though some of us more than others. But it's all relative and sometimes it's the biggest losers that achieve the most because they come to a place of such darkness that they can no longer tolerate it anymore. So they decide their only option is to make a change. Sometimes we need a gun against our head to force us to step out into the light."

"So what happens after the nonplus zero stage?"

"You've felt flashes of it. It's like a strong force flows through you enlightening your whole being, but instead of just flashes, it is continual."

"God."

"Your mother had a lovely idea for distinguishing the different states of being. Picture the moment as an ocean. And we're all on the surface. Everyone is splashing about, some doing lengths, some doggie paddling, some floundering, some swimming in circles, some chasing others, some nearly drowning and some just treading water. She said you need to put all your energy towards getting to a place where you know that if you stop swimming, you won't drown. To just be able to lie comfortably still on the surface, accepting each wave and the current of the water. Though when you get there it feels like such an enormous release of weight, of stress and strain, that you feel like it can't be real or that you must have somehow cheated, because it all seems so easy, so obvious. All you have to do is just realise that you don't need to swim anymore."

"So stop swimming, stop doing anything? Well that suits me fine. Deep down I am a bit of a closet sloth, I hate doing things I don't want to do."

"Who does? We're all just pretending that we love work. We're all lazy daisies, really."

"I don't know, my grandmother was pretty full-on with her continuous cleaning and never-ending list of jobs."

"But you have to look at why she was the way she was. What was she distracting herself from? What thoughts was she running away from? Sometimes if your inside is all messy you feel better making your outside all tidy. It makes sense, especially if you don't know how to spring clean yourself."

"I suppose. So we all need to get to a place of floating on the water's surface?"

"Well, actually that's just the first part. The second part may be a little harder to conceptualise."

"Hit me."

"Well, then you need to fall. To let yourself fall beneath the surface, to sink under it, to surrender into the depths of the moment. Then your surface self will die and you will be reborn. Finally you will find the solid ground you have been searching for. With your feet firmly on the real floor of reality you then realise there was a whole world existing that you were floundering above. This is the real world, and it's more wondrous than you could ever imagine. It is alive and for the first time so are you."

"God, why can't I just fast forward to there? It's not fair that I can feel something, see something, and yet cannot hold onto it, cannot keep it. It's just so cruel."

"You can see the horizon but you can never hold it, let alone keep it, or a rainbow, or the sky or the stars, or in fact most of the beautiful things you see. Even a flower once picked, once taken and owned soon loses the very vibrancy that drew you to it. You don't need to own or consume things in order to connect with them. Don't feel hard done by, you're really not. It's just like seeing your holiday destination before you go. You don't see that as cruel do you? It just adds to the excitement. Don't worry, you will get there, it's inevitable."

"But you don't know that to be an absolute certainty."

"Life will always illuminate the way. It is different for everyone. But everyone gets there. It's just that most get there at the end of their ride. But I think it's more fun to get there halfway through. A chunk of realism, backstory depth for the catapult to fly far, but then also enough time to enjoy the new perspective within the old scene."

"So really it's just as simple as a perspective change?"

"Yeah, well, at the end of the day, isn't everything just the perception of perspective? It is the pain of perspective that forces us to change it, forcing us to go where we fit, to align ourselves with what we are. Until then we just feel like a double hologram, torn between two projections, stuck in some no man's land of being, of self. It's a horrible and extremely uncomfortable place to be in."

"Okay, so instead of having a subjective reality, or several, we should go for more of an objective one?"

"Precisely. Objective means birds-eye view, detached from your one single point of perception, free from the ties of time."

"But what if you lose yourself?"

"How can a self that can be so easily lost ever be your real self? And who is the self that is observing this loss of self?"

"Oh."

"Also, even if you think about it in a very matter of fact way, if you're able to imagine an objective state of being, if the possibility exists for you to go there and adopt that position, if that even exists as an option, an extra gear that we can enter called objective reality, then it must, at the very least, be a half-truth to what we are. It's like a seagull who forgot itself and who is always swimming in the ocean or walking on the beach. If one day it realises it can also fly in the air, then it has to entertain the fact that although it may have lived its life swimming and walking, if it also has the ability to fly, then surely it must consider the possibility that it may well be a bird."

"So you're saying that we've forgotten ourselves and need to look at things from a distance, including ourselves, and kind of regain our old place of perspective, reseat ourselves at the correct angle, the correct view?"

"Exactly, you've got it."

"But conceptualising it is not the same as feeling it, being it, is it, Leo? How long will it take to get there, and stay there?"

"It's a completely unique journey of experience for everyone. But we all reach it, every one of us. It's just that at this point in Earth's arc it's more prevalent to reach it at the moment of the journey's end. However, the ones that do get there early suffer greatly for their prize. For the most part it is pain that initiates their journey, that compels them to leave in search of another path. It can happen in so many different ways. For some, once they have disabled their suffering, it is instantaneous. In one conscious flash they are there. Or it can follow after confronting and overcoming a great injustice. For others, after a lifetime of learning, it can come by unlearning. There are some that are blown around the world, shown their life story from a distance, and grow with each gifted experience helping them to reach their summit. And then there are others, who like a caterpillar, must become hermits, isolating themselves from the world in a cocoon where they can secretly become what they really are."

"So which are you?"

"I've been blown all over the place, and now to here, where I know I am supposed to be for the next step of my evolution."

"Which am I?"

"I can't possibly answer that, and neither can you until you've become."

"Great. So what am I supposed to do now?"

"Just be as sensitive and exposed as you can. Keep cranking open those barriers as much as possible and keep teaching yourself how to let go."

"But how do you let go? I don't know how to do it."

"You do. You do it every night, we all do. Just before we fall asleep we let ourselves fall in the comfort and security of our own beds, let go of all the rushing and pouring of the incessant streams of thought. We all must let go of the day in order to be recharged for the next. You can't fall asleep without letting go, it's impossible."

"Well some people take a few things to help them along."

"Perhaps. But they still need to let go. It's truly astonishing, and in a way slightly implausible, that every night we completely relinquish all control, resigning ourselves to a place of no protection, the exact opposite of how we spend our days. And although we may be tucked up in our nest within our nest, with locks and alarm systems galore, we are still allowing ourselves to be defenceless, unprotected, vulnerable to what beasts may lurk in the night. Surely you must see that it is a little strange that our whole existence of safeguarding ourselves suddenly goes on hold every single night. It's just proof that it is possible for us all to let go. If you can fall asleep, you can fall into the peace of continual present awareness. Whether we realise it or not, we're already practicing it at least once a day and just like with anything else, all it takes is practice. Every time you try you get a little further and even when you fail and close back up you learn how to find your way back along the breadcrumbs until it becomes habit."

"You make it sound nice and straightforward, but it's not going to be is it? It's going to take forever and the breadcrumbs are going to be eaten."

"They won't if you're following them as often as possible. You see, to increase your chance to the max you've really got to put it as top billing in your life. Otherwise it'll slip into third and fourth and then outside the top ten and soon forgotten about, simply passed off as a fad, a phase. But you know it's more than that. It's like locating a lantern in a long dark cave. It's imperative you find it. Your very survival depends upon it."

A flash of that nightmare of a dream stole my mind. That horrible hallway of stone, so cold, so endless. What did it mean? That bridge of light, the immense darkness below. What was that lurking in the dark?

"What is it?"

"Nothing. You just reminded me of a dream."

"A dream you had in here?"

"Yes. I've had a couple."

"That's very interesting."

"Not really, more frightening."

"You don't want to talk about it?"

"No, but you obviously do."

"Not if you don't."

"Whatever. It doesn't matter, they're just dreams. The first was waking up in here alone, except for that stupid old television set. When I turned it on it was broadcasting a feed of me watching it. Then I saw everyone from the room appear behind me, but only in the screen."

"That's really weird. What do you think it means?"

"What do I think it means? I thought you were going to be the translator? I don't know what it means but when I pleaded to join you all... the room filled with water and..."

"And what?"

"And well, I suppose I died."

"You drowned?"

"I told you it wasn't pretty, not like your flying pink elephant dreams."

"Well you know what water signifies in a dream?"

"No, and as you know, I don't have my dream interpreter with me. Would you mind standing in?"

"Not at all. Water, in any form, exposes a fear you are harbouring due to being forced to face unknown changes. These could be mental, physical, emotional or spiritual. Apparently, in your dreams, drowning relates directly to your mind expressing its anguish at being overwhelmed by forces hidden deep within your subconscious. These are usually supressed painful memories and interestingly the fear of the flowering of consciousness itself. So you actually died?"

"Yeah, well I think so."

"Well that's a good thing because death means rebirth. A rebirth, no matter how trying, is a wonderful opportunity to become more yourself."

"I suppose. It was strange but when I was sinking and I saw the television set floating in the water like some fairground balloon, it felt familiar. Like I knew it was the end. But I didn't feel afraid. And then I saw myself in the screen with everyone else."

"Wow. That's pretty trippy to have a déjà vu in a dream. Never heard of that before."

"What do you think the joining everyone else means?"

"Well I suppose the first thing that came to mind was that you died and joined the rest that had passed. But maybe it just means your serious self died, and your real self was allowed to escape. But I don't know, it's your subconscious. Only you can know the way out of that labyrinth. But the accepting death thing is really positive. It's so futile to fear it in any way. Nothing can come from it except wasting your life worrying, which in a way is you manifesting the death of your life right now. So will there be another dream screening today?"

"I'm not sure I want to visit the other one again so soon. It was a bit full on. I didn't have it when I was asleep, I mean, when we were all sleeping at night, if it even was night. Was that just last night? Have we really only been in here for one night? God, it feels like weeks, or months. Time has a different quality to it here, don't you think? Seconds seem stretched, minutes no longer minute. Minute. Is that spelled the same as minute? It is, isn't it? I never thought about that before. How do you read a word which is spelt the same as another word but holds a completely different meaning?"

"Well it's all about the context, I suppose. As the stream flows your mind funnels you into a path that has been created by previous words. Usually, there'll always be a more probable meaning for the word that your mind will then serve to you."

"But what if your mind gets it wrong? What if it makes a mistake and you misunderstand something crucial?"

"I suppose that's all part of the dastardly, and sometimes dangerous, game of Russian roulette of language. We all take that chance when we play. But, at the moment, we have no other alternative. We're stuck with this method of communication and, as a result, are at its mercy of mistaken identity."

"Crazy that something we all rely on so much can be so subjective."

"Like reality."

"Indeed. Aren't words fascinating though? I mean they are so incredibly important. We would be completely lost without them, like some tree stump, not connected, not able to grow, to express ourselves, mentally maimed, stumped. Yet we just use and discard them without a moment's consideration of their invaluable worth. Words are so powerful. Language, understanding, such undervalued tools of humanity."

"Aside from love, they are the most powerful force on the planet. We can destroy and liberate, savage and salvage with just a few understood, or misunderstood, oral sounds."

"Do you think that's in part why we have evolved the way we have? Why our species sits in the hospitality suite of the animal kingdom?"

"Maybe other creatures communicate in as much detail. But we will never know for sure because we just don't speak their lingo. But I think it's more than just the complexities of language that separate man from beast. There are a few intricate details in our makeup that create the divide. For one, we take pleasure in expressing ourselves for the release of the expression itself, not as a means to an end. As far as I know no other species on this planet engages in art to create beauty, for only beauty's sake. Perhaps it's because it is not missing from their world. I also think we have been gifted a very different kind of mind. A questioning mind. A hungry mind. A visualising mind. One that can imagine and foresee, remember correctly or incorrectly events triggered by senses and emotions, one that can conjure and create images never seen before, one that can ultimately create worlds that do not exist."

"I don't know, there was once a tabby cat that used to visit us who had a look of all-knowingness about him, like we were living in a world of his own."

"Maybe we're all playing within the mind of that tabby?"

"Maybe. Not too shabby, for a tabby."

"The quips!"

"I'm here all week, or well, for as long as the clock allows."

"Don't worry your coach won't turn back for a while yet."

"I'm not scared about losing my gilded carriage, just a bit weary that my pumpkin may explode!"

"I won't allow it, fair maiden! I will protect you from every detonating squash or tuber that threatens your safety!"

His theatrical outburst was so loud and so sudden it made me jump. And although I could not subdue my laughter I still succumbed to the classic human reflex of shame control/limitation/inspection and glanced round the room. Thankfully, somehow, no one looked our way. Though I noticed the other thespians of the room wrapped up in their world of worlds. They looked so far from here. I had to take a visit.

"Ahoy there! How's everything going? I hope you've not been bombarded with too many questions. He is a bit of a tough interrogator."

"No, no, we've had a great time. He's a stickler for details. I had to really frisk the old memory banks, but it felt good to remember again. We've had quite an adventure navigating oceans, dodging whirlpools even visiting the Bermuda triangle. He'd make a great first mate."

"Oh, Mummy, please can we go on a sea adventure together? The captain said that when we're finished here, we can go visit him on his ship!"

"Captain?"

"Well, it's small a ship, but she's all mine. You're very welcome to come for a trip sometime."

"Please, Mummy! Please can we go?!"

"Well, why not?"

"Great! Oh wow, I can't wait to see the Redbeard's Cove!"

"We'll have to leave pretty early to catch the sunrise lighting it all up, but it really is a sight."

"Sounds lovely, maybe I could pack a picnic?"

"A pirate picnic!"

"A pirate picnic for my little pirate."

"I love you, Mummy. Well done. You're doing much better now."

"Thank you, darling. I don't think I'll be losing any more points. I might just go and check on the doctor if you guys are okay here?"

"We'll be fine, Mummy. We were actually in the middle of a story."

"Oh well, I'm very sorry to have interrupted. I'll check back in a while."

I veered around them and the conversing clusters as I tried to make my way to the centre of the room. But every avenue seemed to be blocked. It felt like a moving maze. I began to feel a strange sensation slowly flushing through me. It reminded me of that feeling of an anaesthetic wearing off or of a self-induced fruit juice comedown from an overzealous portion of stropharia cubensis. It was like the tide was going back out, like a numbness was leaving me. It was almost like putting your glasses on in the middle of a film, everything looked slightly different, as if the details were only now coming into view. There was a familiarity about it all, the people, this place, this moment, but I couldn't reach it,

I couldn't really see it, I couldn't figure out exactly what it was. As I tried to find it everything all seemed to swirl around and collide into itself like I was watching the scene through some melting kaleidoscope. I felt a motion sickness and the feeling of being put under rise up again. Where was that fruit juice? Then my feet lifted above the ground as my body curled around something solid. I didn't care what it was. I just held on, coiled around my buoy.

"Hey, you still here? Still with me?"

"I... I think so."

"You can't let it drown you. You're at sea for a reason, but it won't be forever."

"What? What do you mean?"

"Take inspiration from your courageous sea pup there. They don't get much braver."

I watched as I saw him enthralled in the web of wonder weaved for him, his eyes alight with delight. He was not on this plain, this world. He had left, he had travelled somewhere else, escaped this prison. My little Houdini. He was inspirational. All children were.

"You're right. He is inspiring."

"I think they show us what we can be, what we were. We've already been that brave, we just forgot."

"We just had to grow up to deal with the big stuff."

"And how did that work out? We're all still controlled by our fear and to be honest I don't of a more terrifying experience of the unknown than being born. I mean, the way I see it these little guys are on the biggest trip of all time. They're just suddenly here, no explanation, nothing. They don't know why or what's going to happen, but yet they're still just chilled with it, just surrendering to it all, no existential crisis whatsoever. It really just blows my mind how they can be so cool with everything without understanding a thing. So really, I think it's our job, all of us big people, to make sure their trip doesn't go bad, be their designated driver. Especially seeing as most of ours did. They need us. After all we are the hosts of this enormous party that they've just wandered into. So we gotta be hospitable, you know, show them where the snacks are, the dip, the drinks, the bathroom. We've got to give them the tour. To them we really are the tour guides, these esteemed ambassadors for this unknown world and so we've really got to welcome them into it, don't you think? Jesus, how could we not? These little guys are the bravest there is, they at least deserve the best tour we can give them. I mean, they literally have no context for anything and yet somehow they're not totally freaking out. You've got to respect them for that. I don't think many of us adults would fare so well submerged in the same depth of unknowns. Yet there they are, just accepting it all, accepting every random thing that enters their reality as just part of the experience, part of the ride, just part of this mad trip they've found themselves on that, by the way, they have no reason not to believe will last indefinitely. Shit, they're fucking heroes. And we're the ones that think they need to be taught? I think we've got it a little backwards. You know I remember as a kid thinking that we should be asking babies things as soon as they can answer. They're the ones just back from wherever we came from. They know stuff that we can never know. Just look at them, the way they handle themselves and their new reality. It's more than inspiring, it's inspiriting. There's something truly magical about them. They've got something going on that we just don't, something we lost, something we traded for experience and knowledge, to help protect us in this big bad world. Well I don't think it's worked. They're doing fine without any of that stuff, not anxious at all that they don't know the all. And here we are, ever thirsty for information, worried we don't have enough of it, won't get enough of it, stressing ourselves sick that we're behind everyone else. These guys are continually surrounded by people who know way more stuff than they can even imagine and they're okay with that. They don't fret over needing to understand it all. In fact they don't exhibit many of the hurdles that we throw in our path. They don't stress or procrastinate, they just do and be. They're little Zen monks, little baby Buddha's. And, you know, their magic really is infectious, you can't help but be yourself when you're around them. Maybe because they don't expect anything from you. They just welcome you and want to play, and you're always left lighter from their company. It's like their fluid sense of reality is contagious and you just get sucked in. Perhaps it's also that faint sense of remembering they impart, that feeling of something important you once knew, something beautiful that got mislaid along the way. I don't know, but when you see that immense purity of innocence unashamedly existing it reaffirms your belief in the humanity of humanity. It makes you realise we were all born that way, we were all free once, we were all ourselves. We just got lost, that's all."

"But how do we find that self?"

"We just have to realise that the other self isn't real. We just need to see the value of our lost selves, then we'll start to return."

"It's all so tragic really, isn't it?"

"I think more poetic actually, majestically poetic. Remember depth of emotion and experience is created by the distance travelled from joy. The greater the distance the more elevated its return, the more meaningful it is, the more existence it holds."

"But surely that doesn't include everything?"

"Woven within every thread are more threads woven within more threads. The story is weaved to complete the circuit, to reach the crescendo. Every beginning has an end, and every end a beginning."

I smiled at his smile. Although I did not understand what he meant, it sounded nice. Maybe there really were no such things as loose ends. Maybe everything was for a reason. How peculiar my thoughts would seem to the girl who had woken up here. They would have seemed so foreign, not my own. But, in truth, were they really more my own than I would care to admit?

Too big a bite for now. Maybe instead something a little more bitesize. I looked around and saw Missy standing up to go to the bathroom. It was time to tie up a loose thread that needed mending. I turned to go towards the doctor, who looked to be still out for the count, when a gloopy guilt filled me. It seemed to pour concrete into my legs and halt my advance. I couldn't, not yet, not now. Instead of facing my remorse I took a cowardly stroll around the room, though as I walked about I felt a bizarre lack of movement as if I were on a treadmill. I was, of course, moving but I felt like I was moving slower than I should have been, like I wasn't really getting anywhere. What would treading water on solid ground be called? Treading ice? Is that like treading on thin ice? What does that even mean? Oh you better be careful, you're treading on thin ice there! Meaning what exactly? That you're pushing it to the extreme? Pushing things to their very limit? Taking the piss? Out of what? Life? But how is that even possible? How could you get one over on life? How could life be any one's fool? It just is what it is. You can't dodge or deceive life. Just like you can't race ahead or fall behind it. You can't help but be in the centre of it at all times. Then why do I always feel like I'm behind, like it's against me and where I want to go, where I want to be? Why does life's direction always seem so different from my own? Does life really know best? Like a child, am I showing my immaturity by questioning my parent's wisdom? Is that all we're doing, just trying to get one up on our guardian, trying to dupe them, do our own thing and not listen when we're being told what's best for us? Perhaps we need to finish growing up and stop pretending that we already have. Just because we've stopped growing physically does not mean we have stopped mentally, emotionally or spirituality. Maybe we never do. Maybe it's time to take responsibility for ourselves, for our lives, for our happiness. Time to stop blaming everything on everything else. Maybe then we'll see where we are, what we are and maybe find some meaning to it all, whatever that means. But, what *does* it mean?

"Your cogs look like they're generating something."

"I was just thinking about meaning."

"Meaning to what?"

"Existence."

"Ah. The big one."

"So?"

"So what?"

"So what is the meaning?"

"Which one?"

"What do you mean which one? The only one!"

"Well there is the over and the under."

"Of course there is. Alright, well give me the under one first."

"Okay. Well, under the parasol of this reality meaning is not fixed. It is fluid. It flows into everything giving it purpose, a reason for existing. Everything has meaning in every moment. That's why it is."

"Okay, so whatever you are experiencing is the reason for that experience, therefore the meaning. So what's the over?"

"I think the over meaning of existence is to give existence meaning."

"Isn't that just answering a question with a question or just mirroring the question?"

"Interesting that you see it that way."

"Is there any other way?"

"My life has brought me to the point where that feels like truth to me."

"But it doesn't tell you anything. It's like saying, why did you bake the cake? To have the cake baked."

"It's not quite the same, but it doesn't matter."

"No, I want to know. Tell me."

"Alright. I believe we've done all this to give meaning to our original timeless existence. Kind of like a holiday makes you appreciate home. The meaning of existence is to give existence meaning."

"Okay... I feel like half of my mind is with you, but it's the day dream half and the signal is a little crackly at the best of times."

"Maybe there's a reason for that."

"For what, the signal being crackly?"

"Yeah, maybe because even though you've finally decided it's time to change the frequency and listen to a new station, when you turn the dial to the frequencies beyond what you know, all you can find is static. Even though you've pushed to the edge of your comfort zone, with the old station still barely audible, you are still out of range of the new one. It lies just beyond the static. But the further you inch towards it, the fainter your old station becomes. And when it disappears entirely, the panic that'll you'll never be able to find it again forces you to turn back."

"Maybe you're right. It's that jumping over the void thing again isn't it?"

"Yep. So now why don't you tell me what is it that we're all searching for?"

"I don't think that's really a question I can answer."

"Why not?"

"Because I can't possibly speak for all of humanity."

"You can't?"

"Of course not!"

"Well, how about you just give it a try, just for fun?"

"Leo, what do you want me to say? Abstract words like 'liberty' and 'freedom'?"

"Why do you think they're abstract?"

"Because they have no sustainable or attainable meaning."

"Of course they do, and they are attainable."

"They're just words."

"Are they? Is that all they are? You don't think they're anything beyond the sounds their letters make?"

"I think their meaning is too vast to quantify."

"Yes, but I also think their meaning is the simplest there is."

"I think your thinking is too simple."

"Maybe I am simple."

"I didn't mean that."

"I know what you meant. But I have no problem with being simple. It's far easier than being complicated."

"I think humans can't be anything but complicated."

"I think we are the ones that complicate our simplicity."

"I don't know if you're seeing the big picture here. Life is infinite complications."

"Yes, life is, but we're not."

"How can you say that? We're all so different so how can we hold the same simplicity?"

"Because we are."

"Are what?"

"Because we just are."

"Are what?"

"Are ourselves."

"You're spiralling out on me again."

"We are existence. We are life. We are awareness. It's no more complicated than that. It's within that where we shade it all up."

"Shade it all up? What does that mean?"

"In order for light to be something other than itself, be different from what it is, it has to obscure parts of itself. It has to shade itself to see itself, to experience itself from the shade. Okay, imagine a balloon. Its round and full. When you see other shaped balloons all they are is a limited version of the original balloon. They become something else because sections, parts of the balloon are eliminated. This process of deconstruction is the construction."

"Are we still talking about the same thing?"

"You don't think so?"

"I think we're having a parallel conversation."

"Isn't that what most conversations are?"

"I don't think so."

"Well, think about it. We engage in conversations primarily to be heard, to express ourselves and to feel someone witness our expression, rarely to listen and learn. It's the easiest, simplest and most convenient method of creativity, of artistic self-expression. Though unfortunately due to our creative constipation we seem to, more often than not, choose quantity over quality. It's also the number one tool of choice to help reaffirm our precarious position, our personal perspective and of course, our selected selves. It is a bit of a schade that conversing is used more to confirm our beliefs rather than to search for the belief we currently deny ourselves."

"And what belief is that exactly?"

"The belief that our current beliefs are not enough, that there's more, much more that lies hidden from us."

"Hidden? Where?"

"Behind our current beliefs."

"So you're saying that I should just stop believing what I believe to be true?"

"Only if your truth does not satisfy you."

"I suppose it has left me more dissatisfied than satisfied."

"The reason for your dissatisfaction is that you know deep down that a version of you must exist who is able to be fully satisfied with life. However, because of the high walls of your current beliefs, you are incapable of seeing and receiving the wisdom necessary to set you free. Put simply, true wisdom will never survive the distortion it will be subjected to as you sieve out anything which threatens your current truth."

"So what should I do?"

"The opposite."

"The opposite of what?"

"Of what you have been doing, thinking, and believing to be true."

"But how?"

"By loosening the grip you have on your perceived truth of reality. Consider new ideas. Be open enough to receive them. Make space available and life will help fill it. By just being open to a new truth, one that truly resonates with you, one that seems more familiar, more real than anything you have previously encountered will show you more than a thousand years of repetitive thought. There is nothing to risk by trying, by sampling the new. You won't diminish, you won't disappear, you won't lose, you'll only gain. It waits for us all. All we have to do is make room for it."

"That sounds hard though. And how do I even do it? How will I know what to do? What if I can't do it?"

"That, there, is a perfect example of your current belief system's security alarm kicking in. Immediately pushing and putting you down, suffocating your wonder, your curiosity, your chance for truth, telling you that it can't be done, that you can't do it, that you're not strong enough."

"Oh."

"But don't worry. Just by questioning your beliefs, you open yourself up to the answers that have been denied to you, blocked by those very beliefs all your life."

"Will I ever know the answers?"

"Yes."

"Can't you just tell me?"

"I am telling you."

"I know, I know, but practically what should I do?"

"Little by little you just remove what currently stands in the way of your happiness, and then little by little you will experience more of it. This is your arc. You must become aware that at every turn our current beliefs hinder the presentation of life's wisdom because what we are presented with does not confirm for us what we currently hold as truth. It is only by stepping beyond the current unhappy version of ourselves to a version who understands the unfolding reality around us, who is in union rather than in conflict with what happens, that we will begin to lead lives which are in sync with our design and the greater design of that which gave rise to us."

"Wow. Okay, so what does that feel like?"

"You know, you've felt it."

"Only flickers. And I don't think I ever fully went to the core, to the deepest I could go. I chickened out a bit. It was a little too much. But, anyway, I was never really there long enough to have much awareness of it. Please. I'd really like to hear it in your words, I kind of like them."

"Alright, but these words that you kind of like may not do themselves justice. The right ones don't really exist, so you have to rummage around for similar parts in order to try and construct some kind of a whole. Okay, well, it's like electricity fills the air, like it comes out of hiding from behind the atoms, from within them, wherever it had hidden itself away. As if light isn't afraid to show itself anymore. Like it's finally safe to completely stretch out, to emerge. Everything looks different, although nothing has changed. But it's like St. Elmo's fire is burning all around you, lighting everything up, igniting your reality in a way you never believed was possible, and you feel just as much a part of it all, of the magic, because you know, you know you're from the same place. It's like you suddenly awake, as though from a dream, only the dream stands apart from you as everything you have ever experienced as your life. Every weight of every worry, which was tied to this life you have been calling your own, now suddenly drops and you experience an elevation which you never even imagined possible. You joyfully become aware that this lightness of being is not something new but the oldest state of being that there is. You realise the heavy, serious business of your life and everything that you have been busy with in an effort to escape anxiety, has only been pushing you further and further into it. You suddenly see this life of yours, this thing that was the most important matter conceivable, as just another pebble on the beach, as just something that you possess, that belongs to you, not the other way round. It is not who you are any more than your face is. You realise that to hold the belief that all you are is your life, is the very thing that restricts you to it. You suddenly recognise that all your life is just a sliver of eternal existence, a star in the sky to be wondered at, enjoyed and, hopefully, perhaps to make a wish upon. You finally understand that the joy that accompanies this occupation of yourself is simply what remains when the agitation you have mistaken for aliveness is shown for what it really is, a sheet of security, the only thing currently standing between where you are and where you belong, as peace without a cause."

"How can you ever come back from that?"

"You don't. Well not fully. It is impossible after such an insight to return to a deeply subjective view of the reality unfolding around you. On the surface reality has not changed but the way in which you relate to it has now changed forever."

"And you really believe that this type of insight is available to everyone?"

"Of course. We are all integral parts of the reality I have just described and as we will soon realise spiritual hierarchy is simply a myth to be dispelled. We are all equal in the eyes of the universe. True reality doesn't play favourites. If it did, well then objective reality would be reduced to a subjective one. Dualism only exists in our consciousness as the illusion of separation from the source of all things. The idea that we could somehow exist on one side of an undefinable vacuum with the source of all things on the other is just, well, completely nonsensical."

"Like thinking ice and clouds are not made of water because they look different."

"Yes."

"I feel like there's two worlds in front of me. Two realities. And both sides are calling the other out as a figment of my imagination. I know which feels the warmest, the most natural and familiar. But it's my fear from the other which prevents me from completely falling. I suppose it's like that walking through hell and heaven thing. Would you prefer to be delusional and happy or delusional and sad? It's not going to come easy, is it?"

"It'll come as easy as you allow it to."

"But it's so hard. You have to set sail and really leave your world behind in the hopes of finding another. But what if you don't? What if you get lost? What if you can't find your way back?"

"Would you even want to?"

"I would, if I were lost."

"But how do you know you will get lost if you've never even hoisted up your anchor?"

"Because there's always a chance."

"You really have to face yourself and ask the question, what is the worst that can happen? What is it that you're so worried you'll lose?"

"My sanity."

"Your perceived sanity you mean. Which has got you where? Leading a life of coping and managing and struggling and surviving? How can that not be something to be risked?"

"Because it's all I have, all I know."

"But is it?"

"It's what I have known the longest."

"It's what you remember knowing the longest. It is a personal decision to make a personal quest. Nothing or no one can force or convince you. You can't go unless you want to. You have to follow your gut, what is it telling you, what is it attracted to, pulling you towards, you just have to sense what feels natural and right and then you'll know what to do. As you become more attuned to listening to it, understanding it, the more you will feel it. If your stomach turns at something, it is not for you. If it leaps at it, then it is. My little leapling. Only you can find your way, only you can sense which direction to go, only you hold the compass. All you have to do is follow it, go towards what feels right, trust yourself and that self will show you. You are your own guide, so allow yourself to be guided. Go follow the trail of breadcrumbs. Welcome the next scene as if it were your own. Because it is, it cannot belong to anybody else. Every scene you enter is all yours, it cannot be anything else but your own. You are the only one holding that camera lens from that exact position so instead of worrying about if it's good enough or trying to look through others, just keep it clean and enjoy your window to the world because that is what it is. It is your window, your portal to existence, to awareness, to a subjective reality, to real life. We are given a pair of portholes to peep through on this trip of an existence called life. So look through them, watch life, watch it unfurl and grow into something that it wasn't. It is a miracle, all of it. You are witnessing a miracle unfold before your very eyes. It is magic. Stop believing that it is a trick, it isn't. It is a wonder and it is happening every second of every day. All for you. All for you to notice it. All for you to live it, so live it."

My feet began walking. I looked around the room, took the whole scene in as one entity, one being, one moving photograph. It all looked so cinematic, so perfect. Every face and every wall, all of it, it all seemed to work. Like it couldn't have been anything else. My beautiful boy was laughing with his entertainer, Missy was talking with her smiling girls, the project fix TV gang were joking together. Everywhere people were just being people, though they seemed more alive than ever before. I was seeing them as more alive. I was seeing them. I saw the doctor, he looked so peaceful in his slumber. I was glad he had been able to stop his whirring mind. Part of me now felt that I hadn't made a mistake. Part of me felt that it was impossible to. Part of me knew something new. And it felt good. I felt good. I felt light. I felt aware. Was this presence? Had I found it? It wasn't so hard, it wasn't so scary. I was still me. I was still the same conscious awareness perceiving but for some reason I wasn't receiving the stream of muddled words which had always clouded my perception. I felt clear. Everything felt clear. For the first time I really felt a complete lightness of being. And there was no reason for it, it was just itself. I had to make sure I remembered this. I couldn't forget. All I had to do was remember to be open, keep my barriers down, walk in a straight line, keep my insides weightless, remove the gravity from myself. Just keep open. But what if I forgot? What if I couldn't remember how to get back? I started feeling a little sick. It was okay. I was okay. But what if I wasn't? I felt a wave of nausea on the horizon. No, I was okay. Everything was okay. Saliva was building up in my mouth. No. No, I was okay. I felt cold. Then too warm. Then dizziness slowly surrounded me. I rested my eyes on the wall of writings, trying to steady myself, but that only made it worse. That stupid wall was mocking me, taunting me for my failure. Were we really going to die in here? Was this really where it was going to end? Was this show all about the final curtain, some grotesque standing ovation in some office somewhere? I felt the room begin to tumble, begin to fall. But I couldn't trust my senses, my mind, my thoughts. Where was Leo?

What was happening to me? Every step I took felt like it had its own gravitational field, its own rules of physics. I couldn't find my balance. Then I noticed my breathing. It felt strange, alien, so unnatural. I was certain that if I didn't remember to breathe I would forget. What if I forgot how to breathe? I tried to calm myself but I couldn't. It felt like my mind was out of sync with what was happening, like it was a step behind or ahead of it. I looked for Leo, but couldn't see him. I felt ill, seasick, like child sitting in the back of a hot car. I was going to be sick. I climbed to the bathroom and closed the door, resting my head on it trying to regain some balance, trying to realign myself with the moment.

"You don't need to steady yourself, it's just your thoughts that are unbalancing you."

I felt a cracking of my perception. Reality seemed to be inverting into itself. What was happening? The motion sickness was immense. Every time I thought a thought to try to rebalance, nausea smothered me. Nothing was working. I had no other choice but to ignore the compulsion to steady myself and allow my core the freedom to turn. I disregarded every instinct in my body that was screaming, demanding me to halt all proceedings. I refused to allow my mind to take back control and I refused to accept that there was anything I could do about the situation. I was not going to look behind that shield and wonder what was going to happen next. I was not going to try to protect my future self. I was going to concentrate on my now self, she needed to stay in the only safe place and not move. So I didn't. Paused, frozen within the moment I found myself becoming to a belonging I didn't understand, existing within an existence I couldn't comprehend, absorbing into a reality where nothing was real, yet more real than it had ever been. I felt I was waking from a dream, from a nightmare I had been having for a very long time, one which had me so under its spell I had been powerless to even recognise its illusion. Now it all just seemed so fake, so ridiculously unbelievable that I felt ashamed I had ever believed in it, so embarrassed that I'd felt anxiety from it. It felt like a prank had been exposed, but one that had lasted far too long. Relief of a truth I had long forgotten rushed out of my eyes and I began to laugh a laugh that had been buried for a forever. I tried to stop it but it just spilled out, wild projectile laughter. I stayed drenched in that absurdity for a while. It felt clean, refreshing, real. I'm sure if the room had seen me the second tranquilliser would have been administered. Was I mad? Was all this lovely lunacy the illusion? Was I completely delusional? Had the stress taken its toll, unhinging me and my hold on reality? Or were those hinges only holding me and reality together because we weren't naturally compatible, because we didn't match, so artificial bonds were needed to connect us? How did I feel? I had to trust my instincts, my intuition. I felt good, like a weight had dissipated. I felt I had touched what I knew was truth and more so, I recognised it. I had felt it before. I knew this, I knew this very well.

I opened my eyes and saw him and for a moment knew who he was. I returned to the dream but with new eyes looking into his. There was so much to say that I couldn't say anything except look through my portals of perception into his and hope he understood. I felt my essence stream towards them. But I didn't fall into their obscurity. Instead I felt myself submerge into the calm blue waters surrounding them. I dived and swam in them, felt the warm clear water cleanse me, fill me, heal me. I may have stayed there for a lifetime, I couldn't be sure. Did it even matter? Did anything anymore? Now. Now mattered. I wanted to tell him, tell him everything, everything that he had conjured inside of me, everything that I had conjured in myself. But words seemed to hold no real meaning, no weight. They just felt worn, over used. Maybe they felt incorrect because they were. Maybe there was no need for words here, no need to scuttle back to that clunky outdated method of communication for connection. Everything was full, everything was complete. And there was certainly no need to press the commentary button again. So I didn't. I decided to leave the commentator sleep. He had been working overtime for all of time, and now, it was time he retired.

Without all the noise and jam of words there was at last space to emanate. I felt I was finally allowed, finally able to completely let myself go, allow my light to shine, to radiate outwards without fear of what might happen. I now sensed a new awareness. It was of not only myself, but the moment, the whole page, the whole scene, everything, the whole of the now. It was like I knew it, remembered it and therefore couldn't be any more at home in it. It was me. It was all, it was it all. I understood that every moment is everything. How could it not be? How could it be a part? How could it be apart? I felt like I was surfing on the very most edge of the crest, barely balanced, but yet somehow still there, keeping with it, even when it barrelled, just coasting through the pit. I knew and I felt truth. This was my new reality. This was true reality. My senses seemed to ignite as I became receptive to all stimuli. I could hear, feel, nearly see the powerful energy of my heart's relentless beat, the electricity animating it. I felt its force and tenacity, its persistence, its compulsion. Its rhythm pumped and pulsed like some kind of tribal Morse code. It carried with it a message, a dream, a belief of surrender and trust absolute.

I stepped towards him. He was now close enough for me to feel the warm breeze of his breath. I imagined fluttering and dancing on its gusts of tenderness, soaring, rising, being. The sparkling spell he cast upon me intensified as it fizzed its way through my entire body severing any last ties to whatever defences I had left. Overcome by a torrent of emotions I closed my eyes and I allowed myself to let go, to finally let go to it all. I allowed my light, not the dark, to guide me, direct me, show me my suppressed self. The secret self that had been cowering in the shadows of an imposter, the deprived, starved, and beaten self that had been hiding for far too long out of fear of rejection, ridicule and a fall too great to ever survive. But now it was time to come out, now it was time to emerge, time to stop hiding my light, to stop being ashamed of its unapologetic vibrancy. It was time to enter life and the scene it had served. After so long I had finally allowed my unbearable hunger a chance to be satisfied, my hunger for connection, for closeness, for becoming.

His arms pulled my whole being towards his. There we stayed wrapped up in each other, our currents joining, completing the circuit of love, of life, of existence. Finally I had found what I had been avoiding, what I had been protecting myself from. Finally I had found what I was too scared to seek, to wish, to hope, to dream. Finally I had found myself, my freedom, my place, home. Just as I was beginning to surrender, to truly trust this feeling, another crossed its path. Loss. It came from nowhere, blindsiding me. This embrace, this wondrous seemingly eternal embrace was now tinged with a faint finality. As much as I tried to submerge it the horrendous feeling kept resurfacing. Instead of a beginning, it now seemed to feel like an end. But it wasn't. It was just my jealous mind soiling the moment, spoiling my chance for happiness, wanting me all for itself. I wasn't going to listen to it, it was not going to have my ear, not this time, not anymore. I was not going to fall for its tricks and let it ruin everything, like it always did. There was no way I was going to pay it any more attention, permit it any more airtime, let alone allow it break out of my head and into this moment. I was not going to help it manifest into this reality and let it wreak its havoc. That would be madness.

"Are you going somewhere?" I hated my weakness.

"We're all going soon."

"I hope you're right. But it's a bit early to say our goodbyes."

"This is not a goodbye. It's more of I enjoyed the hello, very much."

"You're kind of freaking me out a little here. Are you going away?"

Because of my fear of losing the moment I destroyed it, deploying a self-fulfilling self-destructing bomb of insecurity. I pulled away, awaiting for his response. He stroked my cheek with the back of his fingers.

"Hey, it's okay. We've found each other, and we won't ever be apart. I'll never be gone, I'll never leave you. I'll always be with you."

What was I doing? Why was I questioning heaven? This was not hell. I muted my mind's muttering over the possible red flags it had found. I was not going to be pushed around by fear anymore. I was not a child, I knew better. I attached an anvil to my immature insecurities and sunk them. It felt good.

Loud noises shook the room, cracking the moment. I opened the door to a vein of madness I thought we had passed. I felt transported back to where we had started. What was going on? What had happened? They were crawling all over the place like flies, like a swarm infesting the room, tearing and ripping at any edge, any corner they could. As I rushed over to my boy, others stormed passed me into the bathroom. I could hear tiles being hit and smashed with our key. When I got to him he was being shielded from all sides by his brave friend. I crouched down with them and held him tight.

"Is it nearly over, Mummy?"

I didn't know how to respond. I opened my mouth to speak but couldn't.

"You see, kid, this is the storm before the calm, like that night when that ship was ablaze with St. Elmo's fire?"

"Oh yeah. They weren't afraid of the blue fire's flames because they knew it wasn't real."

"Exactly. They didn't take the bait. And then they got to really see it's magic. And after it had finished-"

"They were rewarded with calm seas!"

"You got it. Never forget, it's the greatest storms that make the greatest seamen."

"I won't, captain."

"Now I can't remember, did I yet tell you how I lost my eye?"

"Oh no, not yet. I definitely would have remembered that."

"Well it's a long one, so you'll have to listen very carefully."

Like a hypnotist, he managed to put my son under and bring him to a reality far, far away. He sat behind me against the wall keeping his one eye on the room as my boy watched his story unfold from my shoulder. I stared at the room crumbling before us. What on earth had happened while I was away? What could possibly have caused this complete collapse? The store cupboard was being ripped out, the carpet pulled up in all directions, dust and debris were flying everywhere. The large sound proofing panels on the wall were being torn down. Some started pulling and tearing at one of the panels the writings were on. They were initially stopped but then as more came they continued together in an act of defiance against the room.

As the large panel fell, so did the faces of the vandals. Like a bizarre domino effect people around the room stopped where they stood as they saw what was behind it. I couldn't see what broke the fever, but when they began to step away from the wall, I saw. There, underneath those red writings was something even more terrifying, even more unnerving, even more unbelievable. We thought we had seen it all, that we were desensitised, but now, now we realised we were not. Behind those old wall panels was not a door or an escape or anything new at all. It was exactly, to the letter, what was there before. It was those same red writings.

The wall of reality will fall...

"How...?"

"It can't be."

"But-"

"It's an exact replica! That's impossible!"

"How could they...Why?"

"What does this even mean?!"

"It means we are not the first. It means this has all happened before."

"Oh my God."

"We are in game, just pawns in a game that has been played over and over again and will be played again and again."

The room fell into a deep stillness. Not because we were calm but because seeing those second set of red writings was just too much to digest. How could there be two identical sets of writings, and why? For what possible purpose? Had this really all happened before? It was like a distorted version of Eternal Recurrence. If there were people before us, why leave the old writings there? For us to find? To let us know we weren't special? To make a point of it? To really hit home that we were just another number, figure, result? Were we really just digits on a page? Did it all boil down to that? Was that all we were, all we were meant to be? Was that our sole purpose, our reason, our meaning? I couldn't accept that. It couldn't be true. We were not faceless bodies, these lifeless objects, just puppets on someone else's string. I refused to entertain that truth. So I had to find another.

My mind reacted wildly to this new unknown. It began to over stimulate itself producing any and all possible, not necessary probable, truths; just anything and everything available. Had we been here before? Were we the ones who those hidden set of writings had belonged to? Had we lived this nightmare before? Would we live it again? Was this our life? Had it always been like this? Was this reality? Was this all life had ever been? Was everything else just a dream? Had we dreamt our lives? Were they ever real? Were they only as real as the reality they existed within? Just a false memory, an implanted past, whose sole task was to create context? All to make this more believable, more palatable, to make the deception complete? Just to make us believe we were something we were not? So then, who were we?

A man began scratching and ripping at the wall of replica writings. Everyone just stared as his nails tore and broke, smearing blood over the new writings. No one stopped him. He, like most, had been completely alone. He had nobody here who knew him before the room, no one to confirm his identity, his life, his existence. He had no one to vouch for him, protect him, comfort him. We all just watched, hoping he would not succeed in finding what we refused to believe was there. But he did succeed. And then once he had collapsed down in front of it, he began sobbing violently, baring his tortured soul to a room full of strangers. What an unwavering and unnerving testament to the power of this lifeless room. It could break a man without doing a damn thing. Maybe this guy was the most successful person in the room, and maybe not just in his work, but in every aspect of his life. Maybe he had somehow found the balance to it all, to his whole existence and woke up every day with a smile on his face. Maybe he was a motivational speaker, or even a Zen monk, maybe he was voted most likely to succeed in his graduating year. Or maybe he was just a normal guy, a simple guy who had found happiness in his life, and the room had taken it all away.

The room hadn't just stolen our lives, our world, it had stolen our reality and our grip on it. It had stolen our perspective, our standing and our footing, our beloved bannisters of support. It had taken it all away and left us fragile, unbalanced and raw. But somehow the room's greatest power was that it had managed to steal the very thing we thought could never be stolen - our selves. It had just callously thrown them away, they did not serve as any use. It just left us abandoned, cold and fragile on the side of the road, begging for mercy. We were not the same people we were before the room; that version of ourselves had died. It had been strangled, murdered by these four unmoving walls. We had all mourned for so much, but it is the mourning of oneself that is the hardest, the most confusing. Because how can you? Who does the mourning? Who were we now? Who were we before? And what would we become? Internally abstract questions were breeding wildly, although externally, no one said a word.

Chapter Six

Did we now feel more or less special? It appeared that we had been chosen, selected to be a part of whatever this was, yet now there seemed to be strong possibility that we were not the first. There could have very well been people here before us. My mind could not help but wander down dark alleyways to where their fate had led them. What had happened? Where were they now? Had they done better than us? Or worse? Was that why this all had to be done again? Did they not yield the intended results? Had we? I looked around the ceiling, the corners, the lights, and saw others doing the same. Were we really being watched? The whole thing just seemed so ridiculous, so utterly preposterous. We were all normal people, nothing special. In fact we were such a mix, such an assortment of lives, that you couldn't have had a more speckled segment of society. Maybe that's what they had wanted, a sliver of the spectrum, a full band of what kind of people our supposedly civilised first world had produced. But for what possible purpose? There were no obvious tests to perform. We were just sitting here, rationing our food, trying to pass the time, trying to keep sane. Maybe that was it. Maybe that was the test. All this effort just to see how frail our clasp on sanity was? Maybe to see if we ever really had one at all. Were we always just one room away from madness? Was everything really that tenuous, that delicate, that it could all just crumble, just fall at the first sign of a shake? What did that mean? How could something real ever falter? How could a truth ever be found out as a lie? How could something eternal ever end? What were we protecting? Did that mean then that the fragile reality we had built up around us was, in fact, not protecting us at all but instead preventing us from the truth? Were we hiding from the truth? Had we spent our lives avoiding this question, too scared of what the answer would force us to do, too scared of what we would become? What was the root of that fear? Losing all that we know? Or worse, inescapable insanity? Did we have to walk through the valley of madness in order to find sanity? Were we there already? Were we here to cross it?

We were here, wherever that was, not in the room next to madness, but in it; all of us bubbling together in this cauldron of a reality, everything peeled and chopped away, boiling in a collective soup of fear and uncertainty. Stripped bare, stripped from our identity, stripped from our coping mechanisms, all those carefully positioned handrails which helped to get us through each day, just abandoned and left exposed. Exposed. That's exactly what it felt like. We felt exposed. Like a cut you can't cover, can't protect. Like those horrible dreams where you find yourself naked in the middle of a stadium. Just lost, lost in the wild wild.

Was this the point of it all? To see how a human copes on a stage without their chosen backdrop and props? To expose the actor? To see who they really were? To see who was left? Had we been freed from the scaffolding that had been keeping us up? And was that a good or a bad thing? Would we collapse without it? Were we more than our procured identity? Were we more than our repeated patterns, our routine routines? Was that all our lives consisted of? Was that all we consisted of? What were we without them? What was left? Are we merely a collection of learned responses to stimuli? Just a cluster of programmed actions and reactions? Are we just robotically going through the motions, simply an automaton with a beating heart? Are we more than just a compilation of acquired knowledge, skills learned and memorised moments passed? Is that all a human being is? Is that all a human being can be? Is that really all we were intended to be, created to be?

It cannot be true, it simply cannot. So why do we continue trying to be something we are not? All the time trying to fit a square into a circular hole. We feel constricted, pressured, awkward because we don't fit. No matter how hard we push we will never fit into a mould of something we are not. Our obsession with conformity, equating it with words like perfection and beauty is beyond detrimental to our growth, confidence, security and evolution. Perfection has been placed on a pedestal as the climax of achievement of self. And we strive to embody this image no matter the cost, even at the price of our own happiness. It is because we can't see the perfection in everything that we are forced to conceptualise it. But this is merely a conceived perception of perfection. Perfection does not always denote the most polished, the smoothest or the most streamlined. More often than not it is the irregular, the unusual, the original and the unique that conjures the most beauty. Nature is never formulaic in its formula. Every petal is painted, every tree tailored made, every bird and bee bespoke, every cloud customised. Yet, although we come from this creative chaos we refute our nature, instead preferring to adapt to our amended version of what we deem to be perfection. We strive to be quicker, faster, more efficient. But more efficient at what? Leading lives that we're not even starring in? Sailing ships we're not even aboard? Eating cake we're not even tasting? How can it be that we are continuing the charade without ever stopping, wondering or questioning the why? Never pausing the production line to ponder on what we have become, what we're striving to be and what we really are?

Why are we wearing a mask of machine? To increase efficiency? To decrease humanity? To help us stifle our individuality, our emotions, our essence? For what purpose? To dilute our light? To make it easier to conform to moulds we don't fit? Why are we being damaged in order to get us through the square hole? For what? So that broken beings come out the other side to then be discarded and deemed not worthy? How can this be? How can the world continue to create structures whose only purpose is conformity, when we are all individual in our being, wondrous in our uniqueness and magical in our originality? Aren't we missing a trick? Aren't we misusing the tools we have at our disposal? Disregarding innate ability is not very clever. It's like asking a tortoise to tail a cheetah. Shouldn't ability, talent and aptitude at least be considered? Isn't it far smarter to use things in the way they were intended to be used? We are all different notes on the piano and to compose a piece the right notes must be used at the right time. We can't just keep hitting the same key and call it a tune. Just because we are all part of the same species does not mean we are clones and so should not be treated thus. We are not machines. Not in any way. And we cannot emulate them. We will always fail by measuring ourselves against them. A bird is a terrible fish but it is a marvellous bird. We need to realise what we are in order to be what we can be.

We are not robots. We were not created to be efficient. We were created to be ourselves. Our unique selves. We are all part of the rainbow. And a rainbow can only show it's full brilliance when all the colours are proudly shining as themselves, not hiding or trying to be another, just dazzling within their own splendour. Perfection is not a faultless, flawless existence. Perfection is imagination. And imagination is everything, rough and smooth, hot and cold, light and dark. Imagination is it all and revels in the most bizarre, the most eccentric, the most outlandish and unusual. It is far more challenging to imagine the complex than the simple, far more amusing to create the elaborate than the plain, so then surely it is more interesting, more exciting that we exist in such a complicated existence? Isn't it then the imperfections which make our world what it is, make our world beautiful? Surely it is the perfect imperfect which makes life perfect.

Thoughts grew and scattered seeds which themselves grew into ideas and concepts, generations of branching beliefs joined together, their intermingling roots linking, connecting, soaking up the waters of wisdom flowing in rivers of realisation. I felt my brain rewire, reprogram or perhaps, more accurately, deprogram. It was like just by entering new terrains of thought, new corridors of contemplation, my mind had somehow rerouted all roads towards the new territory. This new land, this untrodden, unexplored place felt familiar, comfortable, safe. But unlike all those other members of this moment's clan, I felt I had reached this on my own. I was not thrust here, but more journeyed, trekked and wandered to it. This gave me confidence that I could return whenever I wished, instead of waiting for another's. Though that did not seem to matter much now as, serendipitously, there seemed to be no escape from this plain, like this was the new default setting. That made me feel even more secure and even more comfortable, maybe even more in control, like I could handle this thing, but on my terms.

Then things began to change. A rushing feeling was building up inside of me, a force, a tugging and a pulling of my being, it was trying to separate me, it felt, I felt like I was being exorcised. I tried to fight it, to hold on. But the intensity just grew, increasing its strength. This energy flowing through me was like a current, but so powerful, so focused, I felt like the EAC was flowing through me. I knew I couldn't hold on, I had no chance to implement my own will. Was this punishment for feeling the regaining of control? Suddenly I felt an increase, like I was in a falling elevator, but horizontally. I left the bathroom, but not through the door, in fact more precisely, it left me. The sensation of speed exited and was replaced by its opposite. I felt I was suspended in time and space and everything within. There was nothing, no light, no mass, no anything. Then a blinding light reversed the polarity with a jolt of clarification hitting, shifting my perception even more, but this time, just enough for me to see through all the keyholes at once. I saw through them all to the very end. But no, it couldn't be? Could it really be true? Was I..? I was barely able to repeat the thought in my head, it was too crazy, too outrageous, but yet... No, I couldn't even entertain it. Too much, too much, it was all too much. I felt a tsunami of nausea rise, my breath was rushing out far too quickly. I ran to the bathroom and expelled all the answers and all the questions, all the anxiety and all the nervousness and, of course, my empty stomach.

I drooped down the side of the cold porcelain bowl and just panted, panted like I was out of breath from running. Maybe I was. Maybe I had been running all my life. Too afraid to stop, too afraid to get off the treadmill for fear I'd fall behind. But fall behind to where? I was the only one walking my road. Why did I feel I had to run it? Who was I against? What was I chasing? Or was it that I felt like the one being chased? Or was it both? But what was I so scared of? What was I running away from? Was it life? Living? Being? Or maybe myself? Maybe it was myself that I had been running from, maybe it was myself that I had been chasing. All this time it was me that had been forcing the chase, the devil and the angel stuck in a loop, caught in my own trap, chasing my tail. Was it really all me? I don't know what I had been doing or why but slumped down in the corner of that old cubicle I felt like I finally stopped.

I didn't move. I literally did not move. I stayed completely still in the gargoyle position I had slumped into. It wasn't a comfortable one, it was cold and hard, but I still didn't move. I didn't care. I just stayed motionless, immobilised by the realisation that I had been running a race that I didn't even know I was in. I stared at the old tiles and the dirty grouting framing them, stared at their grubby uniformity, catching my breath. Every pant felt like such an extraction of grief, a great, great grief. Grief for my former self, my self-inflicted pain and anguish, my sorrow and my loss. There were no details, no nametags on my discarded baggage, they were anonymous.

There was such an unbelievable release of weight, weight that I didn't even know I had been carrying. As it began to lift I suddenly felt like I was in the aftermath of some traumatic ordeal. One that had been haunting me, one that had lasted for many, many years. One that had somehow stayed dormant in its dominance, ruling under the radar. I had been given an awareness that something had happened to me, but not enough to know what. My mind drew blank after blank. I knew I had to stop straying down 'the path of possibilities', but although the medieval stocks had been unlocked and I was free, I wished more than anything to have it back just to get a look at what it was. No, this desire, this curiosity was a trick, a backdoor burglary. I was not going to be so easily fooled. I had to distance myself from my quicksand mind. It only provided false platforms with feigned footing. I had been liberated and nothing could imprison me again.

My mind stilled, my breathing calmed, and to my surprise, I began to cry. My tears contained so much sorrow, so much repressed pain, so much false bravery, the last remnants of a tortured soul. I let go of all the gravity that I had bottled inside me, let it all fizzle out. I did not need it anymore to steady me, to keep me weighted, to keep me safe. After the tide had gone out, carrying with it all the debris, another strange surprise followed, a small smile. The first of its kind. A real smile. An honest, genuine one, not simulated or forged like so many of my smiles had been. How sad I thought, that very likely a larger percentage of all the smiles of my life had been completely counterfeit. What a terribly sad truth. But how had that become a truth? Why had I felt the need to fake a natural response to happiness, to simulate a by-product of joy when I wasn't feeling it? Why did I feel it was so important for me to pretend, to feign my kindness, my friendliness, my happiness? For what reason? To be accepted? To have an easier life? But at what price does this ease come? A fictitious sham? To make other people feel more comfortable in their uncomfortableness? Moments of my past flashed and flushed their way through me. All those misused minutes, all those lost hours and precious days, all wasted, and for what? To keep up the phony veil of cheerfulness for all to see? Why? So that others would then feel compelled to do the same? Each veil being hung up, put out on display to hide the truth, the real reality, the real atmosphere, the real self. Why can't the world just show its true colours all of the time? Why must we all deceive and lie and forge this illusion of what is deemed the perfect life when it is clearly not? What is the point? To continue the charade, all of us together? But even if we all believe it together, even if we all believe in everyone else's act, it doesn't make it, or ours, any more true. It is all still a lie. We are all still living a lie. It is only because we are so skilful in our deception that even we have come to believe it. Why do we continue to live our lives from the outside when they can't be lived from anywhere else but the inside? The madness of the world filled me as I became ignited with a new force, a new energy, a new power of purpose. I was not going to hide anymore. I was not going to play my part in this fantasy any longer. I had a responsibility, an obligation as a member of our species to try my best to be my best. But to do that, I first had to get out. These four concrete walls were not going to stand in my way. I had been awakened to a vista I had never seen before, and then it dawned on me; that it was the room I had to thank.

I now had to face it, whatever it was, whatever it would become. I couldn't shield myself any longer. I pushed the door open to see my son eating his stashed snacks, engrossed in the animated whisperings of his eccentric pirate friend. The rest of the room was in a quiet and meditative state. People were all lost in the reality that their head was projecting. The uncovered duplicate set of writings and the triplicate set behind them tore such a hole in the wall of our reality that it had spilled an intense, surrealistic feeling into the room. It reminded me of when two mirrors are placed opposite one another and you get that weird never-ending reality of never-ending. But what is within a mirror image of a mirrored image of a mirror image? What does it capture? What does it show? Nothingness? Infinite nothingness? But how can there be such a thing? How can infinite nothingness exist?

As a child it always fascinated me. What did a reflection of a reflection of a reflection reflect? I would always come up with new ideas and ways to catch sight of the central most multiplied reflection, trying my best to catch a glimpse of the magic I knew was lying just beyond. But to truly be able to see all the way down that corridor of reflection you would have to view it from the centre, exist in it. Your point of perception would have to be in the middle of one of the mirrors, they would have to capture you. You would have to become the mirror, exist within its reality, its multiple realities. You would then get to see yourself projected and reflected in front and behind and back round again forcing a circuit, a wheel of existence, of self. Would you then be complete? But if you did exist within the mirrored reality, if it was your own, would you too be split across it? Would you feel fragmentation or completion? And what would this self look like? What would I see? Infinity? But what would forever look like? What face would it have? And what expression would that face hold? One of serenity I hoped.

Infinity, time, space. These were all words we threw around, proclaiming to own their understanding, but did we have any real idea of what they meant? Any tangible knowledge of their true essence, their true nature, their true reason for being? After a millennium of studies, were we any closer to finding out their truth, the hidden why within them? Was it imprudent to think we were? Does it serve only to hinder our development when we proclaim full understanding, when we move the unknown into the known column? Isn't it best to, with an open heart and mind, declare that nothing is truly known, nothing is concrete, that all we know is an angle of the picture, not the whole thing. Surely that way we'll always be open to receiving new knowledge, new information, new truths. If we were to view the entirety of Van Gogh's Starry Night from the perspective of one corner we would not see its magic, its inspiring beauty. We would only see the dark clouds and confusion of colour. We may well even be fearful of this perception, this reality, and we would certainly not understand it fully or partially, let alone comprehend it as a celestially celebrated painting hanging in a museum, in a city, in a country, in a world spinning around the brightest star in our sky. We cannot see the big picture from just one corner of it. We must let go of what we have to get the whole. If we cling to what we have, proclaiming it as all, believe what we see is absolute then we'll never be able to catch more. But it's our fear of being left empty handed that prevents our letting go. That corridor of transition terrifies us and keeps us away. We're so scared to be seen as an empty mind, a blank page that we'll do anything to prevent it. We think that somehow we'll be judged negatively, marked down for our lack of accumulated information and facts and figures, deemed an unfit member of society, excluded from the clan. But what clan would do that to his own clansmen? A clan built and based on insecurity and fear.

Is that our greatest folly, our repulsion of ignorance? Is that what forces us to fill our cup to its limit? But surely ignorance is only inexperience, an unfamiliarity, an unawareness. How can anyone be shunned for not experiencing something that they have not experienced? Children are not mocked for their lack of knowledge, so why have we created a hierarchy of comprehension? Surely it is in our best interest, as members of our society and ancestors of the following generations, to encourage growth and understanding, to fan the flames of curiosity and inspiration, not chastise and cast out those who are not in the know. We were all once not in any know, but with patience and kindness we were helped and taught and we learned. We must all do our part in the flowering of this world if we want it to bloom. We must all be open to each person around us, be patient and kind and genuine in all that we do and say. Any other mode of living is counter-productive, suicidal even. Though life may seem to be long at times, in reality we have very little. Its value is incomparable, and we must open our eyes to that every day, not just when it is threatened. We have our time here, as long as that may be, and it is ours. Now is our time.

Time. What is time? We all think about it every day, all the time in fact, continually checking it, planning and moulding our days around it, even sculpting our entire existence out of it. Funny how we live our lives, construct them based upon something we have no true comprehension of. We sew them into something we have never questioned, never even examined. But how can we ever truly understand time? Especially as the only means we have to relate to it is the face of a clock, a mechanical representation of our segmentation of moment. Its purpose is to attempt to capture, categorise and narrate time. In reality all we're doing is trying to keep tabs on it, trying to break it up into little palatable, digestible pieces by using an arbitrary division of one of earth's twirls. But time can never be shattered into these rudimentary components, it is never broken, it just keeps on going immaterial of what we decide that it is. It does not care what we call it, what number we have allocated to at any specific moment. It takes no notice of our need to master and control, it just keeps on moving. We cannot possibly define time by referencing a mechanical device. It can only tell you what time it is, not what time is. So what is it then? Is it simply flow and movement, existence? Is there existence without time? Does time serve to open the portal for creation? Without time would there be anything at all?

Mass and time, time and mass. Which came first? Is it another chicken and the egg conundrum? Or are we looking at it all the wrong way? Instead of who came first, who came before? One generally accepted theory of creation supposes that they were both created by a bang, twins born from the same traumatic birth. Their mother vacuum was lonely and bore them to give meaning to her existence. But then where did she come from? How did she come about or has she always existed?

Always existed, always will exist. Our time shackled linear minds find immense difficulty in grasping and grappling with such a concept as forever going backwards to meet its future self. We live with and within straight lines. We deal in beginnings and ends. To bend time and create a never ending, never beginning loop is nearly beyond our comprehension. We arrogantly believe that the only things that can hold existence are the ones that we can conceptualise. But what if there was more, much more, and we were not even aware of the tip of the iceberg? What if we were the whole iceberg and none of it all at the same time? What if we were the circle, the sphere, and the tesseract within it? What if we were an inverted black hole, the one and the many, the only and the all? What if we were God, and God was us? What if we shattered ourselves into single rays of light to experience life with subjectivity, from only one quaint point of view? What if the uncomfortable feeling of isolation, of disconnection we all felt was natural? What if it was just our understandable feelings of loss from losing ourselves in the darkness, of separation from one another, separation from the whole? What if our task was to find ourselves and then each other, to reconnect and live and be as one? What if it wasn't just words to a song? What if it wasn't just an optimistic dreamer's dream? What if it was possible? What if it were plausible? What if peace on earth was our purpose? What if it was our destiny to reflect our natural, original state of being? What if our big reason, the big why really was to create heaven on earth? What if it was our constant striving, our constant chasing for truth, for happiness, for peace, for ourselves, that only led us further away from it? What if we were already there, already at peace, at one with the universe but we just kept on leaving it, running away from it in the quest to find it? What if all we had to do was stop all the rushing and all the yearning, the grabbing and the grasping, and just stop, just sit, and be, and see the moment, see it for what it is, an opportunity, a chance, an invitation to connect, to go home? See life, existence as just an invitation to return? What if that's all we had to do, just notice the moment, acknowledge it, introduce ourselves to it, and then we would become it. What if that was enlightenment? What if it only meant becoming everything the moment held and recognising your eternal self in it? What if the very thing we have been searching for all our lives, the very thing we have killed and died for was already ours, and we just never checked our back pocket? What if all we had to do to reclaim our divinity was to just see it, to just simply accept it? But easier, far easier said, thought and pondered than done. Talking the talk isn't that hard, it's the putting one foot in front of the other and not falling that's the tough bit.

The room and its strange version of reality had changed mine forever. It had left my perception askew and though I wasn't solidly in any territory, I had certainly left my old one behind. I was in a wandering state of limbo, a kind of positive purgatory. I felt I was seeing and experiencing everything from a distance yet also from its centre. As if bizarrely and quite paradoxically the further I got from myself the closer I was to it. And possibly stranger still, I actually now felt fortunate for this chaos of a calamity that had swallowed me whole. I felt a guilty gratitude for being in the belly of the beast, for its catalytic charm and the emancipating objectivity it had beaten into me.

What was this room? What was it doing? What was its plan? As soon as it allowed us to have any kind of a footing it would immediately rip the rug of reality from beneath us. But I couldn't help feeling that it wasn't accidental. Whilst the sensation of falling was extremely unnerving, in its unbalancing it presented us with something new, something exceptional. With its momentary feeling of weightlessness in the unknown it gave us a possibility to allow ourselves to exist, even just for a second, within that space of complete indefiniteness. For a moment we were allowed a chance to see that we still existed even without anything to hold on to, no footing, no context, no perception. We were still in existence without thought, understanding or opinion on the moment. Within that feeling of uncertainty we were given a rare opportunity to trust, to trust whatever was coming next. It felt like life's trust fall and if we passed, if we believed, then something truly wondrous would be bestowed upon us.

This new crack in the room's reality had not only left a hole but its rich nourishing yolk had spilled out and split my mind in two, with every thought I never knew I had flowing between them. And it was because of this I realised that the room was not just a room, it was a teacher, a healer, a chance to restore our sight, to cure our blindness. I realised that the room was the alarm clock which had been set to wake us from the deepest darkest slumber there was, our unconsciousness.

Now that we had that literal alarm clock counting down above our heads it was time to finish the game. I now felt very differently about it. It wasn't a question of if or when we were going to get out, it was more a curiosity of how it was going to unfold, how we were going to find our rabbit hole. So, instead of swimming upstream, I was now going to try swimming with the current. I had finally decided to let go, to surrender to where this flow was going, it knew better, it was life, I was just the passenger. I wasn't going to man the wheel anymore. That was my last conscious act of freewill.

Freewill. What a curious concept. Like existence, it is such a subjective and speculative thing. If you believe you have it, how is that any different from actually having it? In a strange way isn't there comfort in not being in control, not being the sole driver, the leader, the decision maker? Just as a child is happy to hold its parent's hands trusting them to keep it safe, maybe to achieve true freedom that is what we must do, let go to life and trust it. It created you so how can it not care for you? But maybe to release ourselves from our shackles, from our room, we must first face our greatest fears. What greater fear is there than death? That universal fear hangs over our heads like a fat little demon flying about, knocking and bumping into us, reminding us of our mortality. Maybe that's why extreme sports and situations create such a high? Not only do they force you to give your full attention to the moment, be in a state of complete awareness due to the dangerous content it holds, but because you play so close to the drop off whilst not allowing fear's reins to pull you back, you feel a reward of euphoria from accidentally realising the complete futility in being harnessed. You throw your caution to the wind and the wind carries you on it. Maybe that's what we should all be doing. Maybe by not making death the be all and complete end all, you see it for what it truly is. Maybe then you see its real meaning, that it is nothing more than a changing of the guard, just a stepping stone, a portal back home. If we can conquer all our small fears and then face the ultimate with no hesitation in our hearts, then maybe life will guide us, show us the way, show us ourselves.

My thinking felt like it was being spoken to me, as if they weren't just my thoughts but something that was being shared. As if somehow I had spoken, heard and felt these words before, but not as myself. But what was this voice? And where was it coming from? Everything began to feel more real and more unreal than meaning could ever translate. My mother, her words, her eyes, her being surrounded me. Her voice and Leo's intertwined and became my own. That was the voice speaking to me. It was them, but how? Leo? Where was he?

I pushed open the door and was shockingly met with a perfect metaphor for the maddening voices in our heads. Uncertainty scrambled over confusion with fear and paranoia wrestling, all battling as they fought for dominance. But I did not share their turmoil. Their weary war was no longer mine. I was calm and still, secure amidst the insecurity. I felt a detachment from anxious thoughts, like I was finally out of their reach, too high for their clambering claws. No matter how much they grasped at me, they couldn't touch me. I had risen above them and their torment. I was no longer their prey. They were not going to extinguish my light. Instead, the room chose to extinguish its own.

The solitary candle was not enough to dispel the darkness from the room or in the minds feeding it. Our eyes needed time to adjust. I heard my son. He was laughing at his jester who had now assumed the role of ghoul, a brown blanketed one. I smiled a serene and secure smile as I turned away. I did not know what I had to do, but I knew where I had to go. It was time to confront the biggest fear of all. I walked towards it, towards the bad clock. As I stood in the middle of the store cupboard and closed my eyes the voices of the room quietened and once again I sensed the sphere of red writings surround me.

The looking glass of the door of illusion of time tock ticking over...

I looked down at the grubby grey linoleum. It hadn't been laid down so well and the edges by the doorway were curling. I bent down and tugged at the corner. It was surprisingly stubborn for such a decrepit old thing. I tugged and tugged. It felt like it was pulling against me. But I was stronger. The corner finally ripped away and I stood up pulling it back as hard as I could. Dust flew into the air turning red as it caught the dim light coming from the missing ceiling panel. When it settled, I looked at what had been uncovered. I couldn't believe it. They were so beautiful and old. Why had they been hidden there with their natural majesty concealed by such cheap artificiality? But as elegant as they were those old wooden floorboards would too have to be cast away. They were solid and strong and had been well laid, not buckling or distorting with time. I scratched my head hoping to stimulate a voice of ideas. Then behind me one arrived.

"Maybe we've finally found a use for this."

It was the short bald man and the brothers with the key. I stepped out of the store cupboard and knelt at the doorway behind them. I watched as they pulled off the wooden floor's synthetic wrapping and positioned our key. They pivoted and wiggled it back and forth, but the stiff boards were not cooperating. They had not mellowed with age. But still the three men persevered. They growled and groaned as did their adversary. Neither side was giving up without a fight. One last heave, one last push. The noise of the cracking wood sounded like the air had been torn, ripped in two. I couldn't see exactly what they had unearthed, it was too dark. But once the three of them had lifted the heavy boards away, I saw. I stared at the new ground. I stared and stared, hardly able to believe my eyes. How could it have been hidden underneath that boarding, and why? For what possible purpose? It wasn't even dusty or dirty, in fact it was perfectly polished. The look of shock on the girl's face reminded me of both a dream and a nightmare I had once had. I knelt down closer, still staring at the girl staring back. She looked different from what I remembered, more dishevelled, yet somehow more put together. She seemed older, more wizened, but it was her eyes that had aged the most. They held a distance to them like the person behind them, the entity, the awareness, was further away yet also the closest it had ever been. I thought I saw a flicker of light cross these pupils of paradox, it must have been the candlelight. So, we had finally found it, the looking glass of the door of illusion.

I saw the bald man and the brother's reflection peer over my head. Their faces were full of the same confusion. Why on earth would there be a mirrored floor? The sheer size of it, completely spotless and tilted up at the perfect angle towards us, it just didn't make any sense. How long had it been there, I wondered. How long had it been waiting to fulfil its destiny, its purpose? How long had it been hoping, wishing for someone, a reflection, a reason, meaning? How many years had it been so patiently waiting to reflect this very moment?

"What is it?"

"I don't know."

"I've never seen anything like it before."

"It's like some sort of strange silver glass."

I looked back at them, they couldn't be serious. A few others came and took a look, all concurring on the alien nature of the material that lay before them. I kept blinking, hoping that somehow this scene would reset, return to sanity. Faces poured in behind me, like heavy drops of thunder filled rain, each one crashing down, smashing at my reality. I became more and more uncertain of what I was seeing. Was I going crazy? How could they not see it, see themselves? I stared deeper into my eyes. Were they lying to me? Or was every eye blind to the truth that lay before them? Was I losing my mind? Or were they? Whose program was faulty? Had I already gone crazy and not realised it? I heard his voice before I saw his face.

"You're not crazy. They cannot see what they cannot be."

"I don't understand, they don't see the mirror. How can they not see it?"

"They can only see what they are."

"But they don't see anything?"

He stayed quiet.

"I don't understand. That's impossible. They're right there, I can see them."

"You see what you want to see."

"What? No, I can see them and their reflection."

"You see only what you are."

"I don't understand, Leo. Please just tell me why they can't see themselves."

"You already know."

"No, no I don't. What's going on? Why is this happening?"

"Calm down. It's okay, it's all going to be okay."

"But you see yourself, right? You're there. I can see you and you can see me."

I realised that I didn't have to continue our conversation in the mirror and turned around to face him. But he was not there. I looked back into the mirror. I dared not look away again.

"How? But how are you..? Leo..?"

"It's difficult to explain."

A horrendous feeling of a complete not knowing of anything began to drown me. I felt like I was balancing on a tight rope above death. That with just one false move, one wobble I would fall.

"Relax, it's okay. Nothing has changed."

"What?! Everything has! What's going on, Leo? I don't understand what's happening!"

"You will. You'll understand everything soon."

"I want to understand now."

"You can't, it hasn't finished."

"What hasn't?"

"Your story."

"My story? What does that mean?"

"It means you'll just have to wait a little longer. But don't worry, you'll always be given everything you need."

"But I need you... please."

"I'll always be with you. Please don't cry my little leapling. I'll never leave you. Whenever you feel lost, just close your eyes and stare into the space in front of them, and I'll always be there waiting for you."

"I need you now, Leo, please help me."

"I can't help you anymore. You're the only one who can break the spell."

"Spell? What? What spell?"

"The spell you have cast to keep yourself safe."

"Then why would I want to break it?"

"Because it is the wrong self you are trying to protect."

"Wrong self? Which self am I?"

"You are your only self."

"I can't understand you, Leo! Please stop speaking like this!"

"I am speaking the only way I can, to both parts of you, your shackled and unshackled self."

"But how can I be both?"

"You can't, not anymore."

"What? Leo, please, please, I can't-"

"You have to break it, it's the only way."

"Come on! Let's break it!"

"Yeah, smash it!"

"Destroy it!"

"No, no, what?! Hold on! I'm not ready! I'm too close! Leo!"

They swung the heavy key and hit the mirror hard. I turned away, I was too fragile to witness any more destruction. But when they had finished and I opened my eyes, there wasn't the shattered reality I expected to see before me. All I could see, was myself.

"That's impossible!"

"It bounced right off!"

"But it's glass!"

"It should have smashed!"

"It didn't even crack!"

"It's impenetrable!"

"It's cursed!"

"We'll never get out!"

I looked for Leo's face in the looking glass but he had gone. My heart fell to the floor, several floors below. How could he have left me? Left me to deal with whatever it was that was happening? How do you deal with something if you don't even know what it is? I didn't know, I didn't know anything. Had I ever? Just as every cell in my body seemed to be collapsing in on itself, I felt him speak me. But without words, just presence. It was as if he seemed to be coming from the mirror. I looked into the girls eyes. It felt as if he was calling me from behind them. I could feel him luring me towards their darkest centre, their beyond. I hesitated. What was hidden in the darkness? Was that where we were kept? Were we hiding there? Is that where we existed? Where the perceiver was imprisoned, trapped in a vast continuum of a void, without boundaries of space or time? I felt myself falling into the dark abyss, surrendering, not caring for consequence, knowing this was my destiny, this was what it was all for, this was what my life had all been leading up to, to this exact point, this very moment. This was my great thing. I was to lead a solo mission into the unknown, into the most known, into myself and the creator and everything else in between. Maybe I would never come back, maybe I would cease to exist, or maybe I would find the everything we had all been so desperately searching for. I knew I had to go, accept whatever path I would be taken upon, follow it to its end. I had to trust that this was the way, the only way, that there was no other. It belonged to me and I to it. We could not be separated. We could not exist without the other. All I had to do was accept that truth and allow it to accept me.

Suddenly everything felt familiar. I felt familiar. The music, my dreams, my childhood, Leo, it all seemed to connect, like it always was. As I floated in the obscurity, fragments of long lost memories flew around me. Memories of feelings and experiences in my mother's womb, the faint music and the gliding as they danced, the fizzy feeling as they made love. I remembered my simple self. I remembered the before, the feeling of being enclosed, soaked in a new reality, wanting it even though it felt so artificial, so unnatural. But why? Why would I want that? I tried to understand, but all these newly remembered moments were too disjointed, too muddled to correlate. I couldn't connect them, place or order them. It was impossible, they had no context. Why would I wish to imprison myself?

I then noticed the girl in the mirror. She looked so sad and alone. Her feelings of woe were so great, so intense. I wanted to look after her, shield her from whatever pain had been haunting her. As a tear fell down her cheek, I felt one fall down mine. I saw her pupils dilate as I remembered a shadow of a memory I had long abandoned, long forgotten, long protected myself from. But now uncloaked I felt it coming. It was resurfacing after its burial so long ago, rising up to face me, for me to face it. What face would I see? Would it defeat me? Would I survive? It felt too big. How could I fight it? How could I win? Would it destroy me?

An intensely high pitched noise shattered the moment before I could answer. My ears continued to ring the note as I opened my eyes and saw myself falling in pieces into the darkness. What was happening? Was it happening now? Had it already won? Had it broken me? Had I lost myself? What was left? Fractures of light joined my broken self as it fell away from me. Was this death?

Freedom for all in one key...

Voices collapsed my belief, resurrecting uncertainty.

"How did you do it?!"

"Well done!"

"She's done it!"

"Everyone! We've found it!"

"We've found our door!"

Still on my knees I fell against the side of the doorway, my mind desperately trying to come to terms with what had just happened, what was happening. It was like two jumbled jigsaws were feigning unity. Every piece I tried to match just didn't fit. I couldn't put anything together. I felt numb, blind to reality, shaded from truth. Yet all around me a fantastical fireworks display of emotions was exploding, erasing my identity even more. Blasts of belief sounded, geysers of hope and relief were erupting everywhere I looked. I had never seen such a celebration of elation, such an unbridled and uninhibited overflowing of emotion, such expressive expressions of being, such honest, genuine illustrations of self. People were screaming and shouting out their joy, cheering and sobbing their relief, laughing and crying, nearly bursting in embraces, all falling to the floor in heaps of happiness. Every face I saw was wet, dripping with tears, tears of non-belief, tears of release, of liberation, of alleviation. It was like the night sky had been torn, burst open to reveal its true self, a self that we had only been privy to through pin holes of light. It was so completely overwhelming that I couldn't do anything to stop myself from being swept up in it. It blew uncertainty and disorientation from me, lifted my shaky spirit and took it away with it.

We had won. The darkness had been vanquished. We had made it. We had survived. The room had not beaten us. We had prevailed and crushed our enemy. Our victory overpowered the memory of the whole ordeal, exiling it and its cruel conduct to a place of forget. Maybe it was best to forget. Leave what happened in the room, in the room.

The room, what a strange and curious beast it had been. What a bizarre metamorphosis it had undergone. From hosting an inferno of torment, it had now become the stage for such an outpouring of ecstasy. I doubt anyone here had ever come close to such a feeling. Funny that we never would have felt such elevation without being so awfully exposed to its exact opposite. It was the extremity of experience, of emotion that facilitated this outrageous outpour, this monsoon of tears. My perception of reality was still a little bewildered, but this overwhelming moment, this landslide of emotions, buried that sense of confusion. This extraordinary feeling of feelings lifted my detached apathy and summoned in me an enormous emergence, empathy. I had been presented with a platter of the why, of what was on offer from the pinnacle of people, the crest of civilization, the height of humanity. How could I refuse? I had been ensnared buy its spellbinding trance. It infused my complete being as I felt every cell swell with joy. It was in that moment that I understood, I finally understood the reason for the rhyme.

"Mummy! Mummy! Have we won? Can we go home now?"

I pulled my little sun as close to me as physics would allow. My heart ballooned with the most love possible.

"Yes, darling, it's finished, it's over. We've won. We're going home."

"So do I get my tree house fort?"

"Yes my love, you most certainly do."

I kissed his head as he scrambled out of my embrace.

"Captain! I won!"

He ran straight for him nearly toppling him over with the force of his enthusiasm.

"So, kid, you got a tree in mind?"

He looked up at me smiling as he tried to field a hundred questions a hundred times. He had helped us more than he could have ever known. I still hadn't even had the chance to thank him for everything he had done. As my eyes began to well, his found mine and as he winked a heavy tear cascaded down his face manoeuvring its way through his stubbly cheek. He brushed it away before it fell into my son's reality. It hadn't occurred to me until that very moment that perhaps we had helped him just as much. And maybe it was more than just the distraction we had given him. Maybe we had helped him recover something that he had lost a long time ago. Maybe, in actual fact, it was my son who had been the guardian of his reality, not just in protecting it, but also restoring his sight for a life that he thought had gone forever.

Soft warm arms wrapped themselves around me. Missy squeezed and jiggled as she thanked me over and over again, but for what I did not know. Her wet cheeks pressed against my face as her dripping eyes looked into mine.

"You did this, sugar, you made it possible. You saved us all."

"I didn't do anything. I don't know what happened. I just-"

"It's okay, honey, I know what you did, even if you don't. Now we all finally get to go home. Thank you."

She seemed so earnest, so self-assured, so knowing. I was glad she felt that way but I still didn't know why. She left me in a dumbfounded daze as I watched her hug my son and his loyal captain. I looked around the room. Everywhere strangers acted like family. They were all the reunited now. But we weren't yet free, we were all still in the room. Reality had not changed at all. It was only the promise of a reality that we had. But it seemed that was all that needed to wake them from their nightmare. I saw Missy run back to her post. The doctor was awake. I wasn't surprised, the celebrations had been colossal. Maybe it was the possibility of escape that had allowed his mind to release him from his unconsciousness. I walked towards them but was tackled by the younger brother who lifted me up in the air and swung me around like a doll.

"We're free! We're finally free! I knew it would happen! I just knew it!"

He dropped me down near his older brother who was peering into the void holding the candle in as deep as he could.

"Looks pretty damn dark down there."

Not to allow his older brother's pessimistic slant to dwarf the happy atmosphere the younger switched to his.

"Sure it's dark. But look, you can just about make out the end of it."

"What? Where? I don't see anything. It's complete darkness in there."

"No, it's not. Look, there, just above the centre. There's a pin hole of light."

"What are you talking about? There's nothing there."

"Maybe you're eyes are failing you, old man."

"Hey! I'm only five years older than you! You think maybe you're just seeing what you want to see? There's no light at the end of this tunnel, brother."

"Seriously? You think I'm making this up?"

"I don't doubt you think you can see it, I just doubt it's there."

"I can see it because it is there. And I'm sorry you can't. There's a lot of things you can't see, brother. Maybe sometimes you've gotta believe something's there before you can see it."

"That don't make any sense. If I can't see it, it ain't there."

"Not everything you can't see doesn't exist."

"In my world it don't."

"That's your problem, you're always looking at the dark side of everything, always expecting the worst."

"What you don't understand yet, and you will, is that you gotta go check the dark side first before you can prance around in the light."

"But you never come away from the dark side, you never leave it. I never see you relax and stop all the worry and all that worst case scenario shit. How is that any way to live? You're not living if you're always expecting bad things to happen."

"That's because more times than not they do happen, that's the world we live in, and shit happens, a lot. You just don't see it 'cause I've had you're back. You've never had to check the dark side because I've been the one doing it for the both of us. I'm the one who let you stay in the light and, well, maybe I shouldn't have."

"I never asked you to do that, to do anything."

"Well you didn't have a choice, and neither did I. When they left, I had to step up."

"You don't think I know that, know what you did, what you sacrificed for me? I just wish it hadn't cost you your hope."

"Don't worry, brother, I still got hope. It's the only thing that keeps me going."

"Well, then hope that this is the way out, that there is a light."

"Alright, maybe my eyes are telling me lies. How about we ask the others to take a look?"

The short bald man peered in, swaying side to side, tilting his head back and forth, until he stopped.

"I don't know if my mind's playing tricks on me, but I do see something."

People gathered around our escape. Our promise of liberty now seemed as terrifying as our confinement. Though we had dreamt, prayed for this moment now as we were literally standing on the edge of it, it felt more like a fall to doom than to freedom. Were we just lemmings, blindly falling into the abyss, not questioning the why or the where? Or were we lemmings for staying put and not taking the leap of faith? My doubting

476

thoughts were doubting themselves, as I doubted everything and everyone. Was the escape ever an escape? Was it just another trick, another rouse? Instead of salvation would it lead us to damnation? Was it a punishment for those defying the room, for those who held belief? Were we ever meant to escape? Had it always been a carrot to keep us moving, to keep our hopes high so they could all come crashing down with the final curtain?

The crowd grew as more wanted a peek at our proposed portal home. Curiosity compelled them forward but it was fear that forced them back from the circular void of darkness. An unknown is the most frightening of all things, because within it are all things. I felt I had seen this type of darkness before, felt its depths of despair. What was down there? More and more people began to edge away from it as though it were a dangerous cavity to be avoided, some sinkhole that had just opened up leading straight to the centre of the earth. But it wasn't, it was our door out of here. Maybe we were all experiencing a mild form of Stockholm syndrome. Now that we could finally leave the room whenever we wanted we weren't so eager to. We were questioning our dreams come true, our genie's wish granted, our answered prayer. No matter what we felt about our exit, treating it with such suspicion, felt, well a little ungrateful.

A brave few knelt down by the edge of the precipice, each looking deep into the nothingness, pointing into the empty space.

"I think I see something. Can you see it?"

"I think so."

"There's definitely something there."

"I see it, I see it!"

"Let me have a look."

"I think there's something but it just keeps disappearing."

"It's there alright. Here take a look."

"Yes, its small, but I see it!"

"I see it too, it's definitely there!"

"It's tiny. But it's so bright."

"It's like a twinkling star."

"Wow, it's beautiful."

"Let's have a little look-see."

"Do you see it?"

"See what?"

"There, that twinkling light."

"Twinkling?"

"Well yeah, kind of, just there. That tiny little point of light."

"I don't see it."

"Me neither."

"Nope."

"Really?"

"There's nothing there."

"What?"

"Sorry, it just ain't there."

"What are you talking about? It's just there! Look!"

"There's no light down there at all."

"Hold on... I can see it now!"

"What? I can't see a thing!"

"Do you really not see it?"

"I don't think it's there at all, you're all just imagining things."

"How could we all be imagining the same thing?"

"Obviously y'all just really wanna see it."

"Do you see it, sugar?"

I was lost in all the voices. It took me a second to realise I was being spoken to.

"Honey?"

"Oh sorry, sorry. I haven't had a chance to have a proper look yet."

As absurd as it is there have been many times in my life where I refused to acknowledge or witness things for fear of disappointment. Perhaps I felt that then in some way they wouldn't yet exist, that they wouldn't have yet manifested into reality, well, into my reality anyway; some strange, insecure version of quantum theory. This was one of those moments, but unfortunately I was being forced to see if the cat was still alive. I took a breath and with a small polite smile I bent down, closed my eyes and leaned in. When I opened them all I could see was a vast nothingness. I scanned and scanned the void, desperately searching for a break in the pattern, where there was none. I tried to keep my disappointment at bay as I looked at all the smiling faces awaiting my nod of agreement. I went to look again. But there really was nothing there. Were people so moved and blinded by their optimism that they could have imagined it? Was this a form of mass delusion? Were they all collectively conjuring their projected version of reality? Just as I began to feel pity for them and their unwavering belief, the dark sparkled. Without saying anything, I leaned in further, squinting my eyes, tilting my head as much as was needed to confirm what I thought I'd seen. Had I imagined it? Was I too falling under the spell? If I could only catch just one more glimpse of that speck of light, then I would believe. There it was. My genuine smile answered Missy and all the optimists.

"I see it too, sugar. It's there alright. Our little star of light, guiding us home."

Stars that twinkle colours of view...

I felt a strange weight in my chest. Was it relief or fear grappling for any kind of a grip? I tried to find my strength, the right beast, but voices just trampled over it.

"How can anyone be expected to jump into darkness not knowing what's down there?"

"No one's expected to do anything."

"It could hardly be worse than staying."

"Well, if you think logically about it, there has to be some light, otherwise it would indicate an immensely long tunnel."

"Exactly. The tunnel can't go on forever, can it?"

"Unless it ends in darkness?"

"Or what if that light is just the tunnel getting smaller?"

"What if we get stuck? There's no way we could climb back."

"Would you want to?"

"If I got stuck, I would."

"There won't be any more up to get back to when the timer runs out."

"We don't know that for sure."

"What if we go down too fast and crash at the bottom?"

"It's probably just some old garbage chute."

"Somehow I don't think so."

"What is it then?"

"We won't know until we get down there."

"What if it ends in water?"

"I can't swim!"

"I doubt that'll matter very much."

"We should wait until the lights come back on."

"Yes that'll give us the best chance."

"Maybe there's lights at the end of the tunnel and they'll come back on too. Then we'll get to see how long it is."

"I agree. We need to look at this more, study it a bit better, before we make any rash decisions or do anything drastic."

"Yes, it would be reckless to do otherwise. We don't know where it could lead."

"Yeah, we could die."

"What?! We don't have time for this! If you guys want to talk yourselves, quite literally, to death, be my guest. I'm getting outta here."

The feeling of unrest in the room gave the older brother an idea. He made his way through all the voices to the entrance of the storage cupboard.

"Okay, well let's see how deep this rabbit hole really is."

He took a bolt from his pocket and dropped it into the hole. But it's fall couldn't be heard over the rooms chatter.

"Shush! Hold on a minute."

But no one paid attention. So his brother let out one of his deafening whistles, to which everyone paid immediate attention.

"Thanks. Alright, let me just try this again."

He threw in another bolt and we all listened for the clanging to end. It did, but not as abruptly as we had hoped it would.

The bald man scratched his head.

"That's far, that's very far."

The younger brother stuck his hand down. "It's a tunnel, it'll be okay. It's not a straight drop, there's a bit of an incline. We'll be alright."

He looked at his older brother.

"I don't like it."

"What other choice do we have?"

"I know, but I still don't like it. And we got all those shards of broken glass just waiting for us down there."

"There's no other way out of here."

Sensing, like me, that we could be at this stalemate until the timer ran out, the short bald man turned towards the room.

"It's your choice people. We haven't got much time until the timer finds its way down to zero. We don't know what will happen when it does, and we don't know what's at the end of this tunnel. However you want to play this, you play it. Everyone's got their own ball in their own court."

Surprisingly, it's individual decision making that's the hardest. Group decisions are easy. You can just go with the swell, the biggest flow. But now everyone had to create their own current. Now everyone had their own pressure of choice, of responsibility, of fate. They would have to write their own ending to this tale, and they would have no one to blame.

"What do we do?"

"Well, I'm going down."

"Yeah, I'd rather take my chances than have no chance."

"We don't know for sure what will happen when the timer runs out but we do know that there's a long fall into darkness."

"So basically we need to pick the lesser of two evils."

"No, we need to pick the evil we know less about."

"Seriously, that's what this has come to, hope for the best?"

"Oh God."

"What are we going to do?"

"It's a disaster!"

"What is wrong with you people?! We found our way out, what we've been wishing for since we got here and here you all are complaining about it! This is just typical twenty-first century brat behaviour. 'What do you want Timmy?' 'I want that one!' 'Here you go.' 'No! I don't want it anymore! I don't want anything!' We're so spoilt and what's worse is that we don't even realise it! We've wrapped ourselves in the belief that if it's not the absolute best, then it's the absolute worst! What have we turned into? What have we become? Aren't you embarrassed that you are the product of all your ancestors struggling with trial after trial, overcoming impossible fears, surviving against all odds just to continue their line, to produce you, a little bitch who won't drink anything less than a triple shot, soy, low fat, no foam, hazelnut frappe? The world has gone mad and what's worse is that it doesn't even know it. We have taken freedom of choice to the extreme where we've confused pedanticalness with individuality! When all we are is just hues of grey masquerading as multi-colour."

"What are we supposed to do? Just blindly walk towards our fate?"

"Our fate? When did that word adopt the secondary meaning of demise? Fate is destiny, what is meant to be will be, que sera, sera. I never really believed it until I heard it one day when I needed it the most. A wise highland woman said to me 'What's for you won't pass you', and she's right. I can't help or avoid what is going to happen to me and I'm too old to pretend to be in control anymore. I'm just going to go with it, and anyone who wants to come can come."

"Of course, we all do, but I just think we need some way of finding out what's at the end of that tunnel, other than throwing things into it."

"Yeah, she's right."

"But we don't got rope or chain."

"Maybe if we had a flashlight to drop down-"

"We got candles!"

"We can't throw a lit candle down there."

"A signal! We could do a signal. When someone gets to the bottom they could shout back up or bang on the tunnel or something."

"That's good."

"Yes, that might work."

"Yeah, so who's going to be the guinea pig?"

"I'll do it."

A brave voice came from the back, followed by a small single applause. The crowd turned to thank the volunteer until they realised who it was.

"No, he can't go. He's the only one who knows how to handle the snake."

"Yeah, we need someone else."

"Anyone gonna offer?"

Everyone looked at everyone else. We're all selfless up to a point, that point being when there is an actual possibility of our self becoming less.

"I'll go."

"What? No you won't."

"It's okay. I'm going."

"No. No you can't. I won't let you."

"You won't let me?"

"There is no way that I'm gonna let you go first."

The older brother pushed past the younger as he stood by the doorway.

"Don't listen to him. I'll go instead."

"What? Are you crazy? No! No way!"

"Listen, I don't know what's down there and I don't know if I trust this-"

"So why are you going?"

"Because I trust you, little brother."

"You can't be the first, you can't-"

"Listen to me."

He put both his hands on his little brother's big shoulders and spoke directly into his eyes.

"It makes the most sense. You see, I can't let you go because I don't believe it's safe. But you, you can let me go because you do. And I believe in you. So it's the only way."

The younger brother didn't speak. He just nodded as he stared at his older brother through watery eyes. He looked like a little boy. I felt a sadness well up in me.

"Hey, it's gonna be okay, you know that. Now listen, you won't understand a thing I say from the bottom so I'll do two shouts for no, one for yes, okay?"

The younger brother still couldn't speak, all he could express was a nod.

"Don't worry, I'll see you on the other side, brother."

They both winced in their goodbye embrace. We all did. As he positioned himself on the edge of the drop, a faint red glow shone down, lighting his departure. He gave his brother one last look, one last nod before he fell away into the darkness. And then he was gone. And so was the hundred. We waited. The ninety-nine held their breath, held their hopes, clung onto them as they tried their best to hold their anxiety at bay. After what seemed like too long, worried whispers seeped into the room. The short bald man shushed them as we leaned in closer. Then we heard it. The younger brother exhaled the breath he had been holding. People cheered and clapped, and were shushed again. His voice had echoed as it reached up to us. And now with only our memory of the sound it was impossible to decipher whether it was one or two shouts. Now there was only silence. He obviously didn't repeat the message for fear of throwing us into confusion, but we were already there, trying desperately to separate the memory of the shout from the memory of the echo.

The pessimists were loudly vocalising their shaded opinions.

"It was definitely two shouts."

"He was warning us."

"It's a trap!"

"I knew it wasn't right."

"I'm definitely not going down there now."

"Yeah, I'll take my chances up here."

"That poor boy."

"What's happened to him?"

"What do you think they'll do to him?"

"He's probably..."

The younger brother ignored all the doubting voices, which he seemed quite accustomed to doing.

"Well, he obviously made it. He was wrong. There was a light at the end of it. I knew it wasn't a black hole. I'm gonna go join him, but this time I'll whistle one hell of a bleeder for safe, and a short one for not, okay?"

Before anyone could say a thing he had perched himself on the rim beneath the faint scarlet spotlight. He gave us all a confident nod goodbye before he let himself go. I heard somebody mutter how brave he was and another bravely proclaim how if it were their brother that they would have done the same. But I don't think bravery even came into it. He hadn't triumphed over fear by ignoring it or even facing it. He simply trumped it causing it to cease to exist. The only thing that can overshadow fear, the only thing that blinds us to the ramifications of our actions, the only time our survival instinct seems to stall, is when love enters the stage and, like all true thespians, commands it.

Like an anxious audience awaiting an actors forgotten line, we stayed as still as we could, patiently waiting for the excruciating moment to pass. Unconsciously we all began to move nearer and nearer to the deep silence as if those few centimetres belonged to a new aural space where soundwaves reverberated at a different frequency. Our delicately unfolded eardrums were nearly torn apart as our sign thundered up the tube like a police whistle into a megaphone. It was big and it was long and we were all half deaf, but we had our green light. Now the real evac could begin.

Most ignored the die-hard naysayers and their conspiracy theories of a coerced whistle and began to form a queue, a strange queue that curled around the room like a serpent without end. Everyone slowly shuffled along. They looked a little despondent for people who were waiting in line for salvation. They wouldn't have looked out of place standing at an airport check-in desk. Could we be that easily distracted from salvation by irritation and impatience? People were kicking the floor, sighing, looking up to the ceiling, instinctively looking at their wrists as if they had somewhere to be. Maybe in certain situations we revert to our roles attached to them and act accordingly.

But soon our exodus was in full swing. Down and down they went, splashing into the darkness. It kind of reminded me of a parachute jump, everyone dropping down one after the other, leaping into the fall. I thought of Leo. Leo, where was he? I looked around but I couldn't see him. I asked Missy but she didn't remember if she saw him and said that maybe he had already gone. Maybe he had. But it was her time now. Her two girls had already left and were waiting for her. She shimmied to the edge.

"I ain't so worried about the fall, I'm just worried about gettin' lost along the way!"

I could hear her clucky chuckle bounce up the tunnel long after she had gone, bounding into the room, smothering the serious tone that had settled. Her last spoonful of sugar.

In they fell and then more and more. It was all happening so fast. After so long in our waiting room, we were now finally being seen. I saw the doctor as he was coming up for his turn. I had been subtly avoiding him, a little too ashamed to face up to what I had done. I suspected that he had possibly been feeling the same. I decided to swallow my shame.

"Hey, how are you feeling? Still a bit groggy?"

"No, no much clearer now, thank you. Please excuse my behaviour, it all just overwhelmed me."

"Me too."

"How have you been faring?"

"I'm not sure. I think I'm actually doing quite well. But then again wouldn't a crazy person believe in their sanity?"

"I don't know. There's a bit of disagreement over that. I think it depends on the person and the severity of the madness."

Just as I was about to ask him if he could shed a little light on something, the lights returned. Their clinical glare felt like a needle burrowing through my head, a knitting needle. We didn't need them anymore. We had the candles and they were casting a soft mood for our departure, so I went to find the light switch. I looked at every wall but there was no switch to be found. How could that be? There weren't even markings where a light switch panel could have been removed, it was just void of anything. It felt wrong, like a face without a mouth. Anyone I asked didn't seem to care in the slightest. Was I over dramatizing it? Was I subconsciously trying to hang onto the room, finding more pieces to a puzzle that was already solved? I just wanted the lights off, they were too bright. I saw some silly conscientious people blowing the candles out. What were they afraid of? Starting a fire? I don't know why that annoyed me, but it did. I was beginning to become irritated without any real reason. Maybe the room was grasping at straws, throwing all it had left, trying its best to hold onto me.

With the increase of light and the decrease of people, I could now easily see everyone who was left, and that Leo was not one of them. I checked the bathroom, empty. My heart ached a low ache. Where was he? When was the last time I saw him? The memory felt grainy like an old VHS playback. Was it just before the mirror smashed? What did he say to me? Something about breaking the spell. Did it happen when the mirror broke? Had I done it already? The doctor came over.

"Who are you looking for? Is someone missing?"

"Yes. I don't know, doesn't matter."

"Who is it? Maybe I've seen them."

"He's that kind of surfer looking guy with 'the world is his home' look about him. Crazy mane of hair, you know, the one I have been talking to."

"I never saw you talking to him."

"Well, I suppose you were out for a bit. Did you see him leave by any chance?"

"No, I never saw him."

"Okay, doesn't matter."

"I mean, I have never seen him."

"What? What do you mean?"

"I mean, I have no idea who you're talking about."

"How could you have missed him? You never saw him on your rounds?"

"Never."

The cold hand of reality slapped me hard. Our strange conversation in the mirror came into focus. I rushed over to the inventory pages and ran my finger down the list of names. As the names began to run out, so did my hope in finding his.

"That's impossible. Leo's probably short for something else. He's probably a Leonard or a Leon or even a Leopold."

"Did you see any of those names?"

I checked and rechecked.

"Maybe it's his nickname, it's got to be, there's no other explanation."

I caught the doctor's look of concern in his misty grey eyes. I didn't want an answer, it wasn't a question. I hoped he wouldn't say the words I didn't want to hear. But of course he did.

"It's not abnormal for the mind to supply support during a trauma. It's simply a way to help stabilise the situation."

"I did not imagine him."

"No, no of course you didn't. I'm just saying that sometimes that can happen in certain situations."

I just couldn't take it in. I couldn't question the only piece of steady ground I had. But as it began to give way, so did I. The doctor tried to help me up, but I didn't want to get up. It had all gone, all gone again. Again I was left alone, alone to fend for myself. Anything I let in was taken from me. Everything eventually left, everything, except my baby. As if hearing his mother's silent call for comfort, he ran to me. I swam in his love for me. It filled and mended my broken being. It reminded me who I was and what we were here to do. We were here to get out of this concrete cage. We were here to go home. I walked towards the storage cupboard and looked behind me. There were only five of us left. They pleaded with me to go next but there was something very strange and very strong pulling me to stay until the end, to complete the race. All four males protested but I stood my ground. The short bald man was to go next. He lowered himself over the dark manhole. I bent down and attempted to convey my great gratitude for all he had done for the room.

"Thanks for being such a hero in here. You were one of the very few to never panic."

"I might wobble but I'll never fall down!"

"Oh yeah, like the toy!"

"Yeah, it's the name I got on my first day of work and it's been attached to me like an anchor since. To tell you the truth, it's been weird not hearing it. I used to hate it but now I'm kinda looking forward to hearing the guys holler it again."

"Well, I think it's an honourable nickname. Even superheroes fall sometimes."

A proud smile filled his face as he allowed the darkness to engulf him. The doctor was next. He protested but I told him I had something I needed to face, to overcome. There was something that I had to finish, something that only I could end. He looked into my eyes, as if searching for that something and then nodded.

"Alright. I'll be waiting for you, just don't take too long. I hope everyone made it okay and we haven't got too many injuries. I'll take the kit with me, just in case. I'll see you down there."

I felt a loss as soon as he had slipped into the abyss. At least everyone down there now had him. My son was chasing the eye patch guy around the empty room. It never occurred to me what freedom he must have felt being able to race around like that after being so restricted for so long.

"It's time to go."

He ran full speed into my arms and knocked me back, much to his delight. How much he had grown, even in the room. I felt so guilty about the little time I had given him. But it was all worth it for this moment here, the moment of his freedom. When we got home I was going to spend as much time as he wanted in his tree house fort, maybe we would even camp there if his schematics allowed. I hugged and squeezed him with every ounce of my being. I could have stayed frozen in that moment forever. But a tap on my shoulder reminded me that if I took any longer, my wish may be granted. I wiped my silly tears away.

"Don't be too long, Mummy. I want you to be there when I get my tree house fort."

"I'll be right behind you, sweetheart."

Of course the eye patch guy insisted he should be the last but I just told him that although I had no interest in going down with the ship, I knew I had to be the final one to leave. He seemed to understand. I helped them get into position and did all I could to hold back my heart from jumping out of my chest to join him. I very nearly stopped them, but managed to stop myself first. It was for him I was doing this, though I still didn't know exactly what it was. They slid down full of smiles as if it were a theme park slide. We shouted I love yous for as long as the tunnel would allow them to be delivered.

And then I was alone. I felt strangely comfortable and relaxed, which then made me feel uncomfortable and tense. But it was the first time I had been in my own space, the first time I had truly been by myself, with no one watching, no reputation to uphold, no role to play, no expectations from anyone. I took a deep breath as I turned to face the room. I walked forward a few steps and looked around at the strange stage I had awoken on, where my journey had begun, where I thought it would end. I both cursed and thanked the room. And then I turned and wished it adieu. But the room was not yet ready to let me go.

I heard a beeping coming from the storage cupboard and then the lights went out. I thought I had more time. It was now pitch black, even the faint red glow from the store cupboard had gone. Did that mean it had already happened? Had I just died and not realised it? Maybe this was death? It wasn't as painful as I had imagined. In actual fact it didn't feel too different at all. But surely this wasn't all the afterlife had to offer, was it? I waited for something else to happen. Then I heard a click. I was certain that it came from the room's security door. A flash flood of adrenaline surged through me. I was still in the room. The current increased as I realised I was not dead, not yet anyway. My heart was beating too fast, my breathing too loud. I needed to be quiet. I needed to hear in the dark. I thought I heard a hissing. I held my breath. I hadn't believed in the snake until now. I was blind, cornered and alone. I spun around trying to defend myself from the darkness. I needed to get out of here. If I ran now I could make it. I would have to trust my senses, close my eyes and believe I belonged to escape with everyone else. But I didn't even know which way I was facing. I didn't know which way to turn. I didn't know which way was the right way. Then the room showed me.

A square of black and white dots appeared, dancing together to a crackly tune. They had fixed it. In all the commotion they hadn't even announced it. I scanned the room. I was alone. There was no snake or beast or men with guns. I was safe. But I felt very alone. I immediately turned to walk towards the storage cupboard. But as I glimpsed back into those dots something stopped me. My mesmerised mind seemed to tune to a hypnotic frequency as I became powerless to tear myself away. Gazing deep into that static filled screen I felt like I was a misplaced dot catching a glimpse of my people, my world, my universe. I shook the static from my eyes and untangled my brain from the nets it had been caught in. As I turned away the crackly noise vanished and the lighting dimmed. I looked back at the screen. It had changed. It was now showing a picture of a television set. I looked closer and saw that it was a television set broadcasting a television set within a television set within a television set and there was a silhouette of a girl standing to the side of each set with her hands moving towards her face. There they all stood, hands covering mouths in a poise of shock, each one staring at each other and themselves, stuck within a caged corridor of realities. I wondered for a moment if I were even at the end of this curious conga line. Perhaps I too was being looked at by another self in another reality, who too was being watched by another and another. Or maybe, maybe there was no end to the line, and no beginning. Maybe it connected back round to itself and we were all equally trapped. Either way, I couldn't seem to exit. But nothing except myself was holding me there. Nothing was binding me apart from an overpowering feeling that I had finally found my belonging, that I had finally found my place, my selves, my Now. Time no longer existed here in this reality of now, in this ring of eternity, everything was all of itself all of the time.

Tomorrow is today is yesterday is away...

Just as I began to accept my new reality as being the only truth, the television sets and the girls in the screen began to shrink as the picture panned out to reveal other screens around us. More and more joined until my screen was very small, and only one of many. They were all very different screens with very different scenes. They displayed every act of anarchy the mind could imagine, some too horrific and horrendous to even describe. They were rooms of hell, pure and utter hell and they were all broadcasting for me to see. All those people, all those lives. My heart stung and tore as it bore the deepest sadness it had ever felt. Rooms filled with fire, filled with war, filled with terror, filled with rage, but none empty like ours, not one.

How? How could we do this to each other? How could we unleash such a hell? Who could create a forum for such torment, such torture? How could such a place exist? How could this be permitted? How could people just stand by and allow it? How could every person involved permit this brutality to continue? I wanted to stop them, to stop it all. I screamed and screamed until my voice ran out. It was all I could do, my useless act of rebellion, which now too had left me. I collapsed to the floor. So many people, all those poor people. I began to sob. How many lives ruined, destroyed, and for what? A game? Then the picture began to zoom out again but this time beyond the screen of screens revealing what was watching them. A man and a woman dressed in white lab coats were observing the screens, making notes and ticking clipboards.

"I can't believe they did it. I can't believe they escaped."

"But why hasn't she?"

"I'm not sure why or why she's still staring at the broken television set for that matter."

"What is she doing? The timer has gone off. The door is unlocked. She can leave whenever she wants. It doesn't make sense. Do you think that perhaps she just cracked?"

"Perhaps. I don't know. We've never been this far, so all the results will be new. We finally have a winning room."

"How long until he gets here?"

"He said he was on his way."

The man in the white lab coat perched on his tall white stool.

"It was getting tight there for a while."

"What did he think about the leader's sex?"

"I don't think I mentioned it. He'll get a shock. I think he was expecting it to be male."

The lady in the white lab coat smiled.

"They always do."

Chapter Seven

A loud ringing reverberated around the white crescent observation room as the man in the white coat stretched towards the console and pressed a button.

"That's probably him now. Yes, Margery?"

"Sir, your wife is here and she has your daughter with her."

"My wife? And daughter? Right, right, well send them up."

The lady in the white lab coat peered at him over her small oval glasses.

"I really don't think this is a very appropriate environment for a child. And the timing-"

"There must be something wrong."

He breathed deeply as he rubbed his brow.

"What would you like me to do?"

"We'll just turn the screens off. We'd better start putting the data together, you know he'll want to leave with something."

"Of course. Paper report?"

"Yes, he's never been comfortable with virtual. He doesn't trust things he can't feel."

"For being the head of an organisation piloting progression, he's not quite the progressive."

"People are used to what they're used to. They wear the same pair of slippers until they fall off. We are after all, at our core, creatures of habit."

"But isn't that the very thing we're trying to deviate from?"

"Yes, but as you'll eventually find out, with age your hardwiring becomes even harder. Then the fear of rewiring emerges with the belief that we'll crack and break if bent. You've got to cut them some slack, they've survived this tornado of a life for far longer than you or I. You have to allow them their little eccentricities. God knows which ones we'll end up with."

"I'll remember to memo that to myself the next time he calls me Marie. So, what do you think will happen next?"

"I really don't know. We've been trying to succeed for so long, that now that we have, I really don't know what's going to come next."

"But you do know what his end game is?"

"Well, of course I know that he plans to-"

The door's buzzer interrupted.

"Daddy!"

A young girl bounded into the room completely unaware of the highly classified surroundings she had stormed into.

"Hey, honey! What are you doing here?"

He scooped her up into his arms as he flashed a look to her mother who in turn flashed a look of her own.

"Didn't you have your field trip to the museum today?"

Her mother answered for her.

"Miss Hamersham decided today of all days to have one of her episodes, so everyone had to be picked up early. I'm sorry, Geoffrey, but I-"

"What are all those screens for? Are they TV shows? They look a bit scary. Can we change the channel?"

"Maria? Can you turn them off please?"

"Yes, sorry. I thought I had. Afternoon, Mrs Johnson."

"Hello, Maria. Sorry for interrupting, I-"

"What are they, Daddy?"

"Well, those are the rooms that we test the people in. That's Daddy's work."

"Like exams?"

"Yes, just like exams."

"And did they all pass?"

"No, no they didn't. But today one did, the very first room."

"I'm thirsty, can I go get a drink?"

Maria walked towards her.

"I'll take her downstairs to the machines. Maybe we can see if we can find some naughty treats too."

"Thank you, Maria."

"Don't spoil your dinner too much, sweetheart."

As they left through the thick silver security doors Geoffrey embraced his wife and rubbed her shoulders as he asked a question he hoped he hadn't already guessed the answer to.

"What's wrong?"

"Out of all of the days for her bloody teacher to-"

"What did doctor Liebstein say?"

Her hand instinctively fell to her stomach, as tears that had been held at bay all afternoon were now breaking through the barricades.

"He's gone. Oh, Geoffrey..."

"Oh, honey..."

They held each other close until their pain had subsided enough to let go.

"I don't know if I can have the Kildeegans over tonight. I just-"

"Don't worry. I'll call them."

She took a steadying breath and wiped the leaked mascara from her cheeks.

"Can we talk about it later? I can't do it here. Let's change the subject. So how was your day? You really got your first pass?"

"Yes, yes. I can still hardly believe it myself. We got it. They did it. No fatalities, and they made it out."

"Congratulations, darling. Nice to hear some good news."

"Yes, after all this time, we finally got our first win."

"I'm so glad they all escaped."

"Well, technically not all of them. The leader of the room never did."

"Why not?"

"We don't know. It's all new territory. We'll have to compare it to the next successful room."

"I thought this meant that you could stop the testing."

"I doubt very much he'll want that. But we'll be closer, a lot closer."

"I do hope so. I hate being here, seeing all those people. I don't know how you do it."

"It's all for the future, Ruby's future. We just need to gather enough data on creating successful virgin social structures. Different people, different cultures show us so much. We learn new things from every room."

His wife perched herself on his tall white stool as he continued.

"It's fascinating really. You see how humanity acts when stripped from their natural habitat, torn away from all their safety blankets. You get to see how their real selves begin to emerge as their adopted facades fall away. Obviously there are variables, yet curiously some constants persist. For example, the pessimistic view of the timer is nearly always a recurring theme in every room. The door release timer was there only to show when the test was over. However, in every case, the consensus of the room has always been to approach it with great distrust. They continued to treat it with fear time after time, always presuming that its end would equate to their own. And, of course, it is always fascinating to see how leaders come to the fore, if they are community or self-appointed, how groups form around them, and if there is a struggle for power, how it plays out. Anyone remotely interested in psychology can't help but be completely transfixed."

"It doesn't fascinate me at all. I find the whole thing repulsive."

"Honey, if you just try to see past that first layer and look a little deeper you'll see how truly revolutionary it all is. In a way it's as ground-breaking as the first autopsies. It's simply humans attempting to understand how humans work. The only difference is we're dissecting social bodies instead of physical ones."

"To me they're both grotesque."

"Of course it's hard for you to just come in here without any context and not judge it on face value. But when you're here, immersed in it, day in day out, you can't help but see how immensely thought provoking it all is. We're getting to understand the inner and the outer workings of the isolated human mind within a group mentality. You're being allowed the opportunity to witness innate traits and built-in instincts on such a large scale. You get to glimpse a bird's eye view of humanity in a way that no one ever has. You gain the ability to see and understand so many things that others cannot or simply miss. Trends and patterns form to create pictures, landscapes of the way our species has evolved in order to exist, to survive, to thrive. It's the closest thing to island hopping in the mind of God. You get to see why the tock tics."

"You're sounding like him. Please don't let him swallow your humanity."

"It's my humanity that drives me. If I were passive, I would not find the meaning in the madness, I wouldn't be doing my job properly and would certainly be hindering any advancement. I'm excited by it because it is exciting. After all, it is the core of our very being that I'm attempting to understand, struggling to map out and navigate. What could be more thrilling than that? It really is astonishing when you begin to predict occurrences, guess outcomes, all just by learning the language of ego and instinct. And when you get firsts, it's like watching shooting stars blazing across the dark night's sky. Like today, what a triumph. But I suspected, well, hoped that they would. It was always very different in that room. It was the first time the leader, if you could even call her that, didn't exercise her power. There was never any battle for control, for authority. Although, due to her almost subservient style of leadership, any challenger could have easily stolen command. Perhaps because there wasn't an oppressive governing body, no opposing force was created. Fascinating."

"But I don't understand, what could there possibly be to battle over?"

"There may not have been the obvious crude heavyweights to tussle over but control, respect and the room's ear in a civilisation stripped of all frills, can certainly be things worth fighting for. Even in such a capital driven society as our own, their appeal can be much more alluring than mere money."

"So you think that's what saved them, their disregard for power?"

"One of the main factors, yes. They worked together for the good and sanity of the room. But perhaps, in a way, they received a sense of power from unity. Maybe it was that connection that satisfied their need for dominance because within the security of the group insecurity no longer existed. Therefore, no fight for domination was necessary in order to feel secure. And all this even in spite of our best efforts to rock the proverbial boat! Our baits were never taken. The drinking water, food, blankets and even space were all placed there on a limited basis to see if the balance of benevolence could be maintained. They made their rations last, spread the inadequate bedding given, they shared, and ultimately cared for each other. And that was the simple blueprint for their success. Other rooms did not fare so well because they took the 'every man for himself' approach, which does not work well within the confines of a group. You must assume the identity of the whole and work for it, with it, much like a family. Failed rooms failed because they did not. They isolated themselves, fractured any solidarity, used resources too quickly or unjustly claimed ownership over them usually due to inane, and quite childish, logic based on either close proximity or physical dominance. Resources were regularly used to exercise and wield power over the room, and in many cases as an excuse for violent behaviour."

"But it's just so cruel, all of it. These people believed their loved ones were lost, they believed it all."

"To achieve the results needed they had to believe it all. They had to feel that isolation, truly feel that there was some kind of imminent attack looming and that they may well have been the sole survivors. They had to believe that they were saved, and then they had to question that belief. They then had to entertain the distinct possibility that they might have been forgotten. They had to believe that they were on their own. It was essential to the experiment that they lost hope, time after time. It is easy to have hope for something that has never let you down. But it is very hard to pick yourself up over and over again, allow yourself to believe, to have faith, to regain your lost hope. You're forced to dig deep, to find a very important part of yourself that has been made superfluous in our current world. You are given a chance to find your depth, to see how vast your capacity is to persevere. You get given the rare opportunity to find out how strong your strength really is."

"You can't convince me that the core of all this is altruism!"

"But it is. We not only help people to find themselves, but each other. By creating a fear-filled situation people are forced to choose whether to look beyond themselves and learn the benefits of trusting and caring for others or to just look out for number one. We hoped this experience would lead them to the realisation that togetherness is integral to our survival. If anything, our work here has shown that unity is the greatest force we possess. Unfortunately, the current paradigm doesn't seem to give even a shred of importance to that ideal. But in the room we're finding out, especially today, how truly essential that really is. The room allows the chance for bonds to transcend bloodlines and friendships, to strangers and unknown faces. It shows and helps us to realise that we are all one species, all part of the same family. It serves to remind us that there is a colossal strength in numbers, not just physically, but mentally and emotionally. Can you even imagine the change in the world if everyone recognised this truth, if we all just stopped the petty infighting and bickering and backward behaviour, with everyone adopting this unified approach? What monumental heights would we reach if we all felt a complete belonging to the same tribe? What would our species achieve if we joined together to form one clan all rowing in the same direction?"

"I understand what you're saying, Geoffrey. It all sounds very noble when you articulate your views so passionately, but the bottom line is that you are mentally torturing people. It doesn't matter that it isn't real, to them it is. In their reality they are unable to protect their families. I, I just couldn't bear it."

"As heartless as it may seem, Olivia, it was necessary to create the feeling of helplessness so that they would be forced to find that powerful strength within them. And remember, ten percent of the group have one or two loved ones with them. They're not all completely alone."

"But that makes it even worse for the other ninety percent, it's cruelly unfair."

"Well, then they get the opportunity to work through their injustice, rise above it and connect to the group."

"But why couldn't they all have family with them?"

"Because then we'd just have a room of kin wars. Actually, I'm quite surprised that it was one of the ten percent that emerged as leader of the winning."

"Really? I would have thought they would have had an advantage. I know if I were alone, I would give up sooner."

"Maybe, but we don't always show our true selves to our nearest and dearest. We accumulate and cultivate a persona, an identity that everyone around us reinforces. Essentially, I think we role play within our roles. So to remove these constrictive moulds should, in theory, give the participants more room to expand, allowing them the space and the opportunity to grow beyond the fixed tracks of their lives. It can be very liberating for some. The room can be a fantastic chance for inner development, personal advancement and emotional emergence. Anyway, at the end of the day, they all return to their families, not remembering a thing."

"The ones that make it, you mean."

"Honey, why the third degree? We've talked about this before."

"Have we, Geoffrey? You've talked and you've rationalised, and I've been patient. It was only supposed to be a short-term thing."

"Liv, the end has to justify the means, I have to believe that. Otherwise, otherwise... We are trying to build a better world, you must see that! I can't think of a more commendable vocation!"

"History offers its own cautionary tales of where the path of purification can lead. What if it was us, Geoffrey? In there, without you?"

"Firstly, it's not purification, its gaining understanding to help build better social infrastructures for the future. Secondly, I cannot answer something that is never going to happen or hasn't happened. I have to be a scientist and-"

"I wasn't asking the scientist! I was asking the husband! The father! A family is made better with love and closeness, giving and caring! Not taking, separating and traumatising! That is how you make the world a better place, Geoffrey, you treat it like your family, not like your enemy! The feeling to love and help must come from inside, it cannot be forced into being through fear! That can't possibly be right!"

Just as Geoffrey's cogs were beginning to turn in the opposite direction, the door buzzed and clicked open.

"We're back! Dopamine receptors fully flooded!"

"They had chocolate I'd never even seen before! Oh, Mummy, it was amazing! I saved a bit for you, it has popping candy in it and-"

The door buzzed and clicked open again.

A tall, older gentleman entered the scene dressed in an unusual tweed three piece suit with a dark green tie. Though surprised at the welcome party that greeted him, he adapted seamlessly.

"Oh, hello everyone. Good afternoon, Mrs Johnson, pleasure to see you again. And who is this lovely young lady?"

"I'm very sorry sir, they just popped in to-"

"That's quite alright, Geoffrey, quite alright. Lovely to meet the whole family. Now what's your name?"

"Ruby."

"Well hello there, Ruby, what a beautiful name you have. Ruby always reminds me of poor Dorothy and that terrible cyclone. Do you know it was the first motion picture I ever saw? I was a little younger than you at the time, but I remember it as clear as day, it was truly remarkable. It both terrified and enthralled me in a way nothing had ever before, or maybe even since."

He paused as the old cinema reel in his head began projecting an ancient memory. He smiled a soft smile as he stared into the distance, watching a playback only he could see. The three other adults in the room looked each other, not saying a word, so as not to interrupt the antique flashback. There they all stayed, in silence, waiting for the bizarre moment to end.

"Yes. Now, my dear, shouldn't you be at school?"

"We had a field trip today but my teacher fainted and then-"

"Mr Billington doesn't need to hear all about Miss Hamersham, darling."

Everyone in the room laughed, some more nervously than others.

"So, Ruby, do you like our big laboratory? I bet it's the biggest one you've ever been in. Your daddy does a very important job here, he's the chief tech. It's a very big job. That's why you get to wear such pretty clothes."

"Can I ask you a question?"

"Ruby, leave Mr Billington alone, he's a very busy man."

Her father protested, maybe a little too strongly, but it was to save face for all parties involved. Mr Billington didn't have children, and though he seemed like quite an affable man, his inexperience with filtering information to minors posed a problem. At a glance, you would understandably presume his social skills to be rather polished, but upon further reading, the opposite would soon become clear. This left Ruby's parents in a bit of a predicament as they were now trapped in a unique vortex of a moment created by the fact that their parenting power was trumped by the man who signs the cheques.

"That's quite alright, quite alright. I have never dodged a question in my life and I'm not about to start now, especially one from such a charming young girl. Yes, my dear, what is your corroding query?"

"Well, I was just wondering, why?"

"Why what, my dear?"

"Why do all those people have to be in all those rooms?"

Not even the least bit surprised that she knew about the rooms, he answered, much to the disappointment of everyone else present.

"Yes, yes of course it must seem a little strange. One hundred rooms filled with one hundred people. It does appear to have a slight waft of the dramatics about it. But I guarantee you quite a lot of scientific research has gone behind it, it isn't solely for theatrical effect. So, what is it all for then? Well, in order to answer that question, we'll first have to ask one of our own. How long does it take to make or break a person?"

He paused and looked down at little Ruby, expecting a reaction or quite possibly a guess, none of which he received and so he continued, much to the dismay of the room.

"How long until the veil of civility falls? A month? More? No, no, it takes much less than thirty days. In fact it takes only thirty little hours. Surprising, isn't it? Yes, when they came back with the results, and before you ask I really haven't got the foggiest how they arrived at such a figure, though I must say it has racked my brains over a few late nights, anyway, that is beside the point, I'm rambling again, which I shall warn you, I do a lot. My wife hates it. Oh my goodness, at our dinner parties, the looks she shoots across the room, they'd pierce even the toughest suit of armour, let alone a three piece tweed!"

His hearty laugh echoed about, eclipsing the feigned ones. He looked down smiling at the giggles below, not realising that it was not the quip that had been the cause of the giggling, but the amusing character who had produced it.

"So back to the thirty hours. Yes, I would have estimated more, far more. But you see, what I hadn't brought into consideration was that the world I grew up in has changed significantly over the last few decades. Dare I say it, we've become too comfortable. I know that might sound a little strange, but we have. Imagine you are sitting, enveloped even, in your lovely soft beanbag at home and your favourite chocolate is just out of reach. Well, it takes far more effort to reach over and get it than say if you were sitting at the dinner table. Now then, why do you think that is? Because when we are satisfied, we are incredibly difficult to satisfy. And in this day and age where we are surrounded by all our favourite things all of the time, we've become, well to put it harshly, inept infants. Helpless, unable to function properly outside our distinct and very detailed zones of comfort. We have become so dependant on what we think we need, that we feel we would positively perish without it. Any change or deviation from our norm, is not just seen as a bad, it's seen as sacrilegious, a personal attack against our liberties! And that, my dear, is the beginning of the end when mankind steps along that slippery slope of the inner sloth. Now, when I say inner sloth, I don't mean an abolishment of relaxation. In fact, in a way, I mean quite the opposite. I truly believe people have lost the ability to allow themselves to completely unwind. And because they cannot switch off they have become a mild version of these undead types, aimlessly wandering about, following each other wherever the gradient falls. People have lost their spunk, their get up and go. They have forgotten about their lust for life, they seem to have misplaced their joie de vivre. And this, my dear, will lead to a very unfortunate future for the next few generations. They will bear the brunt of our mistakes and will be born into a collective cloud of irritation in an anxious world full of fear, sadness and great unrest."

He looked down nodding at his small audience of one who nodded back.

"I know, I know, it does sound very bleak indeed. You see, the problem lay in our arrogance. We truly believed we had found the right path, the only path, the greatest path imaginable. We thought that, with just a bit of hard work, we could have it all. We thought we did have it all. But we didn't. And predictably, cracks have begun to appear. These seemingly insignificant cracks that have been passed off as society's growing pains, will explode into unbridgeable chasms into which our whole species will collapse, never to climb out again."

So enveloped was he in his air of dramatics, and so completely unaware of the older audience's looks of shock, that he continued.

"So this is what we have intended to address in our series of experiments here, to determine which method of civilisation proves the most consistently stable. What traits do it and its people exhibit? Can we make a society structurally sound? Can we abolish the weakest link in the chain, and not just outside ourselves but, most importantly, within ourselves. Now, unfortunately, we have had to endure many setbacks in our quest to perfect and polish the process. But I think within this grand altruistic apprenticeship of ours, we are creating a foundation for tomorrow. A foundation for future bridges to be built upon, traversing chasms over to the other side, to mankind's destined design. Which, in my opinion, categorically guarantees that the end undoubtedly justifies the arduous means. We are, after all, attempting to create the true motherland, the most civilised civilisation that has ever walked upon the earth. Now surely that merits a little artistic licence?"

He spoke as if he were addressing members of the board of trustees or potential investors. He was on a roll and he was not going to stop his presentation for anyone. Ruby's parents both took a loud breath in between one of his to try and signal a winding up but, of course, Mr Billington did not notice. He was far too enthralled by the tone of his own voice, while mentally making notes and additions for future speeches.

"Yes, yes, it was, of course, very trying in the beginning as most monumental works usually are. But now we're running a rather smooth operation, all ship shape dare I say it, no more naughty hiccups. Touch wood, of course."

He chuckled as he rapped his knuckles on his head.

"You see, a masterpiece such as The Room takes time, it needs air to breathe, to evolve, to grow. It takes time to work out all the bugs, check all the nooks and crannies, iron out those stubborn creases. Otherwise, well, it would be Harrow all over, and we can't go through that again. Far too much exposure and it really was a very messy clean up. No, no, now we're finally on our feet and in our second year, which no one said we would have the funding for, but low and behold here we are. Truth, integrity and earnestness always finds a way."

He nodded proudly at the older occupants of the room, forcing them to reciprocate.

"So, to answer your question a little better, I would say the reason for all the dire dramatics and distress, deceit and utter destitution, the reason for all the suffering and complete wretchedness, is to guarantee their absolute extinction. To guarantee, my dear, that they will not be the cause of our own. This, all of this, is so that your grandchildren and great grandchildren will grow up in a world filled with peace and harmony, living with true respect and in honest accord with their fellow man. We are crafting a gift for them, the greatest gift of all, the opportunity to live in the most heavenly version of life earth can possess. And they will read about the time before the turn in trajectory of our species, they will learn how close we really were to self-extinction, to self-annihilation and that in our own naïve arrogance we didn't have a clue. They will pity us for our insatiable hunger for unfulfilling things, our delusional fantasies of grandeur, our belief systems based upon fear, our corruption to fight corruption, our vacuous minds and our vacuous ideals, our moaning and our groaning, our fights and our rights, our wars and our bores, our foolish follies and our silly, frilly lives. And they will thank people like your father and I for our unwavering dedication to the cause, to a cause as of yet unknown. A cause, a war we have been desperately waging, fighting on the front lines before the world even knew it had begun. They will remember us for all that we have had to endure and all the insufferable sights we have had to witness and bear along our path to redemption, to liberty."

As though he were on stage, he bent down on one knee, put his hand on Ruby's small shoulder and finished his rousing and ridiculously lengthy reply.

"Your father, Ruby, is the future's hero. And your grandchildren will proudly tell stories to their grandchildren about how brave and honourable a man their great-grandfather was and how he helped to save the world."

Ruby's parents, believing the soliloquy to have come to an end, took a step closer towards their daughter. But Billington hadn't quite finished.

"Songs will be sung, sonnets will be spun, poems penned about our dream for a brighter, lighter, happier future where people will finally be allowed to live!"

He paused for dramatic effect, to allow the mass of his weighty words to settle upon the room, and then stood up, proudly adjusting his waistcoat, satisfied that he had managed to squeeze in as many superfluous words as he could.

"Now, does that answer your question, my dear?"

The other three adults in the room, left speechless from the speech, didn't say a word. But it seemed Ruby's hungry mind was not yet satisfied.

"So why did you pick the room?"

"Good question, good question. She's a bright spark this one! Well, Ruby, originally I had envisaged some sort of hideaway camp in the forests or deepest jungles. Then we thought mountain top or small island to be more preferable for its isolation. But what we found out whilst running the preliminary trials was that, quite unfortunately, our project could not be set in the great outdoors. At first, I rejected my team's views because it was not part of my original vision. But sometimes you need to let go of the ownership of something when it becomes bigger than yourself. After a while, I understood. You see, because mankind left the wilderness so long ago, it is no longer our natural habitat and that displacement of environment would be an external factor to the experiment, a variable we couldn't control. So, in order to compensate for the ease in pressure we had to consider a fear more suited to the age in which we live. And one of the research boys had the ingenious idea of these indistinct, imminent attacks. The occupants of the room are then forced to live in continual fear of an unknown which they don't know if or when will happen. This leaves them with an unnerving current of unfounded anxiety which is very hard to dispel. It's the perfect threat to survival. Due to its indescript nature its power is absolute as it is the individual who fills in the blanks, colouring the picture in, much like you do at school, Ruby. Without us needing to do very much at all suddenly we have managed to switch the room to a frequency of nervousness that not much else can trump for its debilitating effect, tenacity, or its longevity. Remember it is the unknown which houses all the known! Inspired, indeed! It's all been thought out in great detail. The exact sizing of the room, just enough for minimal personal space but not enough to ever really feel it. Then the lighting, it had to be harsh and sterile, unforgiving, penetrating. And, of course, having the ability to remove it at crucial intervals was, well, crucial. The candle challenge was a personal favourite of mine, the chance to regain control over our primary sense. The task of lighting it, coupled with the choice to sacrifice the radio, was ingenious. If they passed the fear based test and completed the trial, they were rewarded with a prize, a soothing ambiance. But that also gifted us something, the power to remove it. Masterful. All of it, my dear, every single detail has had many minds working many hours to bring about its conception. One of the toughest tasks, believe it or not, was in creating credibility of the room itself. You have no idea how long it took to establish that awful look of abandonment, how much detail was involved in achieving a seamlessly aged and dishevelled aesthetic. It then had to be kitted out with discreet state of the art surveillance devices, air ducts fitted to distribute the sleeping gas and to decrease the levels of oxygen. We even had a whole team in charge of fabricating the natural 'odour de room' as it was called. Months and months of tireless, exhausting work. However, we did, of course, enjoy certain aspects of the production. The design process was a definite highlight. We had many a highly entertaining brainstorming sessions together cramped together in our ideas room. The amount of pizza boxes that accumulated was shocking. Charles even referred to it as the leaning tower of pizza! Oh gosh, how we all laughed!"

Ruby burst into laughter, it was her type of humour too.

"Yes, many a great debate was had over many a great nations' cuisine. Good times, eh, Geoffrey?"

Poor Geoffrey nodded and forced an acceptable smile as he wished the large polished white tiles would open up and suck him, or even better Mr Billington, away from this moment.

"I recall many animated arguments were had over whether or not some form of natural light should be present. But the practicalities involved made our decision for us and in the end we all concurred that it was best not to introduce it at all. Little did we know that this would gift us the added bonus of creating a subconscious feeling of being lost in some otherworldly space. Furthermore, it provided us with another offering. Without sunlight the body clock's cogs lose their traction, they seize up, throwing the subject's sense of perception even more. Ah yes, time. Of course, there couldn't be any clocks present. Though we did have one in the preliminary trials, broken obviously, and of course out of reach, just to observe what effect it would have. We really were quite excited to see what they would make of it. How long until they would realise it was broken? Would anyone be led to believe that time itself had stopped? Would it add to their feeling of abandonment? Would it serve as a sad reminder of their old master? Would it torment them, fray their nerves even more? No. In reality it only seemed to mildly annoy, and to some actually served more as a comfort than a disturbance. And we couldn't have that. As they say, even a broken clock is right twice a day."

He gave out a small chuckle, though no one really knew why.

"We kept the television set, though. It was a fantastic hope raising and crushing device. And the research guys were right; it did serve as a talking piece, a bonding exercise, showing us that groups form better and open up whilst tackling a shared problem. As the room evolved, so did the tasks set for the occupants. Though not all groups complete them. For example, the locked storage cupboard. Not every room works out how to use the bracket and fire extinguisher, only about two thirds in fact. And less than half on the first day. And not to forget our rather ambiguous writings. That was actually my wife's idea. She loves games and puzzles, especially riddles. But the team felt a simple riddle would be too formulaic, and so they came up with the startling red writings. Tests showed these to be far more penetrating. I think it both terrified and fascinated. It gave the more higher-minded something to work on, their cerebral bonding exercise, and as expected, helped to separate and cause debate. We were actually thinking about simplifying them because no one as of yet had solved it, until today I hear. Congratulations, Geoffrey, Marie. This really is a triumphant day. I knew it would come, we all knew. It was just a matter of time. We have a lot of work to do and many questions to both ask and answer."

Ruby's mother edged closer to her daughter. But Ruby did not sense her mother's escape plan.

"But how can you do it all without getting into trouble?"

"Trouble? No, no, don't worry, my dear, no danger of that at all. Everything's vetted and backed by the right people. Goodness, it would be very hard to orchestrate completely under the table. It would have to be a very big table! But, fret not, we have friends who understand the intrinsic value of our work. People in the know, know. Of course, it's not public knowledge, heavens no, we would have all kinds of groups on our backs. It would be a literal and legal nightmare. The big players, the kings of commerce, queens of society and princes of politics, appreciate and support our endeavours, share our vision, our belief for the future. They look out for us, protect us, along with their investment. We wouldn't have survived Harrow if they hadn't stepped in. But don't worry. They won't be getting into any trouble either. After all, what it is we are doing here is really not that much different from a member of some governmental police holding you in a cell for twenty-four hours. It is the inhabitants of the room that decide how to use that time, and if it is in a violent and aggressive manner then that only serves to highlight the absolute necessity for our work. The buck of blame lies solely with the individual, I'm afraid. I cannot take any responsibility for their actions, no one can."

Ruby's mother put her hands on Ruby's small shoulders. But Ruby still wasn't done. She was rather enjoying her lengthy moment in the spotlight. And although she did not quite understand why her parents had not yet stopped her and her free rein on questioning such a curious character, she wasn't ready to halt her procession. She was rather enjoying this feeling of freedom, this sense of power, and developing a bit of a taste for this rare experience of untouchability and superiority.

"And don't you ever stop them hurting each other?"

"No, we never intervene. Absolutely not. That would defeat the whole purpose. Under no circumstances can we engage, it would completely defile the findings. It would be impossible to obtain accurate results and then what would it all have been for? All the sacrifice has to be for a purpose. Well, otherwise, otherwise it's just pure brutality, isn't it? No, no, it's all about the science, collecting and processing untainted data; that's our prime objective. But lives are lost here, make no mistake about it. Men and women courageously perish in a war they do not yet even understand. But their lives are not lost in vain. They are martyrs to the cause and we earnestly and respectfully salute them. Don't think for a moment that we don't treat their sacrifice seriously, we treat it very seriously. And I personally regard any loss of life to be a loss. However not as gravely as I do the complete loss of life. That trumps all suits. Ideology, principles, ethics, morality, for what are they with their master? And I know that card of annihilation is still somewhere in the pack, shuffled in with the rest, God knows where, and my job is to prevent it from ever being laid onto the table. Because if it were, if we, as a complete species, were to in actuality become extinct, then we would have failed in the most basic and fundamental of ways any life given creature can. We would have failed as a viable example of life. Destined to forever live in the non-viable pile, categorically deemed unfit to walk the earth, a mistake, just teething pains of this sublunary sphere. And do you know the greatest tragedy of it would not be that it was dear Mother Nature's fault, that genetically, or biologically we were flawed in some way, unable to adapt, inept for survival. No. It would have all been down to our inability, our incapacity to share this great planet of ours, to live together in harmony, to live and breathe as one kind. And all because of our resistance to fully learn the very first lesson we teach a child, to love and be loved.

Isn't that what we do it all for? All that hum and all that drum, every bit of it, every bit of life, well, it's all just for that good stuff isn't it? It's all each and every one of us can hope to have in our lives, the gift to give and receive love. If it's so easy that an infant can do it and its all that we grownups want, then why isn't the whole world loving? Why has it become so hateful, so opposite to its greatest desire? How is it so blind that it cannot see that it has been infected with a virus of vengeance, become its own worst nightmare? The world is complaining of the symptoms of its own disease. It is sick because we are. And yet we continue the game of musical chairs and wonder why it keeps falling. How embarrassing that all our advancement, all our evolution, all our successes and genius could all be taken down by the decision that survival works better when one does not partake in the perceived frivolities and trivialities of caring and sharing, ultimately, of love. Goodness, didn't anyone listen to the song? I mean it was all over the radio when we were young. Doris and I used to sing it as loudly as we could whenever it came on, ta ta da da dah. So simple and yet so true, isn't it always? That friar had a bit of a point with his razor slicing through all the fat. All you need is love. But I suppose people are too busy to listen to the words of songs anymore, let alone of a decades old tune. Though it is such a loss, such a pity humanity finds it so hard to see the wise wheat from the cheap chaff. It really is a tremendous shame that time after time mankind has been given opportunity after opportunity to raise its game, raise the bar of its own humanity, and yet that out reached hand just gets ignored, shoved to the side to make room for the latest and greatest gadget to bring more time and entertainment, meaning and joy into our empty full lives. Oh, Ruby, how can they not see that it doesn't? How can it if it hasn't worked already! I fear, dear Ruby, we are living in a time overrun with snake charmers selling their oil. But the saddest part is that they themselves don't realise that it's them that they are cheating, that it's their kin's world they are ruining. What a legacy for their legacy. Why on earth is everyone setting to ruin their progeny's paradise? I may not be a parent per se, but isn't that quite the opposite of a guardian's mission statement? Everyone is treating this world as disposable, but it certainly is not, it is quite irreplaceable! They are using this planet as though it will never run out. But you can't abuse something and then expect it to last. People are behaving as if it is not their home that it's like some hotel they can trash. Didn't their mothers ever tell them that you leave things the way you found them, if not better? Isn't that just common sense? It's appears not, not common at all, but quite the opposite. Most sense, it seems, has become quite uncommon of late. But where has it all gone to I wonder? Who is squirrelling it away? I do wish they would return some, the general public are in such desperate need for some kind of a bannister, some form of a guiding rail to lean on, to help show the way. Well, I waited for some form of a guiding light, some miracle to come along. I truly and honestly believed it would and possibly naively felt if I had been given the concept of it then surely it was possible, probable even. But as time ticked away and the years etched themselves onto me, I realised that perhaps I was that miracle, that this realisation, this insight I had been gifted so long ago was mine, and only mine, and that it was my duty to follow it through, to carry out my calling, to become what the world needed. And, voilà, the room was born."

Mr Billington seemed to truly believe his rationalisation, his explanation for the extremity of the measures he had signed off on, that he had manifested. Though as he took one of his moments between moments his face revealed that there was perhaps slightly more shades of grey than he would have allowed anyone, including himself, to realise. Maybe it was because of today, because of the rare respite from the relentless determination, that the pressure on the accelerator had eased leaving the leash loose for him to notice the dog at the end of it. But Mr Billington didn't get to where he stood this day by succumbing to his conscience. Whenever it would appear he simply implemented his well-oiled suppression mechanism and buried the voice of reason as deep as he could with more justification, explanation and ingenious excuses. Whatever it took to submerge the knowledge of the crimes he had committed, he took.

"Yes, yes, it's all for the results, those invaluable, lifesaving results. That's our reason, and that's all the reason we need. And if we must take in order to receive, well, then take we must. I suppose it's that old tried and tested divide and conquer template, isn't it? Or perhaps, in actuality, is it dare divide us and you will be conquered? Well, that is what our results are showing us. Humanity is a far more complex organism than we give it credit for. When you try to break us, we hold tighter together. What doesn't kill us makes us stronger. Yes, we do tend to show our truest and undoubtedly most wondrous colours when our very survival is in jeopardy, more so when the tribe is at risk. Once even the most disjointed group is threatened as a whole, we click into a state of understanding, of being, of connection. We protect the whole, and in doing so greatly increase our own odds of survival. It feels right, because it is. We all feel comfort in a unit. We feel that great safety, that great safety in numbers. Therefore, to achieve unification a division must be created, an opposing force to summon the need for union, a threat to wake the threatened. Even if we take just a peak into the back catalogue of mankind, history generously provides us with a plethora of examples where unity has been born through mutual adversity. When we share a common enemy, we, no matter how diverse, no matter how chequered the past between us may have been, now suddenly cease to be enemies, quite readily turning the other cheek to face the new adversary together, stronger and with a higher chance of success. The greater the challenge, the greater the bond."

Billington took a large breath to replenish his overused lungs as the latest train of thought arrived at his old station. As usual it steamed in without inspection, straight to articulation, but as his lips moved to speak no more than a quiet wheeze escaped. His mouth hung open as his watery blue eyes seemed to soften. Sensing the delicate energy in the air, Ruby's mother, who only up until a few moments ago would have taken full advantage of Mr Billington's unexpected intermission, stayed quite still, as did everyone else in the room.

"I remember the war came to us not too long after my mind had been blown away by your friend Dorothy. It was a tremendously terrifying time. I remember my mother's nerves were worn as thin as tissue as my father attempted to preserve his in gin. As much as they tried, as much as everyone did, there wasn't one conversation that succeeded in avoiding the unavoidable. It soaked into all aspects of life, staining it a new colour, obscuring the old. Things were different, there was no denying that. The cover of life had been ripped off with the pages left bare, exposed to the elements, at the mercy of fate. Fate. At that time a shadow seemed to have passed over that once serendipitous word, somehow demonising it, demoting it to the dark side. Make no mistake about it, danger was now everywhere though, perhaps because of my age, its usual companion fear was notably absent. My brothers and I with all the local lads just continued being boys. For us it was mischief as usual, and in a far more fertile setting. Our playground had grown and become far more exciting. And although there was, of course, all the rationing and the air raids, the shared baths and shared shelters, with destruction and devastation everywhere, I really didn't feel as if I was experiencing a traumatic ordeal. I was, though you may not believe me, actually quite happy. Somehow, woe had exposed wonder. Even the dreaded rationing had a charm of its own, conjuring its magic upon our dinner plates. There's no better seasoning than appreciation. Limitation performed alchemy on the basics, turning sugar into diamonds, and chocolate into bars of gold. Throw in free air shows and less baths, and well, for a young boy what's not to like? And those underground shelters of ours, in essence, became more like impromptu gatherings turning into nightly neighbourhood tea parties. A worthy and deserved excuse for a good old knees up, a blank chitty for all kinds of merry merriment. I remember it clearly, that old tube station with everyone's tables all lined up in a row down the centre, each family having their own spot with their own tablecloth, a never-ending patchwork quilt of chintz. All the parents having a jolly good jolly with all us children racing and playing about. It was quite a marvel, a rare flower of its time, never to bloom its colours again. Ah yes, that was it, all you had to do was remember your family's patch. Which, if my memory serves me correctly, was red, no, I believe ours was actually red with white polka dots. Yes, yes that was it, very easy to spot! Pun very much intended!"

It was clear that Mr Billington delighted in his own class of comedy, his particular brand of wit, as he never refused a chance to display it, even if it was solely for his own benefit. But today, very unusually, he did indeed have a supporter among his audience, an ally in his comedic cause. Though unfortunately this only served to cement his belief in being somewhat of a comic crusader, a great hero of humour, when in truth any sense of it he held, had, in the opinion of most, very little sense at all.

"Undoubtedly another page for the project torn straight from that tornado of a time was sense scepticism. A perfect storm had brewed where your tools for perception, the senses, had become rather suspect. Not just the famous five, but also one's own sense of time and space, and well, reality as a whole. All those solid and rather stable things we regularly take for granted, never even giving a second thought to, are suddenly called into question when the very foundations they are built upon begin to crumble. When these pillars of perception become uncertain, a very odd thing happens. You enter foreign territory, your controls are down and you feel like your floating, drifting in the dark. With no more guiding lights directing, you seem to enter a new state of being. A highly aware one where you, most probably due to the inconceivable combinations of unknowns, become very, current. That's the only way I can explain it, it's very bizarre. But I imagine its roots are embedded in some old survival ground. Optimum alertness, of course, providing the optimum chance of continued existence. This enforced focus on the precise moment which is inhabited certainly raises your odds. Yes, being completely tuned in would have been the best course of action in any situation. Interesting that we, in this age, don't avail of that sharpness of self, that mode of being. I would think that it would certainly go a long way to facilitate complete clarity of thought. Anyway, I am on the verge of veering off point. Yes, the room's foundations. Stationed at our subway soiree, as it may well have been called in this country, you were thrust into a very real state of limbo because you never knew how long you were going to be there, when it was going to end. But, for me that is what made it so enlivening. It was all so uncontrollable, it was all just so very live. Obviously that must sound silly as we cannot be living in any other way except live. We're not in a rerun, well, not that we're aware of anyway! But it did feel different, everything really did feel more live. We're coming to you live, ladies and gentlemen!"

Billington chuckled, though he did not follow it with his usual room scan to see what smiles he could catch. Maybe he knew the net would be empty or more likely he was so engrossed in himself, and his reaction to himself, to notice any other.

"Of course, being the boisterous boy that I was, I revelled in the added thrill that our underground picnic could be thrust into darkness without a moment's notice. Sensory deprivation with all its trimmings could befall us in the midst of the festivities, rudely reminding us of why we were there, of the truth of a reality we had been hiding from. But that sudden drop into darkness coerced an astonishing consequence. I had never seen anything like it before. A spirit had been summoned, the human spirit. It was like an inner superpower had shown itself. Even to such a gung-ho boy as myself its force was magnetic. It was raw and rare, and I was hooked. It fascinated me how people could develop such a super strength beyond their own. Where did they find it? And how could they find it when everything else was gone? Perhaps because that's the only place where it can be found. Somehow in the dark the lost were found, light appeared, candles were lit and lanterns shone. A soft breeze of caring blew all around us, revealing a deep love for thy fellow man and a kindred kinship of kindness, the likes of which I had never experienced. The air felt like it was sparkling. It held an authenticity, a deep sincerity, like everyone suddenly stopped pretending to be whoever they were being and just were who they were. It was like all the walls had been pulled down to reveal what you always knew was there. It was incomparable. But how, I imagine you must be thinking, can bad make better and worst make best? Well, somehow that paradigm of a paradox accompanied us through it, like some guardian angel triumphing/conquering its vengeful adversary. Maybe when life is at its darkest, the light seems its brightest, or perhaps because it is when the darkness is so dark that we are forced to seek the light. It's all quite complex in its simplicity. Even in that atrocious aftermath we were awarded something no amount of safe scholarly studies could. That mess of wreckage and rubble imparted upon us a vital life lesson, an indispensable piece of wisdom that no other could have so powerfully and so effectively shown us. It showed us that nothing, not one thing was ever solid or stable, or ever forever. It taught us that landscapes change, that life is fluid, and no matter how fixed it may seem, nothing was concrete. But perhaps the most wondrous of gifts bestowed upon us that winter was that every day we were granted that exceptional life affirming feeling that we may well be living our very last day. That offered us a sense of carpe diem that nothing else could. Sometimes in life you are awarded moments that can change it, and you, forever. You must take them, Ruby, take them with both hands. They are not given often and they are not often given again. They hold more power than any atom bomb. They hold the power to change the way you think, to change your world, and then perhaps the whole world with it."

Mr Billington sighed before deciding to speak again, but then rather unusually appeared to change his mind. His pause lingered mid-air like a gravity taming hover fly. He was so perfectly still that a very unlikely thought glided across all the other minds in the room. Though it was only Ruby's that really entertained it. Maybe he had been frozen, she wondered. Or, maybe, he had run out of words. Perhaps, she thought in her little head, that everyone is given a quota and that it was indeed quite possible he had reached his.

It had now been twice that Mr Billington's locomotive had stopped so abruptly, twice that he had acted so out of character, that his shield of bravado had seemed to slip. Geoffrey looked to his wife. She caught his eyes, their expression of subtle vindication, and the raised eyebrows perched above them. She still didn't like Mr Billington. But she was, rather begrudgingly, beginning to understand him a little better, and beginning to appreciate that he was somewhat of an acquired taste that perhaps with time one could acquire, under the right circumstances of course. She gently held Ruby's shoulders as her gaze found Mr Billington's slightly pained, somewhat pensive expression. Her eyes softened with empathy as she clandestinely hoped that he would continue. Unsurprisingly, her wish was soon granted. But, surprisingly, was as quickly denied. Even more of a surprise was that it was her daughter, Ruby, who had pulled the lever. The uncharacteristic outburst of boldness was reminiscent of someone far older and bolder than her daughter. The realisation of who then prompted her to retract her amended ruling and retreat back to the original opinion her maternal instinct had provided, that Mr Billington was undoubtedly an unsavoury character whose close proximity was enough to decompose the morals of even the most moral of men.

"Obviously, I-"

"Did you see any bombs?"

"Ruby! You know what we said about interrupting someone when-"

"No need for scolding. Passion always trumps politeness in my book. Yes, of course, it's all about the fireworks isn't it? I was very much like you, Ruby. I remember that draw to the dramatics, and luckily I lived through the chaos at an age where my fearless bone had not yet been broken. Though I do remember the faces of those whose had. I can't imagine what a traumatic time of it they must have had, conditioned and commanded by staff sergeants anxiety and fear. Anyway, back to your question. First, of course, you would hear the sirens wail, alerting you to what was to come. Then came the unmistakable drone of the planes overhead. That was the final warning to take cover, though I always tried to delay just long enough to get a peek at them. If you dared stay out any longer, not only would you receive a fair scolding, but you would hear these strange whines coming from the skies. They sounded like screams or cries, almost animal. Though the first time I saw them it was much more of an eerie experience than I had expected. Seeing these dark things falling from the skies they, I'm not quite sure how to put it, well, they seemed to have rather a peculiar effect upon time, as if they somehow managed to jam it, to coagulate and condense the moment. It suddenly became thicker, less fluid, more solid, hardening, like cement, with you still in it. You were stuck in that scene, completely glued to their descent, and although I knew I should run for shelter, I found it nearly impossible to tear myself away, much like a car crash, too scared or disturbed to watch, too captivated to not. But this car crash was falling from the sky, and at great speed directly towards me. Curiosity is a curious trait. Its purpose is to tutor, to attract us towards learning yet sometimes it does so with complete disregard for its pupil's safety. But where would we be without it? Curiosity, no matter how hazardous, is our most valuable tool for progress. It lures us forward toward the next step, the next plain, the next platform of mankind's evolution. It makes us quest and question, and ask and answer, and, and it makes us wonder. Besides, isn't that the whole point? I mean, without wonder where are we? Well, it would appear, exactly where we find ourselves today. Yes, it is the wonder that has to be reinstated, the wonder that has to become a part of our world again, the wonder we all had, that you still have little Ruby. That wonderful wonder you and all your little compatriots hold that all of us wizened big people have lost, declared futile in our own short-sighted search for perfection. Oh to be young again, to feel the complete wonder of the unknown, to really feel it all around, surrounding you with its enchantment. Don't let them siphon it from you, Ruby, from your world. Don't allow them to steal it and replace it with all those appalling facts and figures and ridiculous rules and regulations, it's so indecently inhumane. They want to extinguish the unknown in you, that spark of unpredictability they cannot control, that wild and capricious flame that burns within you, that keeps you alive to life, that keeps you living live. They want it gone because it only serves as a reminder of their fallacies, highlighting their fraudulent being and their dishonour to their own selves. You remind them how frail their clasp on reality truly is, and how pathetic all their justifications really are. Their limp handshake with life leaves them wanting, hollow, ever hungry, but because they have decreed their feeble excuse for a truth as ample fodder, they will never find the sustenance they crave. These starving souls then try to procure as much help as they can get to aid them down their path to perdition. They need as many members as they can to make them feel as safe as possible. And the more they try to invite you, the more unsure they show themselves to be. They take refuge in the amount of light they can snuff, believing that somehow it is proof that only darkness survives. Can they not open their eyes? Don't they realise that they are shut? But what is even more tragic is that in their insecure quest for certainty they are erasing and eradicating the paths and people who have opened their eyes. They're blinding them and any trace of their sight of another way. All just so that no reminder will remain to hold a mirror to a madness that haunts and taunts them as tyrannically and terrifyingly as their attempt at escape. Well, we are that mirror. And we are trying our very best to put an end to that way, that sham our species is shadowing. And slowly but surely we will succeed. Don't you worry, little Ruby, your children will not have to be pushed off their cloud. The whole world will live there without the fear of falling. It will happen! We just need to be a little more patient for a little longer. But that's where the crux lies, I'm afraid, time. We haven't got too much of it left. It's all unravelling so fast and yet the world remains completely oblivious to the countdown. Sometimes, in my more morose moments, I really do fear that it may have fallen so deeply asleep that only the most drastic of measures could wake it from its solemn slumber. That, in order to coax it out of its coma of unconsciousness, we would need the biggest of alarm clocks with the biggest of alarms. Well, especially since the ones that have rung haven't even as much as stirred our collective consciousness, or conscience for that matter. They obviously just haven't been loud enough. Nobody minds that their asphyxiating pollution is decreasing the life expectancy of the world. Nobody seems to care much for the starving or the suffering, or the callous hate-filled cesspools that are breeding in the minds of so many. It appears that it has not as yet impacted or affected people enough in their day to day lives for them to notice, clearly not interfered with their beloved routine, not meddled with their mid-afternoon snack. You know, I do often wonder what would happen, and whether the world would benefit, if one of those extra-terrestrial warmongering type films became a reality. You can bet your bottom dollar, as they would undoubtedly say in such a picture, that if we found ourselves as a planet up against another, all our petty in-fighting and silly arguments over him versus me, lines drawn in sand and soil, disagreements over the truth of reality, over whether one nation has more or less, whether one ideology holds the one true idea, which religion is righteous or not, it wouldn't matter, none of it. There would be no divide, no separation. Whatever nationality, race, creed, sex, sexuality, who and what people we were would not matter tuppence. We would remember, and rather rapidly I should think, that we all belong to the same species, that every last one of us all call the same spinning globe home, as did each one of our many, many ancestors before us, even when they didn't know what it was. Home is home because that is where our family resides. And we are all part of a very old, very big family, the oldest and biggest we know of, and perhaps, the only one. There may well be a few unconventional uncles and eccentric aunts, dithering or grating grandparents, odd cousins and others even odder, but in reality this muddle of mayhem is all we have, and we are all they have. We share this planet like we do a dinner table, and as we all know some family gatherings go smoother than others. Naturally, when livewires mingle there can't help but be a few shocks and even fireworks. The whole spectrum of the dramatics may be performed, but, none of it really and truly matters if we know what we have, if we know what we are, if we know we belong. We are so very fortunate to belong to something, to not be alone. We very easily could have been. Anything could have been. Goodness, I don't need to remind you of how infinitesimal the possibility is of you acquiring a conscious awareness, of you being here, right now. The odds are so highly stacked against every one of us being in the proud possession of consciousness, that it's practically inconceivable. You could even say that it is bordering on the magical. And how, dear Ruby, do we even know that it is not? We may know a great deal about reality, but in reality there is a great deal we do not. And in my own very humble opinion, I trust there to be far more that we do not. Perhaps all that we know is just a concept of a concept. Though, I suppose, how can one not help but to conceptualise reality whilst stuck within it? You cannot possibly see what is outside the box until you first see that you are in one. Maybe if our sense of reality was expanded enough we would see that the sandpit was just in the playground. We would gain a perspective that would blur the lines we have so vigilantly spent and risked our lives to protect and see the big picture, the biggest picture, that we are but one small entity in a sea of entities. But that is what makes us and our lives so special. That is what makes our world special. The wonder and majesty that falling snow summons is due to the many creating the whole. Each floating snowflake, as it dances down from its home in the white sky, brings with it a grace, a wonder that comes from being a singular part of one. If all the snow fell at once the magic would be lost. Or even if it always fell in the same uniform pattern the poetry of it would simply not be there. Its beauty is in its serendipitous nature, just as it is in ours. There's so much truth out there that people just can't see. I do hope that they do not force our hand, that we do not need to burn them in order to make them feel. But if they leave us no choice, then we will have none, and we will be left holding the only card that we can play, plan Z. That would hastily create the unity this planet craves, whilst simultaneously carving a few more notches on that exceedingly short yardstick of ours. But we are not there yet, and hopefully will never find ourselves there. It would make our little test centre here seem like a funfair! Though it is quite interesting, isn't it? That as humans, in order to be made feel that connection, that bond, it must first be threatened. We are strange beings indeed! Such curious creatures, cowering behind the cloak of civility. Why can we not just be what we wish to be? It's all so complicated, Ruby, so very complicated. Life, as you may or may not have realised yet, is a remarkably complicated beast. Simple, of course, incredibly simple, but also frightfully complex. Maybe it's all those damned feelings that get in the way, bouncing us up and down, like little show dogs dancing for treats. It's so very sad. We are given it all, the whole package, the whole deal, and we don't even know what to do with it, like a snail in a sports car. And that is what drives me, the reason I lift these old bones out of my warm womb of a bed every morning. I can no longer bear to be a spectator watching this carnage unfold. I cannot just stand by and watch the world rot. I cannot just sit back in my armchair watching the news, complaining about the travesty and the decaying of decorum, while I just sit idle, unable to even change myself, still stubbornly stuck on repeat, refusing to acknowledge my part in it all, not realising my little turning cog is helping the clock to chime as the whole world turns into a midnight mess. I can't and I won't! I will not continue to be part of the sofa senate governing from living rooms across the world, I abdicate my seat and stand for change. And all the people you have met here have taken a stand. And together we share in the grief for a parent dying without any other sibling so much as fluffing a pillow. As shocking as it may sound we are all to blame for the state of the present. And the turmoil of tomorrow will too be on our hands, unless that is, we start to make a change. It doesn't have to be big and it doesn't have to be grand. Even the smallest falling drop can move a lake. Something as simple as being less grumpy. Just throwing a few more smiles around normally works wonders. It changed my life. Mrs Billington and I are like young finches again, chirping and singing to one another. All it takes is polishing your spectacles for them to become rosy again. Seeing clearly really does change your view. Simply being a little less severe and a little kinder to mankind is the beginning of the cure. Compassion and understanding are powerful instruments and they are always at our disposal. Just a little humanity can raise it. Even seemingly insignificant alterations to your being can culminate to create ripples, that become waves and tsunamis which can then serve to change the course of history. What we forget is that everyone is having a bad day. All they are doing is just trying to better the odds. So instead of confirming and cementing their fears, helping to make their nightmare reality, why not try seeing what happens when you don't? What will happen? Firstly, it will show your fellow man that life may not be the uphill, no light at the end of the tunnel type of existence he believes it to be. Secondly, by offering them that smidgen of hope in existence they may very well feel inspired to do the same. And so on and so forth, further and further, until eventually we reach the furthest regions of the malady and go so far as to eradicate those horrendous hiccups of murderous madness that are becoming more and more prevalent these days. You know I have often found myself wondering if I have ever played a part in saving strangers lives just by being courteous to my valet, allowing the uptight gentleman to go ahead of me in the queue, smiling at the woman sitting alone on the park bench, giving my afternoon coffee and pastry to a weary wanderer who just looked like they needed one small act of kindness to remind them the goodness of the world had not all gone, that they were not alone, that it was not the cold, harsh place it feigned to be, that there were people, like me, who believed in better, who knew better, who wanted a change, even if it meant skipping the highlight of their afternoon. Sometimes all we need is a little help from our friends, even the ones we've yet to meet. As my dearest mother used to instil in us, back in an era where good manners and goodwill were worth far more than in this one, 'Love is the currency of the heart, don't spend your life saving it, save your life spending it.' She had a wonderful way of seeing the world, only on its bright side. 'That's all that's visible,' she'd say, 'the rest that lies in the dark is just the shadow of the world, not the world.' I'd hope she'd be proud of me and the work we are doing. She may not have understood the intricacies, but I know she would have supported our dream to bathe the whole world in light. Who on earth could not? Now, young lady, I'm sure you have seen and heard quite enough for one day. You're a smart one, you take after your father."

Fearing that there may well be the possibility that they could be caught in that room for the rest of the week, Ruby's mother swiftly guided her daughter towards the door.

"Okay, dear, let's leave everyone to get on with their work. Very sorry to have interrupted. We'll see you when you get home, darling."

"Bye, Daddy, see you later."

"Bye, sweetheart."

They left the observation room through the heavy silver door and stepped hand in hand into a pale frosted glass hallway, and then stopped.

"Why are we stopped, Mama?"

"Just a minute, darling."

"But what are we waiting for?"

"Just hold on, sweetie."

"Are we going somewhere?"

"Just hold on one more second."

A strong gust of wind blew through the long glass corridor.

"Mama?"

The opaque hallway lit up as a bright light flashed across it.

"Doctor, she's still unresponsive. Her pupils are non-reactive."

"Give her a dose of the sveluloid serum."

"Done. I still can't see her."

"Shit."

"Why is she still there? No girl has ever not left the hallway."

"This is no ordinary girl. 82 is different."

"Still no change."

"Prepare a second dose."

"But, doctor, that could completely-"

"She can take it. It's far more dangerous for her to be in the hallway any longer."

"A full dose? But she might not be able to-"

"There's no time to discuss it. I'll do it myself."

The doctor grabbed a bottle and syringe from the metal table, filled it and then injected the purple liquid into the tubing and watched as it journeyed down towards the arm of a girl lying motionless on a black hospital bed. The nurse watched the screen next to her as she checked the girl's vitals.

"I still can't find her."

The doctor's scrub cap fell off as he rubbed his balding head. He did not notice its fall nor did he notice the peculiar manner of its decent. It caught the air, billowing as it descended, swinging from side to side like a parachute; though in truth, it looked far more like it was sinking in water, its fall seemed too slow to be falling in the thin sterile air of this patient's room.

The doctor gazed at the screen, half hoping that his observation would collapse possibility. But it did not. Desperate, he leaned over the girl, staring at her with pleading eyes.

"Come on, 82, come back to us. We need you."

He looked at the peaceful expression her face held and, for a second, wondered whether it was right that that peace should be allowed to be disrupted. Who was *he?* And who was *she?* But more to the question, where *was* she? He couldn't just leave her. He couldn't let her go, not now. They had come too far to just jump ship and abandon their voyage, especially as the shore was finally in sight. He instinctively placed his hands upon her shoulders as if it would somehow connect them, allow him to get through to her, bring her back. Though with every second that passed he knew that outcome was drifting further and further away.

"Please, 82, you're the key, the key to it all."

"Hold on. Hold on, I've found her. It's faint but she's there."

"Oh, thank God."

The doctor fell back towards the wall, exhaling loudly as he closed his eyes and rubbed his face.

"Don't worry, doctor, she's left the hallway. She'll be back to REM in a few minutes."

Chapter Eight

The facility was unique, the only one of its kind. It was established under the designation of Eve Project and its purpose was indicant to its name sake. Its objective was simple, though its methods were not. It had been a lengthy and drawn out project, now almost two decades in the making, but it was all about come to an end. They had finally found what they had been looking for, they had finally made the impossible possible.

Their vision had been ridiculed, passed off as an idealistic dream, a fiction of fancy, completely unfeasible and unachievable. But they persevered through the pessimism. They held strong in their belief that they were not delusional dreamers but rational realists who were building an ark for a great, great flood. One that would drown all the world in its tremendous tide of tragedy. One that would leave very few survivors for the solemn cautionary tale to ever be told. Though little did they know, that in their desperate efforts to avoid one, they would be creating a cautionary tale of their own. One that showed how blindness can fall whilst trying to lift it. They did not heed the moral of their story, the warning shots or continuous alarm bells ringing inside their caged conscience, but instead ignored them, leaving those shots and bells only to be heard echoing throughout history's lecture of learning.

Ironically, and most unfortunately, it was their commendable conviction that corroded their credibility, their exemplary determination that deteriorated their decency, their virtuous integrity that destroyed their morality. It was exceptionally unfortunate that roots grown in such goodness would grow branches so twisted. But how? Because they, whilst blinded by vision and blinkered by ambition, as so many revolutionary visionaries often are, became so hypnotised, so entranced by their creation that they became infatuated, consumed with playing creator, with, in their minds eye, becoming God. And when a person succumbs to this belief, when their conscience lapses long enough to allow this new idea to command, nothing or no one is a barrier that cannot be broken. That is why they took steps and crossed lines they swore they would not, with every stride slowly leading them, luring them down the perilous path where ethics fear to tread.

But on what possible grounds could such a project be established? The most honourable there is - fear of a future lost. They believed that our world was spinning on borrowed time. War, suffering, hunger and exploitation were rife and breeding at a tremendous rate. They believed our species was now guided, steered by insecurity, confusing it with instinct, and as a result had found itself trapped, cornered, fighting to get free. So this somewhat controversial project was founded in order to find a way out, a cure, a way to remedy the sickness of the world.

Although they could see the cancer that was eating us from the inside out, they also saw the light the dark was trying to obscure. They held tight onto to their trust and belief in the goodness of the people of the world, and vowed the baby was never to be thrown out with the bathwater. They never lost their unwavering hope or their infallible faith in humanity, even in spite of humanity losing its own.

They understood and accepted the story of life on our planet as one of great drama and challenge, a tale of infinite cycles of change and growth, a book with a beginning, middle and end. But it wasn't the end they feared. They knew the struggle for existence would eventually culminate in a more evolved species. But they feared that in the interim, that during the middle of the story, the human race would be plunged into a suffocating darkness. They believed they had no choice but to intervene and stop this calamity's crescendo.

But how would they begin? How could they hope to avoid such a catastrophe? What could they possibly do to halt the turn of our world? To change the world they first had to change its inhabitants. Instead of having to decide which path they were going to select to assist human progress, instead of having to answer the illusive question of which was more influential upon a person's development, nature or nurture, they chose both. They made the daring, but dangerous, decision to lend Mother Nature a hand in accelerating the natural evolutionary process.

Natural selection was to be the template with, of course, a little assistance from science. They decided to implement Darwin's theories literally, biologically and chemically. A bold plan was created around the forecasted potential a human could embody. DNA manipulation, cell mutation, cerebral programming, instinct encoding, together with continuous calibration and a variation of other dubious tools culminated to produce a hypothetical formula that could push our species up to the next step on evolutions ladder. Science and technology aside, essentially Eve Project, was at its core, a psychological exam. The only difference being that the test and the tested were both designed by the tester.

Females were chosen as the test subjects for the project. They were preferred for their early maturity, flexibility, sensitivity and multi-focus capabilities. They were also less resistant to change, more adaptable, loyal and trusting. They rarely exhibited negative reactions to authority or acted aggressively even under the strenuous conditions they were forced to endure. This created much needed confidence in the project, as well its ambitious mission statement as it was finally becoming evident that the girls were en route to fulfilling it.

The girls were created and bred for one reason and one reason only, to facilitate the creation of the complete human being. The test subjects had to not only be produced, but crafted into the suitable candidates that the project required. After a very bumpy start of many trials and many errors they finally began generating the models they had envisioned. But as this was a maiden flight the project itself had its own evolutionary process. The girls would have to grow and develop as the program did. In order to stay in the project they would have to display highly adaptive capabilities not only at a biological but also at a cerebral and emotional level. Though perhaps this is all too much too soon. Let us maybe explain further the original manifesto, the initial mission statement that Eve Project was founded upon.

The minds behind the creation of Eve Project believed that the key to filling the pool of possibly to its rim was to allow the subjects to thrive in an environment where they were free to discover their own power, free to fulfil their full potential oblivious to any constraints society might place upon them. Ultimately, they wanted to see what would happen if a human being was never held back. Held back by the world's view and accepted parameters of what a person should be, should live, should feel. Held back by archaic ideals, by tepid tradition, by guilt and shame, by fear, by worry, bound by chains of normal, standard, ordinary, conventional, average and the padlock explanation of 'because that's just the way things are'. To see if they could exist and thrive in a world where fear had been the dominator, the dictated commanding force, a world where love and compassion had played second fiddle to uncertainty, anxiety and imagined inadequacy. They wanted to see what a person could be, could embody when not being held back by the strongest opposition of all, themselves.

Although this may have seemed a very noble and benevolent dream, unfortunately within it the seed of a nightmare was beginning to grow. In their striving to better humanity, they soon began to lose their own. They conceitedly bought into the belief that there was a distinct possibility that they were holding in their hands the capability of engineering our species to not just the next rung on the ladder of evolution, but to its furthest, to the highest platform on which a human could stand. Dazzled and distracted by their lust for creation they failed to realise one vital truth, that they themselves were not a part of this new order, and never would be, and thus could never begin to fathom what the mind of such a being could themselves in turn create. They allowed themselves to be infected by the very disease they were trying to cure. They became so consumed by their creation that they created limits to learning and boundaries to belief, the very same limits and boundaries they had so tirelessly torn down at the beginning of the whole operation. But they still held complete faith their work would pioneer a new era, the real age of enlightenment. They had no doubt in their minds that they held the one and only true key to self-unification, to complete and unfaltering self-awareness. They had reached a place where they had indoctrinated in themselves a belief that they were quite literally the hands of God, pushing our species to where it needed to be.

The project, as scientifically minded as it was, was not manned solely by atheists. Quite the contrary. The personnel comprised an amalgamation of many different religions, each believing that it was their divine purpose and destiny in life to work on Eve Project. So convinced were they of their place in mankind's salvation that they wholeheartedly believed that their deity was working through them, and their belief was absolute.

Years of planning, years of patience, years of great sacrifice were consumed all in the hopes that one day their work would show its potential and manifest the perfect blueprint. And that day had come, and that day was today. Finally, a girl had passed the final assessment level. Finally, the tested had beaten the test. Achievement of a perfect result in the current version had been deemed close to impossible. But again, another impossible had been unmasked as possible.

The program was a double layered composition. This dualistic level of reality was chosen in order to submerge the girls' subconscious to a depth that could facilitate maximum realism. This was decided upon after a complication had arisen in the previous version where only a single level existed.

The roots of this problem, in fact, stemmed from the earliest preliminaries where the girls simply did not believe their fictitious world to be real and thus would exit the program prematurely. So an enhancement, a special formula called credulin, was introduced; one that made it impossible for the girls to hold any belief of a reality outside the one they inhabited. This all seemed to work very well until some of the girls, unfortunately the more promising ones, began to sense a simulated quality to their world. And when not being able to conceive of a realm beyond the one they were questioning, the girls lost all hope in existence itself and disengaged from the system entirely. This caused their conscious dot, the cyber collar used to track them, to disappear. And because it could no longer be located, neither could they. Which, very sadly, resulted in the girls being lost, detached from the program yet still stuck within it. They became like living dolls in a dolls house, driven mad by the infinite hollowness of the reality they had exposed.

Therefore, the double layer was decided upon. This added a deeper authenticity and to trap and contain the girls' curiosity. It had worked rather well, except that is, for a few hiccups with emergence. Emergence was always going to be tricky coming from a dual tier. There were too many collapsing realities for the mind to recalibrate. This, regrettably, led to a small group of girls losing the ability to completely trust or accept the real world once they had returned to it. The girls believed our reality to be just another fabrication, one that would also have to be exited. The effects were irreversible. And these poor souls suffered a peculiar fate whereby, trapped in their perceived prison, they were unable to believe any proof or evidence given to the contrary. They remained staunchly convinced that it was simply another ingenious part of an extremely realistic program. It is just as difficult to convince a person of the truth of reality as it is to convince them of its fraudulent nature.

To avoid any more emergence issues a serum was manufactured, a chemical anvil or anchor designed to literally bring them back down to earth. But sveluloid was a very dangerous and delicate compound. And as they found out, the hard way, each girl required a slightly different dose. If too little was administered too late at departure the subject would be at risk of being lost, unattached from both the program and the exit door. If too much was administered, the subject would also be lost. Though this type of loss held no hope of return. It was speculated that, with an anchor so heavy, the girl would continue to fall past the program's reality, then through the platform of our own, though to where no one dared imagine. Nevertheless, despite all the setbacks and casualties along the way, they still fearlessly persevered and finally constructed the successful prototype they needed for the real experiments to begin.

The program was simple in its sophistication. The first layer of reality was confinement, the second was observation. The first layer took place in an abstract, four walled, abandoned space. The second took place within the observation room of the first. By incorporating the two the girls would then be able to express their innate feelings, desires and reactions to the experience from both sides, the inside and the out. The program for the room contained a specific set of fixed parameters such as the other ninety-nine occupants, the facilities, rations, communication devices and the disappearance of the light and heat. These were all timed and orchestrated as part of the software's design. Shadow memories of each character and of the subject's avatar were all imposed and suggested to the subject's subconscious.

Then there was the Eden effect. The timer, the imminent attacks, the venomous snake and, of course, the possible reasoning for their incarceration all came together to create the program's test of trust, the Eden effect; the virtual viper in the nest. Its sole purpose was to create and present psychological fear that had no basis or footing in actual truth. The Eden effect was designed to see if the subject would try to catch the imagined bait, to see if the mirage of fear would dominate and shake the candidate's foundation of belief. It was originally born as just another trial, an obstacle to be overcome in order to categorise the subject's progress. But it grew to become a central player as they soon realised that the further away the future fear lay, the more powerful it became. Due its indistinct nature of the threat, the mind was given free rein to fill in the gaps. This led them to stumble upon something very important, a realisation that was key to unravelling the knots of unconscious behaviour. They discovered that fear is never concerned with what is happening, only what could happen. Now the bark became worth much more than the bite. So they decided to bark.

The realisation that the project could unearth more keys led to an interest in finding more. Though things then began to occur that they could never have foreseen. You see, although the project's team was made up of some the brightest minds our world had ever lit, they were still themselves born from an age of darkness, and therefore could not have forecasted or even comprehended the light such blinding minds could generate. The girl's cerebral capabilities went beyond the pedigree pageantry of jumping over hurdles and through fire lit hoops to impress benefactors, but ventured into a far more complex field of unchartered territory; a territory for which they did not possess a map. A place where things happened separately and simultaneously, collectively and individually, where micro and macro were one, where the word 'paradox' held no meaning and where true comprehension, from a linear point of view anyway, was impossible. But this farfetched find did not steal their direction. It was far too off course to be included in an already ambitious voyage. Anything they did not understand was shelved and deemed, at this point anyway, superfluous. All that mattered was the prize and nothing was going to deviate their attention. So they observed and made notes, collected and assimilated data, sanding down any splinters, polishing their masterpiece, crafting their craft.

In order to elevate the girls to a place where they could realise the fullness of their potential they had to facilitate a structure that allowed them to locate their inner voice of unwavering strength. But to do this the subject needed, not only to entertain but, to consent to their feelings of doubt. They had to believe that their beliefs were unreliable, they had to question everything, allow it all to collapse, leaving only one. The girls had to fall back upon the only true voice in amongst all the pretenders, their instinctual non-cerebral guide. They had to disregard any intellectual assistance, ignore anxiety's crippling counsel and face fear head on, overcoming it through realising its illusory nature.

But it wasn't just their avatar they had to arm. The war of panic went beyond their single subjective perspective. They also had to win the battle raging within each and every other inhabitant of the room. They would have to calm the hundred voices in their head, regain an order, a peace, and maintain a unity between them. They would have to learn to conduct the concerto with an unbridled orchestra of emotions playing in the theatre of their minds, and do it all before the timer ran out.

The wall of red writings was a vital tool in understanding the subject's progression. It was, in essence, a literal blank canvas for the subject to express herself. It would serve as a direct representation of their inner consciousness and feelings toward the program, providing the technicians with a deeper insight into how the girl's cogs were turning, both mentally and emotionally. It was also an opportunity for the girls to allow their subconscious to come to the fore with guidance, resolution and aid.

Once stage one of the program ended, the second stage of observation commenced. In the observation room the candidate would have only two characters through which to express herself, a male and female lab technician. Through the interaction of the two characters, judging and critiquing the hundred occupants, a greater understanding would be gained of the subject's own view on how she performed. Thus gifting invaluable access and insight into the subject's reflection of herself.

Though a relatively simple construct, it consumed a vast amount of the brain power the most dedicated and skilled computer programmers in the world could generate. The software techs comprised an odd collection of esteemed and not so esteemed gentry, some renowned for their work, some for their play, and some for blending both. Though all had two vital things in common - their unquestionable genius and their unwavering dedication to the cause.

And now today, the culmination of the many, many minds that had been burning and churning, night and day, for years was at long last ready to bear fruit. Finally the apple was ripe and it was time for it to fall.

"She's just entered REM. Just a few more minutes and we'll be in the clear. You can go to him."

"No. I'll wait. What's a few more minutes on top of a life's work?"

The doctor sat his tired body and mind on the nearest black chair and contemplated the sudden change in his reality.

"I can't imagine what you must be feeling."

"I don't really know what I'm feeling, what I'm supposed to feel. Anyway, we don't know for absolute sure yet. I'm trying to remain as calm and as detached as possible. Though I must confess my stomach does seems to think it is some sort of an Olympic gymnast."

"Doctor, I may not be a technician but there's something I just don't understand."

"Yes, nurse, what is it?"

"Why, if she discovered the ability to materialise a new character would she create the least powerful one? Why a child? If I was her, I would have created the biggest, baddest guy I could. Surely a child, especially her own, would make her weaker. How could he possibly be of any help to her?"

"You don't have kids yet do you?"

The doctor, pushing his glasses back up onto his nose, leaned back in his chair and smiled.

"No. But I have plenty of nieces and nephews and I've seen how their parents are constantly caved in a cloud of worry, stretched to their limits, just hanging by a thread. They have no attention span for anything else. It's such an Achilles heel."

The doctor, still smiling, removed his gloves.

"When you have a child of your own, you change. Your relationship with the world changes. The world is no longer just a planet, the place in which you live, the backdrop to your expression of self, a thing to be fought against, wrung out and used. It suddenly becomes a thing to fight for, to take pride in, to change for the better. Your playground has become a nursery for your fragile and very precious flower. A force deep within you awakens to a new calling, a new vocation, to be the protector of this new entity no matter the cost, even if it is at your own. So I think she rather masterfully chose him to summon the most powerful version of herself, the only true opponent for the program. And, well it seems, she succeeded."

The doctor peered over his glasses at the screen, smiling a relieved smile when he saw what he wanted to see. He put his hand on the girl's forehead, closing his eyes for a moment, as he seemed to relay some sort of message to her. A small droplet formed in the corner of his right eye as he swallowed the rising emotion. He then turned away from her towards the door.

"Look after our precious flower."

"Yes, doctor. But I still don't understand. She doesn't have a child, she's still practically a child herself. How is it possible for her to summon those powerful instincts?"

The doctor pressed his thumb on a small square of black glass on the wall beside the door as he turned back to the nurse.

"I don't know. When it comes to 82, possible becomes rather hard to define, and even harder to distinguish from impossible. And if she is the one, she'll be dismantling a whole lot more of what we define as truth. God, she'll be deconstructing the very foundations on which our whole world's perceptions of possibility rest. She'll change it all, build her own and we'll all just witness the wonder."

The nurse said nothing as she watched the doctor leave the room. As the doctor closed the steel door marked 82 he caught his reflection in the large polished silver numbers. He saw the old man he had become, the old man his life's work had made him. Yet in his eyes, behind those creased lids, he saw the young man he had been, the young man who had spent his whole life dreaming of this very moment. And here he stood, standing within the bubble of a dream that young man had blown so earnestly with only the bellows of belief. That bubble always seemed so far away. But now it had arrived. And it was real. They had done it, both of them. A colossal feeling of unparalleled relief rose up inside him. He breathed out the depths of a breath that he had been holding for a very long time.

Once ready, he turned and began walking briskly down a long grey hallway lined with doors. Numbers flashed past him as he quickened his step, 77, 69, then faster as his pace increased, 58, 44, and then he began to run, 31, 8, until the numbers and the corridor ran out. He came to an abrupt stop, nearly colliding with the silver glass in front of him. He paused for a second as he saw his full, unforgiving reflection. His thinning hair was dishevelled, his face was red, but for once, he didn't care. His eyes were alight and his smile was alive. The mirror slid open and he stepped into the glossy white box. He pressed his thumb on another small black square of glass and the door closed. The glossy white cube moved vertically at speed. He paced the sleek space as he tried to walk out the excess energy that was building up inside of him. Then, after a small polite beep, the polished door opened and he was again met with another long corridor. This time his walk did not take long to turn into a run. He stopped at the end where a large matte grey door stood. He attempted to tame his disobedient hair and calm his breathing as a small red light scanned his eyes. The door clicked open.

Inside a grey haired man in a grey suit sat behind a stone slab desk at the end of a large room. The entire space was compiled of perfectly arranged, immaculately clean furniture and objects all in different hues of grey. Soft grey, hard grey, silky grey, rough grey, shiny grey, smooth grey. Every shade was purposely arranged and purposely displayed. The doctor walked in a little too excitedly and, in his haste, slipped on one of the expensive soft grey rugs.

"What is it, doctor?"

The man behind the desk did not look up. He was busy manipulating a bright cyan holographic image, of what looked like cell structures, hovering above his desk.

"It's 82."

The man in the grey suit stopped what he was doing and with one dismissive swipe all the images disappeared.

"What about 82?"

Leaning forward on his desk, he was now addressing the doctor directly with both eyes fixed on his.

"The program just finished and... it's just unbelievable."

"Doctor, please, information not emotion."

The doctor knew he had not succeeded in adequately calming himself, or his breathing. He tried to clear his mind as he took a deep steadying breath and continued.

"Yes, yes, of course, sorry. It's just... after all this time. I just can't..."

The doctor wiped his forehead with a red polka dot handkerchief he had produced from his back pocket. The blinding red pierced every shade of grey exposing its feigned spectrum of deceit. It couldn't have been a better reflection of the juxtaposed nature of the two men in the room. Though they were both working for the exact same goal, the exact same prize that had consumed the majority of their adult lives, their whole demeanour could not have been more contrasting. The man behind the grey desk leaned back, waiting for the doctor to compose himself and to remove the jarringly bright cloth from his sight.

"I'm terribly sorry. I thought I was taking it all rather well but…"

He took another deep breath, put his migraine inducing handkerchief back in his pocket and tried to calm himself by submerging into the neutrality of the room.

"I think we've found her."

"You think?"

"Well, she did what no other has."

"Doctor, details, please."

"Yes, of course. She just, well, we just never saw it coming. We could never have guessed it all. I mean, to interact is part of the program, but to adapt it, to modify it to your own needs is, well, it's just outstanding!"

"Quite."

"What I'm trying to tell you is that she altered the program from within. She changed the fixed parameters. She, she free styled!"

"Why didn't you let me know the moment she made the program changes?"

"Well, actually, I have been trying to get you all day, but-

"I was unavoidable detained. Susan… Never mind. Please continue."

"Is everything okay?"

"Please, continue."

"And then the writings. My God, what we didn't realise at the time was that those obscure ramblings of hers did not just represent her cryptic subconscious feelings but, I can hardly believe I'm saying it, they represented her escape plan!"

"Escape plan?"

The man in the grey suit leaned forward in his chair as the doctor took a few steps closer to him.

"Yes, beautiful isn't it? Woven within the seeming nonsense were clues, abstract clues, but still, they helped them, helped her to find an exit."

"Exit? What are you saying, doctor?"

"I'm saying she somehow managed to manipulate the program, to rewrite it to include a new part to the story. It's phenomenal. She actually created a puzzle of her own within the puzzle, a key to help her unlock it. Actually several keys, there was even a second and third set of writings!"

"What? Multiple sets? I don't understand."

"During the hunt for their escape a panel on the writings wall was torn down revealing a second set of identical writings, and then a third! Her subconscious was trying to tell her that she had been in the program before, many times before. She was leaving a message to herself that none of it was real!"

The man in the grey suit slowly shook his head in an attempt to shake the penny free.

"So, let me get this straight. She recalibrated the program, her subconscious tried to communicate with her and what, masterminded an idea of an escape?"

"Not just an idea, Roger, they did it."

The man in the grey suit asked a question he dared not believe he knew the answer to.

"Did what?"

"Escape!"

The man in the grey suit stood up.

"What? The hundred escaped?"

Then he sat down again, adjusting his grey tie as his mind tried to adjust to the new reality he now found himself in.

"Yes, she freed them! She freed them all!"

"But, I don't understand. There is no escape."

"Yes, you're right, there isn't. Not only was she the first to complete the program, completely surpassing the Eden effect, but she managed to create an elaborate exit for the room. Though, peculiarly, not for herself. She remained in the room, deciding instead to use the television set to... Well I don't quite know how to put it, to create a connection, a portal to the next stage, seamlessly. I don't even know how or why yet, but it's remarkable isn't it? She jumped to the observation room on her own terms. Unbelievable."

"Truly."

The man behind the grey desk blinked a slow blink of astonishment as he nodded for the doctor to continue.

As the doctor did, the man in the grey suit's thoughts became heavier and heavier as the full connotations of this conversation were beginning to sink in. He rested his thought laden head upon his clenched fists as his ears listened and his mind processed.

"The other particularly impressive thing was that she somehow managed to manipulate the system to include a character change in the room."

"But the program is fixed, as are the characters. She is one of the hundred. There's no room for change. It isn't possible, or am I mistaken?"

"No, no you're not, it isn't possible. That's what makes her so exciting, she just breaks all the rules, she simply smashes them to pieces."

"What was the new character?"

"A child, her son."

"She gave herself a child?"

The man in grey suit fell back into his chair as his mind broadcasted images only he could see.

"Yes, I knew you would understand. Her addition of a child into the room was inspired, conjuring a female's greatest strength, summoning in her the strongest weapon in her arsenal - the unrivalled power of a mother's protective instinct; downgrading fear to a luxury that could not be indulged."

The man behind the grey desk looked into a space within space. The doctor, torn between not wanting to overload his old friend's brain, yet desperately needing to unload his own, continued.

"And then there was the observation stage. 82 used her creative licence again and instead of sticking to the voice pieces provided, created new ones, changing the entire performance. And then she, I can still barely believe it, actually made a cameo."

"A cameo? What do you mean? She put herself in the program?"

"Yes, exactly, but a younger version. Her mind created a more immature self-projection, possibly as an easier way to handle the scene, I can't be sure. But anyway she decided to masquerade as the chief tech's daughter. Gosh, when she arrived in with her mother, I nearly choked on my flapjack. The backstory behind their sudden appearance, the details, Roger, you wouldn't have believed it. She then decided to send the girl away with the female tech to get chocolate so her parents could talk. She had them arguing for and against the whole project. You have to see it, it's fascinating."

The man in the grey suit just stared at the scene that was unfolding in front of him. For a forever it had always been a tomorrow away. But now that that tomorrow had become a today, his mind was having great trouble in accepting it. But still the doctor continued.

"And then she decided to bring the head honcho in, who quite shockingly bears rather an uncanny resemblance to, well, that's beside the point, she interviews, to be more exact, interrogates him! He rationalises and qualifies it all so skilfully, it's quite an evoking scene. It is as if her subconscious knew what we were doing and somehow burnt a shadow of it into the program. It was like she was laying judgment on us all. I'll send you the entire playback, you really need to see it for yourself."

"Yes."

"Also, I think I have an explanation for her disappearances."

"Yes, you said her dot wasn't fixed properly. Did you administer more credulin?"

"No, I chose not to. I can't explain it but something inside me prevented it. Although we never understood why her conscious dot wasn't embedded correctly in the program I always felt there was something there we weren't seeing, something beyond the usual tech issues. And now, now I think that it was actually her subconscious creating a sheath around her, preventing complete submergence."

"Shrewd."

"Indeed. Then when I studied the details some peculiar patterns began to emerge."

"Go on."

"Well, I noticed how her vitals changed when she went missing, and what was happening in the room before and after her disappearances. And well, separately the figures don't mean too much but, when you put them together, they begin to form a picture. I think she may have created a second character."

"A second character? But wouldn't you have noticed immediately?"

"Not if he were hidden."

"An imaginary friend? Then it's impossible to tell if she did."

"Not exactly."

"But how can you see something that you can't see?"

"I can't, but I can see that she can."

"Doctor?"

"It was her sudden change in breathing, increased heartbeat, rise in body temperature, and then of course the surge in hormones which all pointed to-"

"A lover."

The man in the grey suit leaned back in his chair, smiling.

"Clever girl."

"Well, yes, how do you beat the unbeatable? You play smart, you play a card that trumps them all. You arm yourself with the most powerful force in the world, love. By creating someone to protect and care for, and then someone to be protected and cared by, well then she has all the angles covered, doesn't she?"

"Creating a spherical shield of safety. Ingenious. But why hide it from us?"

"I'm not entirely sure why she would hide it from the room. Maybe that extra intensity that secrecy brings, or maybe because then he was just hers? It's hard to use our mental parameters on her. We can't possibly know for sure. I think what she created here goes far beyond the measuring capabilities of our instruments. She took control of the reins that were not hers to take. She steered her steed off the racetrack to where *she* wanted to go. And we don't even know where that is. All we know is that she gained strength on every disappearance and it was that strength that helped her dismantle the program. There is the possibility that her subconscious created this extra character to serve as some kind of mentor, someone to guide her, to help her break it all down. The mind baffles at how her's does not."

"Fascinating."

"There was one more thing."

"Yes?"

"Her re-entry. It was a little... unorthodox."

The man in the grey suit didn't say anything, but the doctor still heard the words emanating from his expression.

"She didn't exit naturally at the hallway cue. Firstly she exited as the child with her mother so it was never going to go completely to plan."

"Did you administer the sveluloid serum?"

"Of course. But after there was no reaction I had no choice but to give her another. If she had spent any longer in the hallway we wouldn't have been able to get her back."

"Full dose?"

"Yes. Her emergence was a little delayed, but we've got her. She's recovering in REM."

"How long was she in the hallway?"

"No more than a few minutes. We won't know the full effects until the post analysis. I'll let you know as soon as I do. I believe the reason it took so long to get her back was because she was resisting her removal, she was losing control and thus held on tighter. Obviously there are many things left to analyse and hypothesise upon. We'll of course know more after she wakes."

"Let me know the moment she does. I want to speak to her before the post emergence examination."

"Of course."

The doctor paused for a moment and then took a step forward.

"It's all very exciting, isn't it, Roger? All those years ago, working out of those awful derelict offices."

"Yes, we've come quite a way, Henry."

"I can't believe that our vision may finally be coming to fruition. Are you going to call him?"

"Of course. I'll call him immediately. You'd better get a full report ready, you know he'll want one right away."

"I know, I know. I'll prepare one now. I just had to come up and tell you in person."

The doctor turned and walked towards the door, being careful not to tread on the slippery soft rug again. As his hand touched the shiny grey handle the man behind the desk called out to him.

"Henry?"

The doctor turned around smiling, and his old, but austere friend smiled back.

"Thank you."

"My absolute pleasure."

Once the heavy grey door had closed, the man in the grey suit typed a sequence on an imaginary keypad and a cyan holographic number pad appeared hoovering above his desk. He paused for a moment before dialling as he thought a private thought. Once he had finished, he dialled and stood up, pacing as he waited for the call to be answered.

A deep voice spoke.

"Yes? What is it?"

"We think we've found her."

There was a long pause.

"Are you still there?"

"Yes. Yes, I'm still here. What makes you so sure?"

"She took control of the program, altering it and directing it to her own needs."

"Which number?"

"82."

"82. Yes, she always exhibited tendencies. Is she stable?"

"Yes. Yes, now she is."

"Now?"

The throat of the man in the grey suit constricted.

"Because of her interference she didn't take our exit cue so the doctor had to administer two doses of sveluloid. There would have been a small delay in her emergence."

"How long was she in the hallway?"

"The doctor assured me it was no more than a few minutes."

"How many minutes?"

"I don't have an exact number but I will get it to you as soon as I have it."

"Inform me the moment she regains consciousness."

"Certainly. You'll have a preliminary report within the hour."

"Good, thank you. Roger?"

"Yes?"

"Well done. Congratulations."

"Thank you. It's been a long road."

"Well there could be another long one ahead. But at least we've been given a road sign. Give the doctor my felicitations."

"I will and I'll call you the minute she resurfaces."

"Yes. Good. I'll be awaiting your report."

The deep voiced man terminated the call and sat back in his crimson leather arm chair. The sun was shining in from the open glass doors behind him, illuminating his shaggy silver hair. He pivoted off his antique presidential desk and turned to face the wooden doorway and the teal sea framed within it. He rubbed his tanned face with his hands as he stared deep into the horizon, his eyes trying to glimpse beyond it, to the unseen, to the future, where all the answers where hiding. Now that the roulette wheel had finally stopped on his number, what was he going to do with his chips? He felt differently from what he imagined he would. He felt a surprising sense of guilt and a looming calamity. Was this an omen, a grave warning to be heeded? Or was it just his mind soiling the moment? His turquoise eyes sunk into the achingly beautiful scene before him in the hopes of smothering the bad voices in its overwhelming perfection. The setting sun was burning a hole through the baby blue sky as the oceans waves were reaching up to kiss it. The sunlight danced on the crest of each wave like clusters of sparkling diamonds, each one shimmering and shining the brightest light imaginable. A soft warm breeze blew in, blowing a hypnotic melody through the wind chime. The notes played so gently and purposefully as if they had been rehearsed for this very scene. The gust continued to complete its haunting composition, not skipping a note or missing a beat, just masterfully orchestrating its vision. It was an unknown piece by an unknown composer, though more beautiful than any he had ever heard.

Eve's fingers sprang up from her grandfather's old typewriter, tightly frozen with the terror of her realisation that her memoirs could not possibly contain a sea breeze's song, let alone one that had been following her, haunting her all this time. How much of it was real? What else had been sacrificed to selective memory?

Eve's eyes began to glaze as they became transfixed upon the glaringly white page and the letters that filled it; each one callously cutting through their stark reality, each one coldly cutting through her own. None of it seemed familiar, none of the words made sense. All the letters appeared to belong to some foreign tongue, some lost language. Then they became even more obscure as they began to move and sway forming patterns, circling around the page. What was happening? What had happened? What had she been doing?

Eve pushed herself away from her mother's old writing desk as she sensed a realisation was coming. An old book fell to the floor, sounding a shockwave of remembering. She suddenly understood the real reason why her psychiatrist had sent her there. The closure she thought writing the book would bring was not the closure she knew was coming. It did not matter what she did, it only mattered where she was. The end thread had now poked out and she couldn't stop herself from pulling it. Her world began to unravel, her masterfully created world, it was all coming loose and falling apart at the seams. It had all gone too far, the weave had worn too thin, the tale spun too long to conceal the truth. Her illusion had failed, and so had its magic.

Eve felt her breath leave her as her mind raced to try and protect her from the cataclysmic bomb that had just dropped, so unapologetically crashing through all her skilfully crafted layers. She stumbled as she stood up, losing her balance several times until the wall found her. Her fingers grasped and clasped at it until they found the door. She clung to the old wooden door frame as she had done so many times as a child, patiently waiting for her mother to finish writing. It was all a lie. The room spun with her still in it, she grabbed the collar of her loose silk shirt that was now choking her. She needed to get out of there. She needed air. She needed to leave. Now.

Eve ran barefoot across the hallway, through the beaded curtain on the back door and sprinted as fast as she could into the sun soaked garden. No one saw her as she sped silently across the lawn. She ran and ran until her legs ran themselves out of power and purpose in front of the wildflowers meadow and an over grown mound.

Panting, her eyes fell down to where her feet had brought her. She then began to shiver. The mound. She shook her head from side to side, desperately trying to shake her thoughts away. But they wouldn't go. They, like the mound's secret, had been buried for far too long for them to be so easily shaken away. Her legs failed as she fell to her knees, nearer to the source of her trembling. Where was it? Was it still there? Was it ever? Was that too a delusion? What was real? Maybe it was all a bad dream that she would soon awake from. Her thoughts were cancelling each other out, there was nothing to hold onto, nothing to stop her from drowning. She suddenly found herself frantically scraping and digging at the mound, silently hysterical, still trying to keep it all so contained as her past self screamed to be released. She did not care who saw her act of madness. She did not care about her bloodied fingers. She cared for only one thing. To not find what she knew was there. And when her broken nails scraped across the hard wood, then and only then did she finally stop, did she finally stop pretending, did she finally stop holding it all together. She had found it. She had found the door in the dirt. She wept, not only for herself and her wasted years, but for that child that never grieved, for that child that never got to speak, never got to cry. She stopped her tears. They were premature. She needed to open it, needed to make sure. She needed to see if it really was what she hoped it was not. She pushed the earth away from the wooden door and felt her heavy heart sink as a painted white number was revealed, 100. She grabbed onto the dirty brass handles and held them tight as she took a slow deep breath. With all her might she pulled them towards her and the doors cracked open. An unmistakable musty smell blew into her face. She cupped her mouth with her shaking hand as her eyes and the room came into focus.

It was all exactly how she had left it. Exactly how it had been that night, frozen for an age, sealed like a painting. Kept just out of reach from the cruel clutches of time, preserved, reserved for this very moment of complete revelation and realisation. She was now face to face with what she had refused to confront all her life. As the dam's cracks began to grow under the weight of all the repressed pressure of emotion, every supressed, hidden and deleted memory began to flow back from her subconscious. Like a lake being drained, all its lost secrets were now being exposed to the glaring, burning light of day. Her tears ran out, racing to be free. Struggling to contain and silence them, Eve's body shook as she slowly walked down the few steps that had seemed so large so long ago. The sun shone in behind her as her moving shadow touched and shaded different areas of the room. As she reached the last step, the sunlight streamed in, shining like a spotlight on something very old and very forgotten. It was a beautifully ornate antique chest and its pretty key was still in its lock. She twisted it and heard a click.

Eve lifted the wooden lid. There they were, sealed for over twenty years, not disturbed since the day she left them, and her mother had left her. Tears slid down her cheeks over previous tracks made. This time she didn't stop them. How easy they slipped down, how little they knew of the immense difficultly that had brought about their arrival. They knew nothing of it. They just rolled smoothly down as if it were the most natural thing in the world.

Eve stretched her trembling hand into the old chest. She felt a weight inside her expand as she picked up her little baby. Her little baby boy, her poor lost baby. Her body began to heave as it tried to catch up to produce the called for tears. She cuddled it and held its hard plastic body close, clinging tightly to it, protecting it, as her fingers stretched in again and touched something soft. When she saw the worn russet face and the warm smile of her old rag doll, more tears began their advancement. As the doll soaked up her tears Eve tried desperately to soak up some of the great comfort she had always taken from her. Taking a shallow breath, afraid of what was next, she reached in and pulled out the old pirate toy her father had given her. Memories fought for attention as she tried her best to ignore them. But she couldn't. She began grasping at all her long forgotten toys, her kind old doctor and nurse dolls, her courageous soldier and construction worker men, her suited office dolls, so many. Then she saw movement in the corner of the box, her old wobble toy. It knocked against something as she went to grab it. It was only a few notes but she instantly recognised what they were and where they had come from. *All around the mulberry bush.*

Eve picked up her grandmother's old jack-in-the-box and twisted the small lever. She closed her eyes as she heard the familiar sound of the mechanism winding up and then a click. For the first time in her adult life she did something without foreseeing and imagining consequences. She did not know what listening to that tune would do, what would happen next, but still, she let go of the lever. As the little box sang its song, a flickering of remembering blew through her. Every chime chimed deep within her, reverberating in the emptiness, shaking her, beckoning her to awake from her deepest darkest slumber. The music. It was the music that had kept her sane through it all. She remembered how she had played it over and over again, comforting herself, lulling herself into a bubble of protection. She remembered becoming each note and existing within the space between them. That was where she hid, that was where she stayed hiding from all the noise.

The melody was close to finishing its cycle and as it played its last note, a small click followed and then a pop. The hidden figure burst out. Its old plastic blue eyes caught the sunlight as its shaggy mane shook around them. Eve's bubble burst. The jolt furiously shook her and her fragile shell, mercilessly ripping her false reality away leaving her exposed in the void and then, then she began to fall. She fell through the floor of her reality, of her many realities, and tumbled down deep into the burrow of her mind's creation. She fell directly towards the unavoidable fate that had been avoided for so long. And when she reached it, she remembered.

She now remembered it all. They had all been there for her. They had all played their part, helping her, protecting her, keeping her safe. That chest had been her anchor in the raging storm that had started that windy afternoon and ended the following evening, taking away with it her childhood, her security and the very thing in the whole world she held the most dear.

The problem was that no one knew what to say to her, so they didn't say anything at all, anything of substance anyway. Grown-ups are strange beings. They claim that age and experience has given them the answers but back then, little Eve felt they didn't even know the questions. How does a child grieve for a parent lost, especially in such a manner? There was no warning, no goodbye, there was just wind, lots and lots of wind. It was her fault her mother had left the storm shelter, it was her fault the great wind had swept her away, it was her fault her mother had to suffer the unimaginable fate that she did not deserve, and all because of her blinding love for her daughter and her blinkered instinct to keep her safe, compelling her to disregard her own.

As the storm was brewing they had brought down Eve's chest of toys but there was one thing missing, her favourite book, her mother's book, The Little Drop Of Light. Her mother, of course, knew it by heart, any mother would, even one who hadn't written it. But it was the pictures that Eve had wanted to see. She wanted that extra bit of security, that extra bit of assurance. But by wanting it all, she lost it all. In her desire for the maximum, she was punished with the minimum. And instead of learning that incredibly important life lesson, Eve regressed like a little mole as deep as her imagination would allow. And there was where she built her fortress, her tree house fort, high above the pain and trauma of that fateful night.

To be born in a storm of light...

That wild wind had blown the precious pieces of Eve's life so far apart that she couldn't even begin to pick them up again, like some sad scattered jigsaw puzzle left in a park, the pieces couldn't be found, let alone be put back together. Her grandparents were not in the position to help as they too were trying to collect the pieces to their own, to rebuild them, and their home, their family and their reality. Leaving poor Eve to find them alone, to recover the lost pieces that were only now being discovered so many years later. As the years passed and Eve grew, so did her explanation and rationalisation of what had happened. She made the best from the few pieces she had found and simply filled in the rest. She had no siblings and when her grandparents passed, still without discussing the death of their only child, the truth was buried with them.

Eve became highly skilled at masking her guilt and pain and managed to carve out a form of a life for herself. With every year that passed, more dust settled upon her great secret obscuring it from everyone who knew her, even herself. Though from the outside she may have looked like any normal girl, she was incapable of vulnerability and making any real emotional connections, inevitably slashing any relationship that threatened her armour, leaving a trail of fractured hearts behind her. She felt proud she wasn't an affection and attention addict, that she didn't need anyone or anything to complete her. This belief was reaffirmed by her many colleagues' and acquaintances' admiration and respect, revering her for her commendable strength of character and admirable independence.

But under the thick ice a different current was flowing, one that was accumulating force, gathering at great speed, preparing for a collision. Eve's mistake was in believing a castle of feathers would be as strong as stone. She had only started seeing a psychiatrist because of a persistent lump in her throat that had appeared after an emotional connection proved particularly difficult to sever. At the beginning they spoke about him and his relentless hope and naïve belief for their life together. They spoke about why she would be drawn to her exact opposite, why she would be attracted to such an uninhibited and unconventional individual. She blamed it on lust, Mother Nature meddling with her magic potion of pheromones. But her psychiatrist didn't subscribe to her explanation and asked if maybe he represented a symbol of liberation that her subconscious had been seeking, possibly a chance to release repressed feelings of guilt or childhood trauma. She rejected such a cliché claim and dismissed the whole idea as quite pedestrian pop psychology. But this had at least opened a channel into her past, the past that she had allowed herself to believe. Though as she began to explain parts of her unusual history the weight of balancing and carrying so many realities finally began to take its toll. Matter was beginning to appear in her perfect vacuum.

So it was proposed that she to go back to her childhood home and write her shocking memoirs, to get all that unbelievable life journey of hers down in the hopes that she could then let it go. But what she did not realise was that it was going to be an entirely different story that she would be letting go of. For her trapped subconscious had ideas of its own and had been planning a jailbreak for quite some time. What Eve didn't know was that her subconscious had been the one shaking her shaky foundations of false truth, her subconscious that had been the one trying so hard to free her from the layers of confinement that she had wrapped herself within. You see, her overprotective unconscious self believed that by creating a mille feuille reality it would somehow make the illusion stronger, make it tougher to dispel, and the truth far harder to find. With so many safety nets upon safety nets, her mind assumed she would be incapable of falling through to the real reality. Yet, it was arrogance itself that led to its downfall. It was the overly elaborate layer upon layer that had caused such an obvious mound, one that could not be ignored. Her subconscious had repeatedly tried its best to wake her out of her delusion, but her wilful mind stubbornly resisted, it would not allow it. It ignored Leo's pleas, not just the ones her subconscious created in the room, but outside it, in the life they were beginning to build together. He knew that she was hiding a great tragedy from him. But he also knew that picking the fruit before time would always taste sour. So he waited. But after a time, he realised that they could not build a future together upon foundations of sand. When the tide would inevitably come in, their reality would be swept away. So he began trying to piece together the information that he knew, filling in the blanks as best he could, until finally he found out the awful truth.

She remembered the night that she decided it had gone too far, that he had gotten too close, that she had allowed him in too deep. When he arrived home, late, soaking wet, with his own tears mingling with the sky's down his face, she knew something had happened. At first her mind took her to certain infidelity, but when she saw the overwhelming pity in his eyes she knew that it was her mind, and not him, that had strayed. He was not the one who had done something wrong. She didn't know what she had done, she didn't want to know. All she knew was that it was her fault for being too soft in allowing this to go so far. How could any arrangement between two people be positive if it had the potential to cause so much pain? She was never going to be the reason or the receiver of hurt again. So she had no choice but to inflict upon him the most pain he had ever felt in order to protect each other, from each other.

Though his dogged tenacity proved a problem. He was not like the other men. He would not let go of the bone. This also made her feelings harder to digest as his continual interference in her life kept them resurfacing, regurgitating again and again, causing such a burn of the heart, the likes of which she had never felt before. But she had made her decision and she believed it would protect her, even if sometimes, especially late at night, she felt she had jumped from heaven into hell. After months of near unbearable torture she moved apartments in the middle of the night and never saw Leo again. But after a month had passed and her inability to forget him persisted, she decided to see a pain vanquisher, an emotion exorcist. Which, ironically unbeknownst to her, led her down the very path Leo had wished for her all along. All he had wanted was her and her happiness, her peace, to just see her continually content. His only fault was picking the one girl who just couldn't grant his wish. Maybe if they had stayed together, maybe if they had somehow gotten through it, maybe they would have had their happily ever after. Though even with all the love and will in the world Leo still may not have been able to resuscitate her from her comatosed state of consciousness, and then where would they be left? Waiting for the inevitable tide to come in and wash it all away.

Eve had been so enveloped, so stuck within her story's cocoon that she couldn't have conceived any other reality. Strange occurrences, implausibility's and gaping plot holes were simply overlooked, covered up, tarmacked with artistic licence. She had irreversibly trapped herself and the only key to unlock her prison door was in the belly of the very beast she had been running from. She had no choice but to return.

Eve closed the lid on her beloved toy chest and paused as she remembered all the dear friends she would never see again. She then looked at the music box she had kept. She opened the chest one last time. She didn't need its lullaby anymore, it had served its purpose. But had he? As she turned the key in the lock she saw the eight petaled flower symbol on the handle. She remembered the flower's message from the wall. It was meant for her, now, in this moment, when she was aware enough, open enough to understand it. A warm glow of connection surged through her as she finally grasped the correlation of it all. She understood the everything of everything and the nothing of nothing. She was no longer emotional or confused, her waters were now still.

She finally felt she had found the centre of herself and now it all made sense. She felt free, she felt alight, everything felt live and for the first time in her life she felt truly and completely alive. But she knew there was one last thing she had to do. She closed her eyes and went back to the room.

A tear fell down her small cheek as the little girl, who had never been able to leave the room, sat on the edge of the void with her little legs dangling into the darkness. She concentrated her gaze upon the little twinkle of light in the middle of the dark. She could see it clearly now. It twinkled and sparkled for her. She was no longer afraid, she felt safe. She then closed her little eyes and let herself fall. Eve let go of that little girl, let go of her pain and her sorrow. She no longer needed to carry her weight, her identity, her past. She no longer needed to do anything ever again, all she needed to do was fall.

Gravity dissipated as she felt the unbelievable buoyancy of her true self and true freedom's joy. She opened her eyes and saw that she was nearly there. A sigh of relief escaped her. She laughed a laugh for no reason except to let out the happiness contained within her, happiness that had been missing, bottled up, yearning to be freed for longer than she could remember. The release was unimaginable. Her being shimmered and shone, radiated, dissolving into the moment around her. She became light and light became her. They joined and then separated. The penetrating light filled the scene, blinding her in its unwavering glory. As she squinted her eyes to protect both them and her mind from the overload, a calming faint blue seeped into the edges of her view, falling towards the light, forcing it to retreat, squeezing it into a small shining ball of light. The compressed energy emanating from it was immense. Its intensity made her feel like she was being touched by real sunlight for the very first time, as if every other ray she had ever experienced had somehow been artificial. As she bathed in its warm radiance her ears attuned to her new surroundings.

Noises cascaded over each other, singing, vying for her attention. The loveliest of sounds washed through her. The wind, the trees, the vibrating hums and buzzing of bees, the prettiest of bird calls. She recognised their song. Unity penetrated her entire being as she felt a belonging, an acceptance of invitation.

Eve turned around to greet the splendour before her. Her grandest dreams could not have prepared her for the unimaginable beauty, the sheer majesty of it all; it was poetry. She felt like she was in the heart of the feeling of inspiration that had inspired every great artistic piece of work ever created. She was overwhelmed by the completeness of the wondrous beauty that had been bestowed to her. Everywhere her eyes travelled her gaze was met with increasing wonders of magnificence. The glade glistened around her with scattered crystals of light sparkling as the sunlight lit the jewelled, dew sprinkled scene. The lushness of the trees and their leaves was incomparable to anything she had ever seen, real or imagined. She saw nearby bushes bursting with berries so ripe, barely able to contain their sweetness. The kaleidoscope of flora parading every colour of the spectrum, all interspersed so delicately yet so proudly around this wonderland, beckoned her to follow their trails with glazed eyes. The vibrancy of each and every blossoming beauty complimenting each other with their individuality, was beyond dazzling. Each and every flower was so perfectly in bloom their nectar was nearly glowing as it dripped down onto each masterpiece of a petal. Eve barely blinked as so not to miss a second. Even the air seemed to sparkle like its atoms had suddenly learned to reflect light. Magic seemed to be real here. It had its place. This was its home.

The garden was full of a synergy she had never known. The glory of life was everywhere, circling and fluttering all around her, undeterred by her presence, welcoming her into its inner most circle. The scents flooding the air were ethereal. Eve spun around, breathing in as many as she could. Floral notes playing softly upon the fresh fragrance of new growth, tumbling over rich earthy tones, all oozing in the sweet symphonic nectar created together an orchestra of opulence, deafening the senses. This over stimulation of sensation was building to a crescendo. Eve's body pulsed and vibrated with the waves of the whole experience as she looked down at her soft womanly form. How lovely it seemed in this moment. She smiled at the liberation that not only being uncovered gave her but at her own comfort in it. Then, she saw it. Though but one gem in a crown of jewels, it embodied such perfection she felt instantly attracted to it. It was hanging so beautifully, so enchantingly, so invitingly, so purposefully. Perhaps it was due to fall today? Was it best to wait until the fruit has fallen, she thought? Her thought was then answered by a quiet voice.

"Take whatever you wish, it is all yours, you can have it all."

She looked around to ascertain the source of the whisper. But she could not. As she reached out to the apple, the voice returned.

"Yes, yes, pick it, it's everything you've always wanted."

The voice made her stop her advance. She again looked around but no one was there. Once more, the apple's splendour lured her in. She touched and caressed it. It was undeniably beautiful. She could even smell the sweet aroma resonating from it. She leaned closer. Her eyes fluttered to the back of her head as its fragrance filled her lungs, and the voice returned.

"Taste it, it tastes even better than you can imagine."

Trapped in a trance from its scent, and the promise of its taste to come, Eve leaned in and opened her mouth, surrendering to her desire. Though just before she closed her eyes she noticed a caterpillar nearby. He was munching on his succulent apple leaf, then crawling to the other side to get another taste. She watched him toing and froing upon the same leaf and wondered why. In that moment an answer came to her but it did not come from the whisperer. She realised that whilst the caterpillar continued his hunt for the juiciest part of the leaf, he would never be happy. That it was this very quest that would prevent him from ever finding it. There would always be a better leaf, a better side, a juicier, tastier piece, and so he would spend his short life searching for an imaginary prize, chasing an unobtainable goal. Then the whisperer returned to shed his particular shade of light on the subject.

"His quest may keep him striving but it also keeps him living. It is the carrot dangling on the stick that keeps him moving, keeps him alive."

But to where Eve thought, moving to where? Moving like a stubborn mule in a direction that it does not wish to go? Would the mule simply stand still without the carrot to guide him? Would he stay in the same spot forever, completely lost now that his purpose has been removed? Or would he find his own way, decide his own path, find his own food, naturally and instinctively without a need for enticement? Eve leaned back, away from the apple, and the whisperer returned.

"You need the apple. You have needs that must be fulfilled, otherwise you will surely be diminished. You have a hunger that must be satisfied. Hunger exists *only* to be satisfied. You are your desires and they are you. Without them, you are nothing. To strive is to be alive."

Eve arched her head and looked high upon the tree and finally saw where the whisperer was hiding and addressed him directly.

"To be alive is not to strive. To be alive is to live live. My desires are not everything I am. I am more than yearning, more than thoughts and feelings. I will not eat the apple because in this moment I am content with all that surrounds me. You wish for me to bite the apple so you can then bite me, put your poison into my veins and make me your slave. I have been a slave, I know what that means and I will not be tricked again."

Eve turned away from the tree and the whisperer and walked into the wondrous wild before her. She smiled as the grass tickled her ankles and the butterflies flew their bright colours around her. She now knew that she would never listen to the whisperer again, never fall into that slumber of slavery, and never ever find herself waking in the room again. She had changed, she had grown, and she was now impervious to the whispers. And although they would still come and there would be one hundred whispers whispered to her of why she should return to the room, she would listen only to the one voice telling her not to. The one truth amongst all the lies, that she was already home. Her attentions were drawn to the amber sun setting on the horizon. The moment contain such a familiarity to it that she couldn't place. Then she felt a feeling of home call to her, summoning her. Inside a force of energy was building, connecting, pulling her out and away from herself. It was an invitation to return, she knew that now, and as if on autopilot she allowed herself to go.

My core shimmered as I felt a pull towards a growing light on the horizon. Instead of resisting, I allowed myself to gravitate towards it. I felt completely powerless, yet completely protected. Like it was a returning and a completing. All the colours of the scene ran into each other like wet paint. Except the growing light, it just kept on growing. I felt my fragile shell blow away in the breeze, releasing me, allowing me to connect to this strong magnetic force that was beckoning me. I felt time stop and shatter, moments disappeared as they formed into one, everything became and belonged to everything else, time and everything within it became nothing more than just a concept.

As I melted into the light, I remembered. I had been here before, many, many times before. I had completed countless versions of this circuit of experience, in and out, round and round, back and forth. I had lived a thousand lives, a thousand times. I had seen it all, felt it all, been it all, and now it was once again time to return. Time to be the all and the nothing, the full and the empty, the alone and the together, the close and the far, the free and the contained, the forever and the now. Time to return to the place where everything was all of itself, all of the time.

As the little drop of light disappeared into the burning ball it shimmered, and its shimmer echoed across the great ball of light causing it to burn even brighter. As this brightness peaked, the big burning ball of light began to melt. Drops of light gathered at its base awaiting their turn to fall, each one barely able to contain their excitement for the new adventure awaiting them. But each one also remembering not to ever worry or fret on their journey because home was just a moment away. They vowed to hold tight onto that truth whenever fiction felt real. And they vowed to remind all the other drops of light who had forgotten what they truly were, where they really came from. To let them know that they were not the fragile shells they thought they were, that there was a drop of light inside each and every one of them and that drop of light was their true self. They swore to remind them that they were more wondrous than they could possibly imagine, that they always had been and always would be, beautiful shimmering drops of light emanating out from the big burning ball destined to complete the infinite cycle of exit and return, over and over again, soaking up every possible experience imaginable, forever until the end of time or the time of end, or quite possibly, until yesterday becomes tomorrow.

23247114R00358

Printed in Great Britain
by Amazon